THE OLD "FRONT STEPS" HAD NEVER BEEN SO GRACED BEFORE

Without a Home. *Frontispiece*

The Works of E. P. Roe

VOLUME TWO

WITHOUT A HOME

ILLUSTRATED

NEW YORK
P. F. COLLIER & SON

PREFACE

JUST ten years ago I took my first hesitating and dubious steps toward authorship. My reception on the part of the public has been so much kinder than I expected, and the audience that has listened to my stories with each successive autumn has been so steadfast and loyal, that I can scarcely be blamed for entertaining a warm and growing regard for these unseen, unknown friends. Toward indifferent strangers we maintain a natural reticence, but as acquaintance ripens into friendship there is a mutual impulse toward an exchange of confidences. In the many kind letters received I have gratefully recognized this impulse in my readers, and am tempted by their interest to be a little garrulous concerning my literary life, the causes which led to it, and the methods of my work. Those who are indifferent can easily skip these preliminary pages, and those who are learning to care a little for the personality of him who has come to them so often with the kindling of the autumn fires may find some satisfaction in learning why he comes, and the motive, the spirit with which, in a sense, he ventures to be present at their hearths.

One of the advantages of authorship is criticism; and I have never had reason to complain of its absence. My only regret is that I have not been able to make better use of it.

I admit that both the praise and blame have been rather bewildering, but this confusion is undoubtedly due to a lack of the critical faculty. With one acute gentleman, however, who remarked that it "was difficult to account for the popularity of Mr. Roe's books," I am in hearty accord. I fully share in his surprise and perplexity. It may be that we at last have an instance of an effect without a cause.

Ten years ago I had never written a line of a story, and had scarcely entertained the thought of constructing one. The burning of Chicago impressed me powerfully, and obedient to an impulse I spent several days among its smoking ruins. As a result, my first novel, "Barriers Burned Away," gradually took possession of my mind. I did not manufacture the story at all, for it grew as naturally as do the plants —weeds, some may suggest—on my farm. In the intervals of a busy and practical life, and also when I ought to have been sleeping, my imagination, unspurred, and almost undirected, spun the warp and woof of the tale, and wove them together. At first I supposed it would be but a brief story, which might speedily find its way into my own waste-basket, and I was on the point of burning it more than once. One wintry afternoon I read the few chapters then written to a friend in whose literary taste I had much confidence, and had her verdict been adverse they probably would have perished as surely as a callow germ exposed to the bitter storm then raging without. I am not sure, however, but that the impulse to write would have carried me forward, and that I would have found ample return for all the labor in the free play of my fancy, even though editors and publishers scoffed at the result.

On a subsequent winter afternoon the incipient story passed through another peril. In the office of "The New

York Evangelist" I read the first eight chapters of my blotted manuscript to Dr. Field and his associate editor, Mr. J. H. Dey. This fragment was all that then existed, and as I stumbled through my rather blind chirography I often looked askance at the glowing grate, fearing lest my friends in kindness would suggest that I should drop the crude production on the coals, where it could do neither me nor any one else further harm, and then go out into the world once more clothed in my right mind. A heavy responsibility rests on the gentlemen named, for they asked me to leave the manuscript for serial issue. From that hour I suppose I should date the beginning of my life of authorship. The story grew from eight into fifty-two chapters, and ran just one year in the paper, my manuscript often being ready but a few pages in advance of publication. I wrote no outline for my guidance; I merely let the characters do as they pleased, and work out their own destiny. I had no preparation for my work beyond a careful study of the topography of Chicago and the incidents of the fire. For nearly a year my chief recreation was to dwell apart among the shadows created by my fancy, and I wrote when and where I could—on steamboats and railroad cars, as well as in my study. In spite of my fears the serial found readers, and at last I obtained a publisher. When the book appeared I suppose I looked upon it much as a young father looks upon his first child. His interest in it is intense, but he knows well that its future is very doubtful.

It appears to me, however, that the true impulse toward authorship does not arise from a desire to please any one, but rather from a strong consciousness of something definite to say, whether people will listen or not. I can honestly assert that I have never manufactured a novel, and should

I do so I am sure it would be so wooden and lifeless that no one would read it. My stories have come with scarcely any volition on my part, and their characters control me. If I should move them about like images they would be but images. In every book they often acted in a manner just the opposite from that which I had planned. Moreover, there are unwritten stories in my mind, the characters of which are becoming almost as real as the people I meet daily. While composing narratives I forget everything and live in an ideal world, which nevertheless is real for the time. The fortunes of the characters affect me deeply, and I truly believe that only as I feel strongly will the reader be interested. A book, like a bullet, can go only as far as the projecting force carries it.

The final tests of all literary and art work are an intelligent public and *time.* We may hope, dream, and claim what we please, but these two tribunals will settle all values; therefore the only thing for an author or artist to do is to express his own individuality clearly and honestly, and submit patiently and deferentially to these tests. In nature the lichen has its place as truly as the oak.

I will say but a few words in regard to the story contained in this volume. It was announced two years ago, but I found that I could not complete it satisfactorily. In its present form it has been almost wholly recast, and much broadened in its scope. It touches upon several modern and very difficult problems. I have not in the remotest degree attempted to solve them, but rather have sought to direct attention to them. In our society public opinion is exceedingly powerful. It is the torrent that sweeps away obstructing evils. The cleansing tide is composed originally of many rills and streamlets, and it is my hope that this volume may add a little to that which at last is irresistible.

I can say with sincerity that I have made my studies carefully and patiently, and when dealing with practical phases of city life I have evolved very little from my own inner consciousness. I have visited scores of typical tenements; I have sat day after day on the bench with the police judges, and have visited the station-houses repeatedly. There are few large retail shops that I have not entered many times, and I have conversed with both the employers and employés. It is a shameful fact that, in the face of a plain statute forbidding the barbarous regulation, saleswomen are still compelled to stand continuously in many of the stores. On the intensely hot day when our murdered President was brought from Washington to the sea-side, I found many girls standing wearily and uselessly because of this inhuman rule. There was no provision for their occasional rest. Not for a thousand dollars would I have incurred the risk and torture of standing through that sultry day. There are plenty of shops in the city which are now managed on the principles of humanity, and such patronage should be given to these and withdrawn from the others as would teach the proprietors that women are entitled to a little of the consideration that is so justly associated with the work of the Society for the Prevention of Cruelty to Animals. Mr. Bergh deserves praise for protecting even a cat from cruelty; but all the cats in the city unitedly could not suffer as much as the slight growing girl who must stand during a long hot day. I trust the reader will note carefully the Appendix at the close of this book.

It will soon be discovered that the modern opium or morphia habit has a large place in this volume. While

I have tried to avoid the style of a medical treatise, which would be in poor taste in a work of fiction, I have carefully consulted the best medical works and authorities on the subject, and I have conversed with many opium slaves in all stages of the habit. I am sure I am right in fearing that in the morphia hunger and consumption one of the greatest evils of the future is looming darkly above the horizon of society. Warnings against this poison of body and soul cannot be too solemn or too strong.

So many have aided me in the collection of my material that any mention of names may appear almost invidious; but as the reader will naturally think that the varied phases of the opium habit are remote from my experience, I will say that I have been guided in my words by trustworthy physicians like Drs. E. P. Fowler, of New York; Louis Seaman, chief of staff at the Charity Hospital; Wm. H. Vail, and many others. I have also read such parts of my MS. as touched on this subject to Dr. H. K. Kane, the author of two works on the morphia habit.

This novel appeared as a serial in the "Congregationalist" of Boston, and my acknowledgments are due to the editors and publishers of this journal for their confidence in taking the story before it was written and for their uniform courtesy.

I can truly say that I have bestowed more labor on this book than upon any which have preceded it; for the favor accorded me by the public imposes the strongest obligation to be conscientious in my work.

CONTENTS

WITHOUT A HOME

WITHOUT A HOME

CHAPTER I

ONE GIRL'S IDEAL OF LIFE

IT was an attractive picture that Martin Jocelyn looked upon through the open doorway of his parlor. His lively daughter Belle had invited half a score of her schoolmates to spend the evening, and a few privileged brothers had been permitted to come also. The young people were naturally selecting those dances which had some of the characteristics of a romp, for they were at an age when motion means enjoyment.

Miss Belle, eager and mettlesome, stood waiting for music that could scarcely be lighter or more devoid of moral quality than her own immature heart. Life, at that time, had for her but one great desideratum—fun; and with her especial favorites about her, with a careful selection of "nice brothers," canvassed with many pros and cons over neglected French exercises, she had the promise of plenty of it for a long evening, and her dark eyes glowed and cheeks flamed at the prospect. Impatiently tapping the floor with her foot, she looked toward her sister, who was seated at the piano.

Mildred Jocelyn knew that all were waiting for her; she instinctively felt the impatience she did not see, and yet could not resist listening to some honeyed nonsense that her "friend" was saying. Ostensibly, Vinton Arnold was at her side to turn the leaves of the music, but in reality to feast his eyes on beauty which daily bound him in stronger chains of fascination. Her head drooped under his words, but only as the flowers bend under the dew and rain that give them life. His passing compliment was a trifle, but it seemed like the delicate touch to which the subtle electric current responds. From a credulous, joyous heart a crimson tide welled up into her face and neck; she could not repress a smile, though she bowed her head in girlish shame to hide it. Then, as if the light, gay music before her had become the natural expression of her mood, she struck into it with a brilliancy and life that gave even Belle content.

Arnold saw the pleasure his remark had given, and surmised the reason why the effect was so much greater than the apparent cause. For a moment an answering glow lighted up his pale face, and then, as if remembering something, he sighed deeply; but in the merry life which now filled the apartments a sigh stood little chance of recognition.

The sigh of the master of the house, however, was so deep and his face so clouded with care and anxiety as he turned from it all, that his wife, who at that moment met him, was compelled to note that something was amiss.

"Martin, what is it?" she asked.

He looked for a moment into her troubled blue eyes, and noted how fair, delicate, and girlish she still appeared in her evening dress. He knew also that the delicacy and refinement of feature were but the reflex of her nature, and, for the first time in his life, he wished that she were a strong, coarse woman.

"No matter, Fanny, to-night. See that the youngsters have a good time," and he passed hastily out.

"He's worrying about those stupid business matters again," she said, and the thought seemed to give much relief.

Business matters were masculine, and she was essentially feminine Her world was as far removed from finance as her laces from the iron in which her husband dealt.

A little boy of four years of age and a little girl of six,

whose tiny form was draped in such gossamer-like fabrics that she seemed more fairy-like than human, were pulling at her dress, eager to enter the mirth-resounding parlors, but afraid to leave her sheltering wing. Mrs. Jocelyn watched the scene from the doorway, where her husband had stood, without his sigh. Her motherly heart sympathized with Belle's abounding life and fun, and her maternal pride was assured by the budding promise of a beauty which would shine pre-eminent when the schoolgirl should become a belle in very truth.

But her eyes rested on Mildred with wistful tenderness. Her own experience enabled her to interpret her daughter's manner, and to understand the ebb and flow of feeling whose cause, as yet, was scarcely recognized by the young girl.

The geniality of Mrs. Jocelyn's smile might well assure Vinton Arnold that she welcomed his presence at her daughter's side, and yet, for some reason, the frank, cordial greeting in the lady's eyes and manner made him sigh again. He evidently harbored a memory or a thought that did not accord with the scene or the occasion. Whatever it was it did not prevent him from enjoying to the utmost the pleasure he ever found in the presence of Mildred. In contrast with Belle she had her mother's fairness and delicacy of feature, and her blue eyes were not designed to express the exultation and pride of one of society's flattered favorites. Indeed it was already evident that a glance from Arnold was worth more than the world's homage. And yet it was comically pathetic—as it ever is—to see how the girl tried to hide the "abundance of her heart."

"Millie is myself right over again," thought Mrs. Jocelyn; "hardly in society before in a fair way to be out of it. Beaux in general have few attractions for her. Belle, however, will lead the young men a chase. If I'm any judge, Mr. Arnold's symptoms are becoming serious. He's just the one of all the world for Millie, and could give her the home which her style of beauty requires—a home in which not a common or coarse thing would be visible, but all as dainty as herself. How I would like to furnish her house! But Martin always thinks he's so poor."

Mrs. Jocelyn soon left the parlor to complete her arrangements for an elegant little supper, and she complacently felt that, whatever might be the tribulations of the great iron firm down town, her small domain was serene with present happiness and bright with promise.

While the vigorous appetites of the growing boys and girls were disposing of the supper, Arnold and Mildred rather neglected their plates, finding ambrosia in each other's eyes, words, and even intonations. Now that they had the deserted parlor to themselves, Mildred seemed under less constraint.

"It was very nice of you," she said, "to come and help me entertain Belle's friends, especially when they are all so young."

"Yes," he replied. "I am a happy monument of self-sacrifice."

"But not a brazen one," she added quickly.

"No, nor a bronze one, either," he said, and a sudden gloom gathered in his large dark eyes.

She had always admired the pallor of his face. "It set off his superb brown eyes and heavy mustache so finely," she was accustomed to say. But this evening for some reason she wished that there was a little more bronze on his cheek and decision in his manner. His aristocratic pallor was a trifle too great, and he seemed a little frail to satisfy even her ideal of manhood.

She said, in gentle solicitude, "You do not look well this spring. I fear you are not very strong."

He glanced at her quickly, but in her kindly blue eyes and in every line of her lovely face he saw only friendly regard—perhaps more, for her features were not designed for disguises. After a moment he replied, with a quiet bitterness which both pained and mystified her:

"You are right. I am not strong."

"But summer is near," she resumed earnestly. "You will soon go to the country, and will bring back this fall bronze in plenty, and the strength of bronze. Mother says we shall go to Saratoga. That is one of your favorite haunts, I believe, so I shall have the pleasure, perhaps, of drinking 'your very good health' some bright morning before breakfast. Which is your favorite spring?"

"I do not know. I will decide after I have learned your choice."

"That's an amiable weakness. I think I shall like Saratoga. The great hotels contain all one wishes for amusement. Then everything about town is so nice, pretty, and sociable. The shops, also, are fine. Too often we have spent our summers in places that were a trifle dreary. Mountains oppress me with a sense of littleness, and their wildness frightens me. The ocean is worse still. The moment I am alone with it, such a lonely, desolate feeling creeps over me—oh, I can't tell you! I fear you think I am silly and frivolous. You think I ought to be inspired by the shaggy mountains and wild waves and all that. Well, you may think so—I won't tell fibs. I don't think mother is frivolous, and she feels as I do. We are from the South, and like things that are warm, bright, and sociable. The ocean always seemed to me so large and cold and pitiless—to care so little for those in its power."

"In that respect it's like the world, or rather the people in it—"

"Oh, no, no!" she interrupted eagerly; "it is to the world of people I am glad to escape from these solitudes of nature. As I said, the latter, with their vastness, power, and, worse than all, their indifference, oppress me, and make me shiver with a vague dread. I once saw a ship beaten to pieces by the waves in a storm. It was on the coast near where we were spending the summer. Some of the people on the vessel were drowned, and their cries ring in my ears to this day. Oh, it was piteous to see them reaching out their hands, but the great merciless waves would not stop a moment, even when a little time would have given the lifeboats a chance to save the poor creatures. The breakers just struck and pounded the ship until it broke into pieces, and then tossed the lifeless body and broken wood on the shore as if one were of no more value than the other. I can't think of it without shuddering, and I've hated the sea ever since, and never wish to go near it again."

"You have unconsciously described this Christian city," said Arnold, with a short laugh.

"What a cynic you are to-night! You condemn all the world, and find fault even with yourself—a rare thing in cynics, I imagine. As a rule they are right, and the universe wrong."

"I have not found any fault with you," he said, in a tone that caused her long eyelashes to veil the pleasure she could not wholly conceal.

"I hope the self-constraint imposed by your courtesy is not too severe for comfort. I also understand the little fiction of excepting present company. But I cannot help remembering that I am a wee bit of the world and very worldly; that is, I am very fond of the world and all its pretty follies. I like nice people much better than savage mountains and heartless waves."

"And yet you are not what I should call a society girl, Miss Millie."

"I'm glad you think so. I've no wish to win that character. Fashionable society seems to me like the sea, as restless and unreasoning, always on the go, and yet never going anywhere. I know lots of girls who go here and there and do this and that with the monotony with which the waves roll in and out. Half the time they act contrary to their wishes and feelings, but they imagine it the thing to do, and they do it till they are tired and bored half to death."

"What, then, is your ideal of life?"

Her head drooped a little lower, and the tell-tale color would come as she replied hesitatingly, and with a slight deprecatory laugh:

"Well, I can't say I've thought it out very definitely. Plenty of real friends seem to me better than the world's stare, even though there's a trace of admiration in it. Then, again, you men so monopolize the world that there is not much left for us poor women to do; but I have imagined that to create a lovely home, and to gather in it all the beauty within one's reach, and just the people one best liked, would be a very congenial life-work for some women. That is what mother is doing for us, and she seems very happy and contented—much more so than those ladies who seek their pleasures beyond their homes. You see I use my eyes, Mr. Arnold, even if I am not antiquated enough to be wise."

His look had grown so wistful and intent that she could not meet it, but averted her face as she spoke. Suddenly he sprang up, and took her hand with a pressure all too strong for the "friend" she called him, as he said:

"Miss Millie, you are one of a thousand. Good-night."

For a few moments she sat where he left her. What did he mean? Had she revealed her heart too plainly? His manner surely had been unmistakable, and no woman could have doubted the language of his eyes.

"But some constraint," she sighed, "ties his tongue."

The more she thought it over, however—and what young girl does not live over such interviews a hundred times—the more convinced she became that her favorite among the many who sought her favor gave as much to her as she to him; and she was shrewd enough to understand that the nearer two people exchange evenly in these matters the better it is for both. Her last thought that night was, "To make a home for him would be happiness indeed. How much life promises me!"

CHAPTER II

WEAKNESS

VINTON ARNOLD'S walk down Fifth Avenue was so rapid as to indicate strong perturbation. At last he entered a large house of square, heavy architecture, a creation evidently of solid wealth in the earlier days of the thoroughfare's history. There was something in his step as he crossed the marble hall to the hat-rack and then went up the stairway that caused his mother to pass quickly from her sitting-room that she might intercept him. After a moment's scrutiny she said, in a low, hard tone:

"You have spent the evening with Miss Jocelyn again."

He made no reply.

"Are you a man of honor?"

His pallid face crimsoned instantly, and his hands clenched with repressed feeling, but he still remained silent. Neither did he appear to have the power to meet his mother's cold, penetrating glance.

"It would seem," she resumed, in the same quiet, incisive tone, "that my former suggestions have been unheeded. I fear that I must speak more plainly. You will please come with me for a few moments."

With evident reluctance he followed her to a small apartment, furnished richly, but with the taste and elegance of a past generation. He had become very pale again, but his face wore the impress of pain and irresolution rather than of sullen defiance or of manly independence. The hardness of the gold that had been accumulating in the family for generations had seemingly permeated the mother's heart, for the expression of her son's face softened neither her tone nor manner. And yet not for a moment could she be made to think of herself as cruel, or even stern. She was simply firm and sensible in the performance of her duty. She was but maintaining the traditional policy of the family, and was conscious that society would thoroughly approve of her course. Chief of all, she sincerely believed that she was promoting her son's welfare, but she had not Mrs. Jocelyn's gentle ways of manifesting solicitude.

After a moment of oppressive silence, she began:

"Perhaps I can best present this issue in its true light by again asking, Are you a man of honor?"

"Is it dishonorable," answered her son irritably, "to love a pure, good girl?"

"No," said his mother, in the same quiet, measured voice; "but it may be very great folly and a useless waste. It is dishonorable, however, to inspire false hopes in a girl's heart, no matter who she is. It is weak and dishonorable to hover around a pretty face like a poor moth that singes its wings."

In sudden, passionate appeal, he exclaimed, "If I can win Miss Jocelyn, why cannot I marry her? She is as good as she is beautiful. If you knew her as I do you would be proud to call her your daughter. They live very prettily, even elegantly—"

By a simple, deprecatory gesture Mrs. Arnold made her son feel that it was useless to add another word.

"Vinton," she said, "a little reason in these matters is better than an indefinite amount of sentimental nonsense. You are now old enough to be swayed by reason, and not to fume and fret after the impossible like a child. Neither your father nor I have acted hastily in this matter. It was a great trial to discover that you had allowed your fancy to become entangled below the circle in which it is your privilege to move, and I am thankful that my other children have been more considerate. In a quiet, unobtrusive way we have taken pains to learn all about the Jocelyns. They are comparative strangers in the city. Mr. Jocelyn is merely a junior partner in a large iron firm, and from all your father says I fear he has lived too elegantly for his means. That matter will soon be tested, however, for his firm is in trouble and will probably have to suspend. With your health, and in the face of the fierce competition in this city, are you able to marry and support a penniless girl? If, on the contrary, you propose to support a wife on the property that now belongs to your father and myself, our wishes should have some weight. I tell you frankly that our means, though large, are not sufficient to make you all independent and maintain the style to which you have been accustomed. With your frail health and need of exemption from care and toil, you must marry wealth. Your father is well satisfied that whoever allies himself to this Jocelyn family may soon have them all on his hands to support. We decline the risk of burdening ourselves with these unknown, uncongenial people. Is there anything unreasonable in that? Because you are fascinated by a pretty face, of which there are thousands in this city, must we be forced into intimate associations with people that are wholly distasteful to us? This would be a poor return for having shielded you so carefully through years of ill health and feebleness."

The young man's head drooped lower and lower as his mother spoke, and his whole air was one of utter despondency. She waited for his reply, but for a few moments he did not speak. Suddenly he looked up, with a reckless, characteristic laugh, and said:

"The Spartans were right in destroying the feeble children. Since I am under such obligations, I cannot resist your logic, and I admit that it would be poor taste on my part to ask you to support for me a wife not of your choosing."

"'Good taste' at least should have prevented such a remark. You can choose for yourself from a score of fine girls of your own station in rank and wealth."

"Pardon me, but I would rather not inflict my weakness on any of the score."

"But you would inflict it on one weak in social position and without any means of support."

"She is the one girl that I have met with who seemed both gentle and strong, and whose tastes harmonize with my own. But you don't know her, and never will. You have only learned external facts about the Jocelyns, and out of your prejudices have created a family of underbred people that does not exist. Their crime of comparative poverty I cannot dispute. I have not made the prudential inquiries which you and father have gone into so carefully. But your logic is inexorable. As you suggest, I could not earn enough myself to provide a wife with hairpins. The slight considerations of happiness, and the fact that Miss Jocelyn might aid me in becoming something more than a shadow among men, are not to be urged against the solid reasons you have named."

"Young people always give a tragic aspect to these crude passing fancies. I have known 'blighted happiness' to bud and blossom again so often that you must pardon me if I act rather on the ground of experience and good sense. An unsuitable alliance may bring brief gratification and pleasure, but never happiness, never lasting and solid content."

"Well, mother, I am not strong enough to argue with you, either in the abstract or as to these 'wise saws' which so mangle my wretched self," and with the air of one exhausted and defeated he languidly went to his room.

Mrs. Arnold frowned as she muttered, "He makes no promise to cease visiting the girl." After a moment she added, even more bitterly, "I doubt whether he could keep such a promise; therefore my will must supply his lack of decision;" and she certainly appeared capable of making good this deficiency in several human atoms.

If she could have imparted some of her firmness and resolution to Martin Jocelyn, they would have been among the most useful gifts a man ever received. As the stanchness of a ship is tested by the storm, so a crisis in his experience was approaching which would test his courage, his fortitude, and the general soundness of his manhood. Alas! the test would find him wanting. That night, for the first time in his life, he came home with a step a trifle unsteady. Innocent Mrs. Jocelyn did not note that anything was amiss. She was busy putting her home into its usual pretty order after the breezy, gusty evening always occasioned by one of Belle's informal companies. She observed that her husband had recovered more than his wonted cheerfulness, and seemed indeed as gay as Belle herself. Lounging on a sofa, he laughed at his wife and petted her more than usual, assuring her that her step was as light, and that she still looked as young and pretty as any of the girls who had tripped through the parlors that evening.

The trusting, happy wife grew so rosy with pleasure, and her tread was so elastic from maternal pride and exultàtion at the prospects of her daughters, that his compliments seemed scarcely exaggerated.

"Never fear, Nan," he said, in a gush of feeling; "I'll take care of you whatever happens," and the glad smile she turned upon him proved that she doubted his words no more than her own existence.

They were eminently proper words for a husband to address to his wife, but the circumstances under which they were uttered made them maudlin sentiment rather than a manly pledge. As spoken, they were so ominous that the loving woman might well have trembled and lost her girlish flush. But even through the lurid hopes and vague prospects created by dangerous stimulants, Mr. Jocelyn saw, dimly, the spectre of coming trouble, and he added: "But, Nan, we must economize—we really must."

"Foolish man!" laughed his wife; "always preaching economy, but never practicing it."

"Would to God I had millions to lavish on you!" he exclaimed, with tears of mawkish feeling and honest affection mingled as they never should in a true man's eyes.

"Lavish your love, Martin," replied the wife, "and I'll be content."

That night she laid her head upon her pillow without misgiving.

Mrs. Jocelyn was the daughter of a Southern planter, and in her early home had been accustomed to a condition of chronic financial embarrassment and easy-going, careless abundance. The war had swept away her father and brothers with the last remnant of the mortgaged property.

Young Jocelyn's antecedents had been somewhat similar, and they had married much as the birds pair, without knowing very definitely where or how the home nest would be constructed. He, however, had secured a good education, and was endowed with fair business capacities. He was thus enabled for a brief time before the war to provide a comfortable support in a Southern city for his wife and little daughter Mildred, and the fact that he was a gentleman by birth and breeding gave him better social advantages than mere wealth could have obtained. At the beginning of the struggle he was given a commission in the Confederate army, but with the exception of a few slight scratches and many hardships escaped unharmed. After the conflict was over, the ex-officer came to the North, against which he had so bravely and zealously fought, and was pleased to find that there was no prejudice worth naming against him on this account. His good record enabled him to obtain a position in a large iron warehouse, and in consideration of his ability to control a certain amount of Southern trade he was eventually given an interest in the business. This apparent advancement induced him to believe that he might safely rent, in one of the many cross-streets up town, the pretty home in which we find him. The fact that their expenses had always a little more than kept pace with their income did not trouble Mrs. Jocelyn, for she had been accustomed to an annual deficit from childhood. Some way had always been provided, and she had a sort of blind faith that some way always would be. Mr. Jocelyn also had fallen into rather soldier-like ways, and after being so free with Confederate scrip, with difficulty learned the value of paper money of a different color.

Moreover, in addition to a certain lack of foresight and frugal prudence, bred by army life and Southern open-heartedness, he cherished a secret habit which rendered a wise, steadily maintained policy of thrift wellnigh impossible. About two years before the opening of our story he had been the victim of a painful disease, the evil effects of which did not speedily pass away. For several weeks of this period, to quiet the pain, he was given morphia powders; their effects were so agreeable that they were not discontinued after the physician ceased to prescribe them. The subtle stimulant not only banished the lingering traces of suffering, but enabled him to resume the routine of business with comparative ease much sooner than he had expected. Thus he gradually drifted into the habitual use of morphia, taking it as a panacea for every ill. Had he a toothache, a rheumatic or neuralgic twinge, the drug quieted the pain. Was he despondent from any cause, or annoyed by some untoward event, a small white powder soon brought hopefulness and serenity. When emergencies occurred which promised to tax his mental and physical powers, opium appeared to give a clearness and elasticity of mind and a bodily vigor that was almost magical, and he availed himself of the deceptive potency more and more often.

The morbid craving which the drug inevitably engenders at last demanded a daily supply. For months he employed it in moderate quantities, using it as thousands do quinine, wine, or other stimulants, without giving much thought to the matter, sincerely intending, however, to shake off the habit as soon as he felt a little stronger and was more free from business cares. Still, as the employment of the stimulant grew into a habit, he became somewhat ashamed of it, and maintained his indulgence with increasing secrecy—a characteristic rarely absent from this vice.

Thus it can be understood that his mind had ceased to possess the natural poise which would enable him to manage his affairs in accordance with some wisely matured system of expenditure. In times of depression he would demand the most rigid economy, and again he would seem careless and indifferent and preoccupied. This financial vacillation was precisely what his wife had been accustomed to in her early home, and she thoughtlessly took her way without much regard to it. He also had little power of saying No to his gentle wife, and an appealing look from her blue eyes would settle every question of economy the wrong way. Next year they would be more prudent; at present, however, there were some things that it would be very nice to have or to do.

But, alas, Mrs. Jocelyn had decided that, for Mildred's sake, the coming summer must be spent at Saratoga. In vain her husband had told her that he did not see how it was possible. She would reply,

"Now, Martin, be reasonable. You know Mr. Arnold spends his summers there. Would you spoil Millie's chances of making one of the best matches in the city?"

He would shrug his shoulders and wonder where the money was to come from. Meanwhile he knew that his partners were anxious. They had been strong, and had endured the evil times for years without wavering, but now were compelled to obtain a credit more and more extended, in the hope of tiding themselves over the long period of depression.

This increasing business stagnation occasioned a deepening anxiety to her husband and a larger resort to his sustaining stimulant. While he had no sense of danger worth naming, he grew somewhat worried by his dependence on the drug, and it was his honest purpose to gradually abandon it as soon as the financial pressure lifted and he could breathe freely in the safety of renewed commercial prosperity. Thus the weeks and months slipped by, finding him more completely involved in the films of an evil web, and more intent than ever upon hiding the fact from every one, especially his wife and children.

He had returned on the evening of Belle's company, with fears for the worst. The scene in his pretty and happy home, in contrast with the bitter experiences that might be near at hand, so oppressed him with foreboding and trouble that he went out and weakly sought temporary respite and courage in a larger amount of morphia than he had ever yet taken.

While off his guard from the resulting exaltation, he met a business acquaintance and was led by him to indulge in wine also, with the results already narrated.

CHAPTER III

CONFIDENTIAL

MARTIN JOCELYN awoke with a shiver. He did not remember that he had been dreaming, but a dull pain in his head and a foreboding of heart had at last so asserted themselves as to banish the unconsciousness of sleep. His prospects had even a more sombre hue than the cold gray of the morning. All the false prismatic colors of the previous evening had faded, and no serene, steady light had taken their place. The forced elation was followed—as is ever the case—by a deeper despondency. The face of his sleeping wife was so peaceful, so expressive of her utter unconsciousness of impending disaster, that he could not endure its sight. He felt himself to be in no condition to meet her waking eyes and explain the cause of his fears. A sense of shame that he had been so weak the evening before also oppressed him, and he yielded to the impulse to gain a day before meeting her trusting or questioning gaze. Something might occur which would give a better aspect to his affairs, and at any rate, if the worst must come, he could explain with better grace in the evening than in his present wretched mood, that would prove too sharp a contrast with his recent gayety.

He therefore dressed silently and hastily, and left a note saying that a business engagement required his early departure. "She will have at least one more serene day before the storm," he muttered.

"Now wasn't that kind and thoughful of papa to let us all sleep late after the company!" said Mrs. Jocelyn to

Mildred. "He went away, too, without his breakfast," and in her gentle solicitude she scarcely ate any herself.

But weakly hiding trouble for a day was not kindness. The wife and daughter, who should have helped to take in sail in preparation for the threatened storm, were left unconscious of its approach. They might have noticed that Mr. Jocelyn had been more than usually anxious throughout the spring, but they knew so little of business and its risks, that they did not realize their danger. "Men always worry about their affairs," said Mrs. Jocelyn. "It's a way they have."

Mr. Arnold's visits and manner were much more congenial topics, and as a result of the entire confidence existing between mother and daughter, they dwelt at length on these subjects.

"Mamma," said Mildred, "you must not breathe of it to a soul—not even to papa yet. It would hurt me cruelly to have it known that I think so much of one who has not spoken plainly—that is, in words. I should be blind indeed if I did not understand the language of his eyes, his tones, and manner. And yet, and yet—mamma, it isn't wrong for me to love—to think so much of him before he speaks, is it? Dearly as I—well, not for the world would I seem or even *be* more forward than a girl should. I fear his people are too proud and rich to recognize us; and—and—he says so little about them. I can never talk to him or any one without making many references to you and papa. I have thought that he even avoided speaking of his family."

"We have not yet been made acquainted with Mr. and Mrs. Arnold," said Mrs. Jocelyn meditatively. "It is true we attend the same church, and it was there that Vinton saw you, and was led to seek an introduction. I'm sure we have not angled for him in any indelicate way. You met him in the mission school and in other ways, as did the other young ladies of the church. He seemed to single you out, and asked permission to call. He has been very gentlemanly, but you equally have been the self-respecting lady. I do not think you have once overstepped the line of a proper reserve. It isn't your nature to do such a thing, if I do say it. She is a silly girl who ever does, for men don't like it, and I don't blame them. Your father was a great hunter in the South, Millie, and he has often said since that I was the shyest game he ever followed. But," she added, with a low, sweet laugh, "how I did want to be caught! I can see now," she continued, with a dreamy look back into the past, "that it was just the way to be caught, for if I had turned in pursuit of him he would have run away in good earnest. There are some girls who have set their caps for your handsome Mr. Arnold who don't know this. I am glad to say, however, that you take the course you do, not because you know better, but because you *are* better—because you have not lost in city life the shy, pure nature of the wild flowers that were your early playmates. Vinton Arnold is the man to discover and appreciate this truth, and you have lost nothing by compelling him to seek you in your own home, or by being so reserved when abroad."

While her mother's words greatly reassured Mildred, her fair face still retained its look of anxious perplexity.

"I have rarely met Mrs. Arnold and her daughters," she said; "but even in a passing moment, it seemed as if they tried to inform me by their manner that I did not belong to their world. Perhaps they were only oblivious—I don't know."

"I think that is all," said Mrs. Jocelyn musingly. "We have attended their church only since we came up town. They sit on the further side, in a very expensive pew, while papa thinks we can afford only a side seat near the door. It is evident that they are proud people, but in the matter of birth and good breeding, my dear, I am sure we are their equals. Even when poorer than we are now we were welcomed to the best society of the South. Have no fears, darling. When they come to know *you* they will be as proud of you as I am."

"Oh, mother, what a sweet prophetess you are! The

life you suggest is so beautiful, and I do not think I could live without beauty. He is so handsome and refined, and his taste is so perfect that every association he awakens is refined and high-toned. It seems as if my—as if he might take out of my future all that is hard and coarse—all that I shrink from even in thought. But, mamma, I wish he were a wee bit stronger. His hands are almost as white and small as mine; and then sometimes he is so very pale."

"Well, Millie, we can't have everything. City life and luxury are hard on young men. It would be better for them if they tramped the woods more with a gun, as your father did. There was a time when papa could walk his thirty miles a day and ride fifty. But manly qualities may be those of the mind as well as of muscle. I gather from what Mr. Arnold says that his health never has been very good; but you are the one of all the world to pet him and take care of him. Most of the fashionable girls of his set would want to go here and there all the time, and would wear him out with their restlessness. You would be happier at home."

"Indeed I would, mamma. Home, and heaven, are words that to me are near akin."

"I'm glad you are in such a fair way to win the home, but not heaven I trust for a long time yet. Let us think of the home first. While I would not for the world wish you to do a thing which the strictest womanly delicacy did not permit, there are some things which we can do that are very proper indeed. Mr. Arnold has an eye for beauty as well as yourself, and he is accustomed to see ladies well dressed. He noticed your toilet last night as well as your face, and his big brown eyes informed me that he thought it very pretty. I intend that you shall appear as well as the best of them at Saratoga, and what we cannot afford in expensive fabrics we must make up in skill and taste. Luckily, men don't know much about the cost of material. They see the general effect only. A lady is to them a finished picture, and they never think of inventorying the frame, canvas, and colors as a woman does. For quarter of the money I'll make you appear better than his sisters. So get your things, and we'll begin shopping at once, for such nice work requires time."

They were soon in the temples of fashion on Broadway, bent upon carrying out their guileless conspiracy. Nevertheless their seemingly innocent and harmless action was wretched folly. They did not know that it raised one more barrier between them and all they sought and hoped, for they were spending the little money that might save them from sudden and utter poverty.

CHAPTER IV

"PITILESS WAVES"

A DEEPER shadow than that of the night fell upon Mildred Jocelyn's home after the return of her father. Feeling that there should be no more blind drifting toward he knew not what, he had employed all the means within his power to inform himself of the firm's prospects, and learned that there was almost a certainty of speedy failure. He was so depressed and gloomy when he sat down to dinner that his wife had not the heart to tell him of her schemes to secure his daughter's happiness, or of the gossamer-like fabrics she had bought, out of which she hoped to construct a web that would more surely entangle Mr. Arnold. Even her sanguine spirit was chilled and filled with misgivings by her husband's manner. Mildred, too, was speedily made to feel that only a very serious cause could banish her father's wonted good-humor and render him so silent. Belle and the little ones maintained the light talk which usually enlivened the meal, but a sad constraint rested on the others. At last Mr. Jocelyn said, abruptly, "Fanny, I wish to see you alone," and she followed him to their room with a face that grew pale with a vague dread. What could have happened?

"Fanny," he said sadly, "our firm is in trouble. I have hoped and have tried to believe that we should pull through, but now that I have looked at the matter squarely I see no chance for us, and from the words and bearing of my partners I imagine they have about given up hope themselves."

"Oh, come, Martin, look on the bright side. You always take such gloomy views of things. They'll pull through, never fear; and if they don't, you will soon obtain a better position. A man of your ability should be at the head of a firm. *You* would make money, no matter what the times were."

"Unfortunately, Fanny, your sanguine hopes and absurd opinion of my abilities do not change in the least the hard facts in the case. If the firm fails, I am out of employment, and hundreds of as good—yes, better men than I, are looking vainly for almost any kind of work. The thought that we have laid up nothing in all these years cuts me to the very quick. One thing is now certain. Not a dollar must be spent, hereafter, except for food, and that of the least costly kind, until I see our way more clearly."

"Can't we go to Saratoga?" faltered Mrs. Jocelyn.

"Certainly not. If all were well I should have had to borrow money and anticipate my income in order to spend even a few weeks there, unless you went to a cheap boarding-house. If things turn out as I fear, I could not borrow a dollar. I scarcely see how we are to live anywhere, much less at a Saratoga hotel. Fanny, can't you understand my situation? Suppose my income stops, how much ahead have we to live upon?" Mrs. Jocelyn sank into a chair and sobbed, "Oh that I had known this before! See there!"

The bed was covered with dress goods and the airy nothings that enhance a girl's beauty. The husband understood their meaning too well, and he muttered something like an oath. At last he said, in a hard tone, "Well, after buying all this frippery, how much money have you left?"

"Oh, Martin," sobbed his wife, "don't speak to me in that tone. Indeed I did not know we were in real danger. You seemed in such good spirits last evening, and Mr. Arnold showed so much feeling for Millie, that my heart has been as light as a feather all day. I wouldn't have bought these things if I had only known—if I had realized it all."

Mr. Jocelyn now uttered an unmistakable anathema on his folly.

"The money you had this morning is gone, then?"

"Yes."

"How much has been charged?"

"Don't ask me."

He was so angry—with himself more than his wife—and so cast down that he could not trust himself to speak again. With a gesture, more expressive than any words, he turned on his heel and left the room and the house. For hours he walked the streets in the wretched turmoil of a sensitive, yet weak nature. He was not one who could calmly meet an emergency and manfully do his best, suffering patiently meanwhile the ills that could not be averted. He could lead a cavalry charge into any kind of danger, but he could not stand still under fire. The temptation to repeat his folly of the previous evening was very strong, but it had cost him so dearly that he swore a great oath that at least he would not touch liquor again; but he could not refrain from lifting himself in some degree out of his deep dejection, by a recourse to the stimulant upon which he had so long been dependent. At last, jaded and sober indeed, he returned to a home whose very beauty and comfort now became the chief means of his torture.

In the meantime Mildred and her mother sat by the pretty fabrics that had the bright hues of their morning hopes, and they looked at each other with tears and dismay. If the silk and lawn should turn into crape, it would seem so in accordance with their feelings as scarcely to excite surprise. Each queried vainly, "What now will be the future?" The golden prospect of the day had become dark and chaotic, and in strong reaction a vague sense of impending disaster so oppressed them that they scarcely spoke. Deep in Mildred's heart, however, born of woman's trust, was the sustaining hope that her friend, Vinton Arnold, would be true to her whatever might happen. Poor Mrs. Jocelyn's best hope was, that the financial storm would blow over without fulfilling their fears. She had often known her father to be half desperate, and then there was patched up some kind of arrangement which enabled them to go on again in their old way. Still, even with her unbusiness-like habits of thought and meagre knowledge of the world, she could not see how they could maintain themselves if her husband's income should suddenly cease, and he be unable to find a like position.

She longed for his return, but when he came he gave her no comfort.

"Don't speak to me," he said; "I can tell you nothing that you do not already know. The events of the next few weeks will make all plain enough."

The logic of events did convince even Mrs. Jocelyn that making no provision for a "rainy day" is sad policy. The storm did not blow over, although it blew steadily and strongly. The firm soon failed, but Mr. Jocelyn received a small sum out of the assets, which prevented immediate want. Mildred's course promised to justify Arnold's belief that she could be strong as well as gentle, for she insisted that every article obtained on credit should be taken back to the shops. Her mother shrank from the task, so she went herself and plainly stated their circumstances. It was a bitter experience for the poor child—far more painful than she had anticipated. She could not believe that the affable people who waited on her so smilingly a few days before would appear so different; but even those who were most inclined to be harsh, and to feel aggrieved at their small loss in cutting the material returned, were softened as she said, gently and almost humbly:

"Since we could not pay for it we felt that it would be more honorable to bring it back in as good condition as when received." In every instance, however, in which the goods had been paid for, she found that she could effect no exchange for the money, except at such reduced rates that she might as well give them away.

Even Mrs. Jocelyn saw the need of immediate changes. One of their two servants was dismissed. Belle pouted over the rigid economy, now enforced all too late. Mildred cried over it in secret, but made heroic efforts to be cheerful in the presence of her father and mother; but each day, with a deeper chill at heart, she asked herself a thousand times, "Why does not Mr. Arnold come to see me?"

Vinton Arnold was in even greater distress. He had to endure not only the pain of a repressed affection, but also a galling and humiliating sense of unmanly weakness. He, of course, learned of the failure, and his father soon after took pains to say significantly that one of the members of the iron firm had told him that Mr. Jocelyn had nothing to fall back upon. Therefore Arnold knew that the girl he loved must be in sore trouble. And yet, how could he go to her? What could he say or do that would not make him appear contemptible in her eyes? But to remain away in her hour of misfortune seemed such a manifestation of heartless indifference, such a mean example of the world's tendency to pass by on the other side, that he grew haggard and ghost-like in his self-reproach and self-contempt. At last his parents began to insist that his health required a change of air, and suggested a mountain resort or a trip abroad, and he was conscious of no power to resist the quiet will with which any plan decided upon would be carried out. He felt that he must see Mildred once more, although what he would say to her he could not tell. While there had been no conscious and definite purpose on the part of his parents, they nevertheless had trained him to helplessness in mind and body. His will was as relaxed as his muscles. Instead of wise, patient effort to develop a feeble constitution and to educate his mind by systematic courses of study, he had been treated as an exotic all his days. And yet it had been care without tenderness, or much manifestation of affection. Not a thing had been done to develop self-respect or self-reliance. Even more than most girls, he was made to feel himself dependent on his parents. He had studied but little; he had read much, but in a desultory way. Of business and of men's prompt, keen ways he was lamentably ignorant for one of his years, and the consciousness of this made him shrink from the companionship of his own sex, and begat a reticence whose chief cause was timidity. His parents' wealth had been nothing but a curse, and they would learn eventually that while they could shield his person from the roughnesses of the world they could not protect his mind and heart from those experiences which ever demand manly strength and principle. As a result of their costly system, there were few more pitiable objects in the city than Vinton Arnold as he stole under the cover of night to visit the girl who was hoping—though more faintly after every day of waiting—that she might find in him sustaining strength and love in her misfortunes.

But when she saw his white, haggard face and nervous, timid manner, she was almost shocked, and exclaimed, with impulsive sympathy, "Mr. Arnold, you have been ill. I have done you wrong."

He did not quite understand her, and was indiscreet enough to repeat, "You have done me wrong, Miss Millie?"

"Pardon me. Perhaps you do not know that we are in deep trouble. My father's firm has failed, and we shall have to give up our home. Indeed, I hardly know what we shall do. When in trouble, one's thoughts naturally turn to one's friends. I thought perhaps you would come to see me," and two tears that she could not repress in her eyes.

"Oh, that I were a man!" groaned Arnold, mentally, and never had human cruelty inflicted a keener pang than did Mildred's sorrowful face and the gentle reproach implied in her words.

"I—I have been ill," he said hesitatingly. "Miss Millie," he added impulsively, "you can never know how deeply I feel for you."

She lifted her eyes questioningly to his face, and its expression was again unmistakable. For a moment she lost control of her overburdened heart, and bowing her face in her hands gave way to the strong tide of her feelings.

"Oh!" she sobbed, "I have been so anxious and fearful about the future. People have come here out of curiosity, and others have acted as if they did not care what became of us, if they only obtained the money we owed them. I did not think that those who were so smiling and friendly a short time since could be so harsh and indifferent. A thousand times I have thought of that poor ship that I saw the waves beat to pieces, and it has seemed as if it might be our fate. I suppose I am morbid, and that some way will be provided, but *some* way is not *a* way."

Instead of coming to her side and promising all that his heart prompted, the miserable constraint of his position led him to turn from grief that he was no longer able to witness. He went to the window, and, bowing his head against the sash, looked out into the darkness.

She regarded him with wonder as she slowly wiped her eyes.

"Mr. Arnold," she faltered, "I hope you will forgive me for my weakness, and also for inflicting our troubles on you."

He turned and came slowly toward her. She saw that he trembled and almost tottered as he walked, and that his face had become ashen. The hand he gave her seemed like ice to her warm, throbbing palm. But never could she forget his expression—the blending of self-contempt, pitiable weakness, and dejection.

"Miss Mildred," he said slowly, "there is no use in disguises. We had better both recognize the truth at once. At least it will be better for you, for then you may find a friend more worthy of the name. Can you not see what I am—a broken reed? The vine could better sustain a falling tree than I the one I loved, even though, like the vine, my heart clung to that one as its sole support. You suffer; I am in torment. You are sad; I despair. You associate strength and help with manhood, and you are right. You do not know that the weakest thing in the world is a weak, helpless man. I am only strong to suffer. I can do nothing; I am nothing. It would be impossible for me to explain how helpless and dependent I am—you could not understand it. My whole heart went out to you, for you seemed both gentle and strong. The hope would grow in my soul that you might be merciful to me when you came to know me as I am. Good-by, Millie Jocelyn. You will find a friend strong and helpful as well as kind. As for me, my best hope is to die." He bowed his head upon the hand he did not venture to kiss, and then almost fled from the house.

Mildred was too much overcome by surprise and feeling to make any attempt to detain him. He had virtually acknowledged his love for her, but never in her wildest fancy had she imagined so dreary and sad a revelation.

Mrs. Jocelyn, perplexed by Mr. Arnold's abrupt departure, came in hastily, and Mildred told her, with many tears, all that had been said. Even her mother's gentle nature could not prevent harsh condemnation of the young man.

"So he could do nothing better than get up this little melodrama, and then hasten back to his elegant home," she said, with a darkening frown.

Mildred shook her head and said, musingly, "I understand him better than you do, mamma, and I pity him from the depths of my heart."

"I think it's all plain enough," said Mrs. Jocelyn, in a tone that was hard and unnatural in her. "His rich parents tell him that he must not think of marrying a poor girl, and he is the most dutiful of sons."

"You did not hear his words, mamma—you did not see him. Oh, if he should die! He looked like death itself," and she gave way to such an agony of grief that her mother was alarmed on her behalf, and wept, entreated, and soothed by turns until at last the poor child crept away with throbbing temples to a long night of pain and sleeplessness. The wound was one that she must hide in her own heart; her pallor and languor for several days proved how deep it had been.

But the truth that he loved her—the belief that he could never give to another what he had given to her—had a secret and sustaining power. Hope is a hardy plant in the hearts of the young. Though the future was dark, it still had its possibilities of good. Womanlike, she thought more of his trouble than of her own, and that which most depressed her was the fear that his health might give way utterly. "I can bear anything better than his death," she said to herself a thousand times.

She made no tragic promises of constancy, nor did she indulge in very much sentimental dreaming. She simply recognized the truth that she loved him—that her whole woman's heart yearned in tenderness over him as one that was crippled and helpless. She saw that he was unable to stand alone and act for himself, and with a sensitive pride all her own she shrank from even the thought of forcing herself on the proud, rich family that had forbidden the alliance. Moreover, she was a good-hearted, Christian girl, and perceived clearly that it was no time for her to mope or droop. Even on the miserable day which followed the interview that so sorely wounded her, she made pathetic attempts to be cheerful and helpful, and as time passed she rallied slowly into strength and patience.

The father's apparent efforts to keep up under his misfortune were also a great incentive to earnest effort on her part. More than once she said in substance to her mother, "Papa is so often hopeful, serene, and even cheerful, that we ought to try and show a like spirit. Even when despondency does master him, and he becomes sad and irritable, he makes so brave an effort that he soon overcomes his wretched mood and quietly looks on the brighter side. We ought to follow his example." It would have been infinitely better had he followed theirs, and found in prayer, faith, and manly courage the serenity and fortitude that were but the brief, deceptive, and dangerous effects of a fatal poison.

It was decided that the family should spend the summer

at some quiet farmhouse where the board would be very inexpensive, and that Mr. Jocelyn, in the meantime, should remain in the city in order to avail himself of any opening that he might discover.

After a day or two of search in the country, he found a place that he thought would answer, and the family prepared as quickly as possible for what seemed to them like a journey to Siberia.

Mildred's farewell to her own private apartment was full of touching pathos. This room was the outward expression not merely of a refined taste, but of some of the deepest feelings and characteristics of her nature. In its furniture and adornment it was as dainty as her own delicate beauty. She had been allowed to fit it up as she wished, and had lavished upon it the greater part of her spending money. She had also bestowed upon it much thought, and the skilful work of her own hands had eked out to a marvellous extent the limited sums that her father had been able to give her. The result was a prettiness and light, airy grace which did not suggest the resting-place of an ordinary flesh-and-blood girl, but of one in whom the spiritual and the love of the beautiful were the ruling forces of life.

It is surprising how character impresses itself on one's surroundings. Mrs. Arnold's elegant home was a correct expression of herself. Stately, formal, slightly rigid, decidedly cold, it suggested to the visitor that he would receive the courtesy to which his social position entitled him, and nothing more. It was the result of an exact and logical mind, and could no more unbend into a little comfortable disorder than the lady herself. She bestowed upon its costly appointments the scrupulous care which she gave to her children, and her manner was much the same in each instance. She was justly called a strong character, but she made herself felt after the fashion of an artist with his hammer and chisel. Carved work is cold and rigid at best.

Mildred had not as yet impressed people as a strong character. On the contrary, she had seemed peculiarly gentle and yielding. Vinton Arnold, however, in his deep need had instinctively half guessed the truth, for her influence was like that of a warm day in spring, undemonstrative, not self-asserting, but most powerful. The tongue-tied could speak in her presence; the diffident found in her a kindly sympathy which gave confidence; men were peculiarly drawn toward her because she was so essentially womanly without being silly. Although as sprightly and fond of fun as most young girls of her age, they recognized that she was perfectly truthful and loyal to all that men—even bad men—most honor in a woman. They always had a good time in her society, and yet felt the better and purer for it. Life blossomed and grew bright about her from some innate influence that she exerted unconsciously. After all there was no mystery about it. She had her faults like others, but at heart she was genuinely good and unselfish. The gentle mother had taught her woman's best graces of speech and manner; nature had endowed her with beauty, and to that the world always renders homage.

There are thousands of very pretty girls who have no love for beauty save their own, which they do their best to spoil by self-homage. To Mildred, on the contrary, the beautiful was as essential as her daily food, and she excelled in all the dainty handicrafts by which women can make a home attractive. Therefore her own little sanctum had developed like an exquisite flower, and had become, as we have said, an expression of herself. An auctioneer, in dismantling her apartment, would not have found much more to sell than if he had pulled a rose to pieces, but left intact it was as full of beauty and fragrance as the flower itself. And yet her own hands must destroy it, and in a brief time she must exchange its airy loveliness for a bare room in a farmhouse. After that the future was as vague as it was clouded. The pretty trifles were taken down and packed away, with tears, as if she were laying them in graves.

CHAPTER V

THE RUDIMENTS OF A MAN

"MOTHER, I hain't no unison with it at all," said Farmer Atwood, leaning on the breakfast table and holding aloft a knife and fork—formidable implements in his hands, but now unemployed through perturbation of mind. "I hain't no unison with it—this havin' fine city folk right in the family. 'Twill be pretty nigh as bad as visiting one's rich relations. I had a week of that once, but, thank the Lord, I hain't been so afflicted since. I've seen 'em up at the hotel and riding by too often not to know 'em. They are half conceit and half fine feathers, and that doesn't leave many qualities as are suited to a farmhouse. Roger and me will have to be—what was it that lecturin' professor called it—'deodorized' every mornin' after feedin' and cleanin' the critters. We'll have to put on our go-to-meetin's, instead of sittin' down in our shirt-sleeves comfortable like. I hain't no unison with it, and it's been a-growing on me ever since that city chap persuaded you into being cook and chambermaid for his family." And Farmer Atwood's knife and fork came down into the dish of ham with an onslaught that would have appalled a Jew.

"The governor is right, mother," said the young man referred to as Roger. "We shall all be in strait-jackets for the summer."

The speaker could not have been much more than twenty years old, although in form he appeared a full-grown man. As he stood wiping his hands on a towel that hung in a corner of the large kitchen, which, except on state occasions, also served as dining and sitting-room, it might be noted that he was above medium height, broad-shouldered, and strongly built. When he crossed the room his coarse working dress could not disguise the fact that he had a fine figure and an easy bearing of the rustic, rough-and-ready style. He had been out in the tall, dew-drenched grass, and therefore had tucked the lower part of his trousers in his boot tops, and, like his father, dispensed with his coat in the warm June morning. As he drew a chair noisily across the floor and sat down at the table, it was evident that he had a good though undeveloped face. His upper lip was deeply shadowed by a coming event, to which he looked forward with no little pride, and his well-tanned cheeks could not hide a faint glow of youthful color. One felt at a glance that his varying expressions could scarcely fail to reveal all that the young man was now or could ever become, for his face suggested a nature peculiarly frank and rather matter-of-fact, or at least unawakened. The traits of careless good-nature and self-confidence were now most apparent. He had always been regarded as a clever boy at home, and his rustic gallantry was well received by the farmers' daughters in the neighborhood. What better proofs that he was about right could a young fellow ask? He was on such good terms with himself and the world that even the event which his father so deprecated did not much disturb his easy-going assurance. He doubted, in his thoughts, whether the city girls would "turn up their noses" at him, and if they did, they might, for all that he cared, for there were plenty of rural beauties with whom he could console himself. But, like his father, he felt that the careless undress and freedom of their farm life would be criticised by the new-comers. He proposed, however, to make as little change as possible in his habits and dress, and to teach the Jocelyns that country people had "as good a right to their ways as city people to theirs." Therefore the threatened invasion did not in the least prevent him from making havoc in the substantial breakfast that Mrs. Atwood and her daughter Susan put on the table in a haphazard manner, taking it from the adjacent stove as fast as it was ready. A stolid-looking hired man sat opposite to Roger, and shovelled in his food with his knife, with a monotonous assiduity that suggested a laborer filling a coal-bin. He seemed oblivious to everything save the breakfast, and with the exception of heaping his plate from time to time he was ignored by the family.

The men-folk were quite well along with their meal before Mrs. Atwood and Susan, flushed with their labors about the stove, were ready to sit down. They were accustomed to hear the farmer grumble, and, having carried their point, were in no haste to reply or to fight over a battle that had been won already. Roger led to a slight resumption of hostilities, however, by a disposition—well-nigh universal in brothers—to tease.

"Sue," he said, "will soon be wanting to get some feathers like those of the fine birds that will light in our door-yard this evening."

"That's it," snarled the farmer; "what little you make will soon be on your backs or streamin' away in ribbons."

"Well," said Mrs. Atwood, a little sharply, "it's quite proper that we should have something on our backs, and if we earn the money to put it there ourselves, I don't see why you should complain; as for ribbons, Sue has as good right to 'em as Roger to a span-new buggy that ain't good for anything but taking girls out in."

"What made you have the seat so narrow, Roger?" asked Sue; "you couldn't squeeze three people in to save your life."

"I'm content with one girl at a time," replied Roger, with a complacent shrug.

"And the same girl only one time, too, from what I hear. You've taken out all there are in Forestville haven't you?"

"Haven't got quite around yet. And then some prudent mothers do think the seat a trifle narrow, and the ones I'd like to take out most can't go. But there's plenty that can."

"And one is as good as another," added his sister, maliciously, "If she will only talk nonsense, and let you hold her from falling out when you whisk over the thank-e-ma'ams."

"I didn't have to go from home to learn that most girls talk nonsense," laughed Roger. "By the way, how did you learn about the thank-e-ma'ams? I didn't teach you."

"No, indeed! Sisters may fall out for all that brothers care."

"That depends on whose sisters they are," said Roger, rising. "I now perceive that mine has been well taken care of."

"You think other young men have your pert ways," retorted Sue, reddening. "My friends have manners."

"Oh, I see. They let you fall out, and then politely pick you up."

"Come, you are both in danger of falling out now," said the mother reprovingly.

Roger went off whistling to his work, and the hired man lumbered after him.

"Father," said Mrs. Atwood, "who'll go down to the river for the trunks?"

"Well, I s'pose I'll have to," grumbled Mr. Atwood. "Roger don't want to, and Jotham can do more work in the cornfield than me."

"I'm glad you're so sensible. Riding down to the river and back will be a good bit easier than hoeing corn all day. The stage will be along about five, I guess, and I'll get supper for 'em in the sittin'-room, so you can eat in your shirt-sleeves, if that'll quiet your mind."

With the aspect of a November day Mr. Atwood got out the great farm-wagon and jogged down to the landing on the Hudson, which was so distant as to insure his absence for several hours.

It was a busy day for Mrs. Atwood and Susan. Fresh

bread and cake were to be baked, and the rooms "tidied up" once more. A pitcher that had lost its handle was filled with old-fashioned roses that persisted in blooming in a grass-choked flower-bed. This was placed in the room designed for Mrs. Jocelyn and the children, while the one flower vase, left unbroken from the days of Roger's boyish carelessness, adorned the smaller apartment that Mildred and Belle were to occupy, and this was about the only element of elegance or beauty that Susan was able to impart to the bare little room. Even to the country girl, to whom the term "decorative art" was but a vague phrase, the place seemed meagre and hard in its outlines, and she instinctively felt that it would appear far more so to its occupants.

"But it's the best we can afford," she sighed; "and at the prices they'll pay us they shouldn't complain."

Still the day was full of pleasurable excitement and anticipation to the young girl. She was aware that her mother's tasks and her own would be greatly increased, but on the other hand the monotony of the farm-house life would be broken, and in the more distant future she saw a vista of new gowns, a jaunty winter hat with a feather, and other like conditions of unalloyed happiness. Susan had dwelt thus far in one of life's secluded valleys, and if she lost much because her horizon was narrow she was shielded from far more. Her fresh, full face had a certain pleasant, wholesome aspect, like the fields about her home in June, as she bustled about, preparing for the "city folks" whom her father so dreaded.

Roger's buggy was not yet paid for. It was the one great extravagance that Mr. Atwood had permitted for many a year. As usual, his wife had led him into it, he growling and protesting, but unable to resist her peculiar persistency. Roger was approaching man's estate, and something must be done to signalize so momentous an event. A light buggy was the goal of ambition to the young men in the vicinity, and Roger felt that he could never be a man without one.

He also recognized it as the best means of securing a wife to his mind, for courting on a moonlit, shadowy road was far more satisfactory than in the bosom of the young woman's family. Not that he was bent on matrimony, but rather on several years of agreeable preparation for it, proposing to make tentative acquaintances, both numerous and miscellaneous.

In his impatience to secure this four-wheeled compendium of happiness he had mortgaged his future, and had promised his father to plant and cultivate larger areas. The shrewd farmer therefore had no prospect of being out of pocket, for the young man was keeping his word. The acres of the cornfield were nearly double those of the previous year, and on them Roger spent the long hot day in vigorous labor in preference to the easy task of going to the river for the luggage. Dusty and weary, but in excellent spirits over the large space that he and the hired man had "hilled up," he went whistling home through the long shadows of the June evening. The farm wagon stood in the door-yard piled with trunks. The front entrance of the house—rarely used by the family—was open, and as he came up the lane a young girl emerged from it, and leaned for a few moments against the outer pillar of the little porch, unconscious of the picture she made. A climbing rose was in bloom just over her head, and her cheeks, flushed with heat and fatigue, vied with them in color. She had exchanged her travelling-dress for one of light muslin, and entwined in her hair a few buds from the bush that covered the porch. If Roger was not gifted with a vivid imagination he nevertheless saw things very accurately, and before he reached the head of the lane admitted to himself that the old "front steps" had never been so graced before. He had seen many a rustic beauty standing there when his sister had company, but the city girl impressed him with a difference which he then could not understand. He was inclined to resent this undefined superiority, and he muttered, "Father's right. They are birds of too fine a feather for our nest."

He had to pass near her in order to reach the kitchen door, or else make a detour which his pride would not permit. Indeed, the youth plodded leisurely along with his hoe on his shoulder, and scrupled not to scrutinize the vision on the porch with the most matter-of-fact minuteness.

"What makes her so 'down in the mouth'?" he queried. "She doesn't fancy us barbarians, I suppose, and Forestville to her is a howling wilderness. Like enough she'll take me for an Indian."

Mildred's eyes were fixed on a great shaggy mountain in the west, that was all the more dark and forbidding in its own deep shadow. She did not see it, however, for her mind was dwelling on gloomier shadows than the mountain cast.

As he passed he caught her attention, and stepping toward him a little impatiently, she said,

"I suppose you belong to the premises?"

He made an awkward attempt at a bow, and said stiffly, "I'm one of the Atwood chattels."

The answer was not such as she expected, and she gave him a scrutinizing glance. "Surely, if I have ever seen a laborer, he's one," she thought, as with woman's quickness she inventoried his coarse, weather-stained straw hat, blue cotton shirt crossed by suspenders mended with strings, shapeless trousers, once black, but now of the color of the dusty cornfield, and shoes such as she had never seen on the avenue. Even if Roger's face had not been discolored by perspiration and browned by exposure, its contrast with the visage that memory kept before her but too constantly would not have been pleasing. Nothing in his appearance deterred her from saying briefly, "I wish you would bring those trunks to our rooms. We have already waited for them some little time, and Mr. Atwood said that his man would attend to them when he came home from his work."

"That's all right, but I'm not his man," and with another stiff bow he passed on.

"Roger," called Mrs. Atwood from the kitchen door, "where's Jotham?"

"Bringing home the cows."

"The ladies want their trunks," continued his mother, in a sharp, worried tone. "I wish you men-folks would see to 'em right away. Why couldn't you quit work a little earlier to-night?"

Roger made no reply, but proceeded deliberately to help himself to a wash-basin and water.

"Look here, Roger," said his mother, in a tone she seldom used, "if those trunks are not where they belong in ten minutes, Susan and I'll take 'em up ourselves."

"That would be a pretty story to go out," added his sister. "Little use your buggy would be to you then, for no nice girl would ride with you."

"Come, come, what's the use of such a bother!" said the young man irritably. "Mother knows that I'd carry the trunks up on Bald-Top before I'd let her touch them. That's the way it will always be with these city people, I suppose. Everybody must jump and run the moment they speak. Father's right, and we'll have to give up our old free-and-easy life and become porters and waiting-maids."

"I've heard enough of that talk," said Mrs. Atwood emphatically. "Your father's been like a drizzling north-easter all day. Now I give you men-folks fair warning. If you want any supper you must wake up and give me something better than grumbling. I'm too hot and tired now to argue over something that's been settled once for all."

The "warning" had the desired effect, for Mrs. Atwood was the recognized head of the commissary department, and, as such, could touch the secret springs of motives that are rarely resisted.

The open kitchen windows were so near that Mildred could not help overhearing this family jar, and it added greatly to her depression. She felt that they had not only lost their own home, but were also banishing the home feeling from another family. She did but scant justice to Mrs.

Atwood's abundant supper, and went to her room at last with that most disagreeable of all impressions—the sense of being an intruder.

The tired children were soon at rest, for their time of sleepless trouble was far distant. Belle's pretty head drooped also with the roses over the porch as the late twilight deepened. To her and the little people the day had been rich in novelty, and the country was a wonderland of many and varied delights. In the eyes of children the Garden of Eden survives from age to age. Alas! the tendency to leave it survives also, and to those who remain, regions of beauty and mystery too often become angular farms and acres.

Mrs. Jocelyn and Mildred still more clearly illustrated the truth that the same world wears a different aspect as the conditions of life vary. They were going out into the wilderness. The river was a shining pathway, whose beauty was a mockery, for it led away from all that they loved best. The farmhouse was a place of exile, and its occupants a strange, uncouth people with whom they felt that they would have nothing in common. Mrs. Jocelyn merely looked forward to weeks of weary waiting until she could again join her husband, to whom in his despondency her heart clung with a remorseful tenderness. She now almost wished that they had lived on bread and water, and so had provided against this evil day of long separation and dreary uncertainty. Now that she could no longer rest in her old belief that there would be "some way" of tiding over every financial crisis, she became a prey to forebodings equally vague that there might be no way. That *her husband* could spend day after day seeking employment, offering, too, to take positions far inferior to the one he had lost, was a truth that at first bewildered and then disheartened her beyond measure. She felt that they must, indeed, have fallen on evil times when his services went a-begging.

To Mildred the present was dark, and the future most unpromising; but deep in her heart nestled the sustaining thought that she was not unloved, not forgotten. The will of others, not his own, kept her lover from her side. His weaknesses were of a nature that awakened her pity rather than contempt. If he had been a Hercules physically and a Bacon intellectually, but conceited, domineering, untruthful, and of the male flirt genus—from such weaknesses she would have shrunk with intense repugnance. Her friends thought her peculiarly gentle in disposition. They did not know—and she herself might rarely recognize the truth—that she was also very strong; her strength on its human side consisted in a simple, unswerving fidelity to her womanly nature and sense of right; on the Divine side, God's word was to her a verity. She daily said "Our Father" as a little child. Has the world yet discovered a purer or loftier philosophy?

CHAPTER VI

ROGER DISCOVERS A NEW TYPE

YOUNG Atwood rose with a very definite purpose on the following morning. For his mother's sake he would be civil to their boarders, but nothing more. He would learn just what they had a right to expect in view of their business relations, and having performed all that was "nominated in the bond," would treat them with such an off-hand independence that they would soon become aware that he, Roger Atwood, was an entity that could exist without their admiring approval. He meant that they should learn that the country was quite as large as the city, and that the rural peculiarities of Forestville were as legitimate as those which he associated with them, and especially with the young lady who had mistaken him for the hired man. Therefore after his morning work in the barnyard he stalked to the house with the same manner and toilet as on the previous day.

But there were no haughty citizens to be toned down. They were all sleeping late from the fatigues of their journey, and Mrs. Atwood said she would give the "men-folks their breakfast at the usual hour, because a hungry man and a cross bear were nigh of kin."

The meal at first was a comparatively silent one, but Roger noted with a contemptuous glance that his sister's hair was arranged more neatly than he had seen it since the previous Sunday, and that her calico dress, collar, and cuffs were scrupulously clean.

"Expecting company?" he asked maliciously.

She understood him and flushed resentfully. "If you wish to go around looking like a scarecrow, that's no reason why I should," she said. "The corn is too large for the crows to pull now, so if I were you I would touch myself up a little. I don't wonder that Miss Jocelyn mistook you for Jotham."

"It's well," retorted Roger, with some irritation, "that your Miss Jocelyn has no grown brothers here, or you would come down to breakfast in kid gloves. I suppose, however, that they have insisted on a tidy and respectful waitress. Will you please inform me, mother, what my regulation costume must be when my services are required? Jotham and I should have a suit of livery, with two more brass buttons on my coat to show that I belong to the family."

"I think that a little more of the manner and appearance of a gentleman would show your relationship better than any amount of brass," remarked his mother quietly.

Roger was almost through his breakfast, and so, at no great loss, could assume the injured part. Therefore with a dignity that was somewhat in marked contrast with his rather unkempt appearance he rose and stalked off to the cornfield again.

"Umph," remarked Mr. Atwood sententiously, as he rose and followed his son. This apparently vague utterance had for his wife a definite and extended meaning. She looked annoyed and flurried, and was in no mood for the labors of preparing a second breakfast.

"The men-folks had better not roil me up too much," she said to her daughter. "If your father had said No! out and out, I wouldn't have brought strangers into his home. But he kinder wanted me to have their money without the bother of having them around. Now one thing is settled—he must either help me make it pleasant for these people, or else tell them to leave this very day."

"And how about Roger?" asked Susan, still under the influence of pique.

"Oh, Roger is young and foolish. He's a-growing yet," and the mother's severe aspect relaxed. He was her only boy.

Mr. Atwood, brought face to face with the alternative presented by his practical wife, succumbed with tolerable grace. In truth, having had his grumble out, he was not so very averse to the arrangement. He was much like old Gruff, their watch-dog, that was a redoubtable growler, but had never been known to bite any one. He therefore installed himself as his wife's out-of-door ally and assistant commissary, proposing also to take the boarders out to drive if they would pay enough to make it worth the while. As for Roger, he resolved to remain a farmer and revolve in his old orbit.

Mrs. Jocelyn and Mildred were listless and depressed, and time hung heavily on their hands. They were in that condition of waiting and uncertainty which renders cheerful or systematic occupation wellnigh impossible. They daily hoped that a letter would come assuring them that Mr. Jocelyn had secured a position that would change all their future for the better, but the letters received recorded futile efforts only, and often despondency; but occasionally there would come a letter full of vague, sanguine hopes that first produced elation and then perplexity that nothing came of them. His wife found his dejection contagious. If she had been with him she would have made strenuous efforts to cheer and inspirit, but without an unselfish woman's strongest motive for action she brooded and drooped. Belle's irrepressible vivacity and the children's wild delight over the wonders of the fields and farmyard jarred upon her sore heart painfully. She patiently tried to take care of them, but in thought and feeling she could not enter into their life as had been her custom. Belle was too young and giddy for responsibility, and Mildred had many a weary chase after the little explorers. In spite of his clearly defined policy of indifference, Roger found himself watching her on such occasions with a growing interest.

It was evident to him that she did not in the slightest degree resent his daily declaration of independence; indeed, he saw that she scarcely gave him any thoughts whatever—that he was to her no more than heavy-footed Jotham.

"She does not even consider me worth snubbing," he thought, with much dissatisfaction, about a week subsequent to their arrival.

In vain, after the labors of the day, he dressed in his best suit and sported a flaming necktie; in vain he dashed away in his buggy, and, a little later, dashed by again with a rural belle at his side. He found himself unable to impress the city girl as he desired, or to awaken in her a sense of his importance. And yet he already began to feel, in a vague way, that she was not so distant *to* him, as distant *from* him.

Belle soon formed his acquaintance, asking innumerable questions and not a few favors, and she found him more good-natured than she had been led to expect. At last, to her great delight, he took her with him in his wagon to the post-office. The lively girl interested and amused him, but he felt himself immeasurably older than she. With a tendency common to very young men, he was more interested in the elder sister, who in character and the maturity that comes from experience was certainly far beyond him. Belle he understood, but Mildred was a mystery, and she had also the advantage of being a very beautiful one.

As time passed and no definite assurances came from her father, the young girl was conscious of a growing dissatisfaction with the idle, weary waiting to which she and her mother were condemned. She felt that it might have been better for them all to have remained in the city, in spite of the summer heat, than thus to be separated. She believed that she might have found something to do which would have aided in their support, and she understood more clearly than her mother that their slender means were diminishing fast. That she could do anything at a country farmhouse to assist her father seemed very doubtful, but she felt the necessity of employment more strongly each day, not only for the sake of the money it might bring, but also as an antidote to a growing tendency to brood over her deep disappointment. She soon began to recognize that such self-indulgence would unfit her for a struggle that might be extended and severe, and was not long in coming to the conclusion that she must make the best of her life as it was and would be. Days and weeks had slipped by and had seen her looking regretfully back at the past, which was receding like the shores of a loved country to an exile. Since the prospect of returning to it was so slight, it would be best to turn her thoughts and such faint hope as she could cherish toward the vague and unpromising future. At any rate she must so occupy herself as to have no time for morbid self-communings.

Her first resource was the homely life and interests of those with whom she dwelt. Thus far she had regarded them as uncongenial strangers, and had contented herself with mere politeness toward them. In her sad preoccupation she had taken little note of their characters or domestic life, and her mother had kept herself even more secluded. Indeed the poor lady felt that it was hardly right to smile in view of her husband's absence and misfortune, and she often chided Belle for her levity; but Belle's life was like an over-full fountain in spring-time, and could not be repressed.

In her deep abstraction Mildred had seen, but had scarcely noted, certain changes in the farmhouse that would have interested and pleased her had her mind been at rest. Almost unconsciously she had revealed her love of that which is pretty and inviting; therefore Susan, not content with being neat, was inclined to brighten her costume by an occasional ribbon, and to suggest comparisons between her fresh and youthful bloom and an opening flower that she would fasten in her hair as the summer day declined. So far from resenting this imitation of her own habits and tastes, Mildred at last recognized the young girl's awakening perceptions of womanly grace with much satisfaction. Even poor Mrs.

Atwood exhibited a tendency to emerge from her chronic and rather forlorn condition of household drudge. For years she had known and thought of little else save sordid work, early and late. The income from the small farm permitted no extra help except on rare occasions, and then was obtained under protest from her husband, who parted with a dollar as he would with a refractory tooth. His strong and persistent will had impressed itself on his family, and their home life had been meagre and uninviting; the freedom and ease that he and Roger were so loath to lose, consisting chiefly in careless dress and a disregard of the little refinements and courtesies of life.

It was with some self-reproach that Mildred admitted that for nearly a month she had practically ignored these people, and that she was becoming selfish in her trouble; and yet, not so much from a sense of duty, as from a kindling zest in life, she began to take an interest in them and their ways. She was still far too young for her spirit to lose its spring, even under a continuous weight of misfortune. Her nature was not morbid, but sunny and wholesome, and when with the children and Belle unexpected smiles would brighten her face like glints of sunshine here and there on a cloudy day. Deep as had been her wounds, she found that there were moments when she half forgot their pain, and an instinct of self-preservation taught her that it would be best to forget them as far as possible.

When the thought of trying to refine the somewhat rude household in which she dwelt occurred to her, she discovered that the work was already well begun, for the chief condition of success was present—the disposition to do as she would like. The Atwoods soon surmised that the family was in trouble of some kind, and were able to distinguish between pride of caste and a sorrowful preoccupation. It was scarcely in Mrs. Jocelyn and Mildred's nature to speak otherwise than gently and kindly, and so without trying they disarmed their hosts and won their sympathy. Notwithstanding their dejection and lassitude, they maintained the habits of their lives, and unwittingly gave Mrs. Atwood and her daughter a vague impression that neatness, attractiveness, and order were as essential as good morals.

At first Roger had dressed more roughly than ever, in order to assert his right to his old ways, but as Mildred did not protest even by a glance, he next took pains to show her that he had "good clothes" if he chose to wear them. This fact she also accepted without the faintest interest, and so at last he was rather nonplussed. He was not accustomed to being politely ignored, and since he felt a growing interest in this new type of girl, he had an increasing desire to make her aware of his existence. "Hang it all," he would mutter, "I'm no more to her than Jotham and the other farm animals What can a fellow do to make her look at him as if she saw him? She's very kind and polite and all that; she'd as soon hurt the brindle cow as me, but this fact is not very flattering. However, I'll find you out, my lady, and you too shall learn that the one whom you now regard as an object merely has a will and a way of his own."

Therefore it may be guessed that in Roger Mildred might discover more docility and plastic readiness than she desired. Only old Mr. Atwood and Jotham seemed incorrigible material; but she did not despair even of them, and resolved to set about reclaiming this family from barbarism at once.

CHAPTER VII

COMPARISONS

"MRS. ATWOOD," said Mildred one Saturday evening, "I'll go with you to church to-morrow if you'll let me. Belle has been once, and it will be my turn to-morrow."

"Oh, certainly, miss; you will go with Roger in the buggy, I s'pose, like Miss Belle."

"If you please, I'd rather go with you."

"Really, miss, the roads have been muddy of late, and the wagon isn't very nice."

"I would rather go with you," pleaded Mildred, with an appeal in her blue eyes that few resisted.

"Father," said Mrs. Atwood, as soon as her husband came in, "Miss Jocelyn wishes to go with us to meeting to-morrow. Can't you or Roger tidy up the wagon a bit? 'Tain't fit for her to ride in."

"There 'tis again—more time spent in fixing up and fussing than in looking after the main chance. You are all gettin' too fine for plain farmin' people."

"I don't see why plain farming people need enjoy mud more'n other folks. You ought to be ashamed to ask your wife and daughter to ride in such a wagon."

"I don't know why I should be more ashamed to-morrow than on any other Sunday, and you was never ashamed before. Your boarders don't seem inclined to take any rides and pay for them, so I don't see why I should fix up any more'n usual. Anyhow, it's too late now; Jotham's gone home, I'm too tired, and Roger's dressed to go out. Why can't she go with Roger?"

"She says she'd rather go with us, and if you men-folk let her ride in that wagon I hope the minister will give you a scorching sermon"—and she turned toward her son, who, dressed in his rural finery, was finishing an early supper, To her surprise he, from whom she expected no aid, gave her a significant nod and put his finger on his lips. He had already decided upon one bold stratagem, in the hope of opening Mildred's eyes, and if this failed his mother's words suggested another line of policy.

"Sue," he said, with affected carelessness, "I may bring Amelia Stone to spend part of the evening with you."

"Amelia Stone isn't my style, if the young men do say she's the prettiest girl in town."

"If you don't treat her well she'll think you're jealous," said Roger, and with this artful stroke he departed to carry out his experiment. "I'll teach my city lady that I'm not a clodhopper that other girls won't look at," he thought as he drove away.

Everything went according to his mind, for Amelia broke an engagement in order to come with him, and was very friendly. The young fellow thought that Mildred must see that he was not a person to be politely ignored when so handsome a girl was flattering in her favors. Susan would not be thought jealous for the world, and so was rather effusive over Miss Stone. She also imbibed the idea that it might be a good chance to make Mildred aware that they knew some nice, stylish people; therefore, as the rural beauty mounted the steps of the porch she introduced her to Mildred and Belle. Roger meanwhile stood near, and critically compared the two girls. They certainly represented two very different types, and he might have brought a score of his acquaintances that would have been more to Mildred's taste than the florid beauty whose confidence was boldness, and who had inventoried her own pronounced charms more often than had any of her admirers. One girl was a lily, with a character like a delicate, elusive fragrance; the other, a tulip, very striking, especially at a distance. The one no more asserted herself than did the summer evening; the manner of the other the same as button-holed all present, and demanded attention. Her restless black eyes openly sought admiration, and would speedily sparkle with anger and malice should their request be unrewarded. Roger was quick enough to feel Mildred's superiority, although he could scarcely account for it, and he soon experienced so strong a revulsion of feeling toward his unconscious ally that he would have taken her home again with a sense of relief.

"If Miss Jocelyn thinks that's the style of girl that takes with me, I might as well have remained a scarecrow. Amelia Stone seems loud as a brass band beside her," and his gallantries perceptibly diminished.

True to her nature, Amelia assumed toward him what she imagined were very pretty airs of proprietorship. Roger knew well that her manner would have been the same toward the youth with whom, from a sudden caprice, she had broken her engagement for the evening. Her habitual coquetry nevertheless unwittingly carried out his original programme with a success that made him grind his teeth with rage, for he supposed that Mildred would gain the idea that they were congenial spirits drawn together by strong affinities.

And she, half divining his vexation, shrewdly increased it by pretending to associate him with the transparent coquette, while at the same time manifesting disapproval of her by a fine reserve. Amelia felt herself scanned quietly, coldly, and half curiously, as if she belonged to some strange and hitherto unknown type, and her vivacious egotism began to fail her. She was much relieved therefore when Mildred excused herself and went to her room, for careless, light-hearted, and somewhat giddy Belle imposed no restraint. Roger, however, did not recover himself, for he saw that he had made a false step in his effort to win recognition from Mildred, and he waited impatiently until his companion should suggest returning. This she soon did, and they rode toward her home with a mutual sense of dissatisfaction. At last Amelia broke out, "I think she's absurdly proud!"

"Who?" Roger asked demurely.

"You know who well enough. I thank my stars we have no city folks putting on airs around our house. I suppose you think her perfection. You looked as if you did."

"I'm not acquainted with her," he said quietly.

"Not acquainted! Darsn't you speak to her high mightiness then?"

"Oh, yes, I can speak to her when there is occasion, but that does not make one acquainted. I don't understand her."

"I do, perfectly. She thinks herself a wonderful deal better than you or me."

"Perhaps she is," he admitted.

"Well! that's a nice speech to make to *me!* I was a fool to break my engagement and go with you."

"All right," responded Roger, with satirical good-nature, as he assisted her to alight; "we'll both know better next time."

She would not speak to him again, but he escorted her to her door, and bowed in parting with mocking politeness. Instead of inviting him in, as was her custom, she closed the door with a sharpness that spoke volumes.

"I don't believe Miss Jocelyn ever banged a door like that in her life," he muttered with a smile as he hastened homeward.

Hearing unusual sounds in the farmyard before retiring, Mildred peeped out from under her curtain. The moonlight revealed that Roger was washing the wagon with a vigor that made her laugh, and she thought, "After what I have seen this evening, I think I can civilize him."

CHAPTER VIII

CHANGES

BENT upon carrying out her project of introducing among the Atwoods a more gracious and genial family life, and lured by the fresh coolness of the summer morning, Mildred left her room earlier than usual. Mrs. Atwood, whose one indulgence was a longer sleep on the day of rest, came down not very long after and began bustling about the kitchen. Hitherto their meals had been served to the Jocelyns in the sitting-room, the farmer and his family eating as before in the kitchen. Mildred felt that they had no right to impose this extra labor on Mrs. Atwood, especially on the Sabbath, and she also thought it would do her mother good to be roused from the listless apathy into which she was sinking. These were her chief motives, but she knew that at no other place could people be taught the refinements of life more effectually than at the table, and it was her plan to bring about the changes she desired, without appearing to be the conscious cause.

"Mrs. Atwood," she said, "why can we not all take our breakfast together in the sitting-room this morning? I have noticed that your hired man is absent on Sundays"—her zeal for reform would not induce her to sit down with Jotham—"and I can see no reason why you should have the task to-day of preparing two meals. Of course, if this is not agreeable to you let there be no change, but do not put yourself to the extra trouble on our account."

"Well, now, miss, you are very kind, and to tell you

the truth, I was thinking of this very thing, but we don't wish to intrude."

"Intrude, Mrs. Atwood!" exclaimed Mildred, assuming surprise. "I don't understand you, and shall now feel hurt if we do not take our meals together to-day."

"It's very good of you to think of us, and Susan and me will have a more restful day."

Mildred gave her one of her rare smiles, which Mrs. Atwood said "lighted up the old kitchen like a ray of sunshine," and then went to prepare her mother and sister for the change. Belle was pleased, as she ever was with novelty.

"Millie," she cried, "you shall sit next to that great animal, Jotham, and if you don't take care he'll eat you unawares."

"Jotham is not here to-day, and I'll have him fed in the kitchen hereafter."

"Have you become mistress of the farmhouse? Has Roger made proposals? Won't it be fun to hear Mr. Atwood grumble! There is nothing I enjoy more than to hear him grumble and old Gruff growl. They must be chips off the same block."

Mrs. Jocelyn shrank from seeing and speaking to any one, but was much too unselfish to impose extra tasks on Mrs. Atwood.

Susan soon came down to assist her mother, and was delighted at the prospect of taking her meals in the sitting-room, feeling that it was a decided social promotion. Moreover, like all young girls, she longed for companionship, and believed that Mildred would now be more approachable.

By and by Roger came from the barnyard in his working-clothes, and seeing no preparations for breakfast in the kitchen, exclaimed:

"So we heathen must sit down to the second table to-day."

"Yes, if you wish. Susan and me are going to take our

breakfast in the sitting-room with Mrs. Jocelyn and her family."

"Am I not invited?" he asked a little anxiously.

"There's no need of any invitation. You have as much right there as I have, only I would not come in looking like that."

"They won't like it—this new arrangement."

"It seems to me that you have grown very considerate of what they like," put in Susan.

"Miss Jocelyn proposed it herself," Mrs. Atwood said, "and if you and father would fix up a little and come in quietly and naturally it would save a deal of trouble. If I can't get a little rest on Sunday I'll wear out."

Roger waited to hear no more, and went hastily to his room.

Mr. Atwood was more intractable. He distinguished the Sabbath from the rest of the week, by making the most of his larger leisure to grumble.

"I'm in no state to sit down with those people," he growled, after the change and the reasons for it had been explained to him.

"I'm glad you feel so," his wife replied; "but your old clothes have not yet grown fast to you; you can soon fix yourself up, and you might as well dress before breakfast as after it."

He was perverse, however, and would make no greater concession to the unwelcome innovation than to put on his coat. Mildred smiled mentally when she saw him lowering at the head of the table, but an icicle could no more continue freezing in the sun than he maintain his surly mood before her genial, quiet greeting. It suggested courtesy so irresistibly, and yet so unobtrusively, that he already repented his lack of it. Still, not for the world would he have made any one aware of his compunctions. Mrs. Atwood and Susan had their doubts about Roger, fearing that he would rebel absolutely and compel a return to their former habits. They were all scarcely seated, however, before he appeared, a little flushed from his hasty toilet and the thought of meeting one who had been cold and disapproving toward the belle of Forestville, but Mildred said "good-morning" so affably and naturally that he was made quite at ease, and Mrs. Jocelyn, who had seemed unapproachable, smiled upon him so kindly that he was inclined to believe her almost as pretty as her daughter. As for Belle and the children, he already felt well acquainted with them. Mrs. Atwood and Susan looked at each other significantly, for Roger was dressed in his best and disposed to do his best. Mildred saw the glance, and felt that the young fellow deserved some reward, so she began talking to him in such a matter-of-course way that before he was aware he was responding with a freedom that surprised all the family, and none more than himself. Mildred was compelled to admit that the "young barbarian," as she had characterized him in her thoughts, possessed, in the item of intelligence, much good raw material. He not only had ideas, but also the power of expressing them, with freshness and vivacity. She did not give herself sufficient credit for the effects that pleased her, or understand that it was her good breeding and good will that banished his tongue-tied embarrassment. The most powerful influences are usually the most subtle, and Roger found, as had Vinton Arnold and others, that for some cause Mildred evoked the best there was in him.

Poor Mrs. Jocelyn did not have very much to say. Her depression was too deep to be thrown off appreciably, but she replied to Mrs. Atwood's remarks with her wonted gentleness. Belle's spirits soon passed all bounds, and one of her wild sallies provoked a grim smile from even Mr. Atwood, and she exulted over the fact all day. In brief, the ice seemed quite broken between the family and the "boarders."

The old farmer could scarcely believe his eyes when he went out to harness the horses to the three-seated wagon, for it was neat and clean, with buffalo robes spread over the seats. "Well," he ejaculated, "what's a-coming over this here family, anyway? I'm about all that's left of the old rusty times, and rusty enough I feel, with everybody and everything so fixed up. I s'pose I'll have to stand it Sundays, and the day'll be harder to git through than ever. To-morrow I'll be back in the kitchen again, and can eat my victuals without Miss Jocelyn looking on and saying to herself, 'He ain't nice; he don't look pretty'; and then a-showin' me by the most delicate little ways how I ought to perform. She's got Roger under her thumb or he wouldn't have cleaned up this wagon in the middle of the night, for all I know, but I'm too old and set to be made over by a girl."

Thus grumbling and mumbling to himself, Mr. Atwood prepared to take his family to the white, tree-shadowed meeting-house, at which he seldom failed to appear, for the not very devotional reason that it helped him to get through the day. Like the crab-apple tree in the orchard, he was a child of the soil, and savored too much of his source.

Roger was of finer metal, and while possessing his father's shrewdness, hard common-sense and disposition to hit the world between the eyes if it displeased him, his nature was ready at slight incentive, to throw off all coarseness and vulgarity. The greater number of forceful American citizens are recruited from the ranks of just such young men—strong, comparatively poor, somewhat rude in mind and person at the start, but of such good material that they are capable of a fine finish.

Roger had grown naturally, and healthily, thus far. He had surpassed the average boy on the play-ground, and had fallen slightly below him in the school-house, but more from indifference and self-assurance than lack of ability. Even his father's narrow thrift could not complain of his work when he would work, but while a little fellow he was inclined to independence, and persisted in having a goodly share of his time for the boyish sports in their season, and for all the books of travel and adventure he could lay his hands upon. In spite of scoldings and whippings he had sturdily held his own, and at last his father had discovered that Roger could be led much better than driven, and that by getting him interested, and by making little agreements, like that concerning the buggy, the best of the bargain could always be obtained, for the youth would then work with a will and carry out his verbal contracts in a large, good-natured way. Therefore Mildred's belief that he was good raw material for her humanizing little experiment had a better foundation than she knew. Indeed, without in the least intending it, she might awaken a spirit that would assert itself in ways as yet undreamed of by either of them. The causes which start men upon their careers are often seemingly the most slight and causal. Mildred meant nothing more than to find a brief and kindly-natured pastime in softening the hard lives and in rounding the sharp angles of the Atwood family, and Roger merely came in for his share of her attention. Flesh and spirit, however, are not wood and stone, and she might learn in deep surprise that her light æsthetic touches, while producing pleasing changes in externals, had also awakened some of the profoundest motives and forces that give shape and color to life.

In smiling ignorance of such possibilities, she said to him as she came out on the porch dressed for church, "You have given your mother and me also a pleasant surprise, and we shall enjoy our ride to church far more, not only because the wagon is nice and clean, but also because of your thoughtfulness of our pleasure. The wagon looked so inviting from our windows that I have induced my mother to go, and to take the children. I think they will keep still. We will sit near the door, and I can take them out if they get tired."

Her words were very simple, but she spoke them with a quiet grace all her own, while pulling her glove over a hand that seemed too small and white for any of the severer tasks of life. As she stood there in her pretty summer costume, a delicate bloom in her cheeks relieving the transparent fairness of her complexion, she seemed to him, as Amelia Stone had said, perfect indeed—and the young girl could not suppress a smile at the almost boyish frankness of his admiration.

"You gave me a pleasant surprise, also," he said, flushing deeply.

"I?" with a questioning glance.

"Yes. You have brought about a pleasant change, and made breakfast something more than eating. You have made me feel that I might be less nigh of kin to Jotham than I feared."

"I shall imitate your frankness," she replied, laughing; "you are not near so nigh of kin to him as I feared."

"I have not forgotten that you thought me identical with him," he could not forbear saying.

"I did not mean to hurt your feelings," she answered, with deepening color.

"Oh, you were not to blame in the least," he said good-naturedly. "I deserved it."

"You must remember, too," she continued, deprecatingly, "that I am a city girl, and not acquainted with country ways, and so have charity." Then she added earnestly, "We do not want to put a constraint on your family life, or make home seem less homelike to you all."

Mrs. Joselyn with Belle and the children were descending the stairs. "I misunderstood you, Miss Jocelyn," said Roger, with a penitent look, and he hastily strode away.

"I've disarmed him," thought Mildred, with a half smile. She had, a little too completely.

Belle claimed her old place with Roger, and their light wagon was soon lost in the windings of the road.

"Millie," whispered Belle, as the former joined her at church, "what could you have said to Roger to make him effervesce so remarkably? I had to remind him that it was Sunday half a dozen times."

"What a great boy he is!" answered Mildred.

"The idea of my teaching him sobriety seemed to amuse him amazingly."

"And no wonder. You are both giddy children."

"Until to-day, when you have turned his head, he has been very aged in manner. Please let him alone hereafter; he is my property."

"Keep him wholly," and the amused look did not pass from Mildred's face until service began.

Dinner was even a greater success than breakfast. Mrs. Jocelyn had become better acquainted with Mrs. Atwood during the drive, and they were beginning to exchange housekeeping opinions with considerable freedom, each feeling that she could learn from the other. Fearing justly that a long period of poverty might be before them, Mrs. Jocelyn was awakening to the need of acquiring some of Mrs. Atwood's power of making a little go a great way, and the thought of thus becoming able to do something to assist her absent husband gave her more animation than she had yet shown in her exile. Mildred ventured to fill her vase with some hardy flowers that persisted in blooming under neglect, and to place it on the table, and she was greatly amused to see its effect on Roger and Mr. Atwood. The latter stared at it and then at his wife.

"Will any one take some of the flowers?" he asked at last, in ponderous pleasantry.

"I think we all had better take some, father," said Roger. "I would not have believed that so little a thing could have made so great a difference."

"Well, what is the difference?"

"I don't know as I can express it, but it suggests that a great deal might be enjoyed that one could not put in his mouth or his pocket."

"Mr. Roger," cried Belle, "you are coming on famously. I didn't know that you were inclined, hitherto, to put everything you liked in your mouth or pocket. What escapes some people may have had."

"I never said I liked you," retorted the youth, with a

touch of the broad repartee with which he was accustomed to hold his own among the girls in the country.

"No, but if I saw that you liked some one else I might be alarmed"—and she looked mischievously toward Mildred.

For reasons inexplicable to himself, he fell into a sudden confusion at this sally.

With a warning glance at the incorrigible Belle, whose vital elements were frolic and nonsense, Mildred began talking to Mr. Atwood about the great hotel a few miles distant.

"Would you like to go there?" asked Roger after a little.

"No," she said; "I have not the slightest wish to go there." Indeed there was nothing that she shrank from more than the chance of meeting those who had known her in the city.

Later in the day Susan said to her mother, with much satisfaction, "She's not stuck up at all, and we might have found it out before. I can't go back to the kitchen and live in our old haphazard way. I can see now that it wasn't nice at all."

"We'll see," said the politic Mrs. Atwood. "We mustn't drive father too fast."

Roger felt that at last he was getting acquainted, and he looked forward to the long summer evening with much hope. But nothing happened as he expected, for Mildred was silent and preoccupied at supper, and Mrs. Jocelyn appeared to have relapsed into her old depression.

Instead of going out in his buggy to spend the evening with one of his many favorites, as had been his custom, he took a book and sat down under a tree near the porch, so that he might join Mildred if she gave him any encouragement to do so. Belle found him taciturn and far removed from his gay mood of the morning, and so at last left him in peace.

Sue was entertaining a rural admirer in the parlor, which was rarely used except on such momentous occasions, and all was propitious for a quiet talk with the object of his kindling interest. His heart beat quickly as he saw her appear on the porch with her hat and shawl, but instead of noticing him she went rapidly by with bowed head and climbed an eminence near the house, from which there was an extended view to the southward. He felt, as well as saw, that she wished to be alone, that he was not in her thoughts, that she was still as distant from him as he had ever imagined her to be. The shadows deepened, the evening grew dusky, the stars came out, and yet she did not return. For a long time he could see her outline as she sat on the hill top, and then it faded. He knew she was in trouble, and found a vague pleasure in watching with her, in remaining within call should she be frightened, knowing, however, that there was little danger of this in quiet Forestville. Still, the illusion that he was in some sense her protector pleased him in his sentimental mood, and in after years he often recalled this first faint foreshadowing of his lot.

Could he have seen the poor girl, when at last, conscious of solitude and darkness, she gave way to the passionate grief that, for her mother's sake, she had so long repressed, he would have felt that she was distant indeed—far removed by experiences of which he as yet knew nothing. She had been gazing southward, toward the city in which her father was vainly seeking a foothold on the steep incline up which the unfortunate must struggle, and in fancy she saw him lonely, dejected, and deprived of the family life of which he was so fond. Her sympathy for him was as deep as her strong affection. But in spite of her will her thoughts would recur to the beautiful dream which had been shattered in that distant city. Not a word had she heard from Arnold since leaving it, and her heart so misgave her concerning the future that she threw herself on the sod, sobbing bitterly, and almost wishing that she were beneath it and at rest. In the deep astraction of her grief she had scarcely noted the lapse of time, nor where she was, and the moon had risen when she again glided by Roger, her step and bearing suggesting lassitude and dejection.

Soon after he entered the sitting-room, where he found his mother with a troubled look on her face. "Roger," she said, "I feel sorry for these people. When I went upstairs a while ago I heard Mrs. Jocelyn crying in her room, and coming down with the lamp I met the young lady on the stairs, and her eyes were very red. It's certain they are in deep trouble. What can it be? It's queer Mr. Jocelyn doesn't come to see them. I hope they are all right."

"Mother," he burst out impetuously, "they are all right—she is, anyway," and he went abruptly to his room.

"Well," remarked the bewildered woman sententiously, "there never were such goings on in the old house before."

An event momentous to her had indeed taken place—Roger's boyish days were over.

CHAPTER IX

NEITHER BOY NOR MAN

THE two following weeks passed uneventfully at the farmhouse, but silent forces were at work that were as quiet and effective as those of Nature, who makes her vital changes without ever being observed in the act. In respect to the domestic arrangements Mrs. Atwood effected a sensible compromise. She gave the men-folk an early breakfast in the kitchen, so that they might go to their work as usual, and her boarders were thus not compelled to rise at an unaccustomed hour. She and Susan afterward sat down with them, and Mr. Atwood and Roger joined them at dinner and supper. On the Monday following the scenes described in the last chapter, Mildred and Mrs. Jocelyn were listless and unable to recover even the semblance of cheerfulness, for a letter from Mr. Jocelyn informed them that he was making very little headway, and that some agencies which he accepted yielded but a scanty income. Mildred chafed more bitterly than ever over her position of idle waiting, and even grew irritable under it. More than once Roger heard her speak to Belle and the children with a sharpness and impatience which proved her not angelic. This did not greatly disturb him, for he neither "wanted to be an angel" nor wished to have much to do with uncomfortable perfection. A human, spirited girl was quite to his taste, and he was quick-witted enough to see that unrest and anxiety were the causes of her temper. Poor Mrs. Jocelyn was too gentle for irritation, and only grew more despondent than ever at hope deferred.

"Millie," she said, "I have dreadful forebodings, and can never forgive myself that I did not think night and day how to save instead of how to spend. What should we do if we had no money at all?"

"Belle and I must go to work," said Mildred, with a resolute face, "and it's a shame we are not at work now."

"What can you do when your father can do so little?"

"Other poor people live; so can we. I can't stand this wretched waiting and separation much longer," and she wrote as much to her father. In the hope of obtaining a response favorable to her wishes she became more cheerful. Every day increased her resolution to put an end to their suspense, and to accept their lot with such fortitude as they could command.

One morning she found Mr. and Mrs. Atwood preparing to go to the nearest market town with butter, eggs, and other farm produce. She readily obtained permission to accompany them, and made some mysterious purchases. From this time onward Roger observed that she was much in her room, and that she went out more for exercise than from the motive of getting through with the weary, idle hours. For some reason she also gained such an influence over thoughtless Belle that the latter took tolerably good care of little Fred and Minnie, as the children were familiarly called. While she maintained toward him her polite and friendly manner, he saw that he was forgotten, and that it had not entered her mind that he could ever do anything for her or be anything more to her than at the present time. But every hour she gained a stronger hold upon his sympathy, and occasionally, when she thought herself unobserved, he saw a troubled and almost fearful look come into her eyes, as if something were present to her imagination that inspired the strongest dread. At such times he was mastered by impulses of self-sacrifice that would have seemed very absurd if put into plain words. He kept his thoughts, however, to himself, and with an instinctive reticence sought to disguise even from his mother the feelings that were so new, and so full of delicious pain. That he was becoming quite different from the careless, self-satisfied young fellow that he had been hitherto was apparent to all, and after his outburst on Sunday evening his mother half guessed the cause. But he misled her to some extent, and Susan altogether, by saying, "I've had a falling-out with Amelia Stone."

"Well, she's the last girl in the world that I'd mope about if I were a man," was his sister's emphatic reply.

"You're not a man; besides I'm not moping. I'm only cutting my wisdom teeth. I want to do something in the world, and I'm thinking about it."

"He's a-growing," said his mother with a smile, and on this theory she usually explained all of her son's vagaries.

He still further misled his unsophisticated sister by making no special effort to seek Mildred's society. After one or two rather futile attempts he saw that he would alienate the sad-hearted girl by obtrusive advances, and he contented himself by trying to understand her, in the hope that at some future time he might learn to approach her more acceptably. The thought that she would soon leave the farm-house depressed him greatly. She had suggested to him a new and wholly different life from that which he had led hitherto, and he felt within himself no power or inclination to go on with his old ways. These thoughts he also brooded over in silence, and let himself drift in a current which seemed irresistible.

During this period he was under the influence of neither apathy nor dejection. On the contrary, his mind was surging with half-formed plans, crude purposes, and ambitious dreams. His horizon lifted from the farm and Forestville until there seemed space for a notable career. His soul kindled at the thought of winning a position that would raise him to Mildred's side. So far from fearing to burn his ships, and strike out unsupported, the impulse grew strong to make the attempt at any cost. He was sure that his father would not listen to the project, and that he would be wholly unaided, but not many days passed before the thought of such obstacles ceased to influence him. "I'll take my way through the world, and cut my own swath," he muttered a hundred times as he swung the scythe under the July sun.

Moreover, he had a growing belief in his power to climb the heights of success. His favorite books of travel and adventure that he had devoured in boyhood made almost anything seem possible, and the various biographies that the village library furnished revealed grand careers in the face of enormous obstacles. His mind was awaking like a young giant eager for achievement. Even after the toil of long, hot days he took up his old school-books in the solitude of his room, and found that he could review them with the ease with which he would read a story. "I've got some brains as well as muscle," he would mutter, exultantly. "The time shall come when Mildred Jocelyn won't mistake me for Jotham."

Poor Mr. Atwood would have been in consternation had he known what was passing in his son's mind; and Mildred even less pleased, for after all it was she who had inspired the thoughts which were transforming him from a simple country youth into an ambitious, venturesome man.

He knew of but one way to please her, but he made the most of that, and worked quietly but assiduously whenever he could without exciting his father's opposition. After the day's tasks were over the time was his own. He began by cutting all the weeds and grass in the door-yard and around the house. Palings that had disappeared from the fence were replaced, and all were whitewashed.

Mrs. Atwood and Susan were greatly pleased at the changes, but thought it politic not to say much about them; one evening, however, his father began to banter him, remarking that Roger must be intending to "bring home a wife some fine morning." The young fellow reddened resentfully, and brusquely retorted that they "had lived in their old slovenly way long enough. People might well think they were going to the bad."

This practical view somewhat reconciled his father to the new ideas, and suggested that Roger was not so daft as he feared. A little time after he was led to believe his son to be shrewder than himself. Needing some money, he took a note to the bank with much misgiving, but was agreeably surprised when one of the officers said affably, "I think we can accommodate you, Mr. Atwood. I was by your place the other day, and it is so improved that I scarcely knew it. Thrift and credit go together."

But Mildred doubted whether thrift and policy were the only motives which had led to Roger's unwonted action, and believed rather that he had awakened to a perception of the value and attractiveness of those things which hitherto he had not appreciated. This, in a sense, was already true, but had she known to what extent she was in his thoughts she would not have smiled so complacently when, on the Saturday morning after the completion of his other labors, she noted that the weed-choked flower-borders along the walk had been cleaned and neatly rounded up, and the walk itself put in perfect order. "The flower-beds remind me of himself," she thought, as from time to time she glanced at them through her open window. "They contain a good deal of vacant space, and suggest what might be there rather than what is. Would to heaven, though, that Mr. Arnold had more of his muscle and decision. If Vinton were only different, how different all the future might be! But I fear, I fear. We have not enough money to last all summer if we remain here, and father writes so discouragingly. Thank God, I'm no longer idle, whether anything comes of my work or not," and the delicate piece of fancy work grew rapidly in her deft hands.

Toward evening she started out for a walk, but uttered an exclamation of surprise as she saw the flower-borders were bright with verbenas, heliotrope, geraniums, and other bedding plants. Roger's buggy stood near, containing two large empty boxes, and he was just raking the beds smooth once more in order to finish his task.

"Why, Mr. Atwood!" she cried, "it has long seemed to me that a good fairy was at work around the house, but this is a master-stroke."

"If you are pleased I am well repaid," he replied, the color deepening on his sunburned cheeks.

"If I am pleased?" she repeated in surprise, and with a faint answering color. "Why, all will be pleased, especially your mother and Susan."

"No doubt, but I thought these would look more like what you have been accustomed to."

"Really, Mr. Atwood, I hope you have not put yourself to all this trouble on my account."

"I have not put myself to any trouble. But you are in trouble, Miss Jocelyn, and perhaps these flowers may enliven you a little."

"I did not expect such kindness, such thoughtfulness. I do not see that I am entitled to so much consideration," she said hesitatingly, at the same time fixing on him a penetrating glance.

Although he was much embarrassed, his clear black eyes met hers without wavering, and he asked, after a moment: "Could you not accept it if it were given freely?"

"I scarcely understand you," she replied in some perplexity.

"Nor do I understand you, Miss Jocelyn. I wish I did, for then I might do more for you."

"No, Mr. Atwood," she answered gravely, "you do not understand me. Experience has made me immeasurably older than you are."

"Very possibly," he admitted, with a short, embarrassed laugh. "My former self-assurance and complacency are all gone."

"Self-reliance and self-restraint are better than self-assurance," she remarked with a smile.

"Miss Jocelyn," he began, with something like impetuosity, "I would give all the world if I could become your friend. You could do so much for me."

"Mr. Atwood," said Mildred, with a laugh that was mixed with annoyance, "you are imposed upon by your fancy, and are imagining absurd things, I fear. But you are good-hearted and I shall be a little frank with you. We are in trouble. Business reverses have overtaken my father, and we are poor, and may be much poorer. I may be a working-woman the rest of my days; so, for Heaven's sake, do not make a heroine out of me. That would be too cruel a satire on my prosaic lot."

"You do not understand me at all, and perhaps I scarcely understand myself. If you think my head is filled with sentimental nonsense, time will prove you mistaken. I have a will of my own, I can assure you, and a way of seeing what is to be seen. I have seen a great deal since I've known you. A new and larger world has been revealed to me, and I mean to do something in it worthy of a man. I can never go on with my old life, and I will not," he continued, almost passionately. "I was an animal. I was a conceited fool. I'm very crude and unformed now, and may seem to you very ridiculous; but crudity is not absurdity, undeveloped strength is not weakness. An awakening mind may be very awkward, but give me time and you will not be ashamed of my friendship."

He had ceased leaning against a tree that grew near the roadway, and at some distance from the house. In his strong feeling he forgot his embarrassment, and assumed an attitude so full of unconscious power that he inspired a dawning of respect; for, while he seemed a little beside himself, there was a method in his madness which suggested that she, as well as the young man, might eventually discover that he was not of common clay and predestined to be commonplace. But she said, in all sincerity, "Mr. Atwood, I'm sure I wish you twice the success you crave in life, and I've no reason to think you overrate your power to achieve it; but you greatly overrate me. It would be no condescension on my part to give you my friendship; and no doubt if you attain much of the success you covet you will be ready enough to forget my existence. What induces you to think that a simple girl like me can help you? It seems to me that you are vague and visionary, which perhaps is natural, since you say you are just awaking," she concluded, with a little smiling sarcasm.

"You are unjust both to yourself and to me," he replied firmly, "and I think I can prove it. If I shall ever have any power in the world it will be in seeing clearly what is before me. I have seldom been away from this country town, and yet as soon as I saw you with a mind free from prejudice I recognized your superiority. I brought the belle of Forestville and placed her by your side, and I could think of nothing but brazen instruments until I left her loudness at her father's door. I would not go near her again if there were not another woman in the world. I saw at a glance that she was earthenware beside you."

Mildred now could not forbear laughing openly. "If you lose your illusions so rapidly," she said, "my turn will come soon, and I shall be china beside some fine specimen of majolica."

"You may laugh at me, but you will one day find I am sincere, and not altogether a fool."

"Oh, I'm ready to admit that, even now. But you are altogether mistaken in thinking I can help you. Indeed I scarcely see how I can help myself. It is a very poor proof of your keen discernment to associate me with your kindling ambition."

"Then why had you the power to kindle it? Why do I think my best thoughts in your presence? Why do I speak to you now as I never dreamed I could speak? You are giving purpose and direction to my life, whether you wish it or not, whether you care or not. You may always be indifferent to the fact, still it was your hand that wakened me. I admit I'm rather dazed as yet. You may think I'm talking to you with the frankness—perhaps the rashness—of a boy, since you are 'immeasurably older,' but the time is not very distant when I shall take my course with the strength and resolution of a man."

"I should be sorry to be the very innocent cause of leading you into thorny paths. I truly think you will find more happiness here in your quiet country life."

His only answer was an impatient gesture.

"Perhaps," she resumed, "if you knew more of the world you would fear it more. I'm sure I fear it, and with good reason."

"I do not fear the world at all," he replied. "I would fear to lose your esteem and respect far more, and, distant as you are from me, I shall yet win them both."

"Mr. Atwood, I suppose I have as much vanity as most girls, but you make me blush. You are indeed dazed, for you appear to take me for a melodramatic heroine."

"Pardon me, I do not. I've been to the theatre occasionally, but you are not at all theatrical. You are not like the heroines of the novels I've read, and I suppose I've read too many of them."

"I fear you have," she remarked dryly. "Pray, then, what am I like?"

"And I may seem to you a hero of the dime style; but wait, don't decide yet. What are you like? You are gentle, like your mother. You are exceedingly fond of all that's pretty and refined, so much so that you tried to introduce a little grace into our meagre, angular farmhouse life—"

"Thanks for your aid," interrupted Mildred, laughing. "I must admit that you have good eyes."

"You shrink," he resumed, "from all that's ugly, vulgar, or coarse in life. You are an unhappy exile in our plain home."

"All which goes to prove what an ordinary and unheroic nature I have. You will soar far beyond me, Mr. Atwood, for you have portrayed a very weak character—one that is in love with the niceties of life, with mere prettiness."

"You are still laughing at me, but I'm in earnest; and

if you mean what you say, you understand yourself less than you do me. Why will you not go to the hotel occasionally? Because with all your gentleness you are too proud to run the slightest risk of patronage and pity from those who knew you in your more fortunate days. Why do you remain in your little hot room so much of the time? I don't know; but if you will permit a guess, you are working. Every day you grow less content to sit still in helpless weakness. You are far braver than I, for I do not fear the world in the least; but, no matter how much you feared it, you would do your best to the last, and never yield to anything in it that was low, base, or mean. Oh, you are very gentle, very delicate, and you will be misunderstood; but you have the strongest strength there is—a kind of strength that will carry you through everything, though it cost you dear."

"And what may that be?" she asked, looking at him now in genuine wonder.

"I can't explain exactly what I mean. It is something I've seen in mother, plain and simple as she is. It's a kind of enduring steadfastness; it's a patient faithfulness. I should know just where to find mother, and just what to expect from her, under all possible circumstances. I should never expect to see you very different from what you are, no matter what happened. You often have the same look or expression that she has; and it means to me that you would do the best you could, although discouraged and almost hopeless. Very few soldiers will fight when they know the battle is going against them. You would, as long as you could move a finger."

"Mr. Atwood, what has put all this into your head? This seems very strange language from you."

"It is not so strange as it seems. It comes from the gift on which I base my hope of success in life. I see clearly and vividly what is before me, and draw my conclusions. If I see the antlers of a stag above some bushes, it is not necessary to see the whole animal to know he is there, and what kind of a creature he is. I'm not a scholar, Miss Jocelyn, but you must not think I do not know anything because I work in the corn or the hayfield all day. We have long winters up here, and I've studied some and read a great deal more. There are but few books in the village library that I have not read more or less thoroughly, and some of them many times. Because I was a careless, conceited fellow a few weeks since, it does not follow that I'm an ignoramus."

Mildred was decidedly puzzled. She could not account for the change in him; and she did not like to think of that to which his words and feelings pointed. He asked for friendship, but she strongly doubted whether such a placid regard would long satisfy him. Her chief impulse was to escape, for the bare thought of words of love from him or any one except Vinton Arnold was intensely repugnant. As she glanced around, seeking in what direction she might take her flight, she saw a gentleman coming rapidly toward the house. After a second's hesitation she rushed toward him, crying, "Papa, papa, you are welcome!"

CHAPTER X

A COUNCIL

ROGER saw Miss Jocelyn rush into the arms of a tall, florid gentleman, whose dark eyes grew moist at the almost passionate warmth of his daughter's greeting. To Mildred her father's unexpected coming was thrice welcome, for in addition to her peculiarly strong affection for him, his presence ended an interview not at all agreeable, and promised relief from further unwelcome attentions on the part of Roger. Almost in the moment of meeting, she resolved to persuade him that his family would be happier with him in the city. This had been her feeling from the first, but now she was wholly bent on leaving the farmhouse; for with her larger experience and womanly intuition she read in Roger's frank and still half-boyish face the foreshadowing of an unwelcome regard which she understood better than he did.

While his manner for a few weeks past, and especially his words during their recent interview, made it clear that he was not the rough, awkward rustic she had first imagined him to be, he still seemed very crude and angular. In spite of her love for Vinton Arnold, which had not abated in the least, he had ceased to be her ideal man. Nevertheless, his refined elegance, his quiet self-restraint, his knowledge of the niceties and proprieties of the world to which she felt she belonged by right, did combine to produce an ideal in her mind of which she was but half conscious, and beside which Roger appeared in a repulsive light. She shrank with instinctive distaste from his very strength and vehemence, and feared that she would never be safe from interviews like the one just described, and from awkward, half-concealed gallantries. Even the flowers he had set out became odious, for they represented a sentiment the very thought of which inspired aversion.

A coquette can soon destroy the strong instinct of sacredness and exclusiveness with which an unperverted girl guards her heart from all save the one who seems to have the divine right and unexplained power to pass all barriers. Even while fancy free, unwelcome advances are resented almost as wrongs and intrusions by the natural woman; but after a real, or even an ideal image has taken possession of the heart and imagination, repugnance is often the sole reward of other unfortuante suitors, and this dislike usually will be felt and manifested in a proportion corresponding with the obtrusiveness of the attentions, their sincerity, and the want of tact with which they are offered.

To that degree, therefore, that Roger was in earnest, Mildred shrank from him, and she feared that he would not—indeed, from his antecedents could not—know how to hide his emotions. His words had so startled her that, in her surprise and annoyance, she imagined him in a condition of semi-ambitious and semi-amative ebullition, and she dreaded to think what strange irruptions might ensue. It would have been the impulse of many to make the immature youth a source of transient amusement, but with a sensitive delicacy she shrank from him altogether, and wished to get away as soon as possible. Pressing upon her was the sad, practical question of a thwarted and impoverished life—impoverished to her in the dreariest sense—and it was intolerable that one who seemed so remote from her sphere should come and ask that, from her bruised and empty heart, she should give all sorts of melodramatic sentiment in response to his crude, ambitious impulses, which were yet as blind as the mythical god himself.

Had she seen that Roger meant friendship only when he asked for friendship, she would not have been so prejudiced against him; but the fact that this "great boy" was half consciously extending his hand for a gift which now she could not bestow on the best and greatest, since it was gone from her beyond recall, appeared grotesque, and such a disagreeable outcome of her changed fortunes that she was almost tempted to hate him. There are some questions on which women scarcely reason—they only feel intensely.

Mildred, therefore, was heartily glad that Roger did not wait to be introduced to her father, and that he kept himself aloof from the reunited family during the evening. She also was pleased that they were not joined by the Atwoods at the supper-table. That this considerate delicacy was due to the "young barbarian's" suggestion she did not dream, but gave good-hearted but not very sensitive Mrs. Atwood all the credit. As for poor Roger, his quick insight, his power to guess something of people's thoughts and feelings from the expression of their faces, brought but little present comfort or promise for the future.

"I made a bad impression at the start," he muttered, "and it will be long before she loses it, if she ever does. She shrinks from me as from something coarse and rough. She feels that I don't belong to her world at all. In fact, her father's fine bearing, his erect, elegant carriage make me feel as if I were but a country lout in very truth."

The reception given to Mr. Jocelyn satisfied Mrs. Atwood thoroughly that his prolonged absence did not result from any alienation from his family. They overwhelmed him with caresses, and either Fred or Minnie could scarcely be kept out of his arms a moment.

"Fanny," he said to his wife, "I almost made a vow that I would not come here until I had secured a position that would give you all the comforts of life, if not at once its luxuries; but such positions are occupied, and when one becomes vacant they are filled by relatives of the firm, or by those who have stronger claims than I can present. Still my friends are working for me, and I have the prospect of employment where the compensation will be small at first, but if I can draw a considerable Southern trade it will be increased rapidly."

And yet he sighed while revealing this hopeful outlook, and Mildred noticed that he sighed more than once during the evening, in spite of the torrent of affectionate welcome which almost swept him away.

After Belle and the younger children were sleeping, the husband and wife with Mildred talked late over their prospects. Mr. Jocelyn suggested that they should remain in the country, and even that they should rent a small cottage in Forestville or elsewhere, but his gentle wife soon proved that on some occasions she could be decided.

"No, Martin," she said, with the quiet emphasis which reveals a purpose not to be combated, "one thing is settled—there must be no more separation. I have suffered too much during these last few weeks ever to listen again to such an arrangement. Now that you are with us once more, I learn that the ache in my heart was caused not so much by losses and the prospect of poverty as by loneliness and the feeling that you were left to struggle by yourself. It's my place to be with you, and I am willing to live anywhere and in any way. I can see that I might have aided you in providing against this evil time, but it seems now that I thought only of what we wanted for each day as it came, and the trouble was that we all got just what we wanted. Here is the result. Oh, I've thought it over through long sleepless nights till my heart ached with a pain that I hope none of you will ever know. But to sit idly here and wait while you are trying to retrieve my folly is a greater punishment than I can endure. Give me something to do which will be of help to you, and I will do it gladly, even though it be in two attic rooms."

"Mamma's right," added Mildred earnestly. "Papa, you must find a place for us in New York—a place within our means. Let us begin life right this time, and I believe God will bless and prosper us. It won't be many days before Belle and I will find something to do."

Mr. Jocelyn sighed more deeply than ever, and, indeed, appeared so overcome for a few moments that he could not speak. At last he faltered, "I have all of a Southern man's pride, and it's more bitter than death to me that my wife and daughters must work for their bread."

"Papa," exclaimed Mildred, "would it not be infinitely more bitter to us all to eat the bread of charity? I shall pretend to no unnatural heroism, nor say I like toil and poverty. On the contrary, I think I shrink from such things more than most girls do. But I don't propose to sit down and wring my hands. I can put them to a better use. We must just put away all talk of pride and sentiment, and remember only our poverty and self-respect. As Christian and sensible people we are bound to accept of our life and make the best of it. You and mother both know how much this change has cost me," she concluded, with a few half-stifled sobs, "and if I am willing to enter on a cheerful, patient effort to make the best of life as it is, I think all the rest might, too. If we give way to despondency we are lost. Let us be together again, and pull together as one."

"The idea of Nan and the children coming back to the city in August!" said Mr. Jocelyn dejectedly. "You don't either of you realize what you are talking about. We should have to go into a tenement-house."

"Martin, I do realize it," replied his wife earnestly. "The country is doing me no good—indeed I'm failing in health. Nothing does us good when we are unhappy and anxious. Find me two rooms in a tenement-house if we cannot afford more, and let us be together as soon as possible."

"Well," said Mr. Jocelyn, after a long breath, "with such a wife and such children to work for a man ought to be able to do great things; but it's much the same as it was in the army—if one lost his place in the ranks he was hustled about in everybody's way, and if weak and disabled he was left to his fate. The world goes right on and over you if you don't stand aside. I know you've suffered, Nan, and you know that if I had my wish you would never have a care or a pain; but God knows I suffered too. After you all were gone and my duties to my former partners ceased, I began to learn from experience how difficult it is in these cursed times to get a foothold, and I became almost sleepless from anxiety. Then set in that villanous neuralgia, which always strikes a man when he's down, and for a week oı more it seemed that I should almost lose my reason."

"Oh, Martin, Martin!" his wife exclaimed reproachfully, "and you did not let us know!"

"Why should I? It would only have added to your burden, and would not have helped me. I was glad you knew nothing about it."

"This is another proof that we must be together," said his wife, her eyes filling with tears. "How did you come to get better?"

"Oh, the doctor gave me something that made me sleep, and I seldom have neuralgia now."

"Come, papa," cried Mıldred, as she put her arms around his neck and leaned her face against his, "there are thousands worse off than we are, and thousands more have retrieved far worse disasters. Now take courage; we'll all stand by you, and we'll all help you. We will one day have a prettier home than ever, and it will be all our own, so that no one can drive us from it;" and with hope springing up in her heart she tried to inspire hope and courage in theirs.

"Oh, Millie," he said, taking her on his lap, "when you coax and pet one you are irresistible. We *will* begin again, and win back all and more than we have lost."

Then, partly to amuse her father and mother, but more for the purpose of hastening their departure, Mildred told them of Roger's peculiar mood, and her conscience smote her a little as she caricatured rather than characterized the youth. Mrs. Jocelyn, in her kindliness, took his part, and said, "Millie, you are satirical and unjust. I'm sure he's a well-meaning young man."

"The dear little mother!" cried Mildred, laughing; "when she can't think of anything else good to say of a person, she assures us that he is 'well-meaning.' Life may bring me many misfortunes, but I shall never marry what mamma calls 'a well-meaning man.'"

"But, Millie, I'm sure he's been very good and kind to us all, and he's kind to his mother and sister, and he seems steady—"

"Well, mamma, admitting it all, what follows?" asked Mildred.

"It follows that we had better go away," said Mrs. Jocelyn, with her low, sweet laugh, that had been rarely heard of late; "but I don't like you to be unjust to the young fellow. After all, he's not so very much to blame, Millie," she added, with a little nod. "If I were he I fear I might be in the same fix."

"Oh, papa, now we must go; for if mamma's sympathies are once aroused in behalf of this 'steady, well-meaning young man'—there! I will talk no more nonsense to-night, although I often find nonsense a sort of life-preserver that keeps me from sinking. I admit, mamma, that I have been unjust to Mr. Atwood. He's far more clever than I ever imagined him to be, but he's so different"--she finished the sentence with a little repellent gesture that her mother well understood.

They were all comforted, and far more hopeful from their frank interchange of thought and feeling, and both father and mother breathed a fervent "God bless you, Millie," as they separated, long past midnight.

"God will bless us," said the young girl, "if we will just simply try to do what is right and best every day. The blessing will come on doing, not waiting."

She had not been in her room very long before hearing the crunching of gravel under the wheels of Roger's buggy. With a smile she thought, "He must have found a more sympathizing ear and heart than mine to have remained out so late."

CHAPTER XI

A SHADOW

"MRS. ATWOOD," said Mildred the next morning, "I want to thank you for your kindness in giving us our supper alone with papa the first evening of his arrival; but you need not put yourself to any extra trouble to-day."

"Roger is the one to thank," replied Mrs. Atwood. "He's grown so different, so considerate like, that I scarcely know him any more than I do the old place he's so fixed up. He says he's going to paint the house after the summer work slacks off. I don't see what's come over him, but I like the change very much."

Mildred flushed slightly, but said, with some constraint, "Please thank him then from papa and mamma, but do not let us make you further trouble. We shall all return to the city soon, and then you will have easier times every way."

"I'm sorry to hear that, Miss Jocelyn, for we shall miss you all very much. You've done us good in more ways than one."

Roger did not appear at breakfast. "A young horse strayed from the pasture, and Roger is out looking for him," his mother explained when Mrs. Jocelyn asked after him.

Although not a member of any church, Mr. Jocelyn had great respect for his wife and daughter's faith, and accompanied them to service that morning very readily. Roger appeared in time to take Belle, as usual, but she found him so taciturn and preoccupied that she whispered to Mildred, "You've spoiled him for me. He sits staring like an owl in the sunlight, and seeing just about as much. You ought to be ashamed of yourself to make him so glum. I intend to have a dozen beaux, and to keep them all jolly."

Mildred was obliged to admit to herself that the young fellow was very undemonstrative at dinner, and that he did not exhibit the rusticity that she half hoped to see. She gained the impression that he was observing her father very closely, and that no remark of his escaped him. "He has the eyes of a lynx," she thought, with a frown. Still, apart from a certain annoyance at his deep interest in her and all relating to her, she was rather pleased at the impression which such a man as her father must make on one so unsophisticated. Mr. Jocelyn was a finished man of the world, and his large experience left its impress on all that he said and did. Although a little courtly in manner, he was so kindly and frank in nature that his superiority was not at all oppressive, and with true Southern *bonhomie* he made the farmer's family quite at ease, leading them to speak freely of their rural affairs. Susan soon lost all sense of restraint and began to banter her brother.

"You must have had a very affecting time in making up with Amelia Stone to have stayed out so late," she remarked *sotto voce.*

"I've not seen Amelia Stone since the evening she was here," he answered dryly.

"Indeed! what other charmer then tied you to her apron-strings so tightly? You are very fickle."

"Now you've hit it," he answered, with a slight flush. "I was so undecided that I drove by every door, and was not tied at all."

Belle "made eyes" at Mildred, as much as to say, "It's you who are distracting him."

"Next time," Sue continued, "I think it would be well to make up your mind before Sunday morning."

"My mind is made up," replied Roger—Belle looked at

Mildred with an expression of horror, to her intense annoyance—"I shall trouble no one," he added, quietly.

Belle now gave such a great sigh of relief that he turned upon her too swift a glance to leave time for disguise. He smiled a little bitterly, and then began talking in an off-hand way to Mr. Jocelyn about the hotel a few miles distant, saying that it had filled up very rapidly of late. As they rose from the table he remarked, hesitatingly, "My horse and wagon are at your service this afternoon or evening if you would like to take a drive."

Mr. Jocelyn was about to accept, but Mildred trod significantly on his foot. Therefore he thanked Roger cordially, and said he would spend a quiet day with his family.

"I don't wish to be under the slightest obligations to him," explained Mildred when they were alone; "and Belle," she warned, "you must stop your nonsense at once. I won't endure another trace of it."

"Oh, indeed! I didn't know you were so touchy about him," cried the girl. "Is it for his sake or your own that you are so careful? You're stupid not to let him amuse you, since you've spoiled him for me."

Her sister made no reply, but gave the giddy child a glance that quieted her at once. When Mildred was aroused her power over others was difficult to explain, for, gentle as she was, her will at times seemed irresistible.

Roger did not need to be told in so many words that his overtures of "friendship" had been practically declined. Her tones, her polite but distant manner revealed the truth clearly. He was sorely wounded, but, so far from being disheartened, his purpose to win her recognition was only intensified.

"I can at least compel her respect and prove myself her equal," he thought, and instead of lounging or sleeping away the afternoon, as had been his custom, he took a book and read steadily for several hours. At last he left his room to aid his father in the evening labors of the farmyard, and in doing so would have to pass near Mr. Jocelyn, who, with his family, was seated under a wide-spreading tree. The gentleman evidently was in a very genial mood; he was caressing his children, flattering his wife and Mildred, and rallying Belle after her own frolicsome humor. Roger thought, as he looked at them a few moments through the kitchen window, that he had never seen a happier family, and with a sigh wished that it was his privilege to join them without being thought an intruder. Mildred's reserve, however, formed an impassable barrier, and he was hastening by with downcast eyes, when, to his surprise and the young girl's evident astonishment, Mr. Jocelyn arose and said, "Ah, Mr. Atwood, we're glad to see you. Won't you join our little party? I want to thank you again for offering me your horse and carriage, but I assure you that a quiet hour like this with one's family after long separation is happiness enough. Still, as a Southern man, I appreciate courtesy, and am always ready to respond to it in like spirit. Moreover, it gives me peculiar pleasure to see a Northern man developing traits which, if they were general, would make the two great sections of our land one in truth as well as in name."

Roger gave Mildred a quick, questioning glance, and saw that she was regarding her father with much perplexity.

"Mr. Jocelyn," he said quietly, "the little courtesy of which you speak has cost me nothing, and if it had it would not be worth the words you bestow upon it."

"I do not think of the act itself so much as the spirit, the disposition it indicates," resumed Mr. Jocelyn in a manner that was courtly and pronounced, but otherwise natural and quiet enough. "I do not judge superficially, but look past apparent trifles to the character they suggest. Moreover, my wife informs me that you have been very polite to her, and very kind to Belle and the children, whom you have often taken out to drive without any compensation whatever. Since you will not make a business matter of such things, I wish to repay you in the coin which gentleman can always receive—that of friendly acknowledgments."

"Then please consider me amply repaid," and with a smile and a bow he was about to retire.

"Do not hasten away, sir," Mr. Jocelyn began again. "On this day of rest your duties cannot be pressing. I want to assure you further of the pleasure I have in finding a young man who, so far from being rendered callous and material by hard and rather homely work, is alive to all refining influences. The changes in this place for the better since I was here, and those pretty flowers yonder, all prove that you have an eye for the beautiful as well as the practical. My daughter Mildred also informs me that you are cherishing hopes and ambitions that will eventually enlarge your sphere of life and take you out into the great world."

Hitherto Roger's eyes had been fixed keenly and unwaveringly on Mr. Jocelyn's urbane countenance, as if he would detect the cause of such unlooked-for words, but at the mention of Mildred's name his brow and even neck was suffused. "She must have spoken of me kindly," he thought, "or her father would not be so friendly." But when a swift glance around revealed that Mrs. Jocelyn was looking at her husband in perplexity, that Mildred was not even trying to conceal her vexation and amazement, and that Belle had stuffed her handkerchief into her mouth to prevent laughter, a spark of anger glittered in his eyes. His first thought was that Mr. Jocelyn was indulging in unexpected irony at his expense, and the ready youth whose social habits had inured him to much chaffing was able to reply, although a little stiffly and awkwardly, "I suppose most young men have ambitious hopes of doing something in the world, and yet that does not prevent mine from seeming absurd. At any rate, it's clear that I had better reveal them hereafter by deeds rather than words," and with a very slight bow he strode away, but not so quickly that he failed to hear Mildred's voice in the exclamation, "Oh, papa! how could you?" and then followed a paroxysm of laughter from Belle.

Roger was deeply incensed, for he believed that Mr. Jocelyn and Belle were deliberately ridiculing him. That Mildred had repeated his conversation was evident, but her manner showed that she did not expect his words to be used against him so openly, and that she had no part in the cruel sport. The worst he could charge against her was exclusive pride; and he did Mrs. Jocelyn the justice to see that she was pained by the whole affair. His face grew rigid as he finished his work and he muttered, "They shall see that my pride is equal to theirs; I won't go out of my way a hair-breadth for them," and he walked in to supper as if he were at home and had an absolute right to be there. He had been at the table but a few moments, however, before the aspect of the Jocelyn family began to puzzle him exceedingly. Belle appeared as if she had been crying; Mrs. Jocelyn looked perplexed and worried, and in Mildred's eyes there were anxiety and trouble. Mr. Jocelyn had not lost his serenity in the least, but his aspect now was grave, and his manner more courtly than ever. He did not seem inclined to say very much, however, and had an abstracted, dreamy look as if his thoughts were far away. When he did speak, Roger thought that Mildred looked apprehensive, as if fearing that he might again say something embarrassing, but his words were quiet and measured, betraying no excitement. The expression of his face, however, seemed unnatural to Roger's close yet furtive scrutiny. An hour before his eyes had been bright and dilated, and his countenance full of animation; now all the light and cheerfulness were fading, and the man seemed to grow older and graver by moments. Was the dusky pallor stealing across his features caused by the shadows of evening? Roger thought not, but a resentful glance from Mildred warned him to curb his curiosity.

He was curious, but not in a vulgar or prying way, and his anger was all gone. He was sure that something was amiss with Mr. Jocelyn, and that his family also was disturbed and anxious. There had been none of the incoherency and excitement of a man who had drank too much, but only a slight exaggeration of the genial traits manifested at the dinner-table followed by a quietude and abstraction that were not natural. Mental aberrations, even though slight and temporary, are instinctively felt by those who are sound and normal in mind. Still Roger would have charged Mr. Jocelyn's words and manner to the peculiarities of a stranger, had not his family been perplexed and troubled also. "There's something wrong about him," he said to himself as he rose from the table; "he lacks balance, or he's not well. I half believe that the time will come when that young girl will be the stay and support of the whole family. You cannot prevent my friendliness, Miss Jocelyn, any more than you can stop the sun from shining, and some day it will melt all your reserve and coldness." He took his volume of history out on the sward near the porch, resolving to see the end of the domestic drama. His mother had told him during the day that their "boarders" would soon depart. He had made no response whatever, but his sinking spirits revealed to him that in some way his life had become involved with that of the girl now so distant and repellent.

He did not turn many leaves, but he sat with the book in his lap until long after nightfall. The domestic drama apparently had a very prosaic ending. Mr. Jocelyn and his family returned for a time to their seats under the trees, but all except the little children were apparently under some constraint. The latter soon grew sleepy, and Mrs. Jocelyn took them in to bed. Belle was not long in following them, darting an ireful glance at Roger in passing, to which he responded by a rather mocking smile. "We were having a lovely time till you came, you old marplot," she muttered under her breath.

Mr. Jocelyn grew more and more quiet until his head sank on his breast, and it was with difficulty that Mildred aroused him sufficiently to urge his retiring. At last he took his daughter's arm and entered the house as if in a dream. The young girl's face was downcast and averted. As they passed between the youth and the still glowing west they cast a faint shadow upon him. Though by no means imaginative, he noted the shadow and thought about it. It seemed that it still rested on him after they were gone, and that it might never pass away. His was not a dreamy, fanciful nature, that could create a score of improbable contingencies, but his shrewd, strong sense was quick to recognize traces of weakness and untrustworthiness in those he met, and the impression grew upon him that Mr. Jocelyn was not a well-balanced man. "If he fails her, I will not," he murmured. Then with a short laugh he continued, "How is it that I am ready to admit such a far-reaching claim from one who repels and dislikes me? I don't know, and I don't care. She has waked me up; she has the power of calling into action every faculty I have. Already, I scarcely know myself. I never lived before, and I feel that I can become a man—perhaps a great man—if I follow this impulse, and I shall follow it."

Soon all were sleeping, and mother and daughter were alone.

"Mamma," said Mildred, in a low, troubled tone, "it seemed to me that papa acted very strangely this afternoon and evening. Can he be well?"

"Oh, Millie," cried the loving, anxious wife, "I fear he is not well at all; and no wonder, when we think of the long strain he has been under. Haven't you noticed that his appetite is very poor? to-night he scarcely ate a mouthful. He has just been trying to keep up ever since he came, and this afternoon he made unusual effort; reaction of course followed, and at last he was so weary and troubled that he could not hide his feelings from us."

"I suppose you take the right view," said Mildred hesitatingly, "but papa has not seemed the same this afternoon as at other times when tired and worried. His gayety was a little extravagant, and so it might naturally be if it were forced. But I can't understand his speaking to young Mr.

Atwood as he did. Papa never showed such a lack of tact or delicacy before. I would not dare tell him things if he spoke of them afterward so inopportunely. I felt as if I could sink into the ground. And when Belle—who can't help seeing everything in a ridiculous light—began to laugh he turned and spoke to her as he has never spoken to any of us before. And yet he did not seem angry, but his gravity was more oppressive than any amount of natural anger."

"Well, Millie, your father is very kind-hearted, and, like all Southern men, very sensitive to kindness and courtesy. I suppose he thought that you and Belle had not treated Roger well, and that he ought to make amends. The real explanation is that he is overstrained and unhappy, and so cannot act like himself."

"I do hope he is not going to be ill," faltered Mildred. "Such a strange lethargy came over him after you left us. Oh, the day is ending horribly, and it leaves a weight of foreboding on my mind. I wish we could get away to-morrow, for I feel that Roger Atwood is watching us, and that nothing escapes him. I know that papa's manner seemed strange to him as well as to us, and I almost hate him for his obtrusive and prying interest. Why can't he see that he's nothing to us, nor we to him, and let us alone?"

She often recalled these words in after years.

The wife went to her room and found that her husband was sleeping quietly. Returning, she said, more cheerily, "I think papa will be like himself after a good night's sleep, and there's every promise now that he'll get it; so don't look on the dark side, Millie, nor worry about that young man. He don't mean to be obtrusive, and I must say that I think he behaves very well considering. With troubles like ours, why think of such a transient annoyance? If I only knew just how I could help your father I would not think about much else."

It would have been well indeed if she could have known, for she would have taken from his pocketbook a small syringe and a bottle of Magendie's solution of morphia; she would have entreated him upon her knees, she would have bound him by the strongest oaths to die rather than to use it again. The secret of all that was peculiar and unnatural in his conduct can be explained by the fact that early in the afternoon he went apart for a moment, and with a little innocent-looking instrument injected into his arm the amount of the fatal drug which he believed he could enjoy without betraying himself.

CHAPTER XII

VIEWLESS FETTERS

ALTHOUGH Mr. Jocelyn had retired so early and slept heavily until an hour that at the farmhouse was late, the reader knows that his sleep was not the natural repose which brings freshness and elasticity. His wife and Mildred, however, did not know this, and his languor, continued drowsiness, and depression, which even much effort could not disguise, confirmed their dread of an impending illness. He saw their anxiety, and took advantage of their fears to hide his weakness.

"Yes," he sighed, in response to their gentle solicitude as he pushed away his almost untasted breakfast, "I suppose my health has been impaired by worry of mind and the heat in town. I'm better, though, than I have been. I don't see how you are going to endure the city."

They both assured him, however, that they would not even consider any other arrangement except that already agreed upon, and urged that he should return to town that very day, his wife adding that just as soon as he had secured rooms within their means she would join him and prepare them for the family.

"Oh, Nan," he again said dejectedly, "it's a cruel fate which compels me to take you to a tenement-house in August."

"It would be far more cruel to leave me here," his wife answered earnestly. "I could be happy anywhere if you were your old natural self once more. Millie and I can both see that struggling alone and brooding by yourself over your troubles is not good for you," and her gentle but determined purpose carried the day.

Mr. Jocelyn was then directed to a somewhat distant field, where he found Roger, who readily agreed to take him to the steamboat landing in the afternoon. Lifting his eyes from his work a few moments afterward, the young man saw that his visitor, instead of returning to the house, had sat down under a clump of trees and had buried his face in his hands.

"There's a screw loose about that man," he muttered. "He's too uneven. Yesterday at dinner he was the most perfect gentleman ever I saw; in the afternoon he had a fit of pompous hilarity and condescension; then came abstraction, as if his mind had stepped out for a time; and now, after twelve hours of sleep, instead of feeling like a lark, he looks as though he might attend his own funeral before night, and walks as if his feet were lead. He mopes there under the trees when he has but a few more hours with his family. If I had such a wife and such a daughter as he has, I'd cut a swath for them, no matter what stood in the way."

But Roger's censure was slight compared with that which Mr. Jocelyn visited upon himself; and in order to understand his feelings and conduct, it will be necessary to relate some experiences which occurred after the departure of his family to the country. Throughout the entire winter he had been under a severe strain of business anxiety, and then had come the culminating scenes of failure, loss of income, and enforced and unhappy separation. His natural depression had been so increased by the meagre prospect of finding employment which would yield his family an adequate support, that even his increased and more frequent indulgence in his morphia powders failed to give sufficient hopefulness and courage, while at the same time they began to produce some serious disorders in his system. There is a class of diseases which rarely fails to attack one whose system is reduced and enfeebled, and neuralgia began to bind across his forehead a daily pressure of pain that at last became intolerable. Ordinary remedies not giving speedy relief, his physician injected into his arm a few drops of the solution of morphia. Thus far he had never used the drug in solution hypodermically, and he was much surprised by the agreeable effects of a very much smaller quantity than he had been accustomed to use on any one occasion, and his morphia hunger—already firmly established—immediately suggested that the little syringe might become a far more potent agent than the powders. Therefore he induced the physician to give him an order for the instrument, and to explain more fully the methods of its use, saying that attacks of neuralgia were generally rather obstinate in his case, and that he had neither the time nor the means to seek his services very often.

The physician's few words of warning made but slight impression upon the infatuated man at the time. Mr. Jocelyn remembered only that he had an intolerable pain in his head and a heavy weight upon his heart. Many a time during the long civil war he had smilingly led charges wherein the chances of death were greater than those of life, but neither then nor since had he ever displayed any great aptitude for quiet endurance and self-control. Now every day was precious, and he felt he could not give himself up to pain and patient waiting until the disease could be conquered in a slow, legitimate way, when by a wound no more than a pin-prick he could obtain courage, happiness, and prospects illimitable.

Having obtained the syringe and a vial of the solution of morphia, he injected into his arm a much larger quantity than the physician would have dreamed of employing. Not only did the unendurable anguish pass away within a few brief moments, but the world was transfigured; life's grim outlook became full of the richest promise, and discouragement and dread vanished utterly. So far from fearing that he could not provide for his family, he was sure that he could win for them abundance and luxury. A dozen avenues to fortune opened before him, and he felt that his only task was to choose, believing that in some indefinite yet easily discerned way he would achieve more than falls to the lot of most men to accomplish. Instead of a long, sleepless night like those which had preceded, his waking dreams ended in quiet and equally pleasant visions—then oblivion, which did not pass away until the morning sun was shining. But with the new day came a new access of pain and gloom, and the aid of the magic little instrument was invoked once more. Again within a few moments the potent drug produced a tranquil elysium and a transformed world of grand possibilities. With a vigor which seemed boundless, and hopes which repeated disappointments could not dampen, he continued his quest for employment until in the declining day his spirits and energy ebbed as strangely as they had risen in the morning, and after another night of dreams and stupor he awoke in torture. The powerful stimulant enabled him to repeat the experiences of the previous day, and for two or three weeks he lived in the fatal but fascinating opium paradise, gradually increasing the amount of morphia that his system, dulled by habit, demanded. In the meantime, by the lavish use of quinine he gradually banished his neuralgia with its attendant pain.

It is well known to those familiar with the character of opium that its effects are greatly enhanced at first by any decided change in the method of its use; also that its most powerful and immediate influences can be produced solely by the hypodermic needle, since by means of it the stimulant is introduced at once into the system. When taken in powders, the glow, the serenity, and exaltation come on more slowly, and more gradually pass away, causing alternations of mood far less noticeable than those produced by immediate injection of the poison. Therefore it was not at all strange that Mr. Jocelyn's family should remain in complete ignorance of the habit which was enslaving him, or that his behavior failed to excite the faintest suspicion of the threatening influences at work. There is no vice so secret as that of the opium slave's, none that is in its earlier stages more easily and generally concealed from those who are nearest and dearest. The changes produced in Mr. Jocelyn were very gradual, and seeing him daily even his loving wife did not note them.

During the period of unnatural exaltation that has been described he had accepted agencies which promised thousands if he could sell millions of dollars' worth of goods, and after the subtle morphia had infused itself through his system nothing seemed easier; but dreams are not realities, and after grand hopes unfulfilled, and futile efforts, he would sink into a despondency from which nothing could lift him save the little syringe that he carried hidden next to his heart. As its magic never failed him, he went on for a time, blind to the consequences. At last he began to grow more alarmed than ever before at the ascendency of the drug and his dependence upon it, but when he tried to discontinue its use he found that he had been living so long under the influence of a powerful stimulant that without it he sank like a stone. Then came the usual compromise of all weak souls—he would gradually decrease the amount and then the frequency of its use; but, as is generally the case, he put off the beginning of sturdy self-denial until the morrow, and almost every day he poisoned his system with that which also poisoned and demoralized his soul. He dimly saw his danger, but did not realize it. With the fatuity of all self-indulgent natures he thought the day would come when, with better prospects and health renewed, he would throw away the spell which bound him and become a free man, but day after day passed and he did not; his appetite began to flag and his energy also; he would sit dreaming for hours when he might have been at work. At best his agencies would give him but a scanty revenue, although pushed with extraordinary skill and vigor. As it was, they yielded him little more than personal support, and he began to entertain the hope that if he could only obtain regular employment he could then resume his old regular habits. Therefore he had agreed to accept a position which was little more than a foothold, and yet if he would go to work with a determined and patient industry he might, by means of it, win more than he had lost.

Could he do this? The Sunday he had just spent with his family had awakened him as never before to a sense of his bondage. Even with the society of those he loved to enliven and sustain he had felt that he could not get through the day without the help of the stimulant upon which he had grown so dependent. While at church it was not the clergyman's voice he heard, but a low yet imperious and incessant cry for opium. As he rode home, smiling upon his wife and children, and looking at the beautiful and diversified country, between them and the landscape he ever saw a little brass instrument gauged at four or five times the amount that the physician had at first inserted in his arm. At the dinner table he had spoken courteously and well on many subjects, and yet ever uppermost in his mind was one constant thought—opium. The little diabolical thing itself seemed alive in his pocket, and made its faint yet potent solicitation against his heart. At last he had muttered, "I will just take a little of the cursed stuff, and then I must begin to break myself in dead earnest."

The reader knows what followed. Moreover, he was led to fear that the alternations of mood caused by injections of morphia would be so great that they could not fail to excite remark. Although the new day brought every motive which can influence a man, Mr. Jocelyn found the path to freedom so steep and difficult that the ascent seemed well-nigh impossible. His muscles were relaxed, his whole frame so weary and limp that he even dreaded the effort required to return to the house where his family was waiting for him. But the physical oppression was nothing to that which weighed upon his mind. The sense of misery and discouragement was paralyzing, and he was fairly appalled by his lack of energy. And yet he felt his need of power and resolution as keenly as he realized his feebleness. He knew that he had appeared unnatural to his wife and children, and that while they now ascribed his behavior to the long strain he had been under, their loving and charitable blindness could not last if he often exhibited before them such variable moods and conditions. Therefore he felt that he must overcome the habit before they were together permanently, for to permit them to discover his vile weakness in this time of their great need would be a mortal wound to his pride. All his manhood revolted at the bare thought. Their trust, their love, their dependence and unrepining courage in meeting poverty and privation with him imposed the strongest and most sacred of obligations, and his high sense of honor—which hitherto had been his religion—made failure to meet these obligations the most awful disaster that could overwhelm him. The means of escaping from his wretchedness and dejection—from the horrible lassitude of body and soul—could be grasped in a moment, and the temptation to use them and become within a few minutes a strong, sanguine, courageous man was almost irresistible; but he knew well that such an abrupt change from the heavy, dull-eyed condition in which they had seen him at the breakfast table could not fail to arouse suspicion; and should they once discern his crime—for crime he now regarded it—he feared his self-respect would be so destroyed that he would never have the pride and strength for the struggle now clearly foreseen; therefore, with the instinct of self-preservation, and from the impulse of all his native and long-fostered Southern pride, he resolved that they must never know his degradation. He must rally his shattered forces, spend the few hours before his departure with his family in a way to lull all fears and surmises; then when away by himself he would tug at his chain until he broke it. Summoning the whole strength of his will he returned to the house, and succeeded fairly well.

Could he break his chain? The coming pages of this book will reveal his struggle and its termination. Alas! it is no fancy sketch, but a record of human experience that is becoming sadly frequent. The hunger for opium had grown upon Mr. Jocelyn by its almost constant use for nearly two years. During weeks of pain he had almost lived upon the drug, saturating his system with it. It had come to him like an angel of light, lifting him on buoyant pinions out of suffering and despondency, but the light was fading from the wings and brow of this strong spirit, and it was already seen to be an angel of darkness.

At this time Mr. Jocelyn might have escaped from his thraldom, but would he? The world is full of people who are proud and self-respecting in the extreme, who are honorable and virtuous, good and kindly at heart, but whose wills are nerveless, though they may go safely through life without suspecting the truth; but if they fall under the influence of an evil habit—if they pass under this mightiest and darkest of all spells, opium hunger—they may learn their weakness in despair.

Mr. Jocelyn, however, had no thought of despair; he was only surprised, humiliated, and somewhat alarmed; he was satisfied that he must drift no longer, and in perfect sincerity resolved to make the most of his brief separation from his family, hoping that with a physician's advice he could speedily overcome his morbid craving and distressing need. He left the farmhouse with the resolution that he would never touch the drug again, believing that before a week expired the horrible depression, both mental and physical, would so far pass away as to excite no further suspicion.

For an hour he rode at Roger's side, rigid, taciturn, and pale; for except when heated by exercise his wonted ruddy color was passing away from the effects of the poison. Roger drove around to the large hotel, which was not much out of their way, and said, "Mr. Jocelyn, will you please take the lines a few moments? I have an errand here, but it won't keep me long."

Having transacted his business he stood in the office door

watching a young man who sauntered toward him. The stranger was almost as tall as himself, but much slighter. While his carriage was easy and graceful, it was marked by an air of lassitude and weariness, and his step lacked firmness. A heavy mustache relieved his face from effeminacy, but his large, dark eyes were dull and apathetic. Suddenly they lighted up with recognition; he hesitated, and then hastily advanced toward Mr. Jocelyn, but his steps were speedily checked, for the moment the gentleman recognized him he bowed very coldly and turned haughtily away. The young man flushed deeply, stood still a moment in irresolution, and then with a swift glance into Roger's interested face turned and quickly disappeared. Before Roger could resume his place in the wagon the proprietor of the hotel came out and called him back; something had been forgotten.

This interruption was fatal to Mr. Jocelyn's good resolutions. Vinton Arnold, who had won his daughter's affection, but who seemingly had not the manhood to be faithful in her adversity, was the one whom he had repulsed, and the thought of his wealth and luxury, while he was on his way to seek a home in a tenement for his beautiful child, so maddened him that he drove recklessly to an adjacent shed, which shielded him from observation, snatched out his fatal syringe, and in a moment the poison was diffusing itself through all his system. He had returned again before Roger, who had been detained some moments, reappeared, but now his heavy eyes were bright and fiery, and his tongue unloosed.

"Did you see that young man to whom I refused to speak?" he asked as they drove away.

"Yes."

"Well, he's a white-livered scoundrel. He's a type of your Northern gentlemen. A Southern man would starve rather than act so pusillanimously. Of course I'm not going to talk of family secrets, or say anything not befitting a high-toned gentleman, but I taught that snob how a man of honor regards his cowardice and cold-bloodedness. He was one of our fair-weather friends, who promptly disappeared when the sky clouded. Here he is, dawdling around a high-priced hotel, while I'm on my way to seek rooms in a tenement for those to whom he is not worthy to speak; but the time shall come, and speedily, too, when even on the base plane of money—the sole claim of his proud family for consideration—we shall meet him and scorn him as his superiors. I have plans, business prospects—" and he launched forth into such a vague, wild statement of his projects that Roger looked at him in silent amazement, half doubting his sanity.

In his haste Mr. Jocelyn had not carefully gauged his syringe, and the over-amount of morphia thrown into his system so stimulated him that his words appeared exceedingly irrational to the young man, whose judgment was based on unusual shrewdness and common-sense. He was greatly puzzled by the sudden change in his companion. It was evident that he had not been drinking, for his breath was untainted and his utterance was natural. But his face was flushed, and he seemed possessed by a strange, unbalanced mental exaltation which led him to speak as no sensible man ought in any circumstances, and certainly not to a stranger. Roger therefore interrupted him saying, "I shall respect your confidence, Mr. Jocelyn, and will never repeat what you have said. Please let me suggest, however, that it would be wise not to speak so frankly to others, since they might take advantage of you."

"Please let me assure *you*," resumed Mr. Jocelyn, with the most impressive dignity, "that I am a man of the world, and that I have seen a great deal of the world. I can read men as you would read a book. If you were not trustworthy I should know it at a glance. Did you not see how I treated that young jackanapes? His wealth and elegance did not impose upon me in the least. You are trustworthy. You have a large, aspiring mind, and yet you know your station; you would not dream of presuming. What does it signify that we are poor for the moment? True Southern blood is in our veins, and I have a dozen plans for securing large wealth. When that day comes I shall remember those who basely turned their backs on us in our brief obscurity;" and thus he rambled on, while Roger listened coldly and in silence.

"There is method is his madness," he said to himself; "he is not so daft but that he hints broadly I must keep my station and not be 'presuming.' His proud daughter hints as much still more plainly. Well, we'll see whose dreams find the larger fulfilment—his or mine."

By the time they reached the landing the sun was low in the west, and his companion had become comparatively silent, dreamy, and abstracted. Half an hour later Roger went on board of the boat with some solicitude to see how he was faring. Mr. Jocelyn started out of what appeared a deep reverie as Roger addressed him, and said, after a moment's thought, "Please say to my family that you left me well, and safely on my way," and with a quiet and rather distant bow he resumed his absorbing thoughts.

The steamer moved away, but instead of returning directly home Roger went back to the hotel. Even amid the hallucinations of opium the father had too much instinctive delicacy to mention Mildred's name or to make any reference to Arnold's intentions; but the quick-witted fellow gained the impression that the elegant young stranger had been a welcome and favored suitor in the past better days, and he had a consuming wish to see and study the kind of man that he surmised had been pleasing to Mildred. As he rode along, pity for the girl took the place of resentment. "Not our plain little farmhouse, but the fashionable hotel, is the place where she would feel the most at home," he thought. "And yet she is going to a tenement-house! There, too, she'll stay, I fear, for all that her father will ever do for her. If he's not off his balance, I never saw a man that was."

CHAPTER XIII

A SCENE BENEATH THE HEMLOCKS

ROGER sat out on the dusky piazza of the hotel, looking into the large parlor through open windows which came to the floor, bent on making the most of such glimpses as he could obtain of the world to which he felt that Mildred belonged by right. He saw clearly that she would appear well and at home amid such surroundings. A young and elegantly dressed woman crossed the wide apartment, and he muttered, "Your carriage is very fine and fashionable, no doubt, but Miss Jocelyn would have added grace and nature to your regulation gait." He watched the groups at the card-tables with a curious interest, and the bobbing heads of gossiping dowagers and matrons; he compared the remarkable "make up," as he phrased it, of some of them with the unredeemed plainness of his mother's Sunday gown. "Neither the one nor the other is in good taste," he thought. "Mrs. Jocelyn dresses as I intend my mother shall some day." He coolly criticised a score or more of young men and women who were chatting, promenading, flitting through the open windows out upon the piazza and back again into the light, as a small stringed orchestra struck into a lively galop or the latest waltz. He saw a general mustering of the younger guests, even down to the boys and girls, for the lancers, and followed one and another that caught his eye through the mazy intricacies, making little gestures of disgust at those who seemed *outré* and peculiar in manner and appearance, and regarding with the closest observation such as exhibited a happy mean between a certain rusticity and awkwardness with which he was well acquainted, and a conventional artificiality which was to him all the more unnatural and absurd because his perception was not dulled by familiarity with society's passing whims.

The young stranger whom Mr. Jocelyn had repulsed, and who was the real object of his quest, did not appear among the pleasure-seekers, nor could he discover him on the piazza, in the billiard-room, or in other places of resort. At last in much disappointment he returned to his seat, from which he commanded a view of the parlor; and scarcely had he done so before the one he sought mounted the steps near him as if returning from a stroll in the hotel grounds, threw away his cigar, and entered an open window with the same graceful, listless saunter witnessed in the afternoon. He crossed the wide apartment with as much ease and nonchalance as if it had been empty, and sat down on a sofa by a somewhat stout and very elegantly apparelled gentlewoman.

Roger never thought of accounting for the intensity of his interest in this stranger—the young rarely analyze their feelings—but, obedient to an impulse to learn this man's power to win the favor of one so unapproachable by himself, he scanned with keenest scrutiny everything in his appearance and manner, and sought eagerly to gauge his character.

He felt instinctively that the "cold-blooded snob," as Mr. Jocelyn had characterized him, was of the very opposite type to his own. His graceful saunter, which, nevertheless, possessed a certain quiet dignity, suggested a burdensome leisure and an utter lack of purpose to go anywhere or do anything. He dropped on the sofa rather than sat down. The lady at his side spoke rather decidedly to him, and he answered briefly without even looking at her. By and by she spoke again, more energetically; he then slowly arose, approached a young woman sitting near, who in response to something he said sprang up with alacrity, and they glided away in the waltz with an ease and grace scarcely equalled by the others upon the floor. After a few moments they circled around very near Roger's post of observation, and he was able to scan both the features and expression of the man whom he felt inclined to hate. But he was disarmed and perplexed, for the stranger showed no more pleasure or animation than would a fallen leaf that was swept here and there by varying eddies of wind. He kept time and step with perfect accuracy, but evidently from such complete familiarity with the form that he gave it not a thought. He danced as easily as a bird flies, avoiding the others without appearing to notice them. No color came from the exercise, no light kindled in his face. His expression was not *blasé* or cynical, but weary and dejected; the melancholy in his large brown eyes was all the more striking from contrast with the music, the lighted room, and an amusement suggesting gayety. Pale, utterly unresponsive to the brilliant and mirthful scenes, he glided ghost-like here and there, and before very long seated his companion by the elderly woman whose urgency had led to his automaton-like performance. Then with a slight bow he passed through a window near and disappeared. The two lades spoke together for a few moments and seemed annoyed, and Roger now noted such a resemblance between them as to suggest that they were mother and daughter.

He had seen sufficient to satisfy him, and he went away muttering, "There isn't enough of him to hate; he's but the shadow of a man. She fancy him! I couldn't have believed it; I can't account for it, unless he's very gifted in mind or very different when with her. This must be true, and he would be a mummy indeed if she couldn't wake him up."

Roger rode home, however, ill at ease. "He hasn't forgotten her if he has given her up on account of her poverty," he thought. "He could see as well as I that there was no one there who could compare with her; but he mopes instead of trying to win her. If he can dance, why can't he work? I've no reason to ccmplain, however, and

I thank my stars that I have muscle and a will. In the meantime I shall come up here and study your tricks of manner, my elegant nonentity. I believe in force. Force moves the world and carries a man through it; but I now see that it should be well-managed and well-mannered force. Miss Jocelyn compares me with you, and I seem to her uncouth, unfinished, and crude in the extreme. Litheness and grace need not take an atom from my strength, and the time shall come when I will not fear comparisons. I'll win her yet with your own weapons."

Roger's dreams proved that his sympathies with the melancholy stranger were not very deep, and that his idea of the survival of the fittest was the survival of the strongest. His human nature at that time was of the old Saxon type, that went directly for what it wanted, without much thought or sentiment for those weak enough to lose.

Although it was rather late before he reached home, he found his mother, Mrs. Jocelyn, and Mildred waiting for him in the sitting-room.

"What kept you so?" Mrs. Atwood exclaimed.

"I stopped a while at the hotel on my return," he replied.

"Did my husband send any message?" Mrs. Jocelyn asked, with a solicitude she could not disguise.

"He told me to say that I had left him well, and safely on his way to the city."

"Did—did he seem well when you left him?" the anxious wife persisted.

"Quite as well as he did yesterday, I think," was the reply.

"Mr. Atwood," said Mildred, in a tone that startled him a little, and he saw she was looking at him as if she would read his thoughts, "did my father truly appear well when you parted from him?"

Roger's eyes fell before hers, but he replied firmly, "I left him sitting quietly on the steamboat's deck, and when I asked him if he had any message for his family, he said the words I have just repeated. He seemed naturally depressed at leaving you all. If he were not well he did not say anything about it;'' and with a bow he passed up to his room.

''Mother,'' said Mildred, when they were alone, ''was it mere diffidence, or why was it, that he could not look me in the eyes? I wonder if he is concealing anything. It was in the afternoon and evening that papa was unlike himself yesterday. I wish I really knew whether or not that young man is hiding anything, for I have an impression that he is.''

''Oh, it was diffidence, Millie. He would have no motive in hiding the truth from us. I can see that he is both fascinated by you and afraid of you—poor fellow!''

''A few weeks in the cornfield and a few smiles from the girls hereabouts will banish all his nonsense concerning me. I don't give him a thought except that his absurd feelings annoy me. Oh, mamma, you understand me. What he would like to offer is such a grotesque parody on that which I hoped for, on what I imagined I possessed, that it makes me sick. Oh, oh!'' she sobbed, ''I must give it all up. Mr. Arnold acts as if I were dead; and practically I am to him, although he may sigh and mope a little, perhaps. There, I'm wronging him; I know I wrong him. How can I forget his white, deathlike face and look of mortal pain. Oh that he had this young fellow's muscle and courage! I do not care for his money; I would be content with him in one bare room. But as it is I fear, I fear;'' and the poor child buried her face in her mother's lap, and cried away some of her weight of foreboding.

''Millie, darling,'' faltered her mother, ''God knows I'd shield your heart with my own if I could, but I don't know how to help you. You are too much like me. Your love is your life, and you can't stop loving just because it would be wise and thrifty to do so. I think of you almost as much as I do of Martin, and I daily pray the merciful Saviour, who was 'tempted in all points like as we are,' to sustain and comfort you. I don't see how I can help you in any other way, for my own heart shows me just how you suffer."

"There, little mother," said Mildred, raising her head and wiping her eyes, "I've had my cry, and feel the better for it. I'm going to help you and papa and be brave. I'm glad I'm like you. I'm glad I'm a true Southern girl, and that I can love as you loved; and I would despise myself if I could invest my heart and reinvest it like so much stock. Such a woman is cold-blooded and unnatural, and you are the dearest little mother and wife that ever breathed."

"Oh, Millie, Millie, if I had only foreseen and guarded against this evil day!"

"Come, dear mamma, don't always be blaming yourself for what you did not foresee. You are eager to do your best now, and that is all God or man can ask of us. These clouds will pass away some time, and then the sunshine will be all the brighter."

The next few days of waiting and uncertainty were a severer ordeal to Mrs. Jocelyn and Mildred than ever. Mr. Jocelyn, bent on gaining time, kept putting them off. His new duties upon which he had entered, he wrote, left him only the evening hours for his quest of rooms, and he had not succeeded in finding any that were suitable. Thus they expected something definite by every mail, but each day brought renewed disappointment. At last Mildred wrote that she would come down herself if he did not decide upon something at once.

The morning after this letter was despatched the young girl took her work out under some wide-boughed hemlocks that stood beside the quiet country road, along which a farmer occasionally jogged to the village beyond, but which at that hour was usually quite deserted. Fred and Minnie were with her, and amused themselves by building little log huts with the dry sticks thickly scattered around.

To Roger, who was cradling oats in an adjacent field, they made a picture which would always repeat itself whenever he passed that clump of hemlocks; and, as he cut his way down the long slope toward them, under the midsummer sun, he paused a second after each stroke to look with wistful gaze at one now rarely absent from his mental vision. She was too sad and preoccupied to give him a thought, or even to note who the reaper was. From her shady retreat she could see him and other men at work here and there, and she only envied their definite and fairly rewarded toil, and their simple yet assured home-life, while she was working so blindly, and facing, in the meantime, a world of uncertainty. Roger had been very unobtrusive since her father's departure, and she half consciously gave him credit for this when she thought about him at all, which was but seldom. He had imagined that she had grown less distant and reserved, and once or twice, when he had shown some little kindness to the children, she had smiled upon him. He was a hunter of no mean repute in that region, and was famous for his skill in following shy and scarce game. He had resolved to bring the principles of his woodcraft to bear upon Mildred, and to make his future approaches so cautiously as not to alarm her in the least; therefore he won the children's favor more thoroughly than ever, but not in an officious way. He found Belle moping the evening after her father's departure, and he gave her a swift drive in his buggy, which little attention completely disarmed the warm-hearted girl and became the basis of a fast-ripening friendship.

"You need not put on such distant airs," she had said to Mildred; "he never mentions your name any more." But when he asked Mrs. Jocelyn to take a drive with him she had declined very kindly, for she feared that he might speak to her of her daughter in an embarrassing way. Over Belle, Mildred had little control in such matters, but as far as she and her mother were concerned she determined that he should have no encouragement whatever; for, although he made no further efforts either to shun or obtain her society, and had become quite as reserved as herself, he unconsciously, yet very clearly, revealed his state of mind to her womanly intuition.

"There is one thing queer about Roger Atwood," said Belle, joining her sister under the hemlocks; "he now scarcely ever speaks of himself. I suppose he thinks I'd be silly enough to go and tell everything as you did."

"What do you talk about then?" asked Mildred, with a half smile.

"Oh, you are a little curious, are you? perhaps a little jealous, too, that he was so very easily cured of his admiration for you. If it were any secret, I wouldn't tell you. We talk about what we see, and it seems to me he sees everything. If a bird flies across the road he will point out its peculiarities, and he knows so much about the trees and bushes and wild flowers and the little creatures in the woods, how they live, and all that. He says a man's a fool that doesn't see all that's going on around him. Sometimes he makes me ache from laughing over his funny descriptions of the queer characters that live about here. But what interests me most is his accounts of the people at the hotel. Oh, I do wish mother would let me go there with him some evening! He is there nearly every night, and it's as good as a play to hear him take off the affected, snobbish ones. He has caught the English drawl and the 'yeh know' of some young fellows to perfection."

"He *is* a queer fellow," mused Mildred. "I wonder what he goes there for?"

"Oh, Roger Atwood is no fool, I can tell you. He knows country society in perfection, and he would not be long in understanding Fifth Avenue noodledom just as well. He detects sham people and sham ways as quickly as you could, and delights in ridiculing them. He says there's a ghost of a man up there which interests him exceedingly, but that it is such an extremely well-behaved, good-mannered ghost that it is tolerated without remark, and that is all he will say about it, although I have often questioned him. I can't think who or what he means."

Mildred looked up with a sudden access of interest, and then became silent and abstracted.

"Since the children are quiet here," continued Belle, "I'll go back to the house and finish a story in which the hero and heroine are sentimental geese and blind as bats. They misunderstand each other so foolishly that I'd like to bob their empty heads together," and away she went, humming a gay song, with as little thought for the morrow as the birds in the fields around her.

While Roger paused a moment to wipe the perspiration from his brow, the rustling of the grain ceased, and he heard the footfalls of a horse in the adjacent road. With a start he saw riding by the stranger who had been the object of his continued scrutiny at the hotel. The young men restrained to a walk the rather restless horse he bestrode, and seemed musing deeply under the shadow of a broad-brimmed Panama hat. He took no notice of Roger, and passing slowly on entered the shadow of the hemlocks, when an exclamation caused him to raise his head. A second later he sprang from his horse, threw the bridle over the limb of a tree, and seized Mildred's hand with an eagerness which proved that she had indeed the power to "wake him up."

Roger was too distant to see just how she greeted her unlooked-for friend of other days, but thought she appeared so startled that she leaned against a tree for support. He saw, however, that the "ghost of a man" was now flesh and blood in his earnestness, and that he retained her hand in both of his own while speaking rapidly. Before very long, however, the horse became so impatient that he suddenly jerked his bridle loose, wheeled, and came galloping up the road toward Roger, who, after a moment's hesitation, cleared the low stone wall at a bound and stood in the road awaiting him. Mildred's companion made a gesture of annoyance, and then said, with a shrug, "Let the beast go. I'm well content to remain here." When they saw Roger's purpose, however, they stood watching for the outcome of his effort.

As Arnold—for he it was—saw the horse, with broken and flying reins, thundering apparently right upon the motionless form of a man, he exclaimed, "By Jove! but that's a brave fellow."

The vicious brute soon seemed so nearly upon the rash youth that Mildred gave a slight scream of terror, but a second later she saw him spring lightly aside, catch one of the flying reins, hold on for a few yards, half dragged, half running, and then the animal yielded to a master. A cloud of dust obscured them momentarily; then the country-bred athlete vaulted lightly into the saddle and came trotting sharply toward them, riding like a centaur. She was enraged at herself that her face should grow scarlet under his brief glance from one to the other, but without a word he sprang lightly down and began to fasten the horse securely to a tree—an act scarcely necessary, for the animal appeared completely subdued.

"By Jove! my man, that was neatly done," said Arnold. "Here's a bank-note for your trouble."

"The fact that I've caught your horse does not prove me a hostler," Roger replied brusquely, without looking at the speaker.

Arnold now recognized the young man whom he had seen with Mr. Jocelyn, and also at the hotel several times subsequently. He had learned his name, and therefore began, "Oh, I beg pardon; this is Mr. Atwood;" but before he could say more a covered barouche came rapidly down the hill from the opposite direction, turned with the angle of the road, and passed into the shade of the hemlocks. Arnold had become very pale the moment he saw it, and in its occupant Roger recognized the woman whom he had seen at the hotel, and whom he had learned to be the mother of the listless dancer. A brief glance showed him that Mildred knew her also. The lady sharply ordered her coachman to stop, and after a brief but freezing look into Mildred's hot face she said, in a meaning tone, "Vinton, I will esteem it a favor if you will accompany me on my drive."

"I will join you presently," he said irresolutely.

"I will wait politely then until you have concluded your interview," the gentlewoman remarked coldly, leaning back in her carriage.

Her look, tone, and action stung Mildred to the very quick. Gentle and retiring usually, she was capable of a very decided and even an aggressive course under great provocation. For a moment her warm Southern blood boiled at Mrs. Arnold's implication that she was so eager to capture her wealthy son that it was not prudent to leave them alone together a moment. With decision and the dignity of conscious innocence she said, "Good-morning, Mr. Arnold"; then taking little Minnie's hand and calling Fred she led the way toward the house. It happened that the only path of egress led her by the carriage, and the manner in which its occupant ignored her presence was so intolerable in its injustice that she paused, and, fixing her clear, indignant eyes on the flushed, proud face before her, asked, in tones never forgotten by those who heard them, "Mrs. Arnold, wherein have I wronged you or yours?"

The lady was silent and a little embarrassed.

"I know, and you might know," Mildred continued, "if you chose, that you cannot charge me with one unwomanly act, but your look and manner toward me are both unwomanly and unchristian. You insult me in my poverty and misfortune. Without the shadow of right or reason, you cruelly wound one who was wounded already;" and she was about to pass on.

"Mother, as you are a woman, do not let her go without a word of respect and kindness," cried her son, in a hoarse, stifled voice.

"Miss Jocelyn," began Mrs. Arnold in a constrained tone, "I mean you no disrespect. Nevertheless—"

"Nevertheless!" exclaimed Arnold, wrought to frenzy. "Great God! are you going to qualify that grudging sentence?" He struck his hand to his forehead, reeled, and fell prone upon the earth. In a moment Mildred knelt beside him, and Roger saw that she loved him with her whole strong, womanly soul.

"Bring water, bring brandy; mother will give it to you," she said to him in a low voice, and he dashed off to obey.

Mrs. Arnold hastily descended from the carriage and felt her son's pulse with much solicitude. "He has only fainted," she said. "He is apt to have such attacks when overwrought. It's a part of his disease. Miss Jocelyn, you see he is a reed that must be supported, not leaned upon," she added, looking straight into the young girl's troubled eyes. "I mean you kindness as truly as I mean kindness to him. He will soon be better. He has often been in this condition ever since he was a child. With this knowledge you will understand me better. Thomas"—to the coachman—"lift him into the carriage. He will soon revive," she continued to Mildred, "and at the hotel he shall have the best of care. Believe me, I feel for you both, but I know what is right and best."

The coachman did as he was directed, and they drove rapidly away.

Midlred put her hand to her side, and then, with pale and downcast face, led the wondering children toward the house. She soon met Roger returning, and running like a deer.

"They have taken him away," she said briefly, without looking up. "Please care for his horse and accept my thanks," and then she hastened to her room and did not appear again that day.

He complied with her request, then went back to his work, and the grain fell as if the reaper were Death himself.

Mrs. Arnold's course was not so harsh and rude as it seemed, and can readily be explained on the theory by which she governed her feelings and actions toward her son. An obscure weakness in the functions of his heart had rendered him subject to fainting turns from early childhood. Physicians had always cautioned against over-exertion and over-excitement of any kind; therefore he had not been sent to school like the other children, or permitted to indulge in the sports natural to his age. Having been constantly cautioned, curbed, and repressed, he grew into a timid, self-distrustful, irresolute man, and yet was keenly sensible of the defects that separated him from other men. No one ever longed for independence more earnestly than he; few were less able to achieve it. His mother, having shielded him so many years from himself as well as from adverse influences from without, had formed the habit of surveillance. Exaggerating his weakness and dependence, his unfitness to compete with other men in active pursuits, she had almost ignored his manhood. The rest of the family naturally took their tone from her, regarding him as an invalid, and treating him as one. Chafing with secret and increasing bitterness over his misfortune and anomalous position, he grew more and more silent and reserved, dwelling apart in a world created from a literature that was not of the best or most wholesome character. As long as he lived a quiet, monotonous life that accorded with the caution enjoined by physicians, he gave his mother little solicitude, for the woman of the world, versed in all the proprieties of her station, had no comprehension of the sensitive spirit that had been repressed equally with his physical nature. That he should become cold toward her, and cynical toward her world of wealth and fashion, was to her but a proof that his character was defective also, and led to the fear that his "absurd notions" might occasion trouble. His intimacy with the Jocelyns threatened to justify her forebodings, and, while knowing nothing of Mildred personally, she was naturally inclined to the belief that she, like many others, would be glad to escape poverty by allying herself to an old and wealthy family, and she regarded her son as weak enough to become a ready victim. Nevertheless he was of age, and if he should enter into a formal engagement it might be no easy matter to break it or escape the consequences. Therefore she determined at all hazards to prevent such a consummation, and thus far had succeeded. She was greatly angered that, in spite of her precautions and injunctions, he had again met Mildred, and she resolved to end the interview at once, even at the cost of being thought rude and harsh, for if left to themselves that summer day they might realize all her fears. At the same time she proposed to manifest her disapproval so decidedly that if the young woman still sought to enter her family, it would be by a sort of violence; and she also was not unmindful of the fact that, with the exception of an apparent laborer and her coachman, only the parties interested were the witnesses of her tactics. Therefore she had looked at Mildred as coldly and haughtily as only a proud woman can, with the result already narrated. Although compelled to admit that the girl was not what she had imagined her to be, she was none the less bent on preventing further complications, and resolved to take her son elsewhere as soon as he had sufficiently recovered.

The next morning Mildred left her seclusion, and her aspect was pale and resolute, but no reference was made to the events uppermost in the minds of those aware of them. Even the children and Belle had been so cautioned that they were reticent. In the evening, however, as Roger was raking the flower-beds over to prevent the weeds from starting, Mildred came out, and joining him said, a little bitterly, "Well, what did your microscopic vision reveal to you yesterday morning?"

"A brave, proud girl, for whom I have the deepest respect," he replied, looking directly into her eyes.

"Was that all?"

"No, indeed."

"Well, what else?" she persisted, in a tone quite unlike her usual accent.

"I saw the merest shadow of a man and the ghost of a woman who must weigh nearly two hundred."

She flushed hotly as she said, "You pride yourself on your keen perceptions, but the truth is you are blind," and she was turning angrily away when he answered, "Time will show how blind I am," and then he went on quietly with his work.

"Oh, how I detest that man!" she muttered, as she went up to her favorite haunt on the hilltop looking toward the south. "Why did he, of all others, have to be present with his prying eyes at the odious scene? He must know now how I feel toward Vinton Arnold, and yet he has so little sense and delicacy that he expresses contempt for him to my face. Brute strength may be his ideal of manhood, but it's not mine; and he knows so little of women that he thinks I ought to despise one who is simply unfortunate, and through no fault of his own. Poor, poor Vinton! Brief as were the moments before we were interrupted, he had time to assure me that life had become a burden because of our separation, and yet he said that he had no right to see me, no right to send me a line, no right to add his weakness to my other misfortunes. Time shall at least show one thing—that I can be patient and true. That proud, cold woman has no control over me, and as long as he is faithful I shall be."

CHAPTER XIV

THE OLD MANSION

MILDRED'S letter to her father brought a request that she should join him at once and choose between two sets of rooms, of which he had the refusal. She insisted upon going, for she was eager to leave a place that had become hateful to her. She greatly wished to hear of Arnold's welfare before her departure, but would not make any effort to do so.

To her surprise, however, Roger handed her a note the following morning. She knew the handwriting well, and asked, "How do you happen to have this, Mr. Atwood?"

"I supposed you would wish to hear from your friend, and so went up to the hotel. As soon as Mr. Arnold saw me he asked me to give you that letter."

Mildred bit her lip. Was it an officious or a friendly act? She was beginning to doubt whether she had fully gauged the character of this young farmer, but of one thing she was instinctively certain—his motive was personal, and sprung from an interest in her which was now more repugnant than ever. Whether this instance was an obtrusive meddling in her affairs, or an act well meant, but unwarranted by their relations, she could not tell. However it might be, she wished the letter had come by any other hands than his.

She gravely thanked him, and added, "Mr. Atwood, please do not feel called upon to do anything further for me unless requested."

He grew pale and his lips tightened, for her words and manner hurt him. His act had been in truth very generous and self-effacing, but he merely bowed in seeming acquiescence, and turned away.

Arnold's letter ran as follows:

"The memory of that scene yesterday will oppress me forever. Nothing could have happened that would more clearly convince you that I am unworthy of your thought. And yet it will be a life-long agony to know that I am unworthy. When I tell you that I love and honor you above all other women it is but a poor compensation, I fear, for all that I have made you suffer. My mother has *kindly* (?) informed me that she told you how feeble I am, and I proved her words true. I feel that the best service I can render you is to say, Forget me wholly; and yet you can never know what such words cost me. *I* shall never forget, unless death is forgetting. If I had the strength to be of any help to you at all, I would break away at once and take the consequences; but I have been an invalid all my life, and why I still continue to live I scarcely know. If, however, there should ever be a time when one so weak as I am can aid you, give me this one shadowy hope that you will come to me. VINTON ARNOLD."

This was Mildred's reply:

"It is not in my nature to forget, therefore I cannot. It is not my wish to forget, therefore I will not. You will find me ever the same. MILDRED JOCELYN."

Roger would have taken her reply to the hotel that very night, so great was her power over him, but for his sake, as well as her own, she wished to teach him once for all that their ways were apart. She dreaded from what he had said that he would follow her to the city and renew the unwelcome association of his life with hers. Therefore she engaged heavy, blundering Jotham to deliver the note, giving him a dollar from her slender purse as a reward. He lost the note where it was never found, and stolidly concealed the fact lest he should lose the dollar. The little characteristic missive fell to the earth somewhere like a seed that drops into an unkindly soil and perishes. Roger only knew that stupid Jotham had been preferred as her messenger. She made no secret of the fact, but gave the note to the laborer when he came in to his nooning the following day. She knew Roger was watching her from the front porch, and as she turned toward him she saw she had wounded him so deeply that she had some compunctions; but he avoided meeting her, nor did she find a chance to speak to him again. When, an hour later, she was ready to depart with Mr. Atwood for the distant landing, Roger was not to be found. Her conscience smote her a little, but she felt that it would be the best for him in the future, and would probably end his nonsense about leaving home and winning fame out in the world. She had a warm, genuine good-will for Mrs. Atwood and Susan, and even for poor, grumbling Mr. Atwood, at whose meagre, shrivelled life she often wondered; and it would be a source of much pain to her if she became even the blameless cause of Roger's leaving home in the absurd hope of eventually becoming great and rich, and then appearing to her in her poverty, like a prince in fairy lore. "Nothing but the most vigorous snubbing will bring him to his senses," she thought, and she now believed that he would soon subside into his old life, and be none the worse for the summer's episode. Therefore, after embracing her mother again and again in her room, she bade Mrs. Atwood and Susan good-by very kindly, and they saw her depart with genuine regret. For Roger there was nothing more than the quiet remark to Mrs. Atwood, "Please say good-by for me to your son."

Belle and the children accompanied her to the landing, and were in great glee over the long drive. Mildred's spirits rose also. She had learned most emphatically that she was not dead to her lover, and she thought her words, brief as they were, would cheer and sustain him and suggest hope for the future. Although she was a little sorry for Roger, she was glad to think that his dark, searching eyes would no longer follow her, nor she be compelled from day to day to recognize a curbed but ever-present and unwelcome regard. His feeling toward her seemed like something pent up, yet growing, and she was always fearing it might burst forth. In his mastery of the horse he had shown himself so strong and fearless that, not sure of his self-restraint, she dreaded lest in some unguarded moment he might vehemently plead for her love. The very thought of this made her shudder and shrink, and the belief that she would probably never see him again gave decided relief.

Chief of all, she was glad that her weary waiting and uncertainty were over. She was now on her way to seek independence and a home. However humble the latter, it would be a place from which could be excluded all strange and prying looks. When together and alone again, their sorrows and weaknesses could be hidden or seen only with the eyes of love.

The ten days or more that had elapsed since Mr. Jocelyn's departure had made him doubtful whether he could hide his weakness or overcome it very readily. He believed he was gaining ground since he was able to reduce the amount of morphia taken, but in order to keep up he had to employ the stimulant more frequently. By this method he hoped never so to lose self-control as to excite suspicion, and also gradually to wean himself from the drug altogether. Of the two he would rather meet Mildred than his wife; the latter must be kept in ignorance, since to destroy her absolute trust was to be destroyed. Mildred would more quickly suspect his fault than would her mother, and if he could hide his failing from her he surely could from his wife, until complete mastery left nothing to be concealed. That day of liberty always seemed but a little in advance. He surely had the will and the strength to give up a mere drug. He who had led charges amid the smoke and thunder of a hundred cannon, and had warded off sabre-thrusts from muscular, resolute hands, was not going to be pricked to death by a little syringe in his own hand. His very thraldom to the habit seemed an improbable, grotesque dream, which some morning would dissipate, but as a matter of experience each morning brought such a profound sinking and "goneness" that his will-power shrivelled like a paper barricade before the scorching intensity of his desire. After the stimulant began its work, however, all things seemed possible, and nothing more so than his power to abandon the drug when he should fully decide upon the act.

On the morning of Mildred's arrival, having lifted himself out of his chronic dejection by the lever of opium, he went to meet her with the genuine gladness of a proud, loving father asserting itself like a ray of June light struggling through noxious vapors. She was delighted to find him apparently so well. His walk and the heat had brought color to his face, the drug had bestowed animation and confidence, while his heart gave an honest, loving welcome without the aid of any stimulant. They rode uptown together as happily and hopefully as if the nearly empty car were their own carriage, and they were seeking a home in Fifth Avenue instead of a tenement-house; but the hope and happiness of one was based on youth, love, faith, courage, and inexperience, and of the other on a lurid cloud that would darken steadily except as renewed gleams were shot through it by a light that was infernal. Any kindly man or woman would have smiled appreciatively to see the handsome father and beautiful daughter apparently as absorbed in each other's plans and interests as a young couple seeking the home in which their future life would centre. Who would dream that on this sunny morning, and in a prosaic street-car, the actors of a sad, sad tragedy were on their way to its unsuspected scenes? Who would dream that Mildred and her father, of all others, were the actors?

"Millie," said Mr. Jocelyn, "I fear the place to which I shall at first take you may shock you a little. It's an old Revolutionary mansion, gray and rather dilapidated, but it reminded me of some of our residences in the South; and, although perhaps no better—perhaps not so good—it is still quite unlike the stereotyped tenement-house abomination prevailing in this city. This ancient abode of colonial wealth took my fancy. It suggested our own changed fortunes by its fall to its present uses. And yet the carving around and above the doors and windows, much of which still remains, and the lofty ceilings all remind one of past better days that can never return to the poor house, but which we must bring back as soon as possible. I shall never be content or happy, Millie, until I have placed my dear ones in the sphere to which they really belong; but for the present I do not see how we can pay rent for anything much better than rooms in the old mansion. As far as I can learn, the people who live in it are poor, but quiet and respectable.''

Her father's opium-tinged description caught Mildred's fancy also, but when she saw the building her heart sank at the prospect. To her a tenement-house was as yet a vague, untested reality, and the one before her was indeed old and dilapidated, gray and haggard with more than a century's age.

The mansion having been built to face the river, its front was not upon the street, but toward the west. Around its base the mortar was crumbling away, revealing its mingled brick and stone foundation. The hip-roof of weather-beaten shingles still remained, and was surmounted by a wide-railed and wooden platform used by the occupants of the dwelling for the drying of clothes, etc.

''It makes me think of an old, dying, moss-draped white oak standing in the midst of trees of younger and different growth,'' said Mr. Jocelyn, as he and Mildred scanned the gable-end of the house.

Then they entered by two or three stone steps a narrow passage, ascended a forlorn wooden stairway, covered overhead by a few boards nailed lengthwise, and so reached a small landing, where once had been a stately porch or wide veranda, looking no doubt over a broad sweep of lawn and the shining river. The high-arched doorway was still intact, with elaborately carved but now defaced woodwork, which, rising from the sill on either side, was continued in various old-fashioned designs until it culminated over a large square window in the second story. Generations had watched the sunsets from that window, but now high brick walls threw it in shadow much of the day.

A quaint brass knocker which gentlemen—long since dust—had approached wearing laced three-cornered hats, velvet short-clothes, and silver buckles, and upon which they had rapped announcement of their social claims, still hung on the rest from which they had lifted it. It was not often used at present, for people entered without knocking, and the wide hall within was in a sense but a continuation of the street; also the winding stairway, with its ancient rail, which started out on one side and wound up to another square hallway. To each of these open spaces the several families had equal rights.

The lower hall had originally extended through the whole depth of the building to a rear doorway, equally old-fashioned but less elaborately ornamented, but now a partition crossed the raised circle on the ceiling from which had once hung an ancient candelabrum. Upon each hallway opened four suites of two rooms each, and thus the old mansion usually sheltered twelve families instead of one. The doors were high, and surmounted by quaint and worm-eaten carved work.

These halls seemed very dark and close to Mildred, who had just come out of the sunlight and from the country, but they were cool and spacious. They were shown by the janitor to a room over twenty feet square on the second story, whose former occupants had left the *souvenir* of unlimited dirt. "They was dissipated, and we don't let sich stay in the buildin'," said the man. "That's one thing in favor of the place, papa," poor Mildred remarked, and at the moment it seemed to her about the only thing, for the old house was evidently going down hill so fast that it seemed to her as if it might carry its occupants with it. Still, on further inspection, the room was found to be so large and airy and the ceiling so high that it might be made the abode of health and comfort. Opening into the large apartment was another about eight feet by twelve, and this was all.

Mildred drew a long breath. Could the whole domestic life of the family be carried on in those two rooms? "I never realized how thousands of people live," she sighed.

"It will only be for a little while, Millie," whispered her father.

The young girl shrank and shivered even in the summer morning at the ordeal of crowded life, with only intervening doorways and thin partitions between them and all sorts of unknown neighbors.

"Suppose, papa, we look at the other rooms of which you have the refusal," she faltered.

Even in his false buoyancy he could not suppress a sigh as he saw that Mildred, in spite of her determination to make the best of everything, had not imagined what a tenement-house was. "We will be back in an hour or more," he whispered to the janitor, for he believed the other rooms would appear still more repulsive.

And so they did, for when Mildred had climbed up three stairways in a five-story, narrow house, which even at that hour was filled with a babel of sounds, the old mansion seemed a refuge, and when she had glanced around the narrow room and two dark closets of bedrooms, she shuddered and said, "Papa, can we really afford nothing better?"

"Honestly, Millie, we cannot for the present. My income is exceedingly small, although it will soon be increased, no doubt. But if we pay too much for rooms we shall have nothing to live upon while waiting for better times. These rooms are fourteen dollars a month. Those in the old mansion are only eight, and the two rooms there give more chance for comfort than do these three."

"Oh, yes, yes," cried Mildred, "I could not live here at all. Let us go back."

While returning, her father showed her apartments in

other tenements for which rents of ten to sixteen dollars were charged, and she saw that she would not obtain any more in space and light than for half the money in the old house, which had been built when that part of the island was open country.

"Forgive me, papa," she said, smiling, "that I shivered a little at the first plunge. We will go to the old house and stay there until we can do better. It was once evidently a beautiful home, and I believe that within it we can make a happy home, if we will. These other tenements were never homes, and I don't see how they ever could be. They are angular, patent, human packing-boxes, which mock at the very idea of home coziness and privacy. They were never built for homes, they were built to rent. In the old house I noticed that a blank wall near will prevent people staring into our windows, and the space has not been so cut up but that we can keep ourselves somewhat secluded."

Next to a quiet way of earning money, Mildred coveted seclusion beyond everything else. There was one deep hope that fed her life. Her father would work his way up into affluence, and she again could welcome Vinton Arnold to her own parlor. Happiness would bring him better health, and the time would come when he could choose and act as his heart dictated. With woman's pathetic fortitude and patience she would hope and wait for that day. But not for the world must his proud mother know to what straits they were driven, and she meant that the old house should become a hiding-place as well as a home.

Therefore the rooms in the old mansion were taken. A stout, cheery Englishwoman, who with her plump, red arms was fighting life's battle for herself and a brood of little ones, was engaged to clean up and prepare for the furniture. Mildred was eager to get settled, and her father, having ordered such household goods as they required to be sent from their place of storage the following day, repaired to his place of business.

"Now, miss," said sensible Mrs. Wheaton, "I don't vant to do hany more than yer vants done, but hif I was you I'd give hall these 'ere valls a coat hof lime. Vitevash is 'olesome, yer know, and sweetens heverything; hit'll kind o' take haway the nasty taste those drunken people left."

"Please whitewash, then, and use plenty of lime. If you can sweeten these rooms, do so by all means, but I fear that result is beyond your brush or any other."

"You've seen better days, miss, and I 'ave meself; but yer mustn't be down'arted, yer know. See 'ow the sunshine comes in, and ven hit falls hon a carpet, a little furniture, and yer hown people, these 'ere rooms vill soon grow 'omelike, and yer'll come back to 'em hafter yer day's vork's hover gladly henough. I s'pose yer'll vork, since you've come hamong people who must vork hearly and late."

"Yes, indeed, we'll work—that is all we ask for."

"And hit's time I vas habout mine hinstead hof gossiping 'ere. Yer'll soon see 'ow spick and span I'll make heverything."

With a despatch, deftness, and strength that to Mildred seemed wonderful, she bought the lime, made the wash, and soon dark stains and smoky patches of wall and ceiling grew white under her strong, sweeping strokes. It was not in the girl's nature, nor in accordance with her present scheme of life, to be an idle spectator, and from her travelling-bag she soon transformed herself into as charming a house-cleaner as ever waged war against that chief enemy of life and health—dirt. Her round, white arms, bared almost to the shoulder, seemed designed as a sculptor's model rather than to wield the brush with which she scoured the paint and woodwork; but she thought not of sculpture except in the remote and figurative way of querying, with mind far absent from her work, how best she could carve their humble fortunes out of the unpromising material of the present and the near future.

CHAPTER XV

"WELCOME HOME"

MILDRED felt that she had become a working-woman in very truth as she cleaned the dingy closets, vindictively prying into corners and crevices that had been unmolested by generations of tenants, and the rich color produced by summer heat and unwonted exertion deepened at the thought, "What would Vinton Arnold, what would his mother think if they saw me now? The latter would undoubtedly remark," she murmured, in bitterness of spirit, "that I had at last found my true sphere, and was engaged in befitting tasks; but should I lose in his eyes?"

Indeed she would not, either in his eyes or in those of any other man capable of appreciating womanly grace. Genuine beauty is a rare and wonderful gift, and, like genius, triumphs over adverse circumstances, and is often enhanced by them. Even prosaic Mrs. Wheaton was compelled to pause from time to time to admire the slender, supple form whose perfect outlines were revealed by the stooping, twisting, and reaching required by the nature of the labor. But the varying expressions of her face, revealing a mind as active as the busy hands, were a richer study. The impact of her brush was vigorous, and with looks of aversion and disgust she would cleanse away the grimy stains as if they were an essential part of the moral as well as gross material life of the former occupants. To a refined nature association forms no slight element in the constitution of a home; and horrible conjectures concerning repulsive indicaticns of the vulgar people who once kennelled where others would live decently and purely are among the manifold miseries of tenement life. In spite of all her will-power, Mildred shuddered, and shrank from even this remote contact with a phase of humanity peculiarly revolting to her, and the protest of her innate delicacy would often appear strongly upon her face.

"The worst of it is," she muttered, "that soap and water cannot blot out thoughts of the people who were here before us."

But thoughts of other people, some of whom were very dear to her, brought varying expressions, and once she smiled and said to herself, "Roger Atwood now thinks, no doubt, that in me he has seen another 'ghost of a woman,' weighing a little less than 'two hundred.' Of all my little affairs of that nature, his was the most preposterous and absurd. That one human being should expect and seek from another what is so impossible to give produces a certain half-humorous irritation that is indescribable."

Stout Mrs. Wheaton's mind and fancy were not so busy as her hands, and when twelve o'clock came she knew the hour, although carrying no watch. She had interrupted Mildred's musings from time to time, but had received rather absent replies, for the actual inception of a life of toil occasioned many thoughts.

When, however, the practical woman remarked, "I've a hinside 'int that hit's time we took a bite together," Mildred awakened to an honest and hungry approval of the suggestion.

"I don't like to intrude upon you, Mrs. Wheaton," she said. "Isn't there some place near where I can go?"

"Hindeed there his—right down to my room, hif ye're not habove my company. I can brew yer has good a cup o' tea has hany cook in the land, and ve'll find somethin' nourishin' to go vith hit."

"Mrs. Wheaton, you are a genuine friend. I'm so glad you were here and willing to help me, for you make me feel safer and more hopeful. You seem brave and not afraid of being poor, and I want to learn your courage. So far from being above your company, I am very grateful for it, and I shall try to repay your kindness with like neighborly return when I can; but when it comes to actual expense you must let me pay my way. How is it you are so brave and cheery when, as you say, you are alone with several children to support?"

"I'll tell yer vhile ve heat hour dinner; so lock the door and come vith me."

Mrs. Wheaton's room was plain, indeed, but neat and homelike. A variegated and much-patched carpet covered part of the floor, which was bare around the ample cooking-stove, whereon a wholesome dinner soon smoked with appetizing odors. Her daughter, a young girl about twelve years of age, assisted in the preparations, and then went to call the other children, who were playing on the sidewalk.

"'Ow is it I'm so brave and cheery?" Mrs. Wheaton at last answered with a sunshiny smile. "I've a stout pair hof harms, I've a stout body, and I've a downright belief that the Lord means vell by me and mine. I'm tryin' to do my best, and hit's 'is biziness to take care hof the rest. Hand 'E 'as so far. I've been a bit 'ungry meself now and then, but the children halways 'ad enough. So I vork and trust and lose no time and strength ha-vorrying. Things'll all come hout right some day; and I've no time to be doin' the Lord's vork hin carryin' the burden hon my shoulders, hif they are broad. 'Ere's the children; now sit right down with hus, and velcome. Since ve're neighbors ve'll be neighborly and friendly like; and before yer know hit, yer'll be snug and comfortable hin your hown rooms, and yer can be jist as 'appy hin 'em has hever yer vas hin yer life. Bein' poor and 'aving to vork hain't the vorst troubles in the vorld."

The good woman's stout, cheery spirit and homely faith were just the tonics that Mildred needed, and they were all the more effective because combined with the exhilarating tea and wholesome food. Therefore instead of a weary and depressing day, in which body and spirit acted and reacted on each other until the evening brought shadows deeper than the night, her courage and cheerfulness grew with the hours of sustained and healthful toil, and when her father appeared at six o'clock her smile warmed his heart. At the cost of no slight effort he had so reduced his doses of morphia that neither she nor any one could have detected anything unnatural in his manner. He praised their work unstintedly, and thanked Mrs. Wheaton for her kindness with such warm Southern frankness that her eyes grew moist with gratification. Indeed the rooms had grown so clean and wholesome that Mr. Jocelyn said that they looked homelike already. Mrs. Wheaton assured Mildred that if she would be content, she could be made quite comfortable on a lounge in her large living-room, and the young girl won her heart completely by saying that she would rather stay with her than go to the Fifth Avenue Hotel. Her words were sincere, for in accordance with her nature her heart was already drawn toward the place which gave even promise of a home, and the hearty kindness received there made her shrink from the strange, indifferent world without.

Her father asked her to resume her travelling dress, and then by a street-car they soon reached a quiet restaurant near Central Park, from which the outlook was upon trees and shrubbery. The people of New York are singularly fortunate in their ability to reach, at slight expense of money and time, many places where the air is pure, and the sense of beauty can find abundant gratification. Mildred felt that only extreme poverty could rob them in summer of many simple yet genuine pleasures. When, after their frugal supper, she and her father strolled through a path winding around a miniature lake on which swans were floating, she believed that one of her chief fears might be unfounded. Her love of beauty need not be stifled, since there was so much, even in the crowded town, which could be seen without cost.

"Papa," she said, "our lives will not be meagre and colorless unless we make them so. Every tree and shrub—indeed every leaf upon them and every ripple on the water—seems beautiful to me this evening. I do not fear working hard if we can often have these inexpensive pleasures. The thing in poverty that has most troubled me was the fear that one's nature might become blunted, callous, and unresponsive. A starved soul and heart seem to me infinitely worse than a starved body. Thank God, this beautiful place is as free to us now as ever, and I think we enjoy it more than many of those people in yonder carriages. Then at the cost of a few pennies we can get many a breezy outlook, and fill our lungs with fresh air on the ferryboats. So don't let us be downhearted, papa, and mope while we are waiting for better days. Each day may bring us something that we can enjoy with honest zest."

"God bless you, Millie," replied her father. "We'll try to do just as you suggest." Nevertheless he sighed deeply. She was free; he was a slave. In the depths of the placid lake the graceful swans, the pretty wooded shores, were faithfully reflected. In Mildred's clear blue eyes the truth of her words, the goodness and sincerity of her heart, were revealed with equal certainty. His eyes were downcast and fixed on an abyss which no soul has ever fathomed.

"Great God!" he murmured, "I must escape; I shall—I *will* escape;" but while Mildred stepped into a florist's shop to purchase a blooming plant for Mrs. Wheaton, he furtively took from his pocket a small paper of white-looking powder—just the amount which experience had taught him he could take and not betray himself. As a result she was delighted to find him genial and wakeful until they parted rather late in the old mansion wherein, she jestingly said, she proposed to build their nest, like a barn-swallow, the following day.

After a brief consultation with Mrs. Wheaton the next morning Mildred told her father to send for the rest of the family at once, and that she would be ready for them.

The household goods arrived promptly from their place of storage, and she was positively happy while transforming the bare rooms into a home that every hour grew more inviting. They had retained, when giving up their house in the spring, more furniture than was sufficient for the limited space they would now occupy, and Mildred had enough material and taste to banish the impression of poverty almost wholly from their two rooms. She had the good sense, also, to make the question of appearances always secondary to that of comfort, and rigorously excluded what was bulky and unnecessary. "I don't like crowded rooms," she said, "and mamma must have just as little to care for and tax her strength as possible." One side of the large room was partitioned off as a sleeping apartment for her father, mother, and the two children, and was made private by curtains of dark, inexpensive material. The remainder and larger part facing the east was to be kitchen, dining and living room. Mrs. Wheaton did the heavy work, and looked on in delighted wonder as the young girl, with a gift peculiarly her own, gave an air of grace and homelike coziness to every part. Hers was a true woman's touch in woman's undisputed realm, and her father, with strange alternations of sighs and smiles, assisted her after his return from business. Gas had never been introduced in the old house, and so two pretty shaded lamps were bought. One stood on the lofty, old-fashioned mantel, which was so high that Mildred could pass under it without stooping, and the other on the table that was to serve for many uses.

"If we should put a crane in the fireplace," Mr. Jocelyn dreamily mused, "I could imagine that we were at my old home in the South;" but she had said they could not afford that amount of sentiment, and therefore a stove was obtained of the same model that shrewd Mrs. Wheaton had found so well adapted to varied uses.

After two busy days their task was wellnigh completed, and Mildred slept in her own little room, which she was to share with Belle, and her weariness, and the sense that the resting-place was hers by honest right, brought dreamless and refreshing sleep. For the sake of "auld lang syne," her father kindled a fire on the hearth, and sat brooding over it, looking regretfully back into the past, and with distrustful eyes toward the future. The dark commercial outlook filled that future with many uncertain elements; and yet, alas! he felt that he himself was becoming the chief element of uncertainty in the problem of their coming life. There were times when he could distinguish between his real prospects and his vague opium dreams, but this power of correct judgment was passing from him. When not under the influence of the drug everything looked dull, leaden, and hopeless. Thus he alternated between utter dejection, for which there would have been no cause were he in his normal condition, and sanguine hopes and expectations that were still more baseless. He had not gone to a physician and made known his condition, as he had intended while on his brief visit to the country; his pride had revolted at such a confession of weakness, and he felt that surely he would have sufficient strength of mind to break the spell unaided. But, so far from breaking it, every day had increased its power.

The effects of opium and the strength of the habit, as is the case with other stimulants, vary with the temperament and constitution of the victims. A few can use it with comparative moderation and with no great detriment for a long time, especially if they allow considerable intervals to elapse between the periods of indulgence, but they eventually sink into as horrible a thraldom as that which degrades the least cautious. Upon far more the drug promptly fastens its deathly grip, and too often when they awaken to their danger they find themselves almost powerless. Still if they would then seek a physician's advice and resolutely cease using the poison in any form, they would regain their physical and mental tone within a comparatively brief time. I am glad to believe that some do stop at this period and escape. Their sufferings for a time must be severe, and yet they are nothing compared with the tortures awaiting them if they do not abstain. The majority, however, temporize and attempt a gradual reformation. There is not a ray of hope or the faintest prospect of cure for those who at this stage adopt half-way measures. They soon learn that they cannot maintain the moderation which they have resolved upon. A healthful man of good habits may be said to be at par. One indulgence in opium lifts him far above par, but in the inevitable reaction he sinks below it, and wronged nature will not rally at once; therefore she is hastened and spurred by the stimulant, and the man rises above par again, yet not quite so high as before, and he sinks lower in the reaction. With this process often repeated the system soon begins to lose its elasticity; the man sinks lower and more heavily every time; the amount of the drug that once produced a delightful exhilaration soon scarcely brings him up to par, and he must steadily strengthen the fatal leverage until at last even a deadly dose cannot lift him into any condition like his old exhilaration or serenity.

There are a vast number of men and women who ought never to take stimulants at all. They had better die than to begin to use them habitually, and even to touch them is hazardous. There is slumbering in their natures a predisposition toward their excessive use which a slight indulgence may kindle into a consuming, clamorous desire. Opium had apparently found something peculiarly congenial in Mr. Jocelyn's temperament and constitution, and at first it had rewarded him with experiences more delightful than most of its votaries enjoy. But it is not very long content to remain a servant, and in many instances very speedily becomes the most terrible of masters. He had already reached such an advanced stage of dependence upon it that its withdrawal would now leave him weak, helpless, and almost distracted for a time. It would probably cost him his situation; his weakness would be revealed to his family and to the world, and the knowledge of it might prevent his obtaining employment elsewhere; therefore he felt that he must hide the vice and fight it to its death in absolute secrecy. Under the terrible necromancy of his sin the wife from whom he had scarcely concealed a thought in preceding years was the one whom he most feared. As yet the habit was a sin, because he had the power to overcome it if he would simply resolve to do right regardless of the consequences; and these would be slight indeed compared with the results of further indulgence. He had better lose his situation a hundred times; he had better see his family faint from hunger for weeks together, should such an ordeal be an essential part of his struggle for freedom, for only by such an unfaltering effort could he regain the solid ground on which enduring happiness and prosperity could be built. As it was, he was rapidly approaching a point where his habit would become a terrible and uncontrollable disease, for which he would still be morally responsible—a responsibility, however, in which, before the bar of true justice, the physician who first gave the drug without adequate caution would deeply share. He felt his danger as he sat cowering over the dying fire; even with its warmth added to that of the summer night he shivered at his peril, but he did not appreciate it in any proper sense. He resolved again, as he often had before, that each day should witness increasing progress, then feeling that he *must* sleep he bared his arm and sent enough of Magendie's solution into his system to produce such rest as opium bestows.

To her surprise Mildred found the awakening of her father a difficult task the following morning. The boat on which his wife and children were to arrive was probably already at the wharf, and she had thought he would be up with the sun to meet them, but he seemed oppressed with an untimely stupor. When at last he appeared he explained that the fire on the hearth had induced a fit of brooding over the past and future, and that he had sat up late.

"Here's a cup of coffee, papa," she said briskly, "and it will wake you up. I'll have breakfast ready for you all by the time you can return, and I'm so eager to see mamma that I could fly to her."

Mortified that he should even appear dilatory at such a time, he hastened away, but he was far beyond such a mild stimulant as coffee. Even now, when events were occurring which would naturally sustain from their deep personal interest, he found himself reduced to an almost complete dependence on an unnatural support. Before sleeping he had appealed to his dread master, and his first waking moments brought a renewed act of homage. Opium was becoming his god, his religion. Already it stood between him and his wife and children. It was steadily undermining his character, and if not abandoned would soon leave but the hollow semblance of a man.

As the steamboat arrived in the night, Mrs. Jocelyn had no sense of disappointment at not being met, and through Mildred's persistency it was still early when her husband appeared. His greeting was so affectionate, and he appeared so well after his hasty walk, that the old glad, hopeful look came into her eyes. To Belle and the children, coming back to the city was like coming home as in former years, only a little earlier. The farm had grown to be somewhat of an old story, and Belle had long since voted it dull.

"Well, Nan, we've come down to two rooms in very truth, and in an old, old house, too, that will remind you of some of the oldest in the South," and he drew such a humorous and forlorn picture of their future abode that his wife felt that he had indeed taken her at her word, and that they would scarcely have a place to lay their heads, much less to live in any proper sense; and when she stopped before the quaint and decrepit house without any front door; when she followed her husband up the forlorn stairway to what seemed a side entrance with its most dismal outlook, she believed that the time for fortitude had come, in bitter truth. The hall was dark to her sun-blinded eyes, as it had been to Mildred's, yet not so dark but that she saw doors open and felt herself scanned with an unblushing curiosity by slattern-looking women, her near neighbors, and the thought that they were so very near made her shiver. As for Belle, she did not take pains to hide her disgust. With a sinking heart and faltering courage the poor gentlewoman mounted the winding stairs, but before she reached the top there was a rush from an open doorway, and Mildred clasped her in close embrace.

"Welcome home!" she cried, in her clear, sweet, girlish voice.

"Home, Millie! what a mockery that word is in this strange, strange place!" she half whispered, half sobbed in her daughter's ear.

"Courage, mamma. We promised papa we'd ask nothing better than he could afford," Mildred murmured. "Don't let him see tears—he has already put Fred down and is turning to welcome you to the best home he can offer."

Had the rooms been cells only, with but a pallet of straw upon the floors, Mrs. Jocelyn would have responded to that appeal, and she stepped forward resolved to smile and appear pleased with everything, no matter how stifled she might feel for want of space, air, and light.

But when she crossed the threshold into the spacious, sun-lighted room, and looked up at the high ceiling and across its wide area; when she had glanced around and seen on every side the results of the strong spells laid upon stout Mrs. Wheaton by Mildred's domestic magic, and the dainty touches with which the solid work had been supplemented, her face lighted up with a sweet surprise.

"Oh, *oh*, how much better this is than you led me to expect! Is all this really ours? Can we afford so large a room? Here are the dear old things, too, with which I first went to housekeeping." Then stepping to her husband's side she put her arm around his neck as she looked into his eyes and said, "Martin, this is home. Thank God, it is home-like after all. With you and the children around me I can be more than content—I can be very happy in this place. I feared that we might be too crowded, and that the children might suffer."

"Of course you didn't think of yourself, Nan. Millie's the good fairy to thank for all this. The way she and another female divinity have conjured in these rooms the last three days is a matter wholly beyond the masculine mind."

"Father did a great deal, too, and did it much better than you could expect from a man. But, come, I'm mistress of this small fraction of the venerable mansion till after breakfast, and then, mamma, I'll put the baton of rule in your hands. I've burned my fingers and spoiled my complexion over the stove, and I don't intend that a cold breakfast shall be the result."

"Millie," cried Belle, rushing out of the second room, which she had inspected in her lightning-like way before greeting her sister, "our room is lovely. You are a gem, an onyx, a fickle wild rose. It's all splendid—a perpetual picnic place, to which we'll bring our own provisions and cook 'em our own way. No boss biddies in this establishment. It's ever so much better than I expected after you once get here; but as the hymn goes, 'How dark and dismal is the way!' "

It was with difficulty that the children, wild over the novelty of it all, could be settled quietly at the table. It was the family's first meal in a tenement-house. The father's eye grew moist as he looked around his board and said, deep in his heart, "Never did a sweeter, fairer group grace a table in this house, although it has stood more than a century. If for their sakes I cannot be a man—"

"Martin," began his wife, her delicate features flushing a little, "before we partake of this our first meal I want you all to join me in your hearts while I say from the depths of mine, God bless our home."

An hour later, as he went down-town, Mr. Jocelyn finished his sentence. "If for the sake of such a wife and such children I cannot stop, I'm damned."

CHAPTER XVI

BELLE AND MILDRED

THE cosmopolitan bachelor living in apartments knows far more of Sanscrit than of a domestic woman's feelings as she explores the place she must call her home. It may be a palace or it may be but two rooms in a decaying tenement, but the same wistful, intent look will reveal one of the deepest needs of her nature. Eve wept not so much for the loss of Eden as for the loss of home—the familiar place whose homeliest objects had become dear from association. The restless woman who has no home-hunger, no strong instinct to make a place which shall be a refuge for herself and those she loves, is not the woman God created. She is the product of a sinister evolution; she is akin to the birds that will not build nests, but take possession of those already constructed, ousting the rightful occupants.

Mrs. Jocelyn and Mildred were unperverted; they were womanly in every fibre, and the interest with which they planned, consulted, and dwelt upon each detail of their small household economy is beyond my power to interpret. They could have made the stateliest mansion in the city homelike; they did impart to their two poor rooms the essential elements of a home. It was a place which no one could enter without involuntary respect for the occupants, although aware of nothing concerning them except their poverty.

"Mrs. Atwood and Susan actually cried when we came to go," Mrs. Jocelyn remarked as they were all busy together, "and even old Mr. Atwood was wonderfully good for him. He and Roger put a great many harvest apples and vegetables in a large box, and Mrs. Atwood added a jar of her nice butter, some eggs, and a pair of chickens. I told them that we must begin life again in a very humble way, and they just overflowed with sympathy and kindness, and I could scarcely induce them to take any money for the last week we were there. It was funny to see old Mr. Atwood: he wanted the money dreadfully—any one could see that, for a dollar is dear to his heart—but he also wanted to be generous like his wife, and to show his strong good-will. They sent heaps of love to you, Millie, and cordially invited us to visit them next summer; they also offered to board us again for just as little as they could afford. Even Jotham appeared to have something on his mind, for he was as helpful as an elephant, and stood around, and stood around, but at last went off muttering to himself."

"Millie," said Belle indignantly, "I think you treated Roger shamefully. After we returned from seeing you off, mamma and I went mooning up to that hill of yours looking toward the south, because you and papa were in that direction. Suddenly we came upon Roger sitting there with his face buried in his hands. 'Are you ill?' mamma asked, as if his trouble might have been a stomach-ache. He started up and looked white in the moonlight. 'She was cruel,' he said passionately; 'I only asked for friendship. I would have given my life for her, but she treated Jotham better than she did me, and she thinks I'm no better than he is—that I'm one of the farm animals.' 'Mr. Atwood,' mamma began, 'she did not mean to be cruel'—he interrupted her with an impatient gesture. 'The end hasn't come yet,' he muttered and stalked away."

Mildred sat down with a little perplexed frown upon her face. "I'm sure I meant him only kindness," she said; "why will he be so absurd?"

"You had a queer way of showing your kindness," snapped Belle.

"What would you have me to do? Encourage him to leave home, and all sorts of folly?"

"You can't prevent his leaving home. Mark my words, he'll soon be in this city, and he'll make his way too. He's a good deal more of a man than your lily-fingered Mr. Arnold, and if he wants to be friendly to me and take me out sometimes, I won't have him snubbed. Of course all my old friends will cut me dead."

"Oh, if he will transfer his devotion to you, Belle, I'll be as friendly as you wish."

"No, you've spoiled him for me or any one else. He's fool enough to think there's not another girl in the world but Mildred Jocelyn, and he'll get you if you don't look out, for he has the most resolute look that I ever saw in any one's eyes. The day before we came away something happened that took away my breath. A man brought a young horse which he said no one could manage. Roger went out and looked into the beast's eyes, and the vicious thing bit at him and struck at him with his forefoot. Then as he tried to stroke his back he kicked up with both hind feet. Oh, he was a very Satan of a horse, and they had a rope around his head that would have held a ship. Roger went and got what he called a curb-bit, and almost in a twinkling he had slipped it on the horse, and without a moment's hesitation he sprang upon his bare back. The horse then reared so that I thought he'd fall over backward on Roger. Mamma fairly looked faint—it was right after dinner—Susan and the children were crying, his father and mother, and even the owner of the horse, were calling to him to get off, but he merely pulled one rein sharply, and down the horse came on his four feet again. Instead of looking frightened he was coolly fastening the rope so as to have it out of the way. After letting the ugly beast rear and plunge and kick around in the road a few minutes, Roger turned his head toward a stone wall that separated the road from a large pasture field that was full of cows, and he went over the fence with a flying leap, at which we all screamed and shouted again. Then away they went round and round that field, the cows, with their tails in the air, careering about also, as much excited as we were. At last, when the horse found he couldn't throw him, he lay down and rolled. Roger was off in a second, and then sat on the beast's head for a while so he couldn't get up when he wanted to. At last he let the brute get up again, but he was no sooner on his feet than Roger was on his back, and away they went again till the horse was all in a foam, and Roger could guide him easily with one hand. He then leaped the tamed creature back into the road, and came trotting quietly to the kitchen door. Springing lightly down, and with one arm over the panting horse's neck, he said quietly, 'Sue, bring me two or three lumps of sugar.' The horse ate them out of his hand, and then followed him around like a spaniel. His owner was perfectly carried away; 'Jerusalem!' he exclaimed, 'I've never seen the beat of that. I offered you twenty-five dollars if you would break him, and I'll make it thirty if at the end of a month you'll train him to saddle and harness. He wasn't worth a rap till you took him in hand.' 'It's a bargain,' said Roger coolly, and then he whispered to me, 'That will buy me a pile of books.' That's the kind of a man that I believe in," concluded Belle, nodding her head emphatically, "and I want you to understand that Roger Atwood and I are very good friends."

Mildred meditatively bit her lip, and her cheeks had flushed with excitement at Belle's story, but she would make no comment upon it in words. "What does he want with so many books?" she asked, after a moment.

"You'll see before you are gray."

"Indeed! has he taken you into his confidence, also?"

"That's my affair. I believe in him, and so will you some day. He already knows more Latin than you do."

"That's not saying a great deal," replied Mildred, with a short, vexed laugh. "How came he to know Latin?"

"He studied it at school as you did. The fact is, you

are so prejudiced you know nothing about him. He's strong and brave, and he'll do what he attempts."

"He'll find that I am strong, too, in my way," said Mildred coldly. "He said something that hurt me more than I hurt him, and all I ask of him is to leave me alone. I wish him well, and all that, but we are not congenial. Complete success in his wild ambition wouldn't make any difference. He ought to remain at home and take care of his own people."

"Well, I'm glad he's coming to New York, and I hope for my sake you'll treat him politely."

"Oh, certainly for *your* sake, Belle. Let us all stick to that."

"Belle's a mere child," said Mrs. Jocelyn, with her low laugh.

"I'm sixteen years old, I thank you; that is, I shall be soon; and I know a real man from the ghost of one."

"Belle," cried Mildred, in a tone she rarely used, "I will neither permit nor pardon any such allusions."

"Come, girls," expostulated their mother, "our nest is too small for any disagreements, and we have a great deal too much to do for such useless discussions. I'm sorry with Millie that Roger is bent on leaving home, for I think his parents need him, and he could do well in the country. The city is too crowded already."

"He'll make his way through the crowd," persisted Belle.

"Does his father or mother know of his plans?"

"Well, to tell the truth, I don't know very much about his plans. He talks little concerning himself, but when he took me out to drive the day after Millie left, he said he had decided to come to New York and get an education, and that if I'd let him know where we lived he'd come and see me occasionally. I said, 'What will they do at home without you?' and he replied, 'I can do more for them away from home by and by than here.' Now, mamma, you'll let him come to see me, won't you?"

"Certainly, Belle. I'll be reasonable in this respect. I know young people need company and recreation. My only aim has ever been to secure you and Millie good company, and I hope your love for me, Belle, will lead you to shun any other. As we are now situated you must be very, very cautious in making new acquaintances. Young Mr. Atwood is a good, honest-hearted fellow, and I think Millie is a little prejudiced against him."

"Very well, mamma, I'll be all smiles so long as he devotes himself to Belle; but he must stop there most emphatically."

Thus with busy tongues and busier hands they talked of the past and the future while they unpacked and stowed away their belongings with almost the same economy of space that is practiced on shipboard. Mrs. Wheaton was introduced, and she at once became a fast ally of Mrs. Jocelyn as well as of Mildred.

"I 'ope yer'll halways remember yer 'ave a neighbor that's 'andy and villing," she said, as she courtesied herself out. "Hit's too bad," she muttered, on her way back to her room, "that she's 'ad to come down to this, for she's a born lady; she's has much a lady as hany 'oo howned this 'ouse a 'undred years hago."

Thus their life began in the old mansion, and from its humble shelter they looked abroad to see what they could obtain from the great indifferent world without.

"Belle and I must not be idle an hour longer than we can help," said Mildred resolutely, on the following day; "and the only thing is to find what it would be best to do. I am going out to try to sell the work I did in the country, and see if I cannot get orders for more of the same kind. My great hope is that I can work at home. I wish I knew enough to be a teacher, but like all the rest I know a little of everything, and not much of anything. Fancy work will be my forte, if I can only sell it. I do hope I shan't meet any one I know," and heavily veiled she took her way with her dainty fabrics toward the region of fashionable shops.

Those, however, who were willing to buy offered her so little that she was discouraged, and she finally left the articles at a store whose proprietor was willing to receive them on commission.

"You must not calculate on speedy sale," the lady in charge remarked. "People are very generally out of town yet, and will be for some time. Your work is pretty, however, and will sell, I think, later on, although in these hard times useful articles are chiefly in demand."

"Please do your best for me," said Mildred appealingly, "and please let me know what you think will sell. I'm willing to do any kind of work I can that will bring the money we need." After receiving some suggestions she bought more material, and then sat down to work in the hope that the returning citizens would purchase her articles so liberally that she could do her share toward the family's support.

She did not shrink from labor, but with the false pride so general she did shrink morbidly from meeting those who knew her in the past, and from their learning where and how she lived. She was wholly bent on seclusion until their fortunes were greatly mended, fondly hoping that her father would rally such a constituency from his Southern acquaintance that he would soon command a fine salary. And the expectation was not an unreasonable one, had Mr. Jocelyn been able to work with persistent energy for a few years. The South was impoverished, and while a remunerative trade might be built up from it, patient and exceedingly aggressive labor would be required to secure such a result. It is the curse of opium, however, to paralyze energy, and to render all effort fitful and uncertain. He should have written scores of letters daily, and attended to each commission with the utmost promptness and care, but there were times when the writing of a single letter was a burden, and too often it was vague and pointless like the condition of his mind when it was written. Mildred did not dream of this, and his employers felt that they must give him time before expecting very much return for his effort. Since he attended to routine duties fairly well there was no cause for complaint, although something in his manner often puzzled them a little. It was Mildred's belief that renewed prosperity would soon enable them to live in a way entitling them to recognition in the society to which Arnold belonged. If thus much could be accomplished she felt that he own and her lover's faithfulness would accomplish the rest. They were both young, and could afford to wait.

"The world brings changes for the better sometimes," she thought, as she plied her needle, "as well as for the worse; and no matter what his proud mother thinks, I'm sure I could take better care of him than she can. Whether they know it or not, the course of his family toward him is one of cold-blooded cruelty and repression. If he could live in a genial, sunny atmosphere of freedom, affection, and respect, his manhood would assert itself, he would grow stronger, and might do as much in his way as Roger Atwood ever can in his. He has a fine mind and a brilliant imagination; but he is chilled, imbittered, and fettered by being constantly reminded of his weakness and dependence; and now positive unhappiness is added to his other misfortunes, although I think my little note will do him no harm"—she dreamed that it might be carried next to his heart instead of mouldering where the faithless Jotham had dropped it. "I shall not punish him for his family's harsh pride, from which he suffers even more than I do. Turn, turn, fortune's wheel! We are down now, but that only proves that we must soon come up again. Being poor and living in a tenement isn't so dreadful as I feared, and we can stand it for a while. As stout Mrs. Wheaton says, 'There's vorse troubles hin the vorld.' Now that we know and have faced the worst we can turn our hopes and thoughts toward the best."

Poor child! It was well the future was veiled.

The mode of Belle's activity was a problem, but that incipient young woman practically decided it herself. She was outspoken in her preference.

"I don't want to work cooped up at home," she said. "I'd go wild if I had to sit and stitch all day. School half killed me, although there was always some excitement to be had in breaking the rules."

"Naughty Belle!" cried her mother.

"Never naughty when you coax, mamma. I'd have been a saint if they'd only taken your tactics with me, but they didn't know enough, thank fortune, so I had my fun. If they had only looked at me as you do, and put me on my honor, and appealed to my better feelings and all that, and laughed with me and at me now and then, I'd been fool enough to have kept every rule. You always knew, mamma, just how to get me right under your thumb, in spite of myself."

"I hope I may always keep you there, my darling, in spite of this great evil world, out into which you wish to go. It is not under my thumb, Belle, but under my protecting wing that I wish to keep you."

"Dear little mother," faltered the warm-hearted girl, her eyes filling with tears, "don't you see I've grown to be too big a chicken to be kept under your wing? I must go out and pick for myself, and bring home a nice morsel now and then for the little mother, too. Yes, I admit that I want to go out into the world. I want to be where everything is bright and moving. It's my nature, and what's the use of fighting nature? You and Millie can sit here like two doves billing and cooing all day. I must use my wings. I'd die in a cage, even though the cage was home. But never fear, I'll come back to it every night, and love it in my way just as much as you do in yours. You must put me in a store, mamma, where there are crowds of people going and coming. They won't do me any more harm than when I used to meet them in the streets, but they'll amuse me. My eyes and hands will be busy, and I won't die from moping. I've no more education than a kitten, but shop-girls are not expected to know the dead languages, and I can talk my own fast enough."

"Indeed you can!" cried Mildred.

"But, Belle," said her mother, who was strongly inclined toward Mildred's idea of seclusion until fortune's wheel *had* turned, "how will you like to have it known in after years that you were a shopgirl?"

"Yes," added Mildred, "you may have to wait on some whom you invited to your little company last spring. I wish you could find something to do that would be quiet and secluded."

"Oh, nonsense!" cried Belle impatiently. "We can't hide like bears that go into hollow trees and suck their paws for half a dozen years, more or less"—Belle's zoölogical ideas were startling rather than accurate—"I don't want to hide and cower. Why should we? We've done nothing we need be ashamed of. Father's been unfortunate; so have hundreds and thousands of other men in these hard times. Roger showed me an estimate, cut from a newspaper, of how many had failed during the last two or three years—why, it was an army of men. We ain't alone in our troubles, and Roger said that those who cut old acquaintances because they had been unfortunate were contemptible snobs, and the sooner they were found out the better; and I want to find out my score or two of very dear friends who have eaten ice-cream at our house. I hope I may have a chance to wait on 'em. I'll do it with the air of a princess," she concluded, assuming a preternatural dignity, "and if they put on airs I'll raise the price of the goods, and tell them that since they are so much above other people they ought to pay double price for everything. I don't believe they'll all turn up their noses at me," she added, after a moment, her face becoming wistful and gentle in its expression as she recalled some favorites whose whispered confidences and vows of eternal friendship seemed too recent to be meaningless and empty.

The poor child would soon learn that, although schoolgirls' vows are rarely false, they are usually as fragile and transient as harebells. She had dropped into a different world, and the old one would fade like a receding star. She would soon find her that her only choice must be to make new associations and friendships and find new pleasures; and this her mercurial, frank, and fearless nature would incline her to do very promptly.

With Mildred it was different. The old life was almost essential to her, and it contained everything that her heart most craved.

Her courage was not Belle's natural and uncalculating intrepidity. She would go wherever duty required her presence, she would sacrifice herself for those she loved, and she was capable of martyrdom for a faith about as free from doctrinal abstractions as the simple allegiance of the sisters of Bethany to the Christ who "loved" them. Notwithstanding the truth of all this, it has already been shown that she was a very human girl. Brave and resolute she could be, but she would tremble and escape if possible. Especially would she shrink from anything tending to wound her womanly delicacy and a certain trace of sensitive Southern pride. Above all things she shrank from that which threatened her love. This was now her life, and its absorbing power colored all her thoughts and plans. Both conscience and reason, however, convinced her that Belle was right, and that the only chance for the vigorous, growing girl was some phase of active life. With her very limited attainments, standing behind a counter seemed the only opening that the family would consider, and it was eventually agreed upon, after a very reluctant consent from her father.

CHAPTER XVII

BELLE LAUNCHES HERSELF

ONLY the least of Belle's difficulties were past when she obtained consent to stand behind a counter. With her mother she made many a weary expedition through the hot streets, and was laughed at in some instances for even imagining that employment could be obtained at the dullest season of the year. As soon as their errand was made known they were met by a brief and often a curt negative. Mrs. Jocelyn would soon have been discouraged, but Belle's black eyes only snapped with irritation at their poor success. "Give up?" she cried. "No, not if I have to work for nothing to get a chance. Giving up isn't my style, at least not till I'm tired of a thing; besides it's a luxury poor people can't indulge in."

Mrs. Jocelyn felt that the necessity which compelled this quest was a bitter one, and her heart daily grew sorer that she had not resolutely saved part of every dollar earned by her husband in the old prosperous times. As she saw the poor young creatures standing wearily, and often idly and listlessly, through the long summer days, as her woman's eyes detected in the faces of many the impress of the pain they tried to conceal but could never forget, she half guessed that few laborers in the great city won their bread more hardly than these slender girls, doomed in most instances never to know a vigorous and perfected womanhood. "Belle, my child, how can you stand during these long, hot days? It's providential that we can't find any place."

"Well, mamma, I'm not very well up in the ways of

Providence. I fear the dull season has more to do with it. Nevertheless I'm going to make a situation if I can't find one."

She had in her mind a shop on Sixth Avenue, which had the appearance of a certain "go and life," as she phrased it.

"There's a strong-willed, wide-awake man back of that establishment," she had said to herself more than once, "and if I could get at him I believe he'd give me work, but the hateful old foreman stands in the way like a dragon."

She and her mother had been curtly informed by this well-dressed "dragon," which parted its hair like a woman, that "there was no use in bothering the proprietor; he never added to his help in August—the idea was absurd."

One morning after Mrs. Jocelyn had about given up the hope of obtaining a place until the autumn trade revived—as far as it would revive in those languid years—Belle started out alone, heavily veiled, and with her purpose also veiled from her mother and Mildred. She went straight to the shop on Sixth Avenue that had taken her fancy, and walked up to the obnoxious foreman without a trace of hesitation. "I wish to see Mr. Schriven," she said, in a quiet, decisive manner.

"He is very busy, madam, and does not like to be disturbed. I will attend to anything you wish."

"Thank you; then please direct me to the proprietor's office without delay."

After a moment's hesitation the man complied. This veiled presence had the appearance of a gentlewoman and was decided in manner. Therefore he led the way to a small private office, and said, "A lady, sir, who insists on seeing you," and then discreetly closed the door and departed.

The man of business allowed his pen to glide to the end of his sentence before turning to greet his visitor. Belle in the meantime had advanced to a point from which she could look directly into his face, for, child though she was, she understood that it was her difficult task first to obtain a hearing, and then to disarm his anger at her intrusion. Aware, however, that she had nothing to lose and everything to gain by the adventure, her natural fearlessness and quickness of tongue carried her through. She had already guessed that an appeal for employment, even the most pitiful, would meet with a flat, prompt refusal, therefore she had resolved on different tactics.

At last the man lifted his head in his quick, imperious way, asking, as he turned toward her, "What is your business with me, madam?"

"I like your store very much," Belle remarked quietly.

Mr. Schriven now really glanced at her, and he found her brilliant black eyes and fair flushed face such pleasing objects of contemplation that he was content to look for a moment while he puzzled a little over the unexpected apparition. He then smiled satirically and said, "What follows from so momentous a fact?"

"It follows that I would rather be employed here than in other stores that I do not like so well. My mother and I have visited nearly every one, and I like yours best."

"Well, this *is* cool. You and your mother were refused employment at this season at all the others, were you not?"

"Yes, sir."

"And my foreman declined your services here, also, did he not?"

"Yes, sir, but I was sure that if I saw you I should obtain my wish. There's a life and snap about this place that I didn't see elsewhere, and therefore I knew a live man, and not a machine, was back of it, and that if I could see and talk with him he'd give me a chance."

"You are exceedingly flattering," said the man, with another satirical smile. "Has it not occurred to you that your course is just tinged with assurance?"

"Have I said or done anything unbecoming a lady?" asked Belle indignantly.

Mr. Schriven laughed good-naturedly, for Belle's snapping eyes and brusque ways were beginning to interest him. "Oh, I forgot that you American working-women are all ladies. I am told that you speak of certain of your number as 'scrub-ladies' and 'washer-ladies.' "

"You may call me a shop-girl, sir, as soon as I am in your employ."

"And why not now?"

"Because I'm not yet a shop-girl, and never have been one. I've often bought goods with my mother in this very store, and I come from as good blood as there is in the South. A few months ago my social position was as good as yours, and now that we have been unfortunate and I must work, I see no presumption in asking you to your face for honest work."

"Not at all, my dear young lady," resumed Mr. Schriven, still maintaining his half-amused, half-ironical manner, "but I must inform you that I cannot afford to employ my social equals as shop-girls."

"When I enter your employ of my own free will," responded Belle promptly, "I the same as promise to obey all the rules and regulations of your establishment, and I'll do it, too. What's more, I'll sell so many goods in dull times and all times that you can well afford to make a place for me if you have none. One thing is certain—I'm going to get work, and my work will repay those who employ me a hundred times."

"Well, you are an odd fish," Mr. Schriven ejaculated; "I beg your pardon, you are not yet in my employ—you are an eccentric young lady, and a very young one, too, to be making your way in the world in this irresistible style. You mean what you say, that if employed you will put on no airs and conform to rules?"

"I mean just what I say."

Mr. Schriven fell into a foxy fit of musing, and there rose before his mind the pale face and dragged, weary, listless look of a girl now standing at the ribbon counter.

"She'll break down when hard work begins again," he thought; "she's giving way now with nothing much to do. To be sure she has been here a long time, and has done her best and all that, but her day is past, and here's plenty of young flesh and blood to fill her place. This one is rather young, but she's smart as a whip—she's full of mettle and is fresh and healthy-looking. It won't do to have pale girls around, for it gives cursed busybodies a chance to rant about women standing all day. (Out of the corner of his eye he measured Belle from head to foot.) She can stand, and stand it, too, for a long while. She's compact and stout. She's built right for the business." At last he said, aloud, "In case I should so far depart from my usual custom and make a place for you, as you suggest, what do you propose to charge for the services you rate so highly?"

"What you choose to give."

"Well," was the laughing answer, "there's method in your madness. Take that pen and write what I dictate."

Belle wrote a few sentences in a dashing, but sufficiently legible hand.

"You will have to practice a little, and aim at distinctness and clearness. That's more than style in business," Mr. Schriven continued deliberately, for the young creature was so delightfully fresh and original that he began to regard her as an agreeable episode in the dull August day. "I'll make a place for you, as you say, if you will come for three dollars a week and comply with the rules. You are to do just as you are bid by those having charge of your department, and you had better keep on their right side. You are not to come to me again, remember, unless I send for you," he concluded, with his characteristic smile; "an event that you must not look forward to, for I assure you such interviews are rare in my experience. Come next Monday at seven if you agree to these conditions."

"I agree, and I thank you," the girl promptly answered, her brilliant eyes glowing with triumph, for thoughts like these were in her mind: "How I can crow over mamma and Millie, who said this very morning there was no use in trying! Won't it be delicious to hand papa enough money to pay the rent for a month!" No wonder the child's face was radiant.

The thoughts of her employer were of quite a different character. He gave her a look of bold admiration, and said familiarly, "By Jupiter, but you are a daisy!"

Belle's manner changed instantly. He caught a swift, indignant flash in her dark eyes, and then she laid her hand on the door-knob and said, with the utmost deference and distance of manner, "I will try to attend to the duties of my station in a way that will cause no complaint. Good-morning, sir."

"Wait a moment," and Mr. Schriven touched a bell, and immediately the foreman appeared.

"Give this girl a place next Monday at the ribbon counter," he said, in the quick staccato tones of one who is absolute and saves time even in the utterance of words. "I also wish to see you two hours hence."

The man bowed, as if all were a matter of course, but when he was alone with Belle he said sharply, "You think you got ahead of me."

He would indeed have been the most malicious of dragons had not Belle's smiling face and frank words disarmed him.

"I did get ahead of you, and you know it, but you are too much of a man to hold a grudge against a poor girl who has her bread to earn. Now that I am under your charge I promise that I'll do my best to please you."

"Very well, then; we'll see. I'll have my eye on you, and don't you forget it."

Mrs. Jocelyn and Mildred laughed, sighed, and shook their heads over Belle's humorous account of her morning's adventure. They praised her motive, they congratulated her on her success, but her mother said earnestly, "My dear little girl, don't get bold and unwomanly. We had all better starve than come to that. It would wound me to the heart if your manner should ever cause any one to think of you otherwise than as the pure-hearted, innocent girl that you are. But alas! Belle, the world is too ready to think evil. You don't know it yet at all."

She knew it better than they thought. There was one phase of her interview with Mr. Schriven that she had not revealed, well knowing that her gentle mother would be inexorable in her decision that the shop must not even be entered again. The girl was rapidly acquiring a certain shrewd hardihood. She was not given to sentiment, and was too young to suffer deeply from regret for the past. Indeed she turned buoyantly toward the future, while at the same time she recognized that life had now become a keen battle among others in like condition.

"I don't intend to starve," she said to herself, "nor to bite off my own nose because the world is not just what mother and Millie think it ought to be. Papa would be inclined to break that man's head if I told him what he said and how he looked. But what would come of it? Papa would go to jail and we into the street. Unless papa can get up in the world again very fast, Millie and I shall find that we have got to take care of ourselves and hold our tongues. I hadn't been around with mamma one day before I learned that much. Mamma and Millie were never made to be working-women. They are over-refined and high-toned, but I can't afford too much of that kind of thing on three dollars a week. I'm a 'shop lady'—that's the kind of lady I'm to be—and I must come right down to what secures success without any nonsense."

In justice it should be said that Belle's practical acceptance of the situation looked forward to no compromise with evil; but she had seen that she must come in contact with the world as it existed, and that she must resolutely face the temptations incident to her lot rather than vainly seek to escape from them. Alas! her young eyes had only caught a faint glimpse of the influences that would assail her untrained, half-developed moral nature. Body and soul would be taxed to the utmost in the life upon which she was entering.

On the Sunday following Mr. Jocelyn slept so late that none of the family went to church. Indeed, since their old relations were broken up they scarcely knew where to go, and Mildred no more felt that she could return to the fashionable temple in which Mrs. Arnold worshipped than present herself at the elegant mansion on Fifth Avenue. The family spent the after part of the day in one of the most secluded nooks they could find in Central Park, and Mildred often looked back upon those hours as among the brightest in the shrouded past. Mr. Jocelyn gauged his essential stimulant so well that he was geniality itself; Belle was more exuberant than usual; Fred and Minnie rejoiced once more in flowers and trees and space to run. Mrs. Jocelyn's low, sweet laugh was heard again and again, for those who made her life were all around her, and they seemed happier than they had been for many a long, weary day. For a brief time at least the sun shone brightly through a rift in the clouds gathering around them.

Beyond the fact that Belle had found a place, little was said to Mr. Jocelyn, for the subject seemed very painful to him, and the young girl started off Monday morning in high spirits. The foreman met her in a curt, business-like way, and assigned her to her place, saying that the girl in charge of the goods would tell her about the marks, prices, etc. This girl and her companions received Belle very coldly, nor did they thaw out before her sunshine. As a matter both of duty and interest the young woman upon whom the task devolved explained all that was essential in a harsh, constrained voice, and the others ignored the newcomer during business hours. Belle paid no attention to them, but gave her whole mind to the details of her work, making rapid progress. "I'll have time for them by and by," she muttered, "and can manage them all the better when I know as much as they do."

She saw, too, that the foreman had his eye upon her and her companions, so she assumed the utmost humility and docility, but persisted in being told and retold all she wished to know. Since she observed that it was the foreman's eye and not good-will which constrained the cold, unsympathetic instruction received, she made no scruple in taxing the giver to the utmost.

When at last they went to the room in which they ate their lunch, the girls treated her as if she were a leper; but just to spite them she continued as serene as a May morning, either acting as if she did not see them or treating them as if they were the most charming young women she had ever met. She saw with delight that her course aggravated them and yet gave no cause for complaint

As soon as permitted she hastened home, and was glad to lie down all the evening from sheer fatigue, but she made light of her weariness, concealed the treatment she had received from the girls, and the dejection it was beginning to occasion in spite of her courage; she even made the little home group laugh by her droll accounts of the day. Then they all petted and praised and made so much of her that her spirits rose to their usual height, and she said confidently, as she went to a long night's rest, "Don't you worry, little mother; I didn't expect to get broken in to my work without a backache."

The next day it was just the same, but Belle knew now what to charge for the ribbons, or, if she was not sure, the others were obliged, under the eye of the inexorable foreman—who for some reason gave this counter a great deal of attention—to tell her correctly, so she began to lie in wait for customers. Some came to her of their own accord, and they smiled back into her eager, smiling face.

In two or three instances her intent black eyes and manner seemed to attract attention and arrest the steps of those who had no intention of stopping. One case was so marked that the alert foreman drew near to note the result. An elderly lady, whose eye Belle had apparently caught by a look of such vivacity and interest that the woman almost felt that she had been spoken to, came to the girl, saying, "Well, my child, what have you that is pretty to-day?"

"Just what will please you, madam."

"*You* please me, whether your ribbons will or not. It's pleasant for a customer to be looked at as if she were not a nuisance," she added significantly, and in a tone that Belle's companions, with their cold, impassive faces, could not fail to hear. "You may pick out something nice for one of my little granddaughters."

Dimpling with smiles and pleasure, Belle obeyed. Feeling that the eye of the arbiter of their fates was upon them, the young women near might have been statues in their rigid attitudes. Only the hot blood mounting to their faces betrayed their anger. There was evidently something wrong at the ribbon counter—something repressed, a smouldering and increasing indignation, a suggestion of rebellion. So the foreman evidently thought, from his frequent appearances; so the floor-walker clearly surmised, for with imperious glances and words he held each one sternly to her duty. Belle was smiling and working in the midst of a gathering storm, and she was becoming conscious of it. So far from cowering, her indignation was fast rising, and there was an ominous glow kindling in her dark eyes. Their seemingly unwarranted hostility and jealousy were beginning to incense her. She believed she had as much right there as they had, and she resolved to maintain her right. Catching an ireful glance from the girl in charge of the counter, she returned it with interest. Even this spark came very near kindling the repressed fires into an open flame, regardless of consequences. The bread of these girls was at stake, but women are not calculating when their feelings are deeply disturbed.

At last, just as the wretched afternoon was ending, and preparations to close were in progress, a pale, thin girl, with a strange and rather reckless look, came in, and, sitting down before Belle, fixed her gaunt eyes upon her.

"So you were heartless enough to take my place away from me?" she said slowly, after a moment.

"I don't know what you mean," answered Belle indignantly.

"Yes, you do know what she means, you little black snake in the grass," whispered one of the girls in her ear while pretending to put a box upon the shelf.

Belle whirled upon her with such a vivid and instantaneous flash of anger that the girl stepped back precipitately and dropped the box.

Just at this moment Mr. Schriven, in the act of departure, came out of his office and witnessed the whole scene. He stopped and smiled broadly. The foreman had informed him from time to time of the little "comedy" progressing at the ribbon counter, and the two potentates felt quite indebted to Belle for a sensation in the dullest of dull seasons, especially at the girl's conduct was wholly in the line of their wishes, regulations, and interests. "She's as plucky as a terrier," the echo of his chief had said, "and the time will come when she'll sell more goods than any two girls in the store. You made a ten-strike in effecting that exchange."

It was rich sport for them to see her fiery spirit arousing and yet defying the intense and ill-concealed hostility of her companions—a hostility, too, that was extending beyond the ribbon counter, and had been manifesting itself by whispering, significant nods, and black looks toward the poor child all the afternoon; but so far from shrinking before this concentration of ill-will Belle had only grown more indignant, more openly resentful, and unable to maintain her resolute and tantalizing serenity.

Feeling that it would compromise his dignity and authority even to appear to notice what was going forward, Mr Schriven wrapped himself in his greatness and passed down the shop, sweeping the excited group—that was restrained for the moment by his presence—with a cold, nonchalant glance, from which, however, nothing escaped. When in the street his characteristic smile reappeared.

"By the Lord Harry!" he muttered, "if she isn't the gamiest bit of flesh and blood that I've seen in a long time! She's worth looking after."

Since his eye and restraining presence, however, were now absent from the store, there would have been no small tumult at the ribbon counter had not Belle by her straightforward, fearless manner brought things to a speedy issue. There were now no customers in the shop, and the discipline of the day was practically over, therefore the girl on whom Belle had turned so passionately, having reached a safe distance, said, outspokenly, "I'll say it now, so all can hear, even if I lose my place for it. You are a mean, p'isinis little black snake in the grass. We all know how you got this girl out of the place she's had for years, and I want you to understand that if you stay you'll have a hot time of it."

"And I want *you* to understand that if I've a right to stay, I *will* stay," cried Belle, in a ringing voice. "I'm not afraid of you, nor a thousand like you. Either you're all cats to treat a young girl as you've treated me the last two days, or else there's something that I don't understand. But I'm going to understand it here and now. You hold your tongue, and let this girl speak who says I've taken her place. She's the one I'm to deal with. But first let me say how I got this place—I asked for it. That's the whole story, and I didn't know I was taking it from any one else."

Belle's courageous and truth-stamped manner began to create a diversion in her favor, and all near listened with her to what the dismissed girl might say. The latter did not in the least respond to Belle's energy, but after a long, weary sigh she began, without raising her head from her hand as she sat leaning on the counter, "Whether you're right or wrong, I'm too badly used up to quarrel with you or to answer in any such gunpowdery fashion. I'm dead beat, but I thought I'd like to come in and see you all once more, and my old place, and who was standing in it. You are at the beginning, my pert one. If I was as young and strong as you I wouldn't come and stand here."

"How is your mother?" asked the girl in charge of the counter.

"She's dying, starving," was the reply, in the same dreary, apathetic tone, and black looks were again directed toward Belle.

She heeded them not, however. For a moment her eyes dilated with horror, then she sprang to the girl, and taking her hands exclaimed, "Good God! What do you mean? Let me go home with you."

The girl looked at her steadfastly, and then said, "Yes, come home with me. That's the best way to understand it all."

"We'll bring your mother something by and by," said two or three of the girls as the poor creature rose slowly to follow Belle, who was ready instantly, and whose course compelled a suspension of judgment on the part of those even the most prejudiced against her.

CHAPTER XVIII

"I BELIEVE IN YOU"

"COME," cried Belle impatiently, as they made their way down Sixth Avenue, which was crowded at that hour; "why do you walk so slowly? If my mother was as badly off as you say yours is, I'd fly to her."

"No, you wouldn't, if you had scarcely eaten anything for two days."

"What!" Belle exclaimed, stopping short and looking at her companion to see if she were in earnest. Something in her expression caused the impulsive child to seize her hand and drag her into a bakery near. Then snatching out her little purse she thrust it into the girl's hands and said, "Here, take all I have and buy what you like best."

But instead of buying anything, the stranger looked wistfully into the excited and deeply sympathetic face, and said slowly, "I don't believe you're bad after all."

"Oh, I'm bad enough—bad as most girls of my age," said the innocent girl recklessly, "but I'm not bad enough to keep back a penny if I knew any one was hungry. Stop looking at me and buy what you like, or else let me do it. Take home some of this jelly-cake to your mother. That would tempt my appetite if it ever needed any tempting. I half believe you are shamming all this, you act so queer."

"Come with me," said the girl, for the people in the store were looking at them curiously. When in the street she continued, "You are not bad. What is your name?"

"Belle Jocelyn."

"My name is Clara Bute. I *am* hungry. I'm faint for

food, but may it choke me if I eat any before I take something home to mother! Cake is not what either of us need, although it made me ravenous to see it. You haven't much money here, Belle, and small as the sum is, I don't know when I can repay it."

"Oh, stop that kind of talk," cried Belle; "you'll drive me wild. Let us get what your mother *does* want and take it to her without another word."

They purchased bread and milk, a little tea, a bit of beef, a bundle of kindling-wood, and then Belle's slender funds gave out. With these they turned into a side street and soon reached a tall tenement.

"Oh," sighed Clara, "how can I climb those dreadful stairs! We live at the top."

"Drink some of the milk," said Belle kindly, "and then let me carry everything."

"I guess I'll have to or I'll never get up at all." Slowly and painfully she mounted flight after flight, sitting down at last and resting after each ascent. "I didn't—realize—I was so weak," she panted.

"Tell me your room," said Belle, "and I'll come back and help you."

"It's the—last one—back—top floor. I've given out."

Belle left her sitting on the stairs and soon reached the door, which had been left slightly ajar for air, for the evening was sultry. She pushed it open with her foot, since her hands were so full, and with her eyes fixed on the articles she was carrying so as to drop nothing, she crossed the small room to a table and put them down before looking around.

"There's some—mistake," said a very low, hollow voice.

Belle was almost transfixed by eyes as black as her own, gleaming out of cavernous sockets and from the most emaciated face she had ever seen. It seemed as if the dead were speaking to her. At any rate, if the woman were not dead she soon would be, and the thought flashed through Belle's mind that she would be the cause of her death, since she had taken her daughter's place and robbed them of sustenance. She who had been ready to face a whole shopful of hostile people with undaunted eyes was seized with a remorseful panic, and ran sobbing down to Clara, crying, "Oh, do come—let me carry you"; and this she half did in her excitement. "Give your mother something to make her better right away. Let me help you—tell me what to do."

Clara went to her mother and kissed her tenderly, whispering, "Courage, momsy, I've got something nice for you." Then she turned and said, "You are too excited, Belle. I'll do everything, and make the little we have go a great way. You would waste things. I know just what to do, only give me time," and she soaked some of the bread in the milk and began feeding her mother, who swallowed with great difficulty.

"I'll take no more—till—I see you—eat something," gasped the poor woman. "Who gave you all this? Who's that?" pointing feebly at Belle.

"I'm the girl that took Clara's place," Belle began, with a fresh burst of sobs. "I didn't know I was doing it, and now I'll never forgive myself."

Clara looked at her wonderingly as she explained: "The foreman said you asked Mr. Schriven to make a place for you, but I don't believe you meant that he should 'sack' me to do it. Why, you are nothing but a great, warm-hearted child. The girls said you were 'knowing,' and could 'play as deep a game as the next one,' and that the foreman about the same as owned it to them. It's all his doing and his master's. They both care more for a yard of ribbon than for a girl, body and soul."

"Well," said Belle, with bitter emphasis, "I'll never work for them again—never, never."

"Don't say that," resumed Clara, after coaxing her mother to take a little more nourishment, and then sitting down to eat something herself. "If you are poor you must do the best you can. Now that I know you I'd rather you had my place than any one else, for"—she gave a swift glance at her mother's closed eyes, and then whispered in Belle's ear—"I couldn't keep it much longer. For the last two weeks it has seemed I'd drop on the floor where you stood to-day, and every night I've had harder work to climb these stairs. Oh, Lord! I wish mother and I could both stay here now till we're carried down together feet foremost."

"Don't talk that way," pleaded Belle, beginning to cry again. "We'll all do for you now, and you both will get better."

"Who's 'we all'? Would you mind telling me a little about who you are, and how you came to get my place?"

Belle's brief sketch of herself, her history, and how the recent events had come about, was very simple, but strong and original, and left no doubt in her listener's mind.

"My gracious!" Clara cried, as the room darkened, "your folks'll be wild about you. I've nothing to offer you but your own, and I've kept you talking when you must have been tired and hungry, but you are so full of life that you put a bit of life in me. It's ages since I felt as you do, and I'll never feel so again. Now run home with your mind at rest. You have done us more good than you have harm, and you never meant us any harm at all."

"Indeed I did not," cried Belle, "but I'm not through with you yet. I'll bring Millie back with me and a lot of things," and she darted away.

The inmates of the two rooms at the Old Mansion were, indeed, anxious over Belle's prolonged absence. Her father had gone to the shop; Mrs. Wheaton, with her apron thrown over her head, was on the sidewalk with Mildred, peering up and down through the dusk, when the half-breathless girl appeared.

Her story was soon told, and Mrs. Wheaton was taken into their confidence. From trembling apprehension on Belle's behalf, kind Mrs. Jocelyn was soon deep in sympathy for the poor woman and her daughter, and offered to go herself and look after them, but Mildred and Mrs. Wheaton took the matter into their own hands, and Belle, after gulping down a hasty supper, was eager to return as guide. Mr. Jocelyn, who had returned from the closed store on a run, had so far recovered from his panic concerning his child that he said he would bring a physician from the dispensary, and, taking the number, went to do his part for those who had become "neighbors unto them." A woman on the same floor offered to look after Mrs. Wheaton's children for an hour or two, and the two sisters and the stout English woman, carrying everything they could think of to make the poor creatures comfortable, and much that they could ill spare, started on their errand of mercy. It never occurred to them that they were engaged in a charity or doing a good deed. They were simply following the impulses of their hearts to help those of whose sore need they had just learned. Mildred panted a little under her load before she reached the top of those long, dark stairs. "I could never get to heaven this way," muttered Belle, upon whom the day of fatigue and excitement was beginning to tell. "It's up, up, up, till you feel like pitching the man who built these steps head first down 'em all. It's Belle, Clara," she said, after a brief knock at the door; then entering, she added, "I told you I'd come back soon with help for you."

"I'm sorry I've nothing to make a light with," Clara answered; "the moon has been so bright of late that we did without light, and then I got all out of money. We either had to pay the rent or go into the street, unless some one took us in. Besides, mother was too sick to be moved."

"I've brought two candles," said Mrs. Wheaton. "They're heasier managed hon a 'ot night," and she soon had one burning on the table and another on the mantel. "I vant to see vat's to be done," she continued, "because I must give yer a 'arty lift hin a jiffy and be back to my children hagain." Then going to the sick woman she took her hand and felt her pulse. "'Ow do yer find yerself, mum?" she asked.

"Oh, I'm much—better—I shall—get well now," the

poor soul gasped, under the strange hallucination of that disease which, although incurable, ever promises speedy health to its victims.

"That's a splendid; that's the way to talk," cried Belle, who had been oppressed with the fear that the woman would die, and that she in some sense would be to blame. "Clara, this is sister Millie that I told you about," and that was all the introduction the two girls ever had.

"Vy didn't you send yer mother to a 'ospital?" Mrs. Wheaton asked, joining the girls at the table.

"Don't say 'hospital' so mother can hear you. The very word would kill her now, for there's nothing on earth she dreads more than that they'll separate us and send her to a hospital. I've sometimes thought it would have been best, and then it seemed it would kill her at once, she was so opposed to it. That we might keep together and to buy her delicacies I've parted with nearly everything in the room, as you see," and it was bare indeed. A bed from which the element of comfort had long since departed, two rickety chairs, a pine table, a rusty stove, and a few dishes and cooking utensils were about all there was left. With eyes slowly dilating Mildred took in the bleak truth, but said only a few gentle words and was very busy. She lifted Mrs. Bute's head, while Clara gave her a little bread soaked in wine, and then aided Mrs. Wheaton in making the room and bed a little more like what they should be by means of the articles they had brought. Clara wonderingly saw that her little closet was stocked with supplies for days to come. Her mother's preternaturally brilliant eyes followed every movement, also, with a dumb but eager questioning. Tired Belle in the meantime had drawn a chair to the table, and with her head resting on her arms had dropped asleep in a moment.

"Why should your sister work in a store if you're not poor?" Clara asked Mildred. "You can't be poor and spare all these things."

"Yes, we're poor, but not so poor as you are," said Mildred simply. "Belle touched our hearts in your behalf, and we see you need a little neighborly help."

"Well, I was never so mistaken in any one in my life," Clara exclaimed, looking at the sleeping girl, with a remorseful gush of tears. "There isn't a bad streak in her."

At this moment the door opened, and two girls, who had been Clara's companions at the shop, appeared with a few meagre parcels. Before asking them in she pulled them back in the hall and there were a few moments of eager whispering. Then they all came in and looked at Belle, and Clara stooped down and kissed her lightly, at which the girl smiled and murmured, "Dear little mother—always brooding over her chicks."

"She thinks she's home," explained Mildred, with moist eyes.

"This is her sister," said Clara, "and this lady is a friend of theirs. I know they've robbed themselves, they've brought so much."

"Vun's honly ter come to Hameriker ter be a lady," chuckled Mrs. Wheaton under her breath.

"We won't wake your sister," said one of the girls. "She's tired, and no wonder. We haven't treated her right at the store, but we wasn't to blame, for we didn't know her at all. Please tell her that we'll give her a different reception to-morrow," and after another season of whispering in the hall they departed, leaving the simple offerings gleaned from their poverty.

Mr. Jocelyn and the physician soon appeared, and after a brief examination the latter called Mr. Jocelyn aside and said, "Her pulse indicates that she may die at any hour. There is no use in trying to do anything, for the end has come. It has probably been hastened by lack of proper food, but it's too late now to give much, for there is no power of assimilation."

"You had better tell the poor girl the truth, then," said Mr. Jocelyn.

Clara was called, and heard the verdict with a short,

convulsive sob, then was her weary, quiet self again. "I feared it was so," was all she said. She now became aware that Mildred stood beside her with an encircling and sustaining arm. "Don't," she whispered; "don't be too kind or I'll break down utterly, and I don't want to before mother. She don't know—she never will believe she can die, and I don't want her to know. I'll have time enough to cry after she's gone."

"I feel I must stay vith yer to-night," warm-hearted Mrs. Wheaton began; "and if Miss Jocelyn vill look hafter my children I vill."

"No, Mrs. Wheaton," said Mildred decidedly, "I'm going to stay. You ought to be with your children. Don't tell Belle, papa, and take the poor child home. Clara and I can now do all that can be done. Please don't say anything against it, for I know I'm right," she pleaded earnestly in answer to her father's look of remonstrance.

"Very well, then, I'll return and stay with you," he said.

The physician's eyes dwelt on Mildred's pale face in strong admiration as he gave her a few directions. "That's right, Millie, make her well for mercy's sake or I'll have the horrors," Belle whispered as she kissed her sister good-night.

Soon Clara and Mildred were alone watching the gasping, fitful sleeper. "After all that's been done—for me—to-night I'll—surely get well," she had murmured, and she closed her eyes without an apparent doubt of recovery.

Mildred furtively explored the now dimly lighted room. "Merciful Heaven," she sighed, "shall we ever come to this?" Clara's eyes were fixed on her mother's face with pathetic intensity, watching the glimmer of that mysterious thing we call life, that flickered more and more faintly. The difference between the wasted form, with its feeble animation, and what it must soon become would seem slight, but to the daughter it would be wide indeed. Love could still answer love, even though it was by a sign, a glance, a whisper only; but when to the poor girl it would be said of her mother, "She's gone," dim and fading as the presence had been, manifested chiefly by the burdens it imposed, its absence would bring the depths of desolation and sorrow.

Going the poor creature evidently was, and whither? The child she was leaving knew little of what was bright and pleasant in this world, and nothing of the next. "Miss Jocelyn," she began hesitatingly.

"Don't call me Miss Jocelyn; I'm a working-girl like yourself."

"Millie, then, as Belle said?"

"Yes."

"Millie, do you believe in a heaven?"

"Yes."

"What is it like?"

"I don't know very well. It's described to us under every grand and beautiful image the world affords. I think we'll find it what we best need to make us happy."

"Oh, then it would be rest for mother and me," the girl sighed wearily.

"It's surely rest," Mildred replied quickly, "for I remember a place in the Bible where it says, 'There remaineth a rest for the people of God.'"

"That's it," said Clara with some bitterness; "it's always the people of God. What remains for such as we, who have always been so busy fighting the wolf that we've thought little of God or church?"

"You've been no poorer, Clara, than Christ was all His life, and were He on earth now as He was once, I'd bring Him here to your room. He'd come, too, for He lived among just such people as we are, and never once refused to help them in their troubles or their sins."

"Once—once," cried Clara, with a gush of tears. "Where is He now?"

"Here with us. I know it, for we need Him. Our need is our strongest claim—one that He never refused. I have entreated Him in your behalf and your mother's, and do you ask Him also to put heaven at the end of this dark and often thorny path which most of us must tread in this world."

"Oh, Millie, Millie, I'm ignorant as a heathen. I did have a Bible, but I sold even that to buy wine to save mother's life. I might better have been thinking of saving her soul. She's too sick to be talked to now, but surely she ought to find at least a heaven of rest. You could never understand the life she's led. She hasn't lived—she's just been dragged through the world. She was born in a tenement-house. The little play she ever had was on side-walks and in the gutters; she's scarcely ever seen the country. Almost before she knew how to play she began to work. When she was only seventeen a coarse, bad man married her. How it ever came about I never could understand. I don't believe he knew anything more of love than a pig; for he lived like one and died like one, only he didn't die soon enough. It seems horrible that I should speak in this way of my father, and yet why should I not, when he was a horror to me ever since I can remember? Instead of taking care of mother, she had to take care of him. He'd take the pittance she had wrung from the washtub for drink, and then come back to repay her for it with blows and curses. I guess we must have lived in fifty tenements, for we were always behind with the rent and so had to move here and there, wherever we could get a place to put our heads in. Queer places some of them were, I can tell you—mere rat-holes. They served one purpose, though—they finished off the children. To all mother's miseries and endless work was added the anguish of child-bearing. They were miserable, puny, fretful little imps, that were poisoned off by the bad air in which we lived, and our bad food—that is, when we had any—after they had made all the trouble they could. I had the care of most of them, and my life became a burden before I was seven years old. I used to get so tired and faint that I was half glad when they died. At last, when mother became so used up that she really couldn't work any more, father did for us the one good act that I know anything about—he went off on a big spree that finished him. Mother and I have clung together ever since. We've often been hungry, but we've never been separated a night. What a long night is coming now, in which the doctor says we shall be parted!" and the poor girl crouched on the floor where her mother could not see her should she open her eyes, and sobbed convulsively.

Mildred did not try to comfort her with words, but only with caresses. Christ proved centuries ago that the sympathetic touch is healing.

"Oh, Millie, I seem to feel the gentle stroke of your hand on my heart as well as on my brow, and it makes the pain easier to bear. It makes me feel as if the coarse, brutal life through which I've come did not separate me from one so good and different as you are; for though you may be poor, you are as much of a lady as any I've ever waited on at the store. And then to look at your father and to think of mine. I learned to hate men even when a child, for nearly all I ever knew either abused me or tempted me; but, Millie, you need not fear to touch me. I never sold myself, though I've been faint with hunger. I'm ignorant, and my heart's been full of bitterness, but I'm an honest girl."

"Poor, poor Clara!" said Mildred brokenly, "my heart aches for you as I think of all you've suffered."

The girl sprang up, seized the candle, and held it to Mildred's face. "My God," she whispered, "you are crying over my troubles." Then she looked steadfastly into the tearful blue eyes and beautiful face of her new friend for a moment, and said, "Millie, I'll believe any faith *you'll* teach me, for *I believe in you.*"

CHAPTER XIX

BELLE JARS THE "SYSTEM"

SOME orthodox divines would have given Clara a version of the story of life quite different from that which she received from Mildred. Many divines, not orthodox, would have made the divergence much wider. The poor girl, so bruised in spirit and broken in heart, was not ready for a system of theology or for the doctrine of evolution; and if any one had begun to teach the inherent nobleness and self-correcting power of humanity, she would have shown him the door, feeble as she was. But when Mildred assured her that if Christ were in the city, as He had been in Capernaum, He would climb the steep, dark stairs to her attic room and say to her, "Daughter, be of good comfort"—when she was told that Holy Writ declared that He was the "same yesterday, to-day, and forever"—her heart became tender and contrite, and therefore ready for a Presence that is still "seeking that which was lost."

Men may create philosophies, they may turn the Gospel itself into a cold abstraction, but the practical truth remains that the Christ who saves, comforts, and lifts the intolerable burden of sorrow or of sin, comes now as of old—comes as a living, loving, personal presence, human in sympathy, divine in power. As Mildred had said, our need and our consciousness of it form our strongest claim upon Him and the best preparation for Him.

Clara was proving the truth of her words. Life could never be to her again merely a bitter, sullen struggle for bread. A great hope was dawning, and though but a few rays yet quivered through the darkness, they were the earnest of a fuller light.

Before midnight Mr. Jocelyn joined the watchers, and seated himself unobtrusively in a dusky corner of the room. Clara crouched on the floor beside her mother, her head resting on the bed, and her hand clasping the thin fingers of the dying woman. She insisted on doing everything the poor creature required, which was but little, for it seemed that life would waver out almost imperceptibly. Mildred sat at the foot of the bed, where her father could see her pure profile in the gloom. To his opium-kindled imagination it seemed to have a radiance of its own, and to grow more and more luminous until, in its beauty and light, it became like the countenance of an accusing angel; then it began to recede until it appeared infinitely far away. "Millie," he called, in deep apprehension.

"What is it, papa?" she asked, springing to his side and putting her hand on his shoulder.

"Oh!" he said, shudderingly. "I had such a bad dream! You seemed fading away from me, till I could no longer see your face. It was so horribly real!"

She came and sat beside him, and held his hand in both of hers. "That's right," he remarked; "now my dreams will be pleasant."

"You didn't seem to be asleep, papa," said the girl, in some surprise; "indeed, you seemed looking at me fixedly."

"Then I must have been asleep with my eyes open," he answered with a trace of embarrassment.

"Poor papa, you are tired, and it's very, very kind of you to come and stay with me, but I wasn't afraid. Clara says it's a respectable house, and the people, though very poor, are quiet and well behaved. Now that you have seen that we are safe, please go home and rest," and she coaxed until he complied, more from fear that he would betray himself than from any other motive.

In the deep hush that falls on even a great city before

the early life of the next day begins, Mrs. Bute opened her eyes and called, "Clara!"

"Right here, momsy, dear, holding your hand."

"It's strange—I can't see you—I feel so much better, too—sort of rested. It does—seem now—as if I—might get—a little rest. Don't wake me—child—to give me—anything—and rest yourself."

She smiled faintly as she closed her eyes, and very soon Clara could never wake her again. Mildred took the head of the orphan into her lap, and the poor girl at last sobbed herself to sleep.

We will not attempt to follow Mildred's thoughts as she tried to keep up through the long hours. The murmured words, "I would watch more patiently over Vinton Arnold, did not his proud mother stand between us," suggests the character of some of them. At last, when she was faint from weariness, she heard steps coming up the stairs, and her mother entered, followed by Mrs. Wheaton.

"My dear, brave child, this is too much for you. I'd rather it had been myself a thousand times," Mrs. Jocelyn exclaimed.

"It's all right, mamma, but the sight of you and good Mrs. Wheaton is more welcome than I can tell you, for I was getting very lonely and tired."

"I'll stay now hand tend ter heverything," said Mrs. Wheaton, with a stout, cheery kindness that could not be disguised even in her whisper; but Clara awoke with a start and said, "What is it, momsy?"

Then she sprang up, and after a brief glance at her mother threw herself with a long, low cry on the lifeless form.

"Leave hall ter me," said Mrs. Wheaton decidedly, "hand take Miss Jocelyn 'ome, for this'll be too much for 'er."

"Ah, mamma dear," sobbed Mildred, "my heart would be broken indeed if that were you."

"Millie, if you love me, come home at once," Mrs. Jocelyn urged. It was quite light when they gained the street, and after reaching home Mildred was given a warm cup of tea, and left to sleep until late in the day. While she slept, however, there occurred some rather stirring scenes.

Belle, too, slept rather late, but a portentous gloom came into her eyes when told that Mrs. Bute was dead. She did not say very much, but her young face grew older and very resolute while she hastily ate her breakfast. Then she carried something nice to Clara, and found that Mrs. Wheaton had left, a neighbor from the tall tenement having taken her place.

Belle looked at the bereaved girl with half-fearful eyes as if she expected reproaches, and when Clara kissed her in greeting she said "Don't" so sharply as to excite surprise.

"Belle," said Clara gently, "mother's at rest."

"That's more than I am," muttered the girl. "Oh, Clara, I didn't mean to bring all this trouble on you. That man just caught me in a trap."

"Belle, Belle! why do you blame yourself for all this? It would have come just the same, and probably just as soon, and if it hadn't been for you I'd been alone, with no friends and no hope."

"Oh, don't talk to me!" Belle cried; "your mother might have been alive if I hadn't taken your place. I want to see her."

Clara turned back the covering, and the young girl looked at the dead face with a stern, frowning brow.

"Starved!" she muttered. "I understand why they all looked so black at me now; but why couldn't some one have told me? He shall know the truth for once; he's more to blame than I," and she abruptly departed.

Very little later the foreman of the shop on Sixth Avenue was astonished to see her passing hastily toward the private office, regardless of the looks of surprise and interest turned toward her on every side, for the events of the night had been very generally whispered around.

"Mr. Schriven's engaged," he said sharply. "What do you want? Why are you not in your place?"

"I am in my place, but you are not. Stand aside, for I will see Mr. Schriven at once."

"I tell you some one is with him."

"I don't care if the king's with him," and darting on one side she reached the office door, and knocked so sharply that the ireful potentate within sprang up himself to see who the inconsiderate intruder was.

"Oh, it's you," he said, half inclined to laugh in spite of his anger. "I thought I said that, if I employed you, you were not to come to my office again unless I sent for you?"

"I'm not in your employ."

"Indeed! How's that?" he asked very sharply.

"That is just what I've come to explain," was the unflinching reply.

"By-by," remarked Mr. Schriven's visitor maliciously; "I see you are to be interviewed."

"Very briefly, I assure you. Good-morning. Now, miss, I give you about one minute to transact your business with me, then the cashier will pay you for two days' work."

"No, sir, he will not. Do you think I'd take money stained with blood?"

"What do you mean? What kind of a girl are you anyway?"

"I'm an honest girl; I believe in God and the devil—I believe in them both too well to have anything more to do with you unless you can prove you didn't know any more than I did. You think to frighten me with black looks, but I've just come from a greater presence than yours—the presence of one who'll soon be your master—Death, and death for which you are responsible."

"Good God! what do you mean?"

"What did you mean by turning off without a word a poor girl—one who for years had done her best for you? What did you mean by making a place for me in that way?

Her mother died last night—starved—and I'd have you know that I'd have starved before I'd have taken her place had I known what I know now. Go look at your work at the top of a tenement-house! There's more flesh on your arm than on that dead woman's body, and the poor girl herself hadn't eaten anything for two days when she came here last night. She'd have died, too, if sister Millie hadn't stayed with her last night. I hope you didn't know any more than I did. If you did you've got to settle with God and the devil before you're through with this kind of business."

The man was frightened, for he had meant no deliberate cruelty. He was only practicing the sound political economy of obtaining the most for the least, but in the words and stern face of the child he saw how his act must appear to a mind unwarped by interest and unhardened by selfish years. Moreover, he could not bluster in the presence of death, and the thought that his greed had caused it chilled his heart with a sudden dread. He caught at the extenuation her words suggested, and said gravely, "You are right; I did not know. I would send food from my own table rather than any one should go hungry. I knew nothing about this girl, and no one has told me of her need until this moment. A man at the head of a great business cannot look after details. The best he can do is to manage his business on business principles. To prove that I'm sincere, I'll take the girl back again at her old wages, although I do not need her."

The man lied in giving a false impression. It was true that he did not single out individuals as objects of intentional cruelty, but his system was hard and remorseless, and crushed like the wheels of Juggernaut, and he purposely shut his eyes to all questions and consequences save those of profit and loss. When compelled to face, through Belle's eyes, an instance of the practical outcome of his system, he shuddered and trembled, for the moment, and was inclined to ease his conscience by a little ostentatious kindness, especially as the facts in the case bade fair to become known. Men who, unlike Belle, have little fear of God or the devil, do fear public opinion. The girl interpreted him, however, after her own warm, guileless heart, and in strong revulsion of feeling said, tearfully, "Please forgive me, sir, for speaking as I have. I've done you wrong, and I acknowledge it frankly, but I was almost beside myself. We didn't either of us mean them any harm."

The man could not repress a smile at Belle's association of herself with him in the guilt of the affair. In fact, he rather liked the idea, for it made his own part seem quite venial after all—an error of ignorance like that of the child's—so he said kindly, "Indeed, we did not, and now we'll make amends. You go and see what is needed and let me know, and to-morrow, if you wish, you can take your own place and not any one's else. You are a smart, good-hearted girl, and by and by I can give you better wages."

"I did you wrong, sir," repeated Belle remorsefully, "and now that you will take Clara back, I'd work for you almost for nothing. When and where shall I come?" she added humbly; "I don't wish to seem rude any more."

"Come to my house this evening," and he gave her his number.

"I beg your pardon for what I said. Good-by, sir," and with tearful eyes and downcast face she went to the street, without a glance on either side.

The man sat for a few moments with a heavily contracting brow. At last he stretched out his hand and sighed, "I'd give all there is in this store if my heart was like that girl's, but here I am at this hour engaged in a transaction which is the devil's own bargain, and with a firm that can't help itself because it is in my power. Hang it all! business is business; I'll lose a cool thousand unless I carry it through as I've begun." He seized his pen and carried it through.

Belle, attended by her father, was not in the least abashed by the elegance of Mr. Schriven's parlor, as he had rather hoped she would be, but he was much impressed by Mr. Jocelyn's fine appearance and courtly bearing. "No wonder the girl's course has been peculiar," he thought. "She comes from no common stock. If I've ever seen a Southern gentleman, her father's one, and her plump little body is full of hot Southern blood. She's a thoroughbred, and that accounts for her smartness and fearlessness. Where other girls would whine and toady to your face, and be sly and catlike behind your back, she'd look you in the eyes and say all she meant point-blank. I'm glad indeed things are taking their present course, for these people could make any man trouble," and he treated his guests very suavely.

Belle soon told her story in a straightforward manner. One of her generous projects was to have a rather grand funeral, with all the girls in the shop attending in a procession. "What a child she is!" thought Mr. Schriven, with difficulty repressing a laugh, but he proceeded very gravely to induce the girl to take his own practical view.

"In the first place, my child," he said, "that woman died of consumption—she didn't starve at all."

"I think she died the sooner," Belle faltered.

"Possibly. If so, she was the sooner out of her misery. At any rate we are not to blame, since, as you have said, we didn't know. Now a funeral, such as you suggest, would be very costly, and would do no one any good. It would scarcely be in good taste, for, considering the poor woman's circumstances, it would be ostentatious."

"Belle, Mr. Schriven is right," said her father, in a tone of quiet authority.

"Let us rather consider the need of the daughter," Mr. Schriven resumed. "You say she is worn and weak from watching and work. A quarter of the money that a funeral would cost would give her two or three weeks in the country. And now," he concluded impressively—his conscience needed a little soothing, and his purse was plethoric with the thousand dollars wrung from those who had the misfortune to be in his power—"I will pay her board at some quiet farmhouse for three weeks, and then she'll come back fresh and strong to her old place."

Belle's eyes filled with tears of gladness. "You are right, sir, and you are very kind and generous. I know just the place for her to go—the people we've been with all summer. They are kind, and will do everything for her, and take away her strange feeling at once. Oh, I'm so glad it's all ending so much better than I feared! I thought this morning I could never be happy again, but you've made all seem so different and hopeful. I thank you, sir, over and over, and I'll do my best now at the store, and be respectful to every one."

The man was touched. The warm, reflected glow of the girl's heart softened for a moment his own icy organ, and his eyes grew moist momentarily. "You are a good child," he said. "Here are thirty-five dollars for your friend, for you've been a friend to her indeed. Most girls would have let them starve for all they cared. Now send the girl off to the country, and as soon as I can I'll raise your wages to five dollars. I'd do it now, only the others would talk and say it wasn't customary to pay beginners so highly. Mr. Jocelyn, I congratulate you on the possession of such a daughter, and I sincerely hope you may soon retrieve your fortunes and regain the position to which I see that you both naturally belong," and he bowed them out with a politeness and respect that were not by any means assumed.

Belle almost danced home by her father's side, so great was the rebound of her depressed feelings. Thirty-five dollars! How much that would do for poor Clara! Millie would help her make up her mourning, and she would have nothing to pay for but the material. She would write to Mrs. Atwood that very night, and to Roger, telling him he must be kind to Clara, and take her out to drive. Her heart fairly bubbled over with plans and projects for the girl whose "place she had taken."

The poor child had scarcely begun her letter to Mrs.

Atwood before her head drooped, and Mildred said, "Tell me what to say, Belle, and I'll write it all. You've done you part to-day, and done it well."

"That's good of you, Millie. When I get sleepy it's no use to try to do anything. I'd go to sleep if the house was on fire. But you won't write to Roger, I'm afraid."

"No. If he must be written to, you must do that."

"Well, I will to-morrow. He'll do Clara more good than all the rest."

Our story passes hastily over the scenes that followed. A brief service was held over Mrs. Bute's remains by a city missionary, known to Mrs. Wheaton, who was present with Mrs. Jocelyn, Belle, and Mildred. Three or four neighbors from the tenement lent chairs and came in also. The girls at the ribbon counter clubbed together and sent an anchor of white flowers, and at the hour of the funeral they looked grave and were quiet in manner, thus taking part in the solemnity in the only way they could. In due time the city department upon which the duty devolved sent the "dead wagon"; the morsel of human clay was returned to its kindred dust in "Potter's Field," a public cemetery on Hart's Island, in which are interred all who die in the city and whose friends are unable to pay for a grave or a burial plot. Clara, however, had not the pain of seeing her mother placed in the repulsive red box furnished by the department, for Mr. Jocelyn sent a plain but tasteful coffin, with the woman's age and name inscribed upon it.

Mrs. Wheaton went with the girl to the grave, and then brought her to her own little nook in the old mansion, for Clara had said she had no relatives she knew anything about except a few on her father's side, and she had rather go to a station-house than to them. "Don't talk habout station 'ouses till yer can see vat I kin do for yer," the good woman had said in her hearty way, and she did play the good Samaritan so well, and poured the "oil and wine" of kindness into the poor creature's wounds so effectually, that she began to change for the better daily.

Mildred redeemed Belle's promise, and between them all they soon fitted Clara for her trip to the country. By the time Mrs. Atwood's reply reached Mildred, and Roger's hearty answer came back in response to Belle's characteristic note, she was ready to go. "There's a man's hand for you," cried Belle exultantly as she exhibited Roger's bold chirography. "It's a hand that can be depended upon, strong and ready."

Mildred smiled as she replied, "You're welcome to it, Belle."

"You needn't smile so placidly," she retorted, with an ominous nod. "We are not through with Roger Atwood yet."

Perhaps quotations from two letters written by Clara to Mildred and Belle, and received a week later, will form a satisfactory ending to this chapter. Clara had been taught to read and write in the public schools of the city, and but little more. In later years she had occasionally found opportunity to attend some of the night schools established for those whose only leisure came after the busy day was over, and so had learned to use her pen with tolerable correctness. In waiting upon the educated people who frequented the shop she had caught, with the aptness of an American girl, a very fair power of expressing herself in speech. Writing a letter, however, was a formidable affair, in which she had scarcely any experience. Her missives, therefore, were very simple, and somewhat defective in outward form, but they suggested some interesting facts.

"DEAR MILLIE (ran the first): I'm very sad and hapy. The Countrys like heven. All are so kind. Even the dog dosen't grole at me, and Mr. Roger says that's queer for he groles at everybody. I feel so much better, I don't know myself. I feel like takin depe breths of air all the time and I never tasted such milk. Every glass puts life in me. If I can get work up here I'll never go back to town and stand all day again. The girls up here have a chance to live—

they haven't any chance at all in a store. The strongest will brake down and then they are good for nothing. I wish Belle could do something else. I wish thousands would go in the country and do work that would make us look like Susan. Mrs. Atwood thinks she can find me a place with kind people, where I'll be treted almost like one of the family. Anyway I've had enough of standing and bad air and starving and I don't see why working in a farmhouse ain't just as ladylike as wating on folks with the floorwalker awatchin you like a slave driver. Standing all day is deth to most girls and about the hardest deth they can die. I feel as if I could live to be a hundred up here.

"Millie, dear, I read the Bible you gave me and I pray for you and Belle every night and morning and He answers. I know it. I love you very much and I've good reason. Good by. "CLARA BUTE."

Her letter to Belle was more descriptive of her daily life, of the kindness she received on every hand. One brief extract from it will suffice:

"I've got well acquainted with Roger," she wrote. "He's easy to get acquainted with. Now I think of it though he says little or nothing about himself but he leads me to talk and tell about you all in a way that surprises me. If his interest was prying I'm sure I wouldn't have told him anything. I know well now it isn't. Does Millie know how he feels toward her? I saw it all last night. I was telling him about my past life and how poor and forlorn we had been and how I had told Millie all about it and then how Millie had just treted me as if I were as good as she was. As I talked he became so white I thought he'd faint. Suddenly he burst out despairingly, 'I hoped she was proud but she isn't—I could overcome pride. But what can I do when I'm just detested? There, I've made a fool of myself,' he said savagelike after a moment, and he hurried away. For the last two days he's been so quiet and looked so stern and sad that his family don't know what to make of him, but I know what's the matter, and I feel sorry for him, for he seems to me more like a man than any of the young fellows I've seen in town. Don't tell Millie for I don't want to even seem to meddle."

But Belle had no gift of reticence, and she not only showed her sister the letter, but overwhelmed her with reproaches for her "heartless treatment of Roger." As a natural result Mildred was only more irritated and prejudiced against the young man than ever.

"You are all absurdly unreasonable," she cried. "What have I ever done to make him turn white or red, or to 'burst out despairingly,' and all that kind of sentimental nonsense? Because he is lackadaisical and is experiencing strange, vague emotions, must I be afflicted in like manner? Must I break faith with one I do love and do violence to my own feelings, just because this farmer wants me to? You know what's the matter with him—Clara saw at a glance—and the course I'm taking is the only way to cure him. All his talk about friendship is transparent folly. If I took your advice it would make him only more and more infatuated; and now I haven't it on my conscience that I gave him one bit of encouragement. I'm sorry for him, of course. I shall be more sorry for his mother and sister if he is guilty of the folly of leaving home. If, instead of doing his duty by them, he comes mooning after me here, when he knows it is of no use, I shall lose my respect for him utterly."

There seemed so much downright common-sense in this view of the affair that even Belle found no words in reply. Her reason took Mildred's part, but her warm little heart led her to shake her head ominously at her sister, and then sleepily she sought the rest her long, tiresome day required.

CHAPTER XX

SEVERAL QUIET FORCES AT WORK

PRECIPITOUS ascents and descents do not constitute the greater part of life's journey. In the experience of very many they occur more or less frequently, but they conduct to long intervals where the way is comparatively level, although it may be flinty, rough, and hedged with thorns. More often the upward trend or the decline of our paths is so slight as not to be noticed as we pass on, but at the end of years we can know well whether we are gaining or losing.

The Jocelyns, in common with thousands of others, had made a swift descent from a position of comparative affluence to one of real, though not repulsive, poverty. There was nothing, however, in their fall that cast a shadow upon them in the eyes of the world except as the unfortunate are always "under a cloud" to the common herd that moves together in droves only where the sunlight of prosperity falls. If Mr. Jocelyn could regain his former position, or a better one, there had been nothing in his brief obscurity that would prevent his wife and daughters from stepping back into their old social place, with all its privileges and opportunities.

The reader knows, however, that his prospects were becoming more and more dubious—that each day added a rivet to the chain that an evil habit was forging. His family did not even suspect this, although the impression was growing upon them that his health was becoming impaired. They were beginning to accommodate themselves to life at its present level, and the sense of its strangeness was passing slowly away. This was especially true of Belle and the children, upon whom the past had but a comparatively slight hold. Mildred, from her nature and tastes, felt the change more keenly than any of the others, and she could never forget that it raised a most formidable barrier against her dearest hopes. Mrs. Jocelyn also suffered greatly from the privations of her present lot, and her delicate organization was scarcely equal to the tasks and burdens it imposed. As far as possible she sought to perform the domestic duties that were more suited to the stout, red arms of those accustomed to such labors. It seemed essential that Mildred and Belle should give their strength to supplementing their father's small income, for a time at least, though all were living in hope that this necessity would soon pass away. The family was American, and Southern at that, in the idea that bread-winning was not woman's natural province, but only one of the direful penalties of extreme poverty. The working-woman of the South belonged to a totally different class from that in which Mr. and Mrs. Jocelyn had their origin, and prejudices die hard, even among people who are intelligent, and, in most respects, admirable. To Mrs. Jocelyn and her daughters work was infinitely preferable to dependence, but it was nevertheless menial and undignified because of its almost involuntary and hereditary association with a race of bond-servants. He is superficial indeed in his estimate of character who thinks that people can change their views and feelings in response to a brief demonstration of the essential dignity of labor, especially after generations of accumulating pride of caste have been giving the mind a different bent. Moreover, this family of Southern origin had not seen in the city of New York very much confirmation of the boasted Northern ideas of labor. Social status depended too much on the number of servants that people kept and the style in which they lived. Poverty had brought them a more sudden and complete loss of recognition than would have been possible in the South—a loss which they would not have felt so greatly had they wealthy connections in town through whom they might have retained, in part at least, their old relations with people of their own station.

As it was, they found themselves almost wholly isolated. Mrs. Jocelyn did not regret this so much for herself, since her family was about all the society she craved; moreover in her girlhood she had been accustomed to rather remote plantation life, with its long intervals of absence of society. Mr. Jocelyn's business took him out among men even more than he relished, for his secret indulgence predisposed to solitude and quiet. He was living most of the time in an unreal world, and inevitable contact with his actual life and surroundings brought him increasing distress.

With Belle and Mildred it was different. At their age society and recreation were as essential as air and light. Many are exceedingly uncharitable toward working-girls because they are often found in places of resort that are, without doubt, objectionable and dangerous. The fact is ignored that these places are sought from a natural and entirely wholesome desire for change and enjoyment, which are as needful to physical and moral health as sunlight to a plant. They forget that these normal cravings of the young in their own families find many and safe means of gratification which are practically denied to the tenement population. If, instead of harsh judgments, they would provide for the poor places of cheap and innocent resort; if, instead of sighing over innate depravity, they would expend thought and effort in bringing sunshine into the experiences of those whose lives are deeply shadowed by the inevitable circumstances of their lot, they would do far more to exemplify the spirit of Him who has done so much to fill the world with light, flowers, and music.

Mildred began to brood and grow morbid in her monotonous work and seclusion; and irrepressible Belle, to whom shop life was becoming an old, weary story, was looking around for "pastures new." Her nature was much too forceful for anything like stagnation. The world is full of such natures, and we cannot build a dike of "thou shalt nots" around them; for sooner or later they will overleap the barriers, and as likely on the wrong side as on the right. Those who would save and bless the world can accomplish far more by making safe channels than by building embankments, since almost as many are ruined by undue and unwise repression as by equally unwise and idiotic indulgence.

If Mr. Jocelyn had been himself he might have provided much innocent and healthful recreation for his family; but usually he was so dreamy and stupid in the evening that he was left to doze quietly in his chair. His family ascribed his condition to weariness and reaction from his long strain of anxiety; and opium had already so far produced its legitimate results that he connived at their delusion if he did not confirm it by actual assertion. It is one of the diabolical qualities of this habit that it soon weakens and at last destroys all truth and honor in the soul, eating them out with a corrosive power difficult to explain.

For the first week or two Belle was glad to rest in the evenings from the intolerable weariness caused by standing all day, but the adaptability of the human frame is wonderful, and many at last become accustomed, and, in some sense, inured to that which was torture at first. Belle was naturally strong and vigorous, and her compact, healthful organism endured the cruel demand made upon it far better than the majority of her companions. Nature had endowed her with a very large appetite for fun. For a time her employment, with its novelty, new associations, and small excitements, furnished this, but now her duties were fading into prosaic work, and the child was looking around for something enlivening. Where in the great city could she find it? Before their poverty came there were a score of pretty homes like her own in which she could visit schoolmates; her church and Sabbath-school ties brought her into relation with many of her own age; and either in her own home or in those of her friends she took part in breezy little festivities that gave full and healthful scope to her buoyant nature. She was not over-fastidious now, but when occasionally she went home with some of her companions at the shop, she returned dissatisfied. The small quarters in which the girls lived rendered little confidential chats—so dear to girls—impossible, and she was brought at once into close contact with strange and often repulsive people. It seemed that the street furnished the only privacy possible, except as she brought girls to her own abode. Her mother and sister were very considerate in this respect, and welcomed all of her acquaintances who appeared like good, well-meaning girls; and Mildred would either give up her share of their little room for the time, or else take part in their talk in such a genial way as to make the visitors at home as far as they could be with one in whom they recognized their superior. Their light talk and shop gossip were often exceedingly tiresome to Mildred, but she felt that Belle needed every safeguard within their power to furnish. And this privilege of welcoming the best companions her circumstances permitted was of great help to Belle, and, for a time, prevented her restless spirit from longing for something more decided in the way of amusement. Of necessity, however, anything so quiet could not last; but where could the girl find pleasures more highly colored? Occasionally she would coax or scold her father into taking her out somewhere, but this occurred less and less frequently, for she was made to feel that his health required absolute rest when his business permitted it. If she had had kind brothers the case would have been greatly simplified, but thousands of working-girls have no brothers, no male companions save those acquaintances that it is their good or, more often, their evil fortune to make. Without a brother, a relative, or a friend deserving the name, how is a young girl, restricted to a boarding-house or a tenement, to find safe recreation? Where can she go for it on the great majority of the evenings of the year? Books and papers offer a resource to many, and Mildred availed herself of them to her injury. After sitting still much of the day she needed greater activity in the evening. Belle was not fond of reading, as multitudes on the fashionable avenues are not. The well-to-do have many other resources—what chances had she? To assert that working-girls ought to crave profitable reading and just the proper amount of hygienic exercise during their leisure, and nothing more, is to be like the engineer who said that a river ought to have been half as wide as it was, and then he could build a bridge across it. The problem must be solved as it exists.

To a certain extent this need of change and cheerful recreation is supplied in connection with some of the mission chapels, and the effort is good and most commendable as far as it goes; but as yet the family had formed no church relations. Mildred, Belle, and occasionally Mrs. Jocelyn had attended Sabbath service in the neighborhood. They shrank, however, so morbidly from recognition that they had no acquaintances and had formed no ties. They had a prejudice against mission chapels, and were not yet willing to identify themselves openly with their poor neighbors. As yet they had incurred no hostility on this account, for their kindly ways and friendliness to poor Clara had won the goodwill and sympathy of all in the old mansion. But the differences between the Jocelyns and their neighbors were too great for any real assimilation, and thus, as we have said, they were thrown mainly on their own resources. Mrs. Wheaton was their nearest approach to a friend, and very helpful she was to them in many ways, especially in relieving Mrs. Jocelyn, for a very small compensation, from her heavier tasks. The good woman, however, felt even more truly than they that they had too little in common for intimacy.

There is one amusement always open to working-girls if they are at all attractive—the street flirtation. To their honor it can be said that comparatively few of the entire number indulge in this dangerous pastime from an improper motive, the majority meaning no more harm or evil than their more fortunate sisters who can enjoy the society of young men in well-appointed parlors. In most instances this street acquaintance, although unhedged by safe restrictions, is by no means indiscriminate. The young men are brothers or friends of companions, or they are employed in the same establishment, or else reside in the neighborhood, so that usually something is known of their characters and antecedents, and the desire to become friendly is similar to that influencing the young people of country neighborhoods. As a rule these young people have few opportunities of meeting save in the streets and places of public resort. The conditions of life in a great city, however, differ too widely from those of a village or country town, where every one is well known and public opinion is quick and powerful in its restraints. Social circles are too loosely organized in a city; their members from necessity are generally too little known to each other; there are too many of both sexes ready to take advantage of the innocent and unwary, and their opportunities of escape from all penalty invite the crimes suggested by their evil natures. Belle had been often warned, and she had so much affection for her mother and so much pride that she did not fall readily into indiscretions; nor would she in the future respond, without considerable self-restraint, to the frequent advances which she never failed to recognize, however distant she might appear, and she would not have possessed a woman's nature had she been indifferent to admiring glances and the overtures of those who would gladly form her acquaintance. Still it must be admitted that her good resolutions were fast weakening in this direction.

Mildred's dangers were quite different from those which assailed Belle, and yet they were very grave ones. Her mind and heart were preoccupied. She was protected from even the desire of perilous associations and pleasures by the delicacy and refinement of her nature and her Christian principle. She shrank from social contact with the ruder world by which she was now surrounded; she felt and lived like one in exile, and her hope was to return to her native land. In the meantime she was growing pale, languid, morbid, and, occasionally, even irritable, from the lack of proper exercise and change. She was not discouraged as yet, but the day of deliverance seemed to grow more distant. Her father apparently was declining in energy and health, and his income was very small. She worked long hours over her fancy work, but the prices paid for it at the shops were so small that she felt with a growing despondency it was but a precarious means of support. Their first month in the old mansion was drawing to a close, and they had been compelled to draw slightly on the small sum of ready money still remaining after paying for their summer's board. They still had a few articles in storage, having retained them in hope of moving, at no distant time, into more commodious quarters.

In their desire for economy they also fell into the very common error of buying salt fish and meat, and other articles of food that were cheap and easily prepared rather than nutritious, and Belle was inclined to make her lunch on pastry and cake instead of food. In teaching them a better way Mrs. Wheaton proved herself a very useful friend. "Vat yer vant is sumthink that makes blood an' stands by von," she had said; "an' this 'ere salt, dry stuff an' light baker's bread and tea and coffee don't do this hat hall. They's good henough as relishes an' trimmins an' roundins hoff, but they hain't got the nourishin' in 'em that vorking people vants. Buy hoat meal an' corn meal—make good bread of yer hown. Buy good but cheap chunks of beef an' mutton an' wegetables, an' make stews an' meat pies an' rich soups, an' say yer prayers hagainst hall trashy things as hain't vorth the trouble of heatin'. Heggs, too, ven ther're plenty, hare fust-rate, an' milk is better than so much tea an' coffee, heven if the milkman do spill it in the brook an' pick it hout hagain before ve get it. Vorkin' hon tea an' coffee is like keepin' the 'orse hagoin' on a vip hinstead of hoats."

Mrs. Jocelyn and Mildred were sensible enough to take

her advice, and although Belle complained at first over the more simple and wholesome diet, she soon felt so much the better for it that she made no further trouble.

As had been the case at the farmhouse, Mildred at last awakened to the evils of a depressed and sedentary life, and felt that she must look around for objects of interest. She began to spend more time with Mrs. Wheaton, and found considerable amusement in her homely common-sense. The good woman was all the more companionable for the reason that she never presumed on a coarse familiarity or indulged in a prying interest. Mildred also aided the Wheaton children in their lessons, and gave more time to her own little brother and sister, taking them out to walk in the cool of the day, and giving much thought, while she plied her needle, to various little expedients that would keep them content to remain away from the street and the rude children that often made the old house resound with boisterous sport. Mrs. Wheaton's children were in the main well behaved, and there was much visiting back and forth among the little people of the two families, but here the line was drawn, and generally with very good reason. After all, perhaps, the chief horror of tenement life to a family like the Jocelyns consisted in the fact that just outside their door were hordes of prowling little savages ignorant in the main of civilization, but prematurely enlightened as to its vices. To prevent the inevitable contamination which would result from indiscriminate association, and to interest Fred and Minnie in their daily lessons, was the constant effort of both Mildred and Mrs. Jocelyn. And yet, as at the farmhouse, Mildred's conscience began to reproach her for keeping too much aloof from the people who dwelt with her in the old mansion. It was not necessary to make companions of them in order to do them some good, and in aiding them to bear their burdens she might in part forget her own. Mrs. Wheaton's hearty kindness permeated the house like an atmosphere, and from her Mildred learned the character and circumstances of each family quite correctly. "I can get hon with 'em hall hexcept a hold daft German on the top floor, oos a bit crazy hover the 'evens, but don't stand much chance of hever gettin' hup hinto 'em. You've hoften seen 'im a-lookin' at the stars an' things on the roof. 'E 'alf starves 'is family to buy books an' maps an' a telescope. 'E 'ates me cos I tried to talk religion to 'im vonce ven 'e vas sick, an' cos I told 'im 'e 'ad no bizness to take his death a'cold on the roof o' vinter nights; an 'ven 'e vonce gets a grudge hagainst yer 'e never lets hup."

Mildred had already become more interested in this old man than in any other of her neighbors except Mrs. Wheaton, but had found him utterly unapproachable. Not infrequently she spent part of the hot evenings on the platform built over the old hip-roof, and had invariably seen him there on cloudless nights studying the skies with a telescope that appeared to be by no means a toy instrument; but he always took possession of the far end of the platform, and was so savage when any one approached that even Belle was afraid of him. His wife, for a wonder, was a slattern German, and she spoke English very imperfectly. With her several small children she lived in a chaotic way, keeping up a perpetual whining and faultfnding, half under her breath from fear of her irascible husband, that was like a "continual dropping on a very rainy day." Every now and then, Mrs. Wheaton said, he would suddenly emerge from his abstraction and break out against her in a volley of harsh, guttural German oaths that were "henough to make von's 'air riz." Therefore it very naturally happened that Mildred had become acquainted with all the other families before she had even spoken to Mr. or Mrs. Ulph. On the other inmates of the mansion her influence soon began to be felt; for almost unconsciously she exercised her rare and subtle power of introducing a finer element into the lives of those who were growing sordid and material. She had presented several families with a small house-plant, and suggested that they try to develop slips from others that she sedulously tended in her own window. In two or three instances she aided untidy and discouraged women to make their rooms more attractive. The fact, also, that the Jocelyns had made their two apartments, that were little if any better than the others, so very inviting had much weight, and there sprang up quite an emulation among some of the simple folk in making the most of their limited resources.

"Instead of scolding your husbands for going out and perhaps taking a glass too much, try and keep them home by making the living-room homelike," she had said on several occasions to complaining wives who had paved the way by their confidential murmurings. "Have some extra dish that they like for supper—they will spend more if they go out—then be a little smiling and chatty, and tell them to light their pipes and stay with you, for you are a bit lonesome. If they will have their mug of beer, coax them to take it here at home. Try to put a few shillings in the savings bank every week, and talk over little plans of saving more. If you can only make your husbands feel that they are getting ahead a little, it will have a great influence in steadying them and keeping them out of bad company."

Mildred had a genius for everything relating to domestic life, and an almost unbounded belief in good home influences. Although she rarely talked religion directly to the people whom she was trying to benefit—she was much too diffident and self-depreciative for this—her regular attendance at some place of worship on the Sabbath and her course toward poor Mrs. Bute and her daughter had given the impression that she was a very religious girl, and that her motives were Christian in character. People's instincts are quick in discerning the hidden springs of action; and her influence was all the more effective because she gave them the fruits of faith rather than stems of exhortation or which they were required to develop fruit of their own. Much good fruit was eventually produced, but more through her example, her spring-like influence, than from any formal instruction.

CHAPTER XXI

"HE'S A MAN"

MRS. WHEATON, although she had the good taste to ask few questions, was much puzzled over the Jocelyns. Mr. Jocelyn's state of health seemed to her very peculiar, and her shrewd, unprejudiced mind was approaching Roger's conclusion, that he was a little "off." With an insight common to sound, thrifty people, she saw that the outlook for this family was dubious. She believed that the father would become less and less of a reliance, that Mrs. Jocelyn was too delicate to cope with a lower and grimmer phase of poverty, which she feared they could not escape. When alone she often shook her head in foreboding over Belle's brilliant black eyes, being aware from long experience among the poor how dangerous are such attractions, especially when possessed by an impulsive and unbalanced child. She even sighed more deeply and often over Mildred, for she knew well that more truly than any of the house-plants in the window the young girl who cared for them was an exotic that might fade and die in the changed and unfavorable conditions of her present and prospective life. The little children, too, were losing the brown and ruddy hues they had acquired on the Atwood farm, and very naturally chafed over their many and unwonted restrictions.

Nor did the city missionary whom she had called in to attend Mrs. Bute's funeral illumine the Jocelyn problem for the good woman. He was an excellent man, but lamentably deficient in tact, being prone to exhort on the subject of religion in season, and especially out of season, and in much the same way on all occasions. Since the funeral he had called two or three times, and had mildly and rather vaguely harangued Mrs. Jocelyn and Mildred. Instead of echoing his pious platitudes with murmurs of assent and approval, they had been very polite, and also very reticent and distant; and Mr. Woolling—that was his name—had said in confidence to Mrs. Wheaton that "they might be good people, but he fearing they were not yet altogether 'in the light.' They seemed a little cold toward the good cause, and were not inclined to talk freely of their spiritual experiences and relations. Probably it was because they were not altogether orthodox in their views."

It would seem that this worthy person had taken literally the promise of his Master, "I will make you fishers of men," for he was quite content to be a fisher. Let us hope that occasionally, as by a miracle, his lenient Master enabled him to catch some well-disposed sinner; but as a rule his mannerism, his set phrases, his utter lack of magnetism and appreciation of the various shades of character with which he was dealing, repelled even those who respected his motive and mission. Sensitive, sad-hearted women like Mrs. Jocelyn and Mildred could no more open their hearts to him than to a benevolent and impersonal board of trustees sitting around a green baize table. That detestable class, however, who thrive on opening their hearts and dilating on their spiritual experiences, could talk to him, as he would say, in a "most edifying and godly manner," and through him, in consequence, reap all the pecuniary advantages within his power to bestow.

It is not the blatant and plausible poor who suffer, but those who hide their poverty and will starve rather than trade on their faith; and too often Christian and charitable organizations prove they are not the "children of this world" by employing agents so lacking in fitness for the work that a commercial firm, following a like policy, would soon compass its own failure. The Church deserves slight progress if it fails to send its best and most gifted men and women among the poor and vicious. Mr. Woolling was a sincere well-meaning man, but he no more knew how to catch men with a Christ-like magnetism and guile than how to render one of Beethoven's symphonies; and he was so constituted that he could never learn. It was an open question whether he did not do more harm than good; and those who employed him might and ought to have known the fact.

Fortunately for the Jocelyns, there were other workers in that part of the vineyard, and Mrs. Wheaton had said to herself more than once, "Ven my young lady comes 'ome she'll git 'old of these 'ere people and make things better for 'em." One day, about the middle of September, there was a light knock at the door of the large living-room that had been made so inviting. Mildred opened it and admitted a young woman, who appeared not very much older than herself, and who she saw at a glance was of her own class in respect to refinement and cultivation. Although entire strangers, the eyes of the two girls met in woman's intuitive recognition.

"This is Miss Jocelyn, I think," said the visitor in an accent that to the poor girl sounded like her native tongue, so long unheard.

"You are correct," replied Mildred, with exploring eyes and a quiet and distant manner. "Will you please be seated," she added after a moment, as the young lady evidently wished to enter.

It was in the afternoon, and the room had its usual pretty order at that hour. Fred and Minnie were seated by Mrs. Jocelyn, who was giving them their daily lesson from an illustrated primer; and they, with their mother, turned questioning eyes on the unexpected guest, who won their good-will almost instantly by a sunshiny smile. Then turning to Mildred she began, with a quiet, well-bred ease which made her visit seem perfectly natural, "We are now strangers, but I trust we shall not remain such very long.

Indeed, I am already sure that you can help me very much." (This asking help instead of offering it was certainly adroit policy.) "I am a Christian worker in this district. My name is Alice Wetheridge. I am well acquainted with Mrs. Wheaton, and the little she has told me about you has made me wish to know you well; and I trust you will meet me with the spirit in which I come—that of honest friendliness and respect. I shall be just as frank with you as you wish, and I know you have just as much right to your feelings and views as I have to mine. It is our plan of work to co-work cordially, asking each one to choose her own place and kind of effort. I have been around among some of my families in this house, and, if you will permit me to say it, I have seen your influence, and I think it is most Christian and womanly. You can scarcely blame me, then, if I hope to find in you a congenial fellow-worker."

These remarks contained no hint of poverty or inferiority, and might have been made to Mildred in her old home. The sweet, low voice in which they were spoken was soothing and winning, while her visitor's gaze was direct and sincere. Mildred smiled with a little answering friendliness as she said, "Please do not expect much from me. I fear I shall disappoint you."

"I shall not expect anything more than your own feelings prompt and your own conscience can warrant. I and some friends have classes at a mission chapel not far from here, and all I ask at first is that you and Mrs. Jocelyn attend service at the chapel and see how you like us and how you like our minister."

"Is—is his name Mr. Woolling?" faltered Mildred.

A slight, evanescent smile flitted across the visitor's face. "No," she said, "that is not his name. Our minister has just returned from Europe, where he has taken a well-deserved vacation. I, too, have only come in town within the last few days, otherwise I do not think you would have escaped us so long," she concluded, with a bright smile, but after a moment she added earnestly, "Please do not think that we shall try to force upon you associations that may not be pleasant. We only ask that you come and judge for yourselves."

"What you ask is certainly reasonable," said Mildred thoughtfully, and with an inquiring glance at her mother.

"I agree with you, Millie," her mother added with gentle emphasis, for she had been observing their visitor closely; "and I think we both appreciate Miss Wetheridge's motive in calling upon us, and can respond in like spirit."

"I thank you," was the cordial reply. "On this card is written my address and where to find our chapel, the hours of service, etc. Please ask for me next Sabbath afternoon, and I will sit you, so you won't feel strange, you know. After the service is over we will remain a few moments, and I will introduce you to our minister. As I said at first, if you don't like us or our ways you must not feel in the least trammelled. However that may be, I trust you will let me come and see you sometimes. It was my duty to call upon you because you were in my district; but now it will be a pleasure to which I hope you will let me look forward."

"You will be welcome," said Mildred smilingly. "I can at least promise so much."

Miss Wetheridge had slipped off her glove while talking, and in parting she gave a warm, friendly palm to those she wished to win. She had intended only a smiling leave-taking of the children, but they looked so pretty, and were regarding her with such an expression of shy, pleased interest, that she acted on her impulse and kissed them both. "I don't often meet such kissable children," she said, with a bright flush, "and I couldn't resist the temptation."

The room seemed lighter the rest of the day for her visit. If she had kissed the children out of policy Mrs. Jocelyn would have been resentfully aware of the fact; but they *were* "kissable" children, and no one knew it better than the fond mother, who was won completely by the spontaneity of the act.

"Millie, I think I'd go to her church, even if Mr. Woolling were the minister," she said, with her sweet laugh.

"Soft-hearted little mother!" cried Mildred gayly; "if people only knew it, you have one very vulnerable side. That was a master-stroke on the part of Miss Wetheridge."

"She didn't mean it as such, and if some good people had kissed the children I'd have washed their faces as soon as they had gone. The visit has done *you* good, too, Millie."

"Well, I admit it has. It was nice to see and hear one of our own people, and to feel that we were not separated by an impassable gulf. To tell the truth, I feel the need of something outside of this old house. I am beginning to mope and brood. I fear it will be some time before the way opens back to our former life, and one grows sickly if one lives too long in the shade. I *could* work with such a girl as that, for she wouldn't humiliate me. See, her card shows that she lives on Fifth Avenue. If *she* can work in a mission chapel, I can, especially since she is willing to touch me with her glove off," she concluded, with a significant smile.

As the evening grew shadowy Mildred took the children out for their walk, and, prompted by considerable curiosity, she led the way to Fifth Avenue, and passed the door on which was inscribed the number printed on Miss Wetheridge's card. The mansion was as stately and gave as much evidence of wealth as Mrs. Arnold's home. At this moment a handsome carriage drew up to the sidewalk, and Mildred, turning, blushed vividly as she met the eyes of her new acquaintance, who, accompanied by a fashionably-attired young man, had evidently been out to drive. Mildred felt that she had no right to claim recognition, for a young woman making mission calls in her "district" and the same young lady on Fifth Avenue with her financé, very probably, might be, and often are, two very distinct persons. The girl was about to pass on with downcast eyes and a hot face, feeling that her curiosity had been well punished. But she had not taken three steps before a pleasant voice said at her side, "Miss Jocelyn, what have I done that you won't speak to me? This is my home, and I hope you will come and see me some time."

Mildred looked at the speaker searchingly for a moment, and then said, in a low tone and with tearful eyes, "May you never exchange a home like this, Miss Wetheridge, for one like mine."

"Should it be my fortune to do so—and why may it not? —I hope I may accept of my lot with your courage, Miss Jocelyn, and give to my humbler home the same impress of womanly refinement that you have imparted to yours. Believe me, I respected you and your mother thoroughly the moment I crossed your threshold."

"I will do whatever you wish me to do," was her relevant, although seemingly irrelevant, reply.

"That's a very big promise," said Miss Wetheridge vivaciously; "we will shake hands to bind the compact," and her attendant raised his hat as politely as he would to any of his companion's friends.

Mildred went home with the feeling that the leaden monotony of her life was broken. The hand of genuine Christian sympathy, not charity or patronage, had been reached across the chasm of her poverty, and by it she justly hoped that she might be led into new relations that would bring light and color into her shadowed experience.

With her mother and Belle she went to the chapel on the following Sunday afternoon, and found her new friend on the watch for them. The building was plain but substantial, and the audience-room large and cheerful looking. Mr. Woolling was, in truth, not the type of the tall, rugged-featured man who sat on the platform pulpit, and Mildred, at first, was not prepossessed in his favor, but as he rose and began to speak she felt the magnetism of a large heart and brain; and when he began to preach she found herself yielding to the power of manly Christian thought, expressed in honest Saxon words devoid of any trace of affectation, scholasticism, and set phraseology. He spoke as any sensible, practical man would speak concerning a subject in which he believed thoroughly and was deeply interested, and he never once gave the impression that he was "delivering a sermon" which was foreordained to be delivered at that hour. It was a message rather than a sermon, a sincere effort to make the people understand just what God wished them to know concerning the truth under consideration, and especially what they were to do in view of it. The young girl soon reached the conclusion that the religion taught in this chapel was not something fashioned to suit the world, but a controlling principle that brought the rich and poor together in their obedience to Him whose perfect life will ever be the law of the Christian Church. The attention of even mercurial Belle was obtained and held, and at the close of the address she whispered, "Millie, that man talks right to one, and not fifty miles over your head. I'll come here every Sunday if you will."

After the benediction the Rev. Mr. Wentworth came down from the pulpit—not in a bustling, favor-currying style, but with a grave, kindly manner—to speak to those who wished to see him. When he at last reached Mildred, she felt him looking at her in a way that proved he was not scattering his friendly words as a handful of coin is thrown promiscuously to the poor. He was giving thought to her character and need; he was exercising his invaluable but lamentably rare gift of tact in judging how he should address these "new people" of whom Miss Wetheridge had spoken. His words were few and simple, but he made Mrs. Jocelyn and Mildred feel that his interest in them was not official, but genuine, Christian, and appreciative. Belle very naturally shrank into the background. Her acquaintance with clergymen was not extensive, nor would it, I fear, ever have been increased by any efforts of her own; therefore it was with some trepidation that she saw Mr. Wentworth giving her an occasional side glance while talking to her mother.

She was about to bow very formally when introduced, but a smile broke over the man's rugged features like a glow of sunshine, as he held out his hand and said, "Miss Belle, I know you and I would be good friends if we had a chance."

The girl's impulsive nature responded as if touched by an electric spark, and with her usual directness the words in her mind were spoken. "I like you already," she said.

"The liking is mutual then," was Mr. Wentworth's laughing reply; "I'm coming to see you."

"But, sir," stammered the honest child, "I'm not good like my sister."

The clergyman now laughed heartily. "All the more reason I should come," he said.

"Well, then, please come in the evening, for I wouldn't miss your visit for the world."

"I certainly shall," and he named an evening early in the week; "and now," he resumed, "my friend Miss Wetheridge here has informed me of the conditions on which you have visited our chapel. We propose to carry them out in good faith, and not put any constraint upon you beyond a cordial invitation to cast your lot with us. It's a great thing to have a church home. You need not feel that you must decide at once, but come again and again, and perhaps by and by you will have a home feeling here."

"I'm coming whether the rest do or not," Belle remarked emphatically, and Mr. Wentworth gave her a humorous look which completed the conquest of her heart.

"Miss Wetheridge knows that my decision was already made," said Mildred quietly, with an intelligent glance toward her friend; "and if there is any very, very simple work that I can do, I shall feel it a privilege to do the best I can."

She never forgot his responsive look of honest friendliness as he answered, "The simplest work you do in that spirit will be blessed. Miss Wetheridge, I hope you will soon find some more people like Mrs. Jocelyn and her daughters. Good-by now for a short time," and a moment later Mildred saw him talking just as kindly, but differently, to a very shabby-looking man.

Mr. Wentworth was also a "fisher of men," but he fished intelligently, and caught them.

Belle could hardly wait until she was in the street before exclaiming, "He isn't a bit like our old minister. Why —why—he's a man."

CHAPTER XXII

SKILLED LABOR

MISS WETHERIDGE'S visit bade fair to occasion important changes for the better in Mildred's prospects. From Mrs. Wheaton the young lady had learned of her *protegce's* long hours of ill-repaid toil. She was eager to gain Mildred's confidence to an extent that would warrant some good advice, and after another call early in the week she induced the girl to come and see her and to open her heart fully in the privacy thus secured. Of course there was one secret jealously guarded, and the reader can well understand that Vinton Arnold's name was not mentioned, and the disagreeable episode of Roger Atwood was not deemed worth speaking of. He was now but a fast-fading memory, for even Belle rarely recalled him.

That the Jocelyns did not belong to the ordinary ranks of the poor, and that Mildred was not a commonplace girl, was apparent to Miss Wetheridge from the first; and it was her design to persuade her friend to abandon the overcrowded and ill-paid divisions of labor for something more in accordance with her cultivation and ability. Mildred soon proved that her education was too general and superficial to admit of teaching except in the primary departments, and as the schools were now in session it might be many months before any opening would occur. With a mingled sigh and laugh she said, "The one thing I know how to do I shall probably never do—I could make a home, and I could be perfectly happy in taking care of it."

"Pardon me!" cried Miss Wetheridge roguishly, "that

seems to me your inevitable fate, sooner or later. We are only counselling together how best to fill up the interval. My friend almost made me jealous by the way he talked about you the other evening."

A faint color stole into Mildred's face. "All that's past, I fear," she said with low, sad emphasis, "and I would never marry merely for the sake of a home. My future is that of a working-woman unless papa can regain his former means. Even then I should not like to live an idle life. So the question is, What kind of work shall I do? How can I do the most for the family, for I am troubled about papa's health, and mamma is not strong."

Her warm-hearted friend's eyes grew moist as she looked intently and understandingly into the clouded and beautiful face. In one of her pretty impulses that often broke through her polite restraint she exclaimed, "Millie, you are a true woman. Please pardon my familiarity, but I can't tell you how much you interest me, how I respect you, and —and—how much I like you."

"Nor can I tell you," responded Mildred earnestly, "how much hope and comfort you have already brought me."

"Come," said Miss Wetheridge cheerily, "we will go down to the rooms of the Young Women's Christian Association at once. We may get light there. The thing for you to do is to master thoroughly one or more of the higher forms of labor that are as yet uncrowded. That is what I would do."

While she was preparing for the street she observed Mildred's eyes resting wistfully on an upright piano that formed part of the beautiful furniture of her private sanctum. "You are recognizing an old friend and would like to renew your acquaintance," she said smilingly. "Won't you play while I am changing my dress?"

"Perhaps I can best thank you in that way," answered Mildred, availing herself of the permission with a pleasure she could not disguise. "I admit that the loss of my piano has been one of my greatest deprivations."

Miss Wetheridge's sleeping-apartment opened into her sitting-room, and, with the door open, it was the same as if they were still together. The promise of thanks was well kept as the exquisite notes of Mendelssohn's "Hope" and "Consolation" filled the rooms with music that is as simple and enduring as the genuine feeling of a good heart.

"I now understand how truly you lost a friend and companion in your piano," said Miss Wetheridge, "and I want you to come over here and play whenever you feel like it, whether I am at home or not."

Mildred smiled, but made no reply. She could accept kindness and help from one who gave them as did Miss Wetheridge, but she was too proud and sensitive to enter upon an intimacy that must of necessity be so one-sided in its favors and advantages, and she instinctively felt that such wide differences in condition would lead to mutual embarrassments that her enthusiastic friend could not foresee. It was becoming her fixed resolve to accept her lot, with all that it involved, and no amount of encouragement could induce her to renew associations that could be enjoyed now only through a certain phase of charity, however the fact might be disguised. But she would rather reveal her purpose by the retiring and even tenor of her way than by any explanations of her feelings. Thus it came about in the future that Miss Wetheridge made three calls, at least, to one that she received, and that in spite of all she could do Mildred shrank from often meeting other members of her family. But this sturdy self-respect on the part of the young girl—this resolute purpose not to enter a social circle where she would at least fear patronage and surprise at her presence—increased her friend's respect in the secrecy of her heart.

Mildred at once became a member of the Young Women's Association, and its library and reading-room promised to become a continued means of pleasure and help. From among the several phases of skilled labor taught under the auspices of the Association, she decided to choose the highest—that of stenography—if her father thought he could support the family without much help for a few months. She was already very rapid and correct in her penmanship, and if she could become expert in taking shorthand notes she was assured that she could find abundant and highly remunerative scope for her skill, and under circumstances, too, that would not involve unpleasant publicity. She thought very favorably, also, of the suggestion that she should join the bookkeeping class. With her fine mental capacity and previous education Miss Wetheridge believed that Mildred could so far master these two arts as to be sure of an independence, and her kind friend proposed to use no little influence in finding opportunities for their exercise.

Mildred, naturally, lost no time in explaining her projects to her father, and it so happened that she spoke at a moment of peculiar exhilaration on his part. "If it would give you pleasure," he said, "to learn these two accomplishments, you may do so, of course, but I foresee no probability of your ever putting them to use. I now have prospects," etc., etc. Soon after, he was in a deep sleep. She looked at him with troubled eyes, and promptly entered on her studies the following day, working with the assiduity of one who feels that the knowledge may be needed before it can be acquired.

Belle was in quite a flutter of excitement on the evening named for Mr. Wentworth's visit, and the genial clergyman would have laughed again could he have heard one of her reasons for welcoming him. "He is so deliciously homely," she said, "I like to look at him." He came at the hour appointed, and his visit was truly a "spiritual" one, if enlivened spirits, more hopeful hearts, and a richer belief in their Divine Father's goodwill toward them all were the legitimate result of a spiritual visit. Mr. Jocelyn, in expectancy of the guest, had carefully prepared himself in guilty secrecy, and appeared unusually well, but he was the only one who sighed deeply after the good man's departure. Rising from the depths of his soul through his false exhilaration was a low, threatening voice, saying, "That man is true; you are a sham, and your hollowness will become known."

Indeed, Mr. Wentworth went away with a vague impression that there was something unreal or unsound about Mr. Jocelyn, and he began to share Mrs. Wheaton's painful forebodings for the family. Belle enjoyed the visit greatly, for the minister was an apostle of a very sunny gospel, and she was then ready for no other. Moreover, the healthful, unwarped man delighted in the girl's frolicsome youth, and no more tried to repress her vivacity than he would the bubble and sparkle of a spring. Indeed he was sensible enough to know that, as the spring keeps pure by flowing and sparkling into the light, so her nature would stand a far better chance of remaining untainted if given abundant yet innocent scope. His genial words had weight with her, but her quick intuition of his sympathy, his sense of humor, which was as genuine as her own, had far more weight, and their eyes rarely met without responsive smiles. There was nothing trivial, however, in their interplay of mirthfulness—nothing that would prevent the child from coming to him should her heart become burdened with sin or sorrow. She was assigned to Miss Wetheridge's class, and soon became warmly attached to her teacher. Mildred, to her great surprise, was asked to take a class of rude-looking, half-grown boys. In answer to her look of dismay, Mr. Wentworth only said smilingly, "Try it; trust my judgment; you can do more with those boys than I can."

"Were it not for my promise to Miss Wetheridge, I shouldn't even dare think of such a thing," she replied; "but I now feel bound to attempt it, although I hope you will soon give me some very, very little girls."

"In complying you show a high sense of honor, Miss Jocelyn. I will relieve you after a time, if you wish me to," and the student of human nature walked away with a peculiar smile. "When I was a harum-scarum boy," he muttered, "a girl with such a face could almost make me worship her. I don't believe boys have changed."

She was shrewd enough not to let the class see that she was afraid; and being only boys, they saw merely what was apparent—that they had the prettiest teacher in the room. Her beauty and refinement impressed them vaguely, yet powerfully; the incipient man within them yielded its involuntary homage, and she appealed to their masculine traits as only a woman of tact can, making them feel that it would be not only wrong but ungallant and unmannerly to take advantage of her. They all speedily succumbed except one, whose rude home associations and incorrigible disposition rendered futile her appeals. After two or three Sabbaths the other boys became so incensed that he should disgrace the class that after school they lured him into an alleyway and were administering a well-deserved castigation, when Mildred, who was passing, rescued him. His fear induced him to yield to her invitation to accompany her home; and her kindness, to which he knew he was not entitled, combined with the wholesome effect of the pummelling received from the boys, led him to unite in making the class—once known as "the Incorrigibles"—the best behaved in the school.

Everything apparently now promised well for the Jocelyns. Their mistaken policy of seclusion and shrinking from contact with the world during their impoverishment had given way to kindly Christian influences, and they were forming the best associations their lot permitted. All might have gone to their ultimate advantage had it not been for the hidden element of weakness so well known to the reader, but as yet unsuspected by the family.

If Mr. Jocelyn had been able to put forth the efforts of a sound and rational man, he could, with the aid of his daughters, even in those times of depression, have passed safely through the trials of sudden poverty, and eventually—having learned wisdom from the past experience—he could have regained a better and more stable financial position than the one lost. Thus far he had been able to maintain considerable self-control, and by daily experience knew just about how much morphia he could take without betraying himself. His family had become accustomed to its effects, and ascribed them to the peculiar state of his health. Loving eyes are often the most blind, and that which is seen daily ceases to seem strange. Beyond their natural solicitude over his failing appetite, his unwholesome complexion, and his loss of flesh, they had no misgivings. His decline was so very gradual that there was nothing to startle them. Every day they hoped to see a change for the better, and sought to bring it about by preparing such dainty dishes as were within their means to catch his capricious appetite, and by keeping all their little perplexities and worriments to themselves, so that he might have unbroken rest when free from business. He recognized their unselfish and considerate devotion, and it added to the horrible depression into which he sank more and more deeply the moment he passed from under the influence of the fatal drug. He was living over an abyss, and that which kept him from its depths was deepening and widening it daily. He still had the vague hope that at some time and in some way he could escape; but days and weeks were passing, bringing no change for the better, no honest, patient effort to regain the solid ground of safety. He was drifting down, and when at times he became conscious of the truth, a larger dose of morphia was his one method of benumbing the terror that seemed groping for his heart with a death-cold hand.

Mildred soon began to make rapid progress in her studies, and grew hopeful over the fact. If her father would give her the chance she could make a place for herself among skilled workers within a year, and be able, if there were need, to provide for the entire family. Great and prolonged destitution rarely occurs, even in a crowded city, unless there is much sickness or some destructive vice. Wise economy, patient and well-directed effort, as a rule, secure comfort and independence, if not affluence; but continued illness, disaster, and especially sin, often bring with them a train of evils difficult to describe.

Mildred found time between her lessons to aid her mother and also to do a little fancy work, for which, through the aid of Miss Wetheridge, she found private customers who were willing to pay its worth.

Thus the month of October was passing rapidly and rather hopefully away. They received letters from Clara Bute occasionally, wherein she expressed herself well content with the country and the situation Mrs. Atwood had obtained for her. "I'm getting as plump and rosy as Susan," she wrote, "and I'm not coming back to town. Going up and down those tenement stairs tired me more than all the work I do here. Still, I work hard, I can tell you; but it's all sorts of work, with plenty of good air and good food to do it on. I'm treted better than I ever was before—just like one of the family, and there's a young farmer who takes me out to ride sometimes, and he acts and talks like a man."

Whether this attentive friend were Roger or a new acquaintance she did not say. For some reason a reticence in regard to the former characterized her letters.

CHAPTER XXIII

THE OLD ASTRONOMER

ONE Saturday night Mildred was awakened from time to time by the wailing of a child. The sounds came from the rooms of the Ulphs, which were directly overhead, and by morning she was convinced that there was a case of serious illness in the German family. Led by her sympathies, and also by the hope of thawing the reserve of the eccentric old astronomer, she resolved to go and ask if she could be of any help.

In response to her light knock a shock-headed, unkempt boy opened the door and revealed a state of chaos that might well have driven mad any student of the heavenly bodies with their orderly ways. There seemed to be one place for everything—the middle of the floor—and about everything was in this one place. In the midst of a desolation anything but picturesque, Mrs. Ulph sat before the fire with a little moaning baby upon her lap.

"I heard your child crying in the night," said Mildred gently, "and as we are neighbors I thought I would come up and see if I could help you."

The woman stared a moment and then asked, "You Miss Schoslin?"

"Yes, and I hope you will let me do something, for I fear you've been up all night and must be very tired."

"I'm shust dead; not von vink of schleep haf I had all der night. He shust cry und cry, and vat I do I don't know. I fear he die. Der fader gone for der doctor, but he die 'fore dey gets here. Schee, he getten gold now."

Truly enough, the child's extremities were growing chill indeed, and the peculiar pinched look and ashen color which is so often the precursor of death was apparent.

"Let me call my mother," cried Mildred, in much alarm. "She knows about children."

Mrs. Jocelyn soon became convinced from the mother's account that the child's disease was cholera infantum, and some previous experience with her own children taught her just what to do. Before very long the little one gave evidence of a change for the better. After the crisis of danger was past, and while her mother and Mrs. Ulph were working over the infant, Mildred began quietly to put the room into something like order, and to dress the other children that were in various transition stages between rags and nakedness. As the German woman emerged from a semi-paralyzed condition of alarm over her child she began to talk and complain as usual.

"It vas von shudgment on der fader," she said querulously. "He care more for der schpots on der sun dan for his schilder. For der last veek it's all peen schpots on der sun, notting put schpots. Vat goot dey do us? Dare's peen light to vork py, put efry minit he schtop vork to run to der roof und see dem schpots vot he says on der sun. He says dere ish—vat you call him—pig virl-a-rounds up dere dat vould plow all der beoples off der earth in von vink, und ven I tells him dat he ish von pig virl-a-round himself, runnin' und runnin', und lettin' der vork schstand, den von of der schpots come outen on him und I dink he plow my hed offen."

By and by she began again: "If it ish not schpots it ish someding else. Von year he feel vorse dan if I die pegose vat you call a gomet did not gome ven he said it vould gome. He near look his eyes outen for it, und he go efry morning 'fore preakfast for der bapers to get vord of dat gomet. I dought ve all schtarve 'fore he got done mit dot gomet, and ven he give oup all hope of him, he feel vorse dan he vould if dis schild die. He vas so pad to me as if I eat der gomet oup, und ve had not mooch else to eat till he sure der gomet gone to der duyvil. It might haf been vorse if der gomet come; vat he done den der goot Lord only know—he go off mit it if he gould. He tink notting of sittin' oup mit a gomet, put he get der schpots on him ven I ask to nurse der schild in der night."

Mrs. Jocelyn and Mildred paid little attention to her plaints; and the former, having done what she could, returned to her own family cares. Mildred took the little sick boy in her arms, saying that she would hold him while Mrs. Ulph prepared breakfast.

It was at this stage of affairs that the door opened, and the pinched and grizzled visage of Mr. Ulph appeared, followed by the burly form of a German physician whom he had insisted on finding. The former stopped short and stared at Mildred, in grim hesitation whether he should resent an intrusion or acknowledge a kindness. His wife explained rapidly in German, with a deferential manner, but in a sub-acidulous tone.

"I do not wish to intrude, but only to help as a neighbor should," Mildred began, during a lull between Mrs. Ulph's shrill notes. "I fear your little boy was very ill when I first came—indeed my mother thought he was dying. She knows, I think, for my little brother nearly died of an attack like this."

Beyond her explanation of Mildred's presence he seemingly had given no heed to his wife's words, but now he started and exclaimed, "Mein Gott! Vat you say? Die?" and he turned with intense anxiety to the doctor, who without ceremony began to investigate the case, asking the mother questions and receiving answers that Mildred did not understand. The woman evidently claimed all the credit she deserved for her care of the patient in the night, and suggested that Mr. Ulph had been very oblivious until the child seemed sinking, for the old man grew excessively impatient during the interrogations. As if unconscious of Mildred's ignorance of their language, he said earnestly to her, "I did not know—I vould gif my life for der schild—der boor leedle poy—I no dink dat he vas so sick," and his eager words and manner convinced Mildred that his wife misrepresented him, and that his interest in the mystery of the comet's fate would be slight compared with that which centred in his son.

The phlegmatic physician continued his investigations with true German thoroughness and deliberation. It was well that the child's worst symptoms had been relieved before he came, for he seemed bent on having the whole history of the case down to the latest moment before he extended his heavy hand to the aid of nature, and he questioned Mildred as minutely as he had Mrs. Ulph, while she, unlike the former, did not take any credit to herself.

If the doctor was a little slow, he was sure, for he said something emphatically to the father, who in turn seized Mildred's hand, exclaiming, with explosive energy, "Gott pless you! Gott pless you!"

"But it was mamma who did everything," protested the young girl.

"Yah, I know, I know; put who prought mamma? Who listen ven der boor leetle poy gry in der night? Who gome in der morning? Mine paby vould haf been ded if you haf not gome. Gott pless you; Gott pless your moder. I vant to dank her mooch."

The grateful father had called down God's blessings so lavishly that Mildred very naturally said, "You have more reason to thank God than any one else, Mr. Ulph, for no doubt it was His blessing on our efforts that has made your child better. The disease is such a dangerous one that the best human skill is often in vain."

The physician shrugged his shoulders and looked significantly at Mr. Ulph, whose visage wrinkled into an odd grimace.

"You may dink vat you please and say vat you please, Miss Schoslin. Men dink different off dese dinks vrom vomans. I haf a vay off saying Gott pless beoples ven I feels goot dowards 'em, put I means 'em no harm. Vat you American beoples somedimes say—dank my schtars? Dat will do shust so vell for me. It vas dis vay: der schild vas seek; you und your moder gome, und you make gauses und dere are der evvects. I perlieve in gause und evvect, und you vas a very goot gause."

"We certainly should be very poor neighbors had we not come and done all we could, and with your permission mother and I will help your wife to-day so she can get some rest."

"I dank you vrom mine heart. You make me dink off der heafenly podies—you make order put no noise. I vill do for you vatefer you vish und pe honest."

Mildred now believed that she had gained the key to the old German's character, and such a hold upon his feelings that he would eventually permit her to become his companion in his star-gazing on the roof. Denied so much of the beauty she craved on the earth, she believed that she could find in an intelligent study of the skies a pleasure that would prove an antidote for the depressing circumstances of her lot. She had often longed with intense curiosity to look through his telescope, and to penetrate some of the bright mysteries that glittered above her with such tantalizing suggestion. She was adroit, however, and determined that the invitation should come unsolicited from him, so that his suspicions and cynical nature could give no sinister interpretation to her kindness.

The physician evidently shared in Mr. Ulph's estimate of the mother of the child, for he explained to Mildred how the remedies he left should be used. She and Mrs. Jocelyn acted as nurse most of the day, and the patient improved steadily. After her return from the chapel in the afternoon, Mildred found the old German smoking his pipe in quite a placid mood, and she skilfully led him to talk on his favorite theme. He soon became so interested and so confidential that he unlocked a small, closet-like room and showed her his treasures—the telescope and other instruments, Argelander's maps, and many books written by the most eminent authorities.

"I haf gone mitout mine dinner many und many der day to puy dese. Mine pody schtays in dis hole in dis old house, put mit dese vat I gather since ven I vas young, I go to heafen every night. Hah, hah, hah! dot Engleesh voman on der virst vloor dink she know a petter vay off going to heafen; und she dalk her reeleegious schargon to me, ven she know notting at all put vat der briests dell her. If dey dell her de moon von pig green scheese she swar it ish so; put dese dings dell der druf, und der great laws vork on for efer no matter vat voolish beoples perlieve. It vas all law und vorce, und it vould be von pig muddle in der heafens if it vas all vat der briests say."

Mildred was in a dilemma, for she felt that she could not be silent under his outspoken scepticism, and yet if she revealed her mind she doubted whether there would be any result except the alienation of the man whose friendship she was bent on securing. After a moment's hesitation she saw but one honorable course, and so said firmly, "Mr. Ulph, I believe you are an honest man, but I want you to think of me as an honest girl, also. If I wanted to know about astronomy—and I do want to know very much—I would come to you. If I wanted to know about some other things I would go to my minister. I believe in law as truly as you do, but I believe God made the laws—that they are simply His will. If I respect your unbelief, you must respect my faith—that is fair; and I think you are one who would deal fairly and do justice to all. Mrs. Wheaton knows little of astronomy and many other things, no doubt, but she has known how to be a very kind, good neighbor to us, and her religion is mine."

The old German stared at her a moment, then scratched his head as he replied, half apologetically and half pityingly, "You vas notting put a leedle schild, put you haf a goot heart. You vas honest, und you schtands oop vor your vriends, und I likes dot. You may perlieve all der vables you vish; und I vill dells you more vables apout der schtars dat ish shust so goot und shust so old."

"But you will tell me the truth about them, too, won't you?" pleaded Mildred, with a smile that would have thawed a colder nature than Mr. Ulph's. "I want to learn a wee bit of what you know. I have so little that is bright and pretty in my life now that I just long to catch some glimpses of what you see in the skies. Perhaps I could help you by writing down your observations. I would ask questions only when you said I might."

"Vell, now, dot's a good idea. Mine eyes vas getten old, und you vas young, put it von't last; you vas a young ding, und girls vas vlighty and vant—vat you call him?—peaux und vrolics ven der nights vas goot and glear."

"Try me," said Mildred, with a little emphatic nod.

"Vell, you don't seem likes von silly girl, und I vill dry you; put you moost pe very schteady und batient, und but down shust vhat I say. Von leedle schlip, und I vas all vrong in mine vigures. Von preadth off hair down here ish oh—so vide oop dere. Und now, gome, I tells you apout der schpots—der sun schpots," and with many odd gesticulations and contortions of his quaint visage he described the terrific cyclones that were sweeping over the surface of the sun at that time, and whose corresponding perturbations in the astronomer's mind had so exasperated his wife. She and the sick child were now sleeping, and the other children, warned by the threatening finger of the father, played quietly in a corner. It was an odd place to conjure up images of whirling storms of fire so appallingly vast that the great earth, if dropped into one of them, would be fused instantly like a lump of ore in a blast furnace; but the grotesque little man was so earnest, so uncouth, yet forcible, in his suggestions as he whirled his arms around to indicate the vast, resistless sweep of the unimaginable forces working their wild will millions of miles away, that their truth and reality grew painfully vivid to the young girl, and she trembled and shuddered. The roar of the wildest storm, he told her, and the bellowing of mountainous waves combined, would be but a murmur compared with the far-reaching thunder of a sun hurricane as it swept along hundreds of times faster than clouds are ever driven by an earthly tornado. There was nothing in her nature which led her to share in his almost fierce delight in the far-away disturbances, and he suddenly stopped and said kindly, "Vy I vrighten you mit sooch pig gommotions? You shust von leedle schild off a voman; und I likes you pegause you haf prain so you see und know vat I say. You see him too mooch, und so you dremble. Dot's goot. If you vas silly you vould giggle. Der schpots ish a goot way offen, und vill nefer virl you away; und next dime I dells you someding schmooth und britty."

Mildred was glad to hasten through the gathering dusk to her own natural and homelike abode, for the old man's strong descriptions and vivid manner had oppressed her with a vague terror, and it was a long time before she could escape from the spell of his words. Indeed they followed her into her dreams, and in one of these dreadful visions she imagined herself shot by the old astronomer through his telescope straight into the centre of a "sun schpot." Whom should she find there in her uncurbed imagination but Roger Atwood? He seemed to be standing still, and he coolly remarked that "a man had no business to be whirled about by any force in the universe." She, however, was carried millions of miles away—a fact she did not so much regret, even in her dream, since he was left behind.

CHAPTER XXIV

ROGER REAPPEARS

ROGER ATWOOD had entered Mildred's mind as a part of a grotesque dream, but he had no place in her waking thoughts. With Vinton Arnold, however, it was very different, and scarcely an hour passed that she was not wondering where he was, and again questioning his prolonged silence. Often her heart beat quick as she imagined she caught a glimpse of him in the street; and it must be admitted that she looked for him constantly, although she took pains never to pass his residence. Could he be ill, or was he patiently waiting like herself, secure in her good faith? She longed to see him, even though unseen herself, and one Sunday early in November she yielded to her strong desire to look upon one in reality who had become an abiding presence in her mind. She believed that from a certain part of the gallery in the church they both had attended in former days she could look down upon the Arnold pew. If he were not ill she felt quite sure he would be in his old place.

It was almost with a sense of guilty intrusion that she crossed the threshold of her old church-home and stole to the thinly occupied gallery. She saw familiar faces, but shrank from recognition in almost trembling apprehension, scarcely feeling secure behind her thick veil. The place, once so familiar, now seemed as strange as if it belonged to another world; and in a certain sense she felt that it was part of a world with which she would never willingly identify herself again. It was a place where fashion was supreme, and not the spirit of Christ, not even the spirit of a broad, honest, and earnest humanity. The florid architecture, the high-priced and elegantly upholstered pews, sparsely occupied by people who never wished to be crowded under any possible circumstances, and preferred not to touch each other except in a rather distant and conventional way, the elaborately ritualistic service, and the cold, superficial religious philosophy taught, were all as far removed from the divine Son of Mary as the tinsel scenery of a stage differs from a natural landscape. Mildred's deep and sorrowful experience made its unreality painfully apparent and unsatisfactory. She resolved, however, to try to give the sacred words that would be uttered their true meaning; and, in fact, her sincere devotion was like a simple flower blooming by the edge of a glacier. She felt that the human love she brought there and sought to gratify was pure and unselfish, and that in no sense could it be a desecration of the place and hour. To a nature like hers, her half-pitying love for one so unfortunate as Vinton Arnold was almost as sacred as her faith, and therefore she had no scruple in watching for his appearance.

Her quest was unrewarded, however, for no one entered the pew except Mr. Arnold and one of his daughters. The absence of Mrs. Arnold and the invalid son filled her with forebodings and the memory of the past; the influence of the place combined with her fears was so depressing that by the time the service ended her tears were falling fast behind her veil. With natural apprehension that her emotion might be observed she looked hastily around, and, with a start, encountered the eyes of Roger Atwood. Her tears seemed to freeze on her cheeks, and she half shuddered in strong revulsion of feeling. She had come to see the man she loved; after months of patient waiting she had at last so far yielded to the cravings of her heart as to seek but a glimpse of one who fed her dearest earthly hope; but his place is vacant. In his stead she finds, almost at her side, one whom she hoped never to see again; and she knew he was offering through his dark eyes a regard loathed in her inmost soul. She was oppressed with a sudden, superstitious fear that she could not escape him—that he was endowed with such a remorseless will and persistence that by some strange necessity she might yield in spite of herself. Belle's words, "He'll win you yet," seemed like a direful prophecy. How it could ever be fulfilled she could not imagine; but his mere presence caused a flutter of fear, and the consciousness that she was followed by a man preeminently gifted with that subtle power before which most obstacles crumble made her shiver with an undefined dread.

She believed her veil had been no protection—that he had seen her emotion and divined its cause, indeed that nothing could escape his eyes. She also felt sure that he had come to the city to carry out the projects which he had vaguely outlined to her, and that henceforth she could never be sure, when away from home, that his searching eyes were not upon her. However well-intentioned his motive might be, to her it would be an odious system of espionage. There was but one way in which she could resent it—by a cold and steadily maintained indifference, and she left the church without any sign of recognition, feeling that her lowered veil should have taught him that she was shunning observation, and that he had no right to watch her. She went home not only greatly depressed, but incensed, for it was the same to her as if she had been intruded upon at a moment of sacred privacy, and coldly scrutinized while she was giving way to feelings that she would hide from all the world. That he could not know this, and that it was no great breach of delicacy for a young man to sit in the same church with a lady of his acquaintance, and even to regard her with sympathy, she did not consider. She was in no mood to do him justice, and circumstances had imbued her mind with intense prejudice. She was by no means perfect, nor above yielding to very unjust prejudices when tempted to them by so unwelcome an interest as that entertained by Roger Atwood.

"What's the matter, Millie?" her mother asked, following her into her room where Belle was writing a letter to Clara Bute.

Mildred concluded to tell all, for she feared Roger might soon appear and occasion awkward explanations, so she said, "I felt, this morning, like having a glimpse of our old church and life. I suppose it was very weak and foolish and I was well punished, for toward the end of the service I was thinking over old times, and it all very naturally brought some tears. I looked around, and who, of all others, should be watching me but Roger Atwood!"

Belle sprang up and clapped her hands with a ringing laugh. "That's capital," she cried. "Didn't I tell you, Millie, you couldn't escape him? You might just as well give in first as last."

"Belle," said Mildred, in strong irritation, "that kind of talk is unpardonable. I won't endure it, and if such nonsense is to be indulged in Roger Atwood cannot come here. I shall at least have one refuge, and will not be persecuted in my own home."

"Belle," added Mrs. Jocelyn gravely, "since Mildred feels as she does, you must respect her feelings. It would be indelicate and unwomanly to do otherwise."

"There, Millie, I didn't mean anything," Belle said, soothingly. "Besides I want Roger to come and see us, for he can be jolly good company if he has a mind to; and I believe he will come this afternoon or evening. For my sake you must all treat him well, for I want some one to talk to once in a while—some one that mamma will say is a 'good, well-meaning young man.' The Atwoods have all been so kind to us that we must treat him well. It would be mean not to do so. No doubt he's all alone in the city, too, and will be lonely."

"There is no need of his being in the city at all," Mildred protested. "I've no patience with his leaving those who need him so much. I think of them, and am sure they feel badly about it, and likely enough are blaming me, when, if I had my way, he'd live and die in sight of his own chimney smoke."

"Millie, you are unreasonable," retorted Belle. "Why hasn't Roger Atwood as good a right to seek his fortune out in the world as other young men? Papa didn't stay on the old plantation, although they all wanted him to. What's more, he has as good a right to like you as you have to dislike him. I may as well say it as think it."

It was difficult to refute Belle's hard common-sense, and her sister could only protest, "Well, he has no right to be stealthily watching me, nor to persecute me with unwelcome attentions."

"Leave it all to me, Millie," said her mother gently. "I will manage it so that Belle can have his society occasionally, and we show our goodwill toward those who have been kind to us. At the same time I think I can shield you from anything disagreeable. He is pretty quick to take a hint; and you can soon show him by your manner that you wish him well, and that is all. He'll soon get over his half-boyish preference, or at least learn to hide it. You give to his feelings more importance than they deserve."

"I suppose I do," Mildred replied musingly, "but he makes upon me the queer impression that he will never leave me alone—that I can never wholly shake him off, and that he will appear like a ghost when I least expect it."

Belle smiled significantly. "There, you might as well speak plainly as look in that way," Mildred concluded irritably. "I foresee how it will be, but must submit and endure as best I can, I suppose."

Belle's anticipation proved correct, for just as they were nearly ready to start for the chapel Roger appeared, and was a little awkward from diffidence and doubt as to his reception. Mrs. Jocelyn's kindness and Belle's warm greeting somewhat reassured him, and atoned for Mildred's rather constrained politeness. While answering the many and natural questions about those whom he had left in Forestville, he regained his self-possession and was able to hold his own against Belle's sallies. "You have come to the city to stay?" she asked, point-blank.

"Yes," he said briefly, and that was the only reference he made to himself.

She soon began vivaciously, "You must go with us to church and Sunday-school. Here you are, an innocent and unprotected youth in this great wicked city, and we must get you under good influence at once."

"That is my wish," he replied, looking her laughingly in the face, "and that is why I came to see you. If you have a class and will take me into it, I will accept all the theology you teach me."

"Mr. Wentworth's hair would rise at the idea of my teaching theology or anything; but I'll look after you, and if you get any fast ways I'll make you sorry. No, I'm only a scholar. Millie has a class of the worst boys in school, and if—" A warning glance here checked her.

"Well, then, can't I join your class?"

"Oh, no, we are all girls, and you'll make us so bashful we wouldn't dare say anything."

"I think Mr. Atwood had better go with us to the chapel, accepting the conditions on which we first attended," suggested Mrs. Jocelyn. "If he is pleased, as we were, he can then act accordingly."

"Yes, come," cried Belle, who had resumed at once her old companionable and mirthful relations with Roger. "I'll go with you, so you won't feel strange or afraid. I want you to understand," she continued, as they passed down the quaint old hallway, "that we belong to the aristocracy. Since this is the oldest house in town, we surely should be regarded as one of the old families."

"By what magic were you able to make so inviting a home in such a place?" he asked.

"Oh, that's Millie's work," she replied.

"I might have known that," he said, and a sudden shadow crossed his face. Quickly as it passed away, she saw it.

"Yes, ' she resumed in a low, earnest tone—for she had no scruple in fanning the flame of his love which she more than half believed might yet be rewarded—"Millie is one of a million. She will be our main dependence, I fear. She is so strong and sensible."

"Is—is not Mr. Jocelyn well?" he asked apprehensively.

"I fear he isn't well at all," she answered with some despondency. "He is sleeping now; he always rests Sunday afternoon, and we try to let him rest all he can. He sleeps, or rather dozes, a great deal, and seems losing his strength and energy," and she spoke quite frankly concerning their plans, projects, and hopes. She believed in Roger, and knew him to be a sincere friend, and it was her nature to be very outspoken where she had confidence. "If Millie can learn thoroughly what she is now studying," she concluded, "I think we can get along."

"Yes," said Roger, in low, sad emphasis, "your sister is indeed one of a million, and my chance of winning one friendly thought from her also seems but one in a million. Belle, let us understand each other from the start. I have come to the city to stay, and I intend to succeed. I have an uncle in town who has given me a chance, and he'll do more for me, I think. He's peculiar, but he's shrewd and sensible, and when he is convinced that I intend to carry out certain plans he will aid me. He is watching me now, and thinks I am here only from a restless impulse to see the world; by and by he will know better. He has the obstinate Atwood blood, and if he takes a notion to give me a chance to get a first-class education, he will see me through. I'm going to have one anyway, but of course I'd rather be able to get it in five or six years than in eight or ten years, as would be the case if I had to work my own way. I am now employed in his commission store down town, but I am studying every spare moment I can get, and he knows it, only he thinks it won't last. But it will, and I shall at least try to be one of the first lawyers in this city. What's more, I shall work as few young men are willing to work or can work, for I am strong, and—well, I have motives for work that are not usual, perhaps. You see I am frank with you as you have been with me. You often talk like a gay child, but I understand you well enough to know that you are a whole-souled little woman, and thoroughly worthy of trust; and I have told you more about myself and present plans than any one else. Clara Bute informed me all about your courage at the store, and I felt proud that I knew you, and don't intend that you shall ever be ashamed of me. You may tell your mother all this if you please, because I wish her to know just what kind of a young fellow I am, and what are my connections and prospects. I would much like to come and see you and go out with you now and then; and if you and your—well, your family should ever need any service that it was in my power to render, I should like you all to feel that I am not altogether unfit to give it, or to be your associate."

"You needn't talk that way," said Belle; "you are up in the world compared with us."

"I mean every word I say. I respect your mother as I do my own, for I have seen her beautiful life and beautiful face for weeks and months. I never expect to see a more perfect and genuine lady. I am not well versed in society's ways, but I assure you I would make every effort in my power to act as she would think a young man ought to act. I'd rather fight a dragon than displease her."

Tears of gratified feeling were in Belle's eyes, but she said brusquely, "Not versed in society's ways! Account, then, for that fashionable suit of clothes you are wearing."

"They were not cut in Forestville," he replied dryly.

"Roger," she said impulsively, "I'm wonderfully glad you've come to New York to live, for I was dying for a little society and fun that mother and Millie wouldn't disapprove of. They are so particular, you know, that I fairly ache from trying to walk in the strait and narrow path which is so easy for them. I want a lark. I must have a lark before long, or I'll explode. What can we do that will be real genuine fun? It will do you good, too, or you'll become a dull boy with nothing but work, work, work. You needn't tell me the world was only made to work in. If it was, I've no business here. You must think up something spicy, and no make-believe. I want to go somewhere where I can laugh with my whole heart. I can't go on much longer at this old humdrum, monotonous jog, any more than your colts up at the farm could go around like the plow-horses, and I know it isn't right to expect it of me. And yet what has been the case? Off early in the morning to work, standing all day till I'm lame in body and mad in spirit—stupid owls to make us stand till we are so out of sorts that we are ready to bite customers' heads off instead of waiting on 'em pleasantly. When I come home, mamma often looks tired and sad, for this life is wearing on her, and she is worrying in secret over papa's health. Millie, too, is tired and downhearted in spite of her trying to hide it. She won't go out anywhere because she says there are no places where young girls can go unattended that are within our means. I've got tired of the other shop-girls. A few of them are nice; but more of them are stupid or coarse, so I just sit around and mope, and go to bed early to get through the time. If I even try to romp with the children a little, mamma looks distressed, fearing I will disturb papa, who of late, when he comes out of his dozing condition, is strangely irritable. A year ago he'd romp and talk nonsense with me to my heart's content; but that's all passed. Now is it natural for a young girl little more than sixteen to live such a life?"

"No, Belle, it is not, and yet I have seen enough of the city during the week I have been here to know that your mother and sister are right in their restrictions."

"Well, then, it's a burning shame that in a city called Christian a poor girl is not more safe outside of her own door than if she were in a jungle. Do you mean to say that girls, situated as Millie and I are, must remain cooped up in little rooms the year round when our work is over?"

"The street is no place for you to take recreation in after nightfall; and where else you can go unattended I'm sure I don't know. If there is any place, I'll find out, for I intend to study this city from top to bottom. A lawyer is bound to know life as it is, above all things. But you needn't worry about this question in the abstract any more. I'll see that you have a good time occasionally. You sister will not go with me, at least not yet—perhaps never—but that is not my fault. I've only one favor to ask of you, Belle, and I'll do many in return. Please never, by word, or even by look, make my presence offensive or obtrusive to Miss Mildred. If you will be careful I will not prove so great an affliction as she fears."

"Roger Atwood, do you read people's thoughts?"

"Oh, no, I only see what is to be seen, and draw my conclusions," he said, a little sadly.

"Well, then, if you can have the tact and delicacy to follow such good eyesight, you may fare better than you expect," she whispered at the chapel door.

He turned toward her with a quick flash, but she had stepped forward into the crowd passing through the vestibule. From that moment, however, a ray of hope entered his heart, and in quiet resolve he decided to conform his tactics to the hint just received.

Mrs. Jocelyn and Mildred followed half a block away, and the former said to her daughter: "There they go, Millie, chattering together like two children. You surely take this affair too seriously. His sudden and boyish infatuation with you was the most natural thing in the world. He had never seen a girl like you before, and you awoke him into something like manhood. Very young men are prone to fall in love with women older than themselves, or those who seem older, and speedily to fall out again. Martin has often said his first flame is now a gray-headed lady, and yet he was sure at one time he never could endure life without her. You know that I consoled him quite successfully," and Mildred was pleased to hear the old, sweet laugh that was becoming too rare of late. Even now it ended in a sigh. Mr. Jocelyn was losing his resemblance to the man she had accepted in those bright days that now seemed so long ago.

"I hope you are right, mamma. It seems as if I ought to laugh at the whole affair and good-naturedly show him his folly, but for some reason I can't. He affects me very strangely. While I feel a strong repulsion, I am beginning to fear him—to become conscious of his intensity and the tenacity and power of his will. I didn't understand him at first, and I don't now, but if he were an ordinary, impulsive young fellow he would not impress me as he does."

"Don't you think him true and good at heart?"

"I've no reason to think him otherwise. I can't explain to you how I feel, nor do I understand it myself. He seems the embodiment of a certain kind of force, and I always shrank from mere force, whether in nature or people."

"I can tell you how it is, Millie. Quiet and gentle as you seem, you have a tremendous will of your own, and very strong-willed people don't get on well together."

"Astute little mother! Well, explain it in any way that pleases you, only keep your promise not to let him become the bane of my life."

"I'm not at all sure but that Belle will soon usurp your place in his regard, nor would I object, for I am very anxious about the child. I know that her present life seems dull to her, and the temptations of the city to a girl with a nature like hers are legion. He can be a very useful friend to her, and he seems to me manly and trustworthy. I'm not often deceived in my impressions of people, and he inspires me with confidence, and has from the first. I never saw anything underhand in him at the farm."

"Oh, no, he's honest enough, no doubt."

"There, Millie," resumed her mother, laughing, "you have a woman's reason for your feelings—you don't like him, and that is the end of it. You must admit, however, that he has improved wonderfully. I never saw a young fellow so changed, so thoroughly waked up. He has sense, too, in little things. One would think from his dress he had been born and bred in the city. They didn't palm off an old-fashioned suit on him, if he was from the country.

"Chant his praises to Belle, mamma, and she will greatly appreciate this last proof of his superiority. To me he seems like his clothes—a little too new. Still I admit that he can be of very great service to Belle; and if he will restrict his attentions to her I will be as polite as either of you can wish. I, too, feel a very deep sympathy for Belle. She is little more than a child, and yet her life is imposing upon her the monotonous work of a middle-aged woman, and I fear the consequences. It's contrary to nature, and no one knows it better than she. If he will help us take care of her I shall be grateful indeed; but if he grows sentimental and follows me as he did this morning, I could not endure it—indeed I could not."

"Well, Millie dear, we won't cross any bridges till we come to them."

CHAPTER XXV

THE DARK SHADOW OF COMING EVENTS

DURING the sermon it must be admitted that Belle's thoughts wandered from the text and its able development by Mr. Wentworth. In fact, she was developing a little scheme of her own, and, as the result, whispered at the close of service, "Mamma, Roger and I are going to take a walk in the Park. Can't I ask him home to supper? This is his first Sunday in town, and it will be so dismal—"

"Yes, child, go and have a good time."

Within the next five minutes radiant Belle was an unconscious embodiment of foreordination to Roger. He had had no idea of going to the Park, but Belle had decreed he should go, and as he smilingly accompanied her he certainly remained a very contented free agent.

It was a clear, bracing afternoon and evening, wherein were blended the characteristics of both autumn and winter, and the young people returned with glowing cheeks and quickened pulses.

"Oh, Millie!" cried Belle, "such a walk as I have had would make you over new. I felt as if I were a hundred this morning, but now I feel just about sixteen—that was my last birthday, wasn't it, mamma?"

Both mother and sister smiled to see her sparkling eyes and bubbling happiness; and the latter thought, "For her sake I must certainly either master or conceal my dislike for that young fellow."

Indeed, she herself appeared sadly in need of a little vigorous exercise in the frosty air. The events of the day had been exceedingly depressing; despondency had taken the place of the irritation and the hopes and fears that had alternated in the morning hours; but she unselfishly tried to disguise it, and to aid her mother in preparing an inviting supper for Belle and her guest.

Mildred was obliged to admit to herself that Roger had very little of the appearance and manner of an uncouth countryman. There was a subtle, half-conscious homage for her mother in his every look and word, and for herself a politeness almost as distant and unobtrusive as her own. Once, when a sigh escaped her as she was busy about the room, she looked apprehensively at him, and, as she feared, encountered a glance from which nothing could escape. She now felt that her assumed cheerfulness deceived him so little that, were it not for Belle, she would wholly forego the effort, and end the long, miserable day in her own room.

Suddenly the thought occurred to her: "I will learn from his microscopic eyes how papa appears to others not blinded by love as we are; for, in spite of all my efforts to look on the bright side, I am exceedingly ill at ease about him. I fear he is failing faster than we think—we who see him daily. Mr. Atwood has not seen him for months, and the least change would be apparent to him."

Immunity from business induced Mr. Jocelyn to gratify his cravings more unstintedly on Sunday; and as he was often exceedingly irritable if disturbed when sleeping off the effects of an extra indulgence, they usually left him to wake of his own accord. Unfortunately the walls of his apartment were but curtains, and his loud breathings made it necessary to rouse him. This Mrs. Jocelyn accomplished with some difficulty, but did not mention the presence of Roger, fearing that in his half-wakened condition he might make some remark which would hurt the young man's feelings. She merely assisted him to arrange his disordered hair and dress, and then led the way to the supper-table, he in the meantime protesting petulantly that he wished no supper, but would rather have slept.

As he emerged from the curtained doorway, Mildred's eyes were fastened on Roger's face, determined that nothing in its expression should escape her. He at the moment was in the midst of a laughing reply to one of Belle's funny speeches, but he stopped instantly and turned pale as his eyes rested on the visage of her father. Had that face then changed so greatly? Had disease made such havoc that this comparative stranger was aghast and could not conceal the truth that he was shocked?

It was with sharp anguish that these queries flashed through Mildred's mind, and, with her own perceptions sharpened and quickened, she saw that her father had indeed changed very greatly; he had grown much thinner; his complexion had an unnatural, livid aspect; his old serene, frank look was absent, and a noticeable contraction in the pupils of his eyes gave an odd, sinister aspect to his expression.

There were other changes that were even more painful to witness. In former days he had been the embodiment of genial Southern hospitality; but now, although he made a visible effort for self-control, his whole body seemed one diseased irritable nerve.

Roger almost instantly overcame his pained surprise, yet not so quickly but that it was observed by all, and even by him who had been the cause. "I am very sorry to learn you are not in good health," he was indiscreet enough to say as he offered his hand in greeting.

"From whom have you learned this?" demanded Mr. Jocelyn, looking angrily and suspiciously around. "I assure you that you are mistaken. I never was in better health, and I am not pleased that any one should gossip about me."

They sat down under a miserable constraint—Belle flushed and indignant, Mildred no longer disguising her sadness, and poor Mrs. Jocelyn with moist eyes making a pitiful attempt to restore serenity so that Belle's happy day might not become clouded. Roger tried to break the evil spell by giving his impressions of the Park to Mrs. Jocelyn, but was interrupted by her husband, who had been watching the young man with a perplexed, suspicious look, vainly trying to recall the name of one whose face was familiar enough, remarking at last very satirically, "Has it ceased to be the style to introduce people, especially at one's own table? I might appreciate this gentleman's conversation better if I knew his name."

They all looked at each other in sudden dismay, for they could not know that opium impairs memory as well as health and manhood. "Martin," cried his wife, in a tone of sharp distress, "you *are* ill, indeed. There is no use in trying to disguise the truth any longer. What! don't you remember Roger Atwood, the son of the kind friends with whom we spent the summer?" and in spite of all effort tears blinded her eyes.

The wretched man's instinct of self-preservation was aroused. He saw from the looks of all about him that he was betraying himself—that he was wholly off his balance. While vividly and painfully aware of his danger, his enfeebled will and opium-clouded mind were impotent to steady and sustain him or to direct his course. He had much of the terror and all the sense of helplessness of a man who finds himself in deep water and cannot swim. He trembled, the perspiration started out on his brow, and his one impulse now was to be alone with his terrible master, that had become the sole source of his semblance of strength as well as of his real and fatal weakness. "I—I fear I am ill," he faltered. "I'll go out and get a little air," and he was about to leave the room almost precipitately.

"Oh, Martin," expostulated his wife, "don't go out—at least not alone."

Again he lost control of himself, and said savagely, "I will. Don't any one dare to follow me," and he almost rushed away

For a moment Mrs. Jocelyn tried to bear up from instinctive politeness, but her lip quivered like that of a child; then the tide of her feeling swept her away, and she fled to the adjoining apartment. Mildred followed her at once, and Belle, with a white, scared face, looked into Roger's eyes. He rose and came directly to her and said, "Belle, you know you can always count on me. Your father is so ill that I think I had better follow him. I can do so unobserved."

"Oh, Roger—why—is—is papa losing his mind?"

His quick eye now noted that Fred and Minnie had become so impressed that something dreadful had happened that they were about to make the occasion more painful by their outcries, and he turned smilingly to them, and with a few reassuring words and promises soon quieted their fears. "Be a brave little woman, Belle," he at last said to her. "There is my address, and please promise to let me know if I can do anything for you and for—for Mrs. Jocelyn."

"Don't go—please don't go yet," Belle pleaded. "Papa's looks and words to-night fill me with a strange fear as if something awful might happen."

"Perhaps if I follow your father I may prevent—"

"Oh, yes, go at once."

He was intercepted at the door by the entrance of Mr. Jocelyn, who had had ample time in the few brief minutes that had elapsed to fill his system with the subtle stimulant. He now took Roger by the hand most cordially, and said, "Pardon me, Mr. Atwood. My health has become somewhat impaired of late, and I fear I have just had a rather bad turn; but the air has revived me, and the trouble now has passed. I insist that you stay and spend the evening with us."

"Oh, papa," cried Belle, rushing into his arms, "how you frightened us! Please go into my room, there, and comfort mamma by telling her you are all well again."

This he did so effectively that he soon led her out smiling through her tears, for her confidence in him was the growth and habit of years, and anything he said to her seemed for the moment true. And, indeed, the man was so changed that it was hard to realize he was not well. His face, in contrast with its aspect a few moments since, appeared to have regained its natural hue and expression; every trace of irritability had passed away, and with his old-time, easy courtesy and seeming frankness he talked so plausibly of it all that Belle and his wife, and even Roger, felt that they had attached undue importance to a mere temporary indisposition.

Mildred made great effort to be cheerful for her father's sake, but the pallor did not pass from her face, nor the look of deep anxiety from her eyes. The shadow of coming trouble had fallen too heavily upon her, and that the marked exhibition of her father's failing powers should have occurred at this time added to the impression that Roger Atwood was their evil genius. She recalled the fact that he seemingly had been the first exciting cause of her father's unnatural behavior, and now his reappearance was the occasion of the most convincing proof they had yet received that the one upon whom they all depended was apparently failing in both mind and body. Even now, while he was doing his best to reassure and render happy his family, there was to her perception an unreality in his words and manner. She almost imagined, too, that he feared to meet her eye and shunned doing so. Not in the remotest degree, however, did she suspect the cause of his suddenly varying moods and changed appearance, but regarded all as the result of his misfortunes; and the miserable presentiment grew strong upon her that soon—alas! too soon—she would be the slender reed on which they all would lean. If she could have six months, only, of careful preparation she would not so dread the burden; but if now, or soon, the whole responsibility of the family's support should come upon her and Belle, what would they do? Her heart sank, and her very soul cowered at the prospect. She could not live in the present hour like Belle, but with too keen a foresight realized how dark and threatening was the future.

The night was clear and beautiful, and Roger and Belle went up to the platform built over the roof. Not long afterward there was a knock at the door, and Mr. Ulph appeared. "Der night vas goot," he said to Mildred, "und I vill gif you von leedle glimpse off hefen if you vould like him."

The poor girl felt that she certainly needed a glimpse of something bright and reassuring, and wrapping herself warmly she followed her quaint friend to the roof.

Roger grew taciturn as he watched the dim outline of her form and her white, upturned face. She seemed as cold and distant to him as the stars at which she gazed, and he thought dejectedly, "The least of them have an interest for her greater than I shall ever be able to inspire."

He overrated her interest in the stars on that occasion, however, for though she did her best to follow the old astronomer's words, her heart was too sorrowful and preoccupied, and her eyes too often blinded by tears, which once glittered so distinctly in the rays of a brilliant planet that her companion stopped in the midst of a sentence and looked at her keenly.

"You vas not habby, my leedle schild," he said kindly. "Dere's someding droubling you heart; put you gan no see vay inter der hefens drew dears do' dey vas glear as der lens off my glass."

"I fear I shall have to see through tears very often, if I see at all," Mildred replied, with a low, suppressed sob. "Forgive me to-night. I *do* feel grateful that you are willing to show me—but—I—I—well, I am troubled to-night about something, and I can't control myself. To-morrow night I'll be braver, and will help you. Please don't feel hurt if I leave you now."

"Ah, mine leedle girl, learn vrom der sohtars dot der great laws moost be opeyed, und don't you vorry und vret ober vat you gannot help. Shust you go along quiet und easy like Shupiter oup dere. Lots off dings vill dry to bull dis vay and dot vay outen der right orpt, put dond you mind 'em, und shust go right schtrait along und not care. You veels too mooch apout oder beoples. Der schtars deach you petter; dey goes right on der own vay und about der own pisness, unless dey vas voolish leedle schtars, like dot von dere dots shust gone to der duyvel vrom runin outen his vay toward der earth."

She might have reminded him that, if she had acted upon this cold and selfish philosophy, his little child would now be sleeping in a distant cemetery instead of in his warm crib, but she only said, "Good-night, Mr. Ulph; I'll do better next time," and she hurried away. She felt that the sun and centre of their family life was passing under a strange and lasting eclipse, and the result might be darkness—chaos.

She wiped her eyes carefully, that no traces of grief might appear, and then entered their room. Her mother was putting the children to bed, and her father looking dreamily out of the window. She kissed him, and said briefly, "I'm tired and think I will retire early so as to be ready for my work." He made no effort to detain her. She clasped her mother in a momentary passionate embrace, and then shut herself up to a night of almost sleepless grief.

CHAPTER XXVI

WAXING AND WANING MANHOOD

BOTH Belle and Roger saw that Mildred had not been reassured by Mr. Jocelyn's return and manner; and as they thought it over they found it difficult to account for his strangely varying moods. After a rather lame effort to chat cheerily, Roger bad Belle good-night, and assured her that she now had a friend always within call.

His uncle's modest residence was in a side street and not far away, but the young fellow walked for hours before applying his night-key to the door. What he had seen and heard that day touched his heart's core, and the influences that were so rapidly developing his manhood were greatly strengthened. For Belle he now had a genuine liking and not a little respect. He saw her foibles clearly, and understood that she was still more a child than a woman, and so should not be judged by the standards proper for those of mature age; but he also saw the foundations on which a noble womanhood might be built. She inspired a sense of comradeship and honest friendliness which would easily deepen into fraternal love, but Mrs. Jocelyn's surmise that she might some day touch that innermost spring which controls the entire man had no true basis. Nor would there have been any possibility of this had he never seen Mildred. A true man—one governed by heart and mind, not passion—meets many women whom he likes and admires exceedingly, but who can never quicken his pulse. On Mildred, however—although she coveted the gift so little—was bestowed the power to touch the most hidden and powerful principles of his being, to awaken and stimulate every faculty he possessed. Her words echoed and re-echoed in the recesses of his soul; even her cold, distant glances were like rays of a tropical sun to which his heart could offer no resistance; and yet they were by no means enervating. Some natures would have grown despondent over prospects seemingly so hopeless, but Roger was of a different type. His deep and unaccepted feeling did not flow back upon his spirit, quenching it in dejection and despair, but it became a resistless tide back of his purpose to win her recognition and respect at least, and his determination to prove himself her peer. A girl so beautiful and womanly might easily gain such power over several men without any conscious effort, remaining meanwhile wholly indifferent or even averse herself, and Roger had indeed but little cause for hope. He might realize every ambitious dream and win her respect and admiration, and her heart continue as unresponsive as it had been from the first. Many a man has loved and waited in vain; and some out of this long adversity in that which touched their dearest interests have built the grandest successes of life and the loftiest and purest manhood.

A few months before, Roger seemingly had been a good-natured, pleasure-loving country youth, who took life as it came, with little thought for the morrow. Events had proved that he had latent and undeveloped force. In the material world we find substances that apparently are inert and powerless, but let some other substance be brought sufficiently near, and an energy is developed that seems like magic, and transformations take place that were regarded as supernatural in times when nature's laws were little understood. If this be true concerning that which is gross and material, how much more true of the quick, informing spirit that can send out its thoughts to the furthest star! Strong souls—once wholly unconscious of their power—at the touch of adequate motives pass into action and combinations which change the character of the world from age to age.

But in the spiritual as in the physical world, this development takes place in accordance with natural law and within the limitations of each character. There is nothing strange, however strange it may appear to those who do not understand. Roger Atwood was not a genius that would speedily dazzle the world with bewildering coruscations. It would rather be his tendency to grow silent and reserved with years, but his old boyish alertness would not decline, or his habit of shrewd, accurate observation. He thus would take few false steps, and would prove his force by deeds. Therefore he was almost predestined to succeed, for his unusually strong will would not drive him into useless effort or against obstacles that could be foreseen and avoided.

After Mildred's departure from the country he carried out his plans in a characteristic way. He wrote frankly and decidedly to his uncle that he was coming to the city, and would struggle on alone if he received no aid. At the same time he suggested that he had a large acquaintance in his vicinity, and therefore by judicious canvassing among the farmers he believed he could bring much patronage with him. This looked not unreasonable to the shrewd commission merchant, and, since his nephew was determined to make an excursion into the world, he concluded it had better be done under the safest and most business-like circumstances. At the same time recalling the character and habits of the country boy, as he remembered him, he surmised that Roger would soon become homesick and glad to go back to his old life. If retained under his eye, the youth could be kept out of harm's way and returned untainted and content to be a farmer. He therefore wrote to Roger that, if his parents were willing, he might secure what trade he could in farm produce and make the trial.

At first Mr. and Mrs. Atwood would not hear of the plan, and the father openly declared that it was "those Jocelyn girls that had unsettled the boy."

"Father," said Roger, a little defiantly and sarcastically,

doesn't it strike you that I'm rather tall for a boy? Did you never hear of a small child, almost of age, choosing his own course in life?"

"That is not the way to talk," said his mother reprovingly. "We both very naturally feel that it's hard, and hardly right, too, for you to leave us just as we are getting old and need some one to lean on."

"Do not believe, mother, that I have not thought of that," was the eager reply; "and if I have my way you and father, and Susan too, shall be well provided for."

"Thank you," Mr. Atwood snarled contemptuously. "I'll get what I can out of the old farm, and I don't expect any provision from an overgrown boy whose head is so turned by two city girls that he must go dangling after them."

Roger flushed hotly, and angry words rose to his lips, but he restrained them by a visible effort. After a moment he said quietly, "You are my father, and may say what you please. There is but one way of convincing you whether I am a boy or a man, and I'll take it. You can keep me here till I'm twenty-one if you will, but you'll be sorry. It will be so much loss to me and no gain to you. I've often heard you say the Atwoods never 'drove well,' and you found out years ago that a good word went further with me than what you used to call a 'good thrashing.' If you let me have my way, now that I'm old enough to choose for myself, I'll make your old age cozy and comfortable. If you thwart me, as I said before, you'll be sorry,' and he turned on his heel and left them.

Politic Mrs. Atwood had watched her son closely for weeks and knew that something was coming, but with woman's patience she waited and was kind. No one would miss him so much as she, and yet, mother-like, she now took sides against her own heart. But she saw that her husband was in no mood to listen to her at present, and nothing more was said that day.

In the evening Roger drove out in his carriage and returned on horseback.

"There's the money you paid for the buggy, with interest," he said to his father.

"You aren't gone yet," was the growling answer.

"No matter. I shall not ride in it again, and you are not the loser."

Roger had a rugged side to his nature which his father's course often called out, and Mrs. Atwood made her husband feel, reluctant as he was to admit it, that he was taking the wrong course with his son. A letter also from his brother in town led him to believe that Roger would probably come back in the spring well content to remain at home; so at last he gave a grudging consent.

Ungracious as it was, the young man rewarded him by a vigorous, thorough completion of the fall work, by painting the house and putting the place in better order than it had ever known before; meanwhile for his mother and sister he showed a consideration and gentleness which proved that he was much changed from his old self.

"I can see the hand of Mildred Jocelyn in everything he says and does," Susan remarked one day after a long fit of musing, "and yet I don't believe she cares a straw for him." Her intuition was correct; it was Roger's ambition to become such a man as Mildred must respect in spite of herself, and it was also true that she was not merely indifferent, but for the reasons already given—as far as she had reasons—she positively disliked him.

Roger brought sufficient business from the country to prevent regretful second thoughts in the mind of his thrifty uncle, and the impression was made that the young fellow might steady down into a useful clerk; but when as much was hinted Roger frankly told him that he regarded business as a stepping-stone merely to the study of the law. The old merchant eyed him askance, but made no response. Occasionally the veteran of the market evinced a glimmer of enthusiasm over a prime article of butter, but anything so intangible as a young man's ambitious dreams was looked upon with a very cynical eye. Still he could not be a part of New York life and remain wholly sceptical in regard to the possibilities it offered to a young fellow of talent and large capacity for work. He was a childless man, and if Roger had it in him to "climb the ladder," as he expressed it to himself, "it might pay to give him the chance." But the power to climb would have to be proved almost to a demonstration. In the meantime Roger, well watched and much mistrusted, was but a clerk in his store near Washington Market, and a student during all spare hours.

He had too much sense to attempt superficial work or to seek to build his fortunes on the slight foundation of mere smartness. It was his plan to continue in business for a year or more and then enter the junior class of one of the city colleges. By making the most of every moment and with the aid of a little private tutoring he believed he could do this, for he was a natural mathematician, and would find in the classics his chief difficulties. At any rate it was his fixed resolve not to enter upon the study of the law proper until he had broadened his mind by considerable general culture. Not only did his ambition prompt to this, but he felt that if he developed narrowly none would be so clearly aware of the fact as Mildred Jocelyn. Although not a highly educated girl herself, he knew she had a well-bred woman's nice perception of what constituted a cultivated man; he also knew that he had much prejudice to overcome, and that he must strike at its very root.

In the meantime poor Mildred, unconscious of all save his unwelcome regard, was seeking with almost desperate earnestness to gain practical knowledge of two humble arts, hoping to be prepared for the time—now clearly foreseen and dreaded—when her father might decline so far in mind and health as to fail them utterly, and even become a heavy burden. She did not dream that his disease was a drug, and although some of his associates began to suspect as much, in spite of all his precautions, none felt called upon to suggest their suspicions to his family.

Causes that work steadily will sooner or later reach their

legitimate results. The opium inertia grew inevitably upon Mr. Jocelyn. He disappointed the expectations of his employers to that degree that they felt that something was wrong, and his appearance and manner often puzzled them not a little even though with all the cunning which the habit engenders he sought to hide his weakness.

One day, late in November, an unexpected incident brought matters to a crisis. An experienced medical acquaintance, while making a call upon the firm, caught sight of Mr. Jocelyn, and his practiced eye detected the trouble at once.

"That man is an opium-eater," he said in a low tone, and his explanation of the effects of the drug was a diagnosis of Mr. Jocelyn's symptoms and appearance. The firm's sympathy for a man seemingly in poor health was transformed into disgust and antipathy, since there is less popular toleration of this weakness than of drinking habits. The very obscurity in which the vice is involved makes it seem all the more unnatural and repulsive, and it must be admitted that the fullest knowledge tends only to increase this horror and repugnance, even though pity is awakened for the wretched victim.

But Mr. Jocelyn's employers had little knowledge of the vice, and they were not in the least inclined to pity. They felt that they had been imposed upon, and that too at a time when all business men were very restless under useless expenditure. It was the man's fault and not misfortune that he had failed so signally in securing trade from the South, and, while they had paid him but a small salary, his ill-directed and wavering efforts had involved them in considerable expense. Asking the physician to remain, they summoned Mr. Jocelyn to the private office, and directly charged him with the excessive and habitual use of opium.

The poor man was at first greatly confused, and trembled as if in an ague fit, for his nerve power was already so shattered that he had little self-control in an emergency. This, of course, was confirmation of guilt in their eyes.

"Gentlemen, you do me a great wrong," he managed to say, and hastily left the office. Having secreted himself from observation he snatched out his hypodermic syringe, and within six minutes felt himself equal to any crisis. Boldly returning to the office he denied the charge in the most explicit terms, and with some show of lofty indignation. The physician who was still present watched him closely, and noticed that the cuff on his left hand was somewhat crumpled, as if it had been recently pushed back. Without a word he seized Mr. Jocelyn's arm and pulled back his coat and shirt sleeve, revealing a bright red puncture just made, and many others of a remoter date.

"There is no use in lying about such matters to me," said the physician. "How much morphia did you inject into your arm since you left us?"

"I am a victim of neuralgia," Mr. Jocelyn began, without any hesitation, "and the cruel and unreasonable charge here made against me brought on an acute paroxysm, and therefore I—"

"Stop that nonsense," interrupted the doctor, roughly. "Don't you know that lying, when lying is of no use, is one of the characteristic traits of an opium-eater? I am a physician, and have seen too many cases to be deceived a moment. You have all the symptoms of a confirmed morphia consumer, and if you ever wish to break your chains you had better tell doctors the truth and put yourself under the charge of one in whom you have confidence."

"Well, curse you!" said Mr. Jocelyn savagely, "it was through one of your damnable fraternity that I acquired what you are pleased to call my chains, and now you come croaking to my employers, poisoning their minds against me."

"Oh, as to poisoning," remarked the physician sarcastically, "I'll wager a thousand dollars that you have absorbed enough morphia within the last twenty-four hours to kill every one in this office. At the rate you are going on, as far as I can judge from appearances, you will soon poison yourself out of existence. No physician ever advised the destroying vice you are practicing, and no physician would take offence at your words any more than at the half-demented ravings of a fever patient. You are in a very critical condition, sir, and unless you can wake up to the truth and put forth more will-power than most men possess you will soon go to the bad."

"I sincerely hope you will take this experienced physician's advice," said the senior member of the firm very coldly. "At any rate we can no longer permit you to jeopardize our interests by your folly and weakness. The cashier will settle with you, and our relations end here and now."

"You will bitterly repent of this injustice," Mr. Jocelyn replied haughtily. "You are discharging a man of unusual business capacity—one whose acquaintance with the South is wellnigh universal, and whose combinations were on the eve of securing enormous returns."

"We will forego all these advantages. Good-morning, sir. Did you ever see such effrontery?" he continued, after Mr. Jocelyn had departed with a lofty and contemptuous air.

"It's not effrontery—it's opium," said the physician sadly. "You should see the abject misery of the poor wretch after the effects of the drug have subsided."

"I have no wish to see him again under any aspect, and heartily thank you for unmasking him. We must look at once into our affairs, and see how much mischief he has done. If he wants the aid and respect of decent men, let him give up his vile practice."

"That's easier said than done," the physician replied. "Very few ever give it up who have gone as far as this man."

CHAPTER XXVII

A SLAVE

THE physician was right. A more abject and pitiable spectacle than Mr. Jocelyn could scarcely have been found among the miserable unfortunates of a city noted for its extremes in varied condition. Even in his false excitement he was dimly aware that he was facing a dreadful emergency, and following an instinctive desire for solitude so characteristic of those in his condition, he took a room in an obscure hotel and gave himself up to thoughts that grew more and more painful as the unnatural dreams inspired by opium shaped themselves gradually into accord with the actualities of his life.

For a month or two past he had been swept almost unresistingly down the darkening and deepening current of his sin. Whenever he made some feeble, vacillating effort to reduce his allowance of the drug, he became so wretched, irritable, and unnatural in manner that his family were full of perplexed wonder and solicitude. To hide his weakness from his wife was his supreme desire; and yet, if he stopped —were this possible—the whole wretched truth would be revealed. Each day he had been tormented with the feeling that something must be done, and yet nothing had been done. He had only sunk deeper and deeper, as with the resistless force of gravitation.

His vague hope, his baseless dream that something would occur which would make reform easier or the future clearer, had now been dissipated utterly, and every moment with more terrible distinctness revealed to him the truth that he had lost his manhood. The vice was already stamped on his face and manner, so that an experienced eye could detect it at once; soon all would see the degrading brand. He, who had once been the soul of honor and truth, had lied that day again and again, and the thought pierced him like a sword.

And now, after his useless falsehoods, what should he do? He was no longer unacquainted with his condition—few opium victims are, at his advanced stage of the habit—and he knew well how long and terrible would be the ordeal of a radical cure, even if he had the will-power to attempt it. He had, of late, taken pains to inform himself of the experience of others who had passed down the same dark, slippery path, and when he tried to diminish instead of increasing his doses of morphia, he had received fearful warnings of the awful chasm that intervened between himself and safety.

A few opium consumers can go on for years in comparative tranquillity if they will avoid too great excess, and carefully increase their daily allowance so as not to exhibit too marked alternations of elation and depression. Now and then, persons of peculiar constitution can maintain the practice a long time without great physical or moral deterioration; but no *habitué* can stop without sufferings prolonged and more painful than can be described. Sooner or later, even those natures which offer the strongest resistance to the ravages of the poison succumb, and pass hopelessly to the same destruction. Mr. Jocelyn's sanguine, impulsive temperament had little capacity for resistance to begin with, and he had during the last year used the drug freely and constantly, thus making downward advances in months that in some instances require years of moderate indulgence. Moreover, as with alcohol, many natures have an unusual and morbid craving for opium after once acquiring the habit of its use. Their appetite demands it with an imperiousness which will not be denied, even while in soul they recoil and loathe the bondage.

This was especially true of Mr. Jocelyn. The vice in his case was wrecking a mind and heart naturally noble and abounding in the best impulses. He was conscious, too, of this demoralization, and suffered almost as greatly as would a true, pure woman, if, by some fatal necessity, she were compelled to live a life of crime.

He had already begun to shrink from the companionship of his family. The play and voices of his little children jarred his shattered nerves almost beyond endurance; and every look of love and act of trust became a stinging irritant instead of the grateful incense that had once filled his home with perfume. In bitter self-condemnation he saw that he was ceasing to be a protector to his daughters, and that unless he could break the dark, self-woven spells he would drag them down to the depths of poverty, and then leave them exposed to the peculiar temptations which, in a great city, ever assail girls so young, beautiful, and friendless. Mildred, he believed, would die rather than sin; but he often groaned in spirit as he thought of Belle. Their considerate self-denial that he might not be disturbed after his return from business, and their looks of solicitude, pierced him daily with increasing torture; and the knowledge that he added to the monotony of their lives and the irksomeness of their poverty oppressed him with a dejection that was relieved only by the cause of all his troubles.

But the thought of his loving, trusting, patient wife was the most unendurable of all. He had loved her from the first as his own soul, and her love and respect were absolutely essential to him, and yet he was beginning to recoil from her with a strange and unnatural force. He felt that he had no right to touch her while she remained so true and he was so false. He dreaded her loving gaze more than a detective's cold, searching eye. He had already deceived her in regard to the marks of the hypodermic needle, assuring her that they were caused by a slight impurity in his blood, and she never questioned anything he said. He often lay awake through interminable nights—the drug was fast losing its power to produce quiet sleep—trembling and cold with apprehension of the hour when she would become aware that her husband was no longer a man, but the most degraded of slaves. She might learn that she was leaning, not even on a frail reed, but on a poisoned weapon that would pierce her heart. It seemed to him that he would rather die than meet that hour when into her gentle eyes would come the horror of the discovery, and in fact the oft-recurring thought of it all had caused more pain than a hundred deaths.

Could he go home now and reveal his degradation? Great drops of cold perspiration drenched him at the bare thought. The icy waters, the ooze and mud of the river seemed preferable. He could not openly continue his vice in the presence of his family, nor could he conceal it much longer, and the attempt to stop the drug, even gradually, would transform him almost into a demon of irritability and perhaps violence, so frightful is the rebellion of the physical nature against the abstinence essential to a final cure.

At last he matured and carried out the following plan: Returning to the firm that had employed him, he told them of his purpose to go South among his old acquaintances and begin life anew, and of his belief that a sea voyage and change of scene would enable him to break the habit; and he so worked upon their sympathies that they promised to say nothing of his weakness, and not to let the past stand in his way if he would redeem himself.

Then fortifying his nerves carefully with morphia he went home and broached the project to his wife and Mildred, plausibly advancing the idea that the change might restore his failing health. To his relief they did not oppose his scheme, for indeed they felt that something must be done speedily to arrest his decline; and although the separation would be hard for the wife to endure, and would become a source of increased anxiety for a time, it was much better than seeing him fail so steadily before her eyes. His plan promised improvement in their fortunes and cure of the mysterious disease that was slowly sapping his life. Therefore she tearfully consented that he should go, and if the way opened favorably it was decided that the family should follow him.

The only question now was to raise the money required; and to accomplish this they sold the household effects still in storage, and Mildred, without a word, disposed of the most of her jewelry and brought the proceeds to her father; for the gold and gems worn in days that accorded with their lustre were as nothing to her compared with her father's life and health.

"I would turn my blood into gold if I could, father," she said, with swimming eyes, "if it would only make you well and strong as you once were."

The man's hand so trembled that he could scarcely receive the money. When by himself he groaned, "Oh, how awful and deep will be the curse of God if I turn this money against her by using it for the damnedest poison the devil ever brewed!" and he wrapped it up separately with a shudder.

A few days later, with many tears and clinging embraces, they parted with him, his wife whispering in his ear at the last moment, "Martin, my every breath will be a prayer for your safety and health."

Under the influence of the powerful emotions inspired by this last interview he threw his hypodermic syringe and morphia bottle overboard from the deck of the steamer, saying, with a desperate resolution which only an opium slave could understand, "I'll break the habit for one week if I die for it," and he sailed away into what seemed a region of unimaginable horrors, dying ten thousand deaths in the indescribable anguish of his mind and body. The winter storm that soon overtook the ship was magnified by his disordered intellect until its uproar was appalling in the last degree. The people on the vessel thought him demented, and for a few days the captain kept him under a continuous guard, and considerately suppressed the cause of his behavior, that was soon revealed by requests for opium that were sometimes pitiful pleadings and again irritable demands. He soon passed into a condition approaching collapse, vomiting incessantly, and insane in his wild restlessness. Indeed he might have died had not the captain, in much doubt and anxiety, administered doses of laudanum which, in his inexperience, were appalling in their amount.

At last, more dead than alive, with racking pains, shiverings and exhaustion from prolonged insomnia, he was taken ashore in a Southern city and a physician summoned, who, with a promptness characteristic of the profession, administered a preparation of morphia, and the old fatal spell was renewed at once. The vitiated system that for days had been largely deprived of its support seized upon the drug again with a craving as irresistible as the downward rush of a torrent. The man could no more control his appetite than he could an Atlantic tide. It overwhelmed his enervated will at once, and now that morphine could be obtained he would have it at any and every cost. Of course he seemingly improved rapidly under its influence, and cunningly disguising his condition from the physician, soon dismissed him and resumed his old habits. He felt that it was impossible to endure the horrors of total abstinence, and, now that he was no longer under the observation of his family, he again tried to satisfy his conscience by promising himself that he would gradually reduce the amount used until he could discontinue it utterly—delusive hope, that has mocked thousands like himself. If he could have gone to an asylum and surrounded his infirm will by every possible safeguard, he might have been carried through the inevitable period of horrible depression; but even then the habit had become so confirmed that his chances would have been problematical, for experience sadly proves that confirmed opium-consumers are ever in danger of a relapse.

CHAPTER XXVIII

NEW YORK'S HUMANITY

MRS. JOCELYN drooped in her husband's absence, for every year had increased her sense of dependence. She felt somewhat like one who is drifting on a wreck. If the sea would only remain calm, all might be well; but the sea never is at rest very long, and if storms, dangers, and emergencies occurred what would she do?

Each day that passed without word from her husband grew longer, and when at last a letter came it was vague and unsatisfactory. He hoped he was better; he hoped to find a foothold; and then came again several days of silence which were almost as oppressive to Mildred as to herself.

Meanwhile their funds were failing fast, and they both felt that they ought not to sell anything else for mere living expenses. More critical emergencies might arise and find them destitute. If Mr. Jocelyn should become seriously ill in the South, they must be in a position to have him cared for and brought home. Mildred with extreme reluctance was compelled to face the necessity of giving up her studies so that she might earn something at once. She had about decided to reveal her troubles to Miss Wetheridge, when a hasty note from her friend swept away all immediate chance of aid in that direction. "The gentleman to whom I was soon to be married," she wrote, "has not been strong for a year past, and a few days since he was taken with a hemorrhage from his lungs. His physician ordered him to go immediately to Nassau. In accordance with our mutual wishes we were married quietly in the presence of a few relatives, and by the time this note reaches you we shall be on our way to the South. My heart is burdened with anxiety, and my hourly prayer is that God will spare the life of one so dear to me. I wish I could see you before I sail, but it is impossible. I have had to leave almost everything undone. Write me often."

This note threw Mildred on her own resources. She felt that Mr. Wentworth could do little for her beyond certifying to her character, for he was the pastor of a congregation of which a large proportion were as poor as herself. There was naught to do but go to work like the others in uncomplaining silence and earn her bread.

One evening she learned from Belle that the increased trade incident to the approaching holiday season had rendered more help necessary, and that one large shop on Sixth Avenue had already made known this need. When the doors opened the following morning, Mildred was among the crowd of applicants, and her appearance was so much in her favor that she was engaged at once on a salary of six dollars a week. Only immediate necessity could have induced her to take this step, for she justly doubted her ability to endure the strain of standing continuously. The shop, however, was full of girls as frail-looking as herself, and it was the only certainty of support within her reach. Her mother cried bitterly over the step, and she, also, could not hide a few tears, brave as she tried to be; but she said resolutely, "I'm no better than hundreds of others, and if they can endure it I can and will, for a while at least."

The first day was one that she never forgot. The bright sun and clear, bracing atmosphere brought out crowds of shoppers, but the air of the store soon became vitiated, hot, and lifeless. In this close, stifling place she was compelled to stand, elbowed by other girls who were strangers to her, and too busy or too indifferent to aid materially her inexperienced efforts to learn her duties. She made blunders, for which she was scolded; she grew bewildered and faint, and when the few moments of nooning came she could not eat the lunch her mother had prepared. If she could only have had a cup of strong coffee she might have got through the day; but her employers were much too thrifty to furnish such a luxury, and she was too tired, and the time allotted her much too brief to permit its quest. Therefore she tried to rest a little from the intolerable fatigue and pain of standing, and to collect her thoughts.

The afternoon crush of customers was greater even than that which had crowded the counters in the morning, and she grew more and more bewildered under the confused fire of questions and orders. If any one had had the time or heart to observe, there would have been seen in her eyes the pathetic, fearful look of some timid creature of the woods when harried and driven to bay by hounds.

Suddenly everything grew black before her eyes; the piled-up goods, the chattering throng, faded, and she sank to the floor—there was no room for her to fall.

When she revived she found that she had been carried to the cloak-room, in which the girls ate their lunch, and that a woman was kneeling beside her applying restoratives. In a few moments one of the managers looked in and asked, in an off-hand way, "How is she getting on?"

With the instinct of self-preservation Mildred sat up, and pleaded, "Indeed, sir, I'm better. It was all so strange —the air was close. I beg of you not to discharge me. I will learn soon."

"Oh, don't be so worried," the man replied good-naturedly. "It's nothing new to have a girl faint on the first day. You'll get used to it by and by like the rest. Will you be well enough to walk home, or shall I have a carriage ordered?"

"Please don't get a carriage. It would frighten mamma terribly, and she would not let me come back, and I *must* come, for we need every penny I can earn."

"Well, now, that's sensible, and you save the carriage hire also. You're a fine-looking, plucky girl, and I'll give you a place at the lace counter, near the door, where the air is better and the work lighter (and where her pretty face will do us no harm," he added mentally).

"You are very kind, sir, and I can't tell you how much I thank you."

"All right, you'll get into training and do as well as the best, so don't be discouraged," and the man had the grace or business thrift—probably a blending of both—to send her a cup of coffee.

She was then left to rest, and go home when she felt like it. As early as she dared without exciting her mother's suspicions, she crept away, almost as the wounded slowly and painfully leave a field of battle. Her temples still throbbed; in all her body there was a slight muscular tremor, or beating sensation, and her step faltered from weakness. To her delicate organization, already reduced by anxiety, sedentary life, and prolonged mental effort, the strain and nervous shock of that day's experiences had been severe indeed.

To hide the truth from her despondent mother was now her chief hope and aim. Her fatigue she would not attempt to disguise, for that would be unnatural. It was with difficulty she climbed the one flight of stairs that led to their room, but her wan face was smiling as she pushed open the door and kissed her mother in greeting. Then throwing herself on the lounge she cried gayly, "Come, little mother, give me an old maid's panacea for every ill of life—a cup of strong tea."

"Millie," cried Mrs. Jocelyn, bending over her with moist eyes, "you look pale and gone-like—"

"Oh no, mamma, I'm here—a good hundred and ten pounds of me, more or less."

"But how did you get through the day?"

"You will hardly believe it," was the reassuring reply; "I've been promoted already from work that was hard and coarse to the lace counter, which is near the door, where one can breathe a little pure air. If the goods were as second-hand as the air they would not have a customer. But come, mamma dear, I'm too tired to talk, and would rather eat, and especially drink. These surely are good symptoms."

"Millie, you are a soldier, as we used to say during the war," said Mrs. Jocelyn, hastening the preparations for supper; "but you cannot deceive a mother's eyes. You are more exhausted than you even realize yourself. Oh, I do wish there was some other way. I'd give all the world if I had Mrs. Wheaton's stout red arms, for I'd rather wash all day and half the night than see you and Belle so burdened early in life."

"I wouldn't have my beautiful mamma changed even by one gray hair," was the very natural response.

Belle nearly rendered futile all of Mildred's efforts to hide the worst from her mother; for, after her duties were over, she went eagerly to the shop where she expected to find her sister. Having learned that Miss Jocelyn had fainted and had gone home some time in the afternoon, she sped almost breathlessly after her, and burst into the room with the words, "Millie! Millie!"

Fortunately Mrs. Jocelyn was busy over the stove at the moment and did not see Mildred's strong cautionary gesture; but Belle's perceptions were almost instantaneous, and with one significant glance of her dark eyes she entered into the loving conspiracy.

"What is it, Belle?" was Mrs. Jocelyn's anxious query.

"I'm wild to know how Millie has got on the first day, and whether she has a big fight on her hands as I had. If she has, I declare war, too, against all the powers and principalities—not of the air, for there wasn't a breath of it in our store to-day. We've had a crush, and I'm half dead from trying to do two days' work in one. Ten minutes for lunch. Scores of cross customers all wanting to be waited on at once, and the floor-walkers flying around like hens bereft of heads, which, after all, are never of much use to either. In spite of all, here we are, mamma, ready for a cup of your good tea and other fixin's. Now, Millie, it's your turn. I've let off enough steam to be safe till after supper. Have you made cruel enemies to-day, from whom you desire my protection?"

"No, Belle," said Mildred, laughing; "I haven't your force and brilliancy, and have made but a humdrum beginning. I was so stupid at one counter that they transferred me to another, and I'm glad of it, for laces are pretty, and taking care of them wouldn't seem like drudgery at all. Best of all, it's near the door, and every customer will give me a sustaining breath."

"Millie is standing it capitally for a beginner," Belle remarked, with the air of a veteran, as Mildred eagerly drank her cup of tea and asked for more. "I was so tired the first night that it seemed as if I could scarcely swallow a mouthful."

Thus they carried out the little ruse, careful not to exaggerate, for Mrs. Jocelyn's intuitions were quick.

As it was she looked at her child with many misgivings, but she tried for their sakes to be cheerful, and praised the courage and spirit of both the girls, assuring them that they showed their true Southern blood, and that they reminded her of their father when, during his brief visits, he talked over the long, hard campaigns.

At last they were in the privacy of their own room, and Mildred, as if she were the weaker and younger, buried her face on her sister's shoulder and sobbed despairingly, "Oh, Belle, you are the stronger. I fear I can't stand it at all. I've suffered more to-day than in all my life, and my feet and back still ache—oh, I can't tell you."

The child soothed and comforted her, and said she had suffered just the same at first, and often still she felt that if she could not sit down for a few moments she would drop down; "but there, Millie," she concluded, with the best philosophy the case admitted of, "you get used to it gradually—you can get used to anything."

"I don't believe I can," was the dejected reply, "and

yet I must, if we would have shelter and bread. Oh that we might hear some good news from papa! Why don't he write oftener?. I fear it is because he has nothing cheering to tell us."

The next morning, in spite of all effort, Mildred was too ill and lame to rise, but she instructed Belle to assure her employer that she would come the following day.

Mrs. Jocelyn tried hard to persuade her not to go back at all, and at last Mildred grew a little stern and said emphatically, "Please say no more, mamma. We can afford none of this weak nonsense. I must earn my bread, as do other girls, and have no time to lose."

The following day, fortunately, was so stormy that customers were scattering, and Mildred had a chance to gain an idea of her duties and to rest a little from time to time, for out of consideration of the facts that she had been ill and was a beginner, she was permitted to sit down occasionally. She was so attractive in appearance, and had brought such an excellent certificate of character, that the proprietors were inclined to be lenient, and smooth a little the harsh and thorny path of a beginner.

And so the weary days dragged on, and she slowly acquired the power to stand as did the others. They were days, however, which ended in a close approach to agony, from which the nights brought but slight and temporary relief, for so great was the pain in her feet and back that she would moan even in her sleep. Her sufferings were scarcely less than at first, but, as Belle said, she was "getting used" to them.

It is a well-known fact that many would persist in living in spite of all the tortures of the Inquisition. I wonder if the old-time inquisitors and their "familiars" were ingenious enough to compel delicate women to stand and talk all day, and sometimes part of the night?

In very truth, the poor girl was earning her bread by torture, and she soon found that she had many companions in suffering who, with woman's capacity for the patient endurance of pain, made the best of their lot, often trying to forget themselves in jests, laughter, and gossip, planning, meanwhile, in odd moments, for some snatch at the few pleasures that their brief evenings permitted—pleasures, too often, in which Mildred could or would take no part. While her gentleness and courtesy to all gave no cause for hostility, her air of quiet aloofness and her recognized superiority prevented her from becoming a favorite, nor did the many admiring looks and even open advances that she received from the young men in the store, and occasionally from customers, add to her popularity. The male clerks soon found, however, that beyond the line warranted by their mutual duties she was utterly unapproachable, and not a few of them united in the view held by the girls, that she was "stuck up"; but since she was not in the least above her business, no one could complain openly.

As one long, exceedingly busy and weary day was drawing to a close, however, she received a sharp reprimand. A gentleman had agreed to meet his wife at the shop as he came up town, in order that they might together make provision for Christmas. The lady having nearly accomplished her round, and having proved herself a liberal purchaser, she was naturally accompanied toward the door by a very amiable foreman, who was profuse in his thanks. Suddenly it occurred to her that she would look at the laces, and she approached Mildred, who, in a momentary respite, was leaning back against the shelves with closed eyes, weary beyond all words of description.

"Will you please wake that young woman up," the lady remarked, a little sharply.

This the foreman did, in a way that brought what little blood the poor girl had left into her face. The shopper sat down on the plush seat before the counter, and was soon absorbed in the enticing wares, while her husband stood beside her and stole sidelong glances at the weary but beautiful face of the saleswoman.

"Jupiter Ammon," he soliloquized mentally, "but she

is pretty! If that flush would only last, she'd be beautiful; but she's too pale and fagged for that—out to a ball last night, I imagine. She don't even notice that a man's admiring her—proof, indeed, that she must have danced till near morning, if not worse. What lives these girls lead, if half the stories are true! I'd like to see that one rested, fresh, and becomingly dressed. She'd make a sensation in a Fifth Avenue drawing-room if she had the sense to keep her mouth shut, and not show her ignorance and underbreeding."

But he was growing impatient, and at last said, "Oh, come, my dear, you've bought enough to break me already. We'll be late for dinner."

The lady rose reluctantly, and remarked, "Well, I think I'll come and look at these another day," and they were bowed out of the door.

"You must be more alert," said the foreman, imperatively, to Mildred. "These people are among the best and wealthiest in town."

"I'll try," was the meek answer.

The gentleman had hardly reached the sidewalk, however, before all his chivalry and indignation were aroused. Under the press of Christmas times a drayman had overloaded his cart, and the horse was protesting in his dumb way by refusing to budge an inch; meanwhile the owner proved himself scarcely equal to the animal he drove by furious blows and curses, which were made all the more reckless by his recent indulgence in liquor.

The poor beast soon found many champions, and foremost among them was the critic of the weary shop-girl, who had suffered more that day than the horse was capable of suffering in his lifetime. The distinguished citizen, justly irate, I grant, sent his wife home in their carriage, and declared that he would neither eat nor sleep until he had seen the brute—the drayman, not the horse—arrested and locked up, and he kept his word.

Much later, the wronged and tortured human creature of

whom he had surmised evil, and on whom he had bestowed at best only a little cynical admiration, crept home with steps that faltered, burdened with a heaviness of heart and a weariness of body which could be measured only by the pitiful eye of Him who carries the world's sins and sorrows.

The rescued horse munched his oats in stolid tranquillity; the woman raised to heaven her eyes, beneath which were dark, dark lines, and murmured, "'O God, how long?"

CHAPTER XXIX

THE BEATITUDES OF OPIUM

AT least once each week Roger took Belle to some evening entertainment, selecting places that, while innocent, were in keeping with their years—full of color, life, and interest. The young girl improved at once, as the result of this moderate gratification of a craving that was as proper as it was natural. The sense of being restricted and arbitrarily shut away from the pleasures belonging to her youth no longer worked like a subtle and evil ferment in her mind. The repressed and unhappy are in tenfold more danger from temptation than those who feel they are having their share of life's good. The stream that cannot flow in the sunshine seeks a subterranean channel, and in like manner when circumstances, or the inconsiderate will of others, impose unrelenting restraint upon the exuberant spirit of youth, it usually finds some hidden outlet which cannot bear the light. Until Roger came, circumstances had restricted Belle within such a narrow and colorless life, and she was growing very discontented with her lot—a dangerous tendency. Through all this long ordeal her mother and Mildred had retained her sympathy, for she knew that they were not to blame, and that they were right in protesting against all acquaintances and amusements which involved danger. Now that she and Roger occasionally had a merry time together, and a confidenial chat on Sunday, she accepted her long days of toil without complaint.

The wholesome and tonic influence of a few hours of

positive and unalloyed enjoyment in a busy or burdened life is properly estimated by a very few. Multitudes would preach better, live better, do more work and die much later, could they find some innocent recreation to which they could often give themselves up with something of the whole-hearted *abandon* of a child.

Belle now had pleasures to look forward to, or some bright scene to live over again, and, were it not for her sympathy for her sister and anxiety on her father's behalf, her brow would have been serene.

To Mildred, however, the days were growing darker and the way more thorny. She was gaining only in the power of endurance; she was unconsciously developing the trait that bade fair to become the keynote of her life—fidelity. It was her absolute loyalty to her long-cherished love that prevented her from accepting invitations to go with Belle and Roger. Through all disguises she saw that the latter was a lover and not a friend, and while she had learned to respect him much more, she shrank from him none the less. True, therefore, to her womanly instincts, and pathetically patient with a life full of pain and weariness, she faltered on toward a future that seemed to promise less and less. Roger did not need to be told by Belle of Mildred's burdened life, although the young girl did speak of it often with sad and indignant emphasis. "Beautiful Millie, who would grace the finest house in the city," she said, "is as much out of place in this life as if a gazelle were made to do the work of a cart-horse. It's just killing her."

"It's not the work that's harming her so much as the accursed brutality which permits more cruelty to white women than was ever inflicted on black slaves. If the shop-keepers owned these girls who serve their counters they would provide them seats instantly, on the same principle that some of your Southern people, who had no humanity, cared well for their human property; but these fellows know that when a girl breaks down they can take their pick from twenty applicants the next morning. If I could scalp a few of these woman-murderers, I'd sleep better to-night. Oh, Belle, Belle, if you knew how it hurts me to see such advantage taken of Miss Mildred! I sometimes walk the streets for hours chafing and raging about it, and yet any expression of my sympathy would only add to her distress. You must never speak to her of me, Belle, except in a casual way, when you cannot help it, for only as I keep aloof, even from her thoughts, can she tolerate me at all."

"Be patient, Roger. Millie is unlike many girls, and wants only one lover. Now I'd like half a dozen, more or less, generally more. She's too infatuated with that weakling, Vinton Arnold, to care for any one else. And to think he hasn't sent her one reassuring word since last summer! There isn't enough of him to cast a shadow. Catch me moping after such a dim outline of a man! But it's just like Millie. If he'd only vanish into thin air she might give him up, and perhaps he has."

"No, he's in Europe, and has been there ever since he left the hotel at Forestville. I learned the fact the other day. He's living in luxury and idleness, while the girl who loves him is earning her bread in a way that's infernal in its cruelty."

"How did you find that out?" Belle asked quickly.

"It was in no mean or underhand way, and no knowledge of my inquiries will ever reach him. I thought she'd like to know, however, and you can tell her, but give her no hint of the source of your information."

"Who told you?" was Mildred's prompt response to Belle's news that night, while a sudden bloom in her pale face showed how deeply the tidings interested her.

"No matter how I learned the fact," replied Belle a little brusquely; "it's true. He wouldn't lift his little finger to keep you from starving."

"You wrong him," cried Mildred passionately; "and I don't wish you ever to speak of him again. I know who told you: it was Roger Atwood, and I wish he would leave me and my affairs alone. He is singularly stupid and ill-bred to meddle in such a matter."

"He has not meddled," retorted Belle indignantly, and wholly off her guard; "he thought you might like to know the truth, and he learned it in a way that left no trace. When you are in the streets you are always looking for Mr. Arnold (it's a pity he wasn't doing a little looking, too), and now your mind can be at ease. He isn't sick or dead; he's entirely safe and having a good time, faring sumptuously every day, while you are dying by inches for little more than bread and a nook in a tenement-house. I don't care what you say, I detest such a man."

Mildred's overtaxed nerves gave way at Belle's harsh and prosaic words, and throwing herself on her couch she sobbed so bitterly that the inconsiderate child, in deep compunction, coaxed and pleaded with her not "to take it so hard," and ended by crying in sympathy, almost as heartily as Mildred herself. The latter was completely disarmed of her anger by Belle's feelings, and, indeed, as she came to think it all over, it did not seem so like desertion on Arnold's part, since he might have written from Europe and the letter have failed to reach her. That he should have been in New York all this time and have made no effort to find her would seem heartless indeed. At any rate, with her rare fidelity and faith, she would believe nothing against him without absolute proof.

But of Roger Atwood she thought resentfully, "He reads my very thoughts. He has seen me looking for Vinton half-unconsciously when in the streets. He keeps himself in the background, and no doubt thinks himself very distant and considerate; but I can scarcely turn in any direction but I see his shadow, or meet with some indication that he is watching and waiting."

There was more truth in her words than she half suspected. His duties required that he should be down town very early in the morning, but he was usually released in the afternoon, for his uncle tacitly humored his desire for study. Scarcely an evening elapsed that the young man did not pass and repass the shop in which Mildred was employed, for through the lighted windows he could see the object of his thoughts unobserved, and not infrequently he followed her as she wearily returned homeward, and his heart ached with the impotent desire to lighten the burdens of her life. He feared that she would never accept of his watchful care or thank him for it; but love is its own reward, and impels to action that does not well stand the test of the world's prosaic judgment. Beyond this brief and furtive gratification of his passion, he lost no time in sighing or sentiment, but bent his mind to his tasks with such well-directed and persistent energy that the commission merchant occasionally nodded significantly; for, in accordance with his habit, he took counsel of no one except himself.

It was Roger's hope that, eventually, Mildred, for her own sake, could be persuaded to accompany Belle on some of their pursuits of evening recreation, and he suggested that the latter should persistently try to induce her to go, saying that her health and success in the future required more change and cheerfulness; but Mildred always said "No," with a quiet emphasis which admitted of no argument.

In truth, when evening came she was too weary to go with him or with any one else, and the first Sunday after her duties at the shop began she could not be present at the chapel and meet her class.

Mr. Wentworth called, fearing she was ill. She explained in part, and he was quick to understand. His brow darkened in such a frown that the poor girl grew frightened, and began: "Indeed, Mr. Wentworth, do not judge me harshly, or think that I let a trifle keep me—"

Then he awakened to her misapprehension, and coming directly to her side he took her hand, with a face so kind, so full of deep, strong sympathy, that her eyes filled at once.

"My poor child," he said, "could you imagine I was frowning at you?—brave little soldier that you are, braver and stronger in your way and place than I in mine. God bless you, no. I felt savage to think that in this nineteenth century, and right under the shadow of our church spires, this diabolical cruelty is permitted to go on year after year. Oh, I know all about it, Miss Mildred; you are not the first one by hundreds and hundreds. I wish I could give you more than sympathy, and that some other way would open—we must find some other way for you—but you have no idea how many are worse off in these bad times than you are—worthy people who are willing to work, but cannot get work. If it seems to you that I cannot do very much for you, remember that there are scores who, for the time, seem to have no resources at all. I trust you may soon hear such tidings from your father as will bring relief to both body and mind. And now, my child, don't let a morbid conscience add to your burdens. When you are as greatly in need of rest as you were last Sunday, don't come to the chapel. I'll take your class, or find a substitute."

In a few minutes he was gone; but they were not alone, for he had made them conscious of One who is touched with the feeling of our infirmities.

How was the absent husband and father fulfilling the hopes that daily turned to him, but found no reward? He was literally writhing under chains that, to his horror, he could not break. He had found on shipboard that sudden and complete abstinence from the drug brought a torture of mind and body that he could not endure, and now he was learning, in sickening fear, that he could not gradually reduce his daily allowance below a certain point without immediate sufferings beyond his fortitude to sustain.

The room in the Inquisition, whose circular walls, studded with long, sharp spikes, gradually closed upon and pierced the victim, had its spiritual counterpart in his present condition. He was shut in on every side. If he made a push for liberty by abstaining from the drug, he was met and driven back by many nameless agonies. He seemed to recoil, inevitably, as if from steel barbs. Meanwhile the walls were closing in upon him. In order to prevent life from being a continuous burden, in order to maintain even the semblance of strength and manhood, so that he might have some chance of finding employment, he had to increase the quantity of morphia daily; but each succeeding indulgence brought nearer the hour when the drug would produce pain—pain only, and death. After a week or two of futile and spasmodic effort he drifted on in the old way, occasionally suffering untold agony in remorse and self-loathing, but stifling conscience, memory, and reason, as far as possible, by continuous stimulation.

His quest of employment was naturally unsuccessful. The South was impoverished. Weak from the wounds of war, and the deeper enervation of a system that had poisoned her life for generations, she had not yet begun to rally. There was not enough business in the city for the slow and nerveless hands of its citizens, therefore there was little prospect for a new-comer, unless he had the capital and energy to create activity in the midst of stagnation. A few were slightly imposed upon at first by Mr. Jocelyn's exalted moods, and believed that he might do great things if he were given the chance; but they soon recognized that he was unsound and visionary, broaching plans and projects that varied widely with each succeeding interview. The greater number of his former friends and acquaintances were scattered or dead, and those who remembered him had their hands too full to do more than say a good word for him—saying it, too, more and more faintly as they saw how broken and untrustworthy he was. The story of his behavior on the ship, and correct surmises of the true cause of his manner and appearance, soon became current in business circles, and the half-pitying, half-contemptuous manner of those with whom he came in contact at last made it clear, even to his clouded mind, that further effort would be utterly useless.

Meanwhile his habit now began to inflict a punishment that often seemed beyond endurance. The increased quantities of morphia with which he sought to sustain himself, combined with his anxiety, remorse, and solicitude for his family and his own future, filled the hours of darkness with one long nightmare of horror. His half-sleeping visions were more vivid and real than the scenes of day. From some harrowing illusion he would start up with a groan or cry, only to relapse a few moments later into an apparent situation more appalling and desperate.

The earth would open and swallow him in fathomless darkness; then he was on a ship caught in a maelstrom and whirled down with a speed imaginable only by a mind as disordered and morbid as his own. Panting, struggling, drenched with a cold perspiration, he would struggle back into a brief and miserable consciousness. With scarcely any respite his diseased imagination would seize him again, and now the ship, with tattered sails and broken masts, would be becalmed in the centre of a cyclone. All around him was the whirling tornado from which the vessel had passed into awful silence and deceptive peace. Although viewless, a resistless volume was circling round him, a revolving torrent of air that might at any second make its existence known by wrenching the ship in some direction with such violence as to destroy it at once. When would the awful suspense be over, and the cyclone, with a peal of thunder through the rigging, again lay its frenzied grasp on the ill-fated ship? In unspeakable dread he seemed to spring from the deck in the hope of ending all, and would find himself gasping on his couch, which vice had made a place of torture, nor rest.

But the visions which most shook his soul were those connected with his wife and children. He saw them starving; he saw them turned into the street, mocked and gibed at by every passer-by. He saw them locked up in prison-cells, under the charge of jailers that were half brute, half fiend; he saw Fred and Minnie carried off by an Italian padrone to a den reeking with filth, and loud with oaths and obscenity. With a hoarse shout of rage he would spring up to avert blows that were bruising their little forms; he saw his wife turn her despairing eyes from heaven and curse the hour of their union; he saw Mildred, writhing and resisting, dragged from her home by great dark hands that were claws rather than hands; worse than all, he saw Belle, dressed in colors that seemed woven from stains of blood, stealing out under the cover of night with eyes like livid coals.

Such are the beatific visions that opium bestows, having once enchained its victims. Little wonder that, after spending nights upon a poisoned rack, Mr. Jocelyn was in no condition to meet his fellow-men and win their confidence.

The dark thought crossed his mind more than once that he had better never return home—that, since he had lost his manhood, life had better go too; but in these darkest and most desperate moments the face of his wife would rise before him, and from her white lips came the cry, "No! no! no!" with such agonized intensity that he was restrained.

Moreover, he had not given up hope altogether, and he determined to return, and, unknown to his family, consult his old physician, who had inadvertently led him into this terrible dilemma, and adjure him to undo his work. He might aid in concealing the truth from those from whom, of all others, the unhappy man would hide his shame. This seemed his one last chance.

CHAPTER XXX

THE SECRET VICE REVEALED

ON the day preceding Christmas, late in the afternoon, Roger Atwood boarded a steamer which had just arrived from a Southern city. His uncle, the commission merchant, was expecting a consignment of tropical fruits, and as the young man stood among others waiting to see the freight clerk, he overheard one of the vessel's officers remark, "His name is Jocelyn—so papers on his person indicate—and he must be sent to a hospital as soon as possible."

Advancing promptly to the speaker, Roger said, "I overheard your remark, sir, and think I know the gentleman to whom you refer. If I am right, I will take him to his family immediately."

The officer acted with such alacrity as to prove that he was very glad to get the sick man off his hands, and Roger noted the fact. A moment later he saw Martin Jocelyn, sadly changed for the worse, and lying unconscious in a berth.

"I am right, I am very sorry to say," Roger said, after a moment, with a long, deep breath. "This will be a terrible shock to his family."

"Do you think he is dying?" the officer asked.

"I don't know. I will bring a physician and take Mr. Jocelyn home on one condition—that our consignment of produce is delivered at once. I must be absent, and my employer's interests must not suffer in consequence. I am doing you a favor, and you must return it just as promptly."

The freight clerk was summoned, and Roger was assured

that his uncle's consignment should take the precedence as fast as it could be reached. The young man then hastened to find the nearest physician, stopping a moment at his place of business to give a hurried explanation of his course. Mr. Atwood listened in silence, and nodded merely; but, as Roger hastened away, he muttered, "This mixing himself up with other people's troubles isn't very shrewd, but his making capital out of it so that my consignment will all be delivered to-night is—well, we'll call it even. He's no fool."

The physician was rather young and inexperienced, and he pronounced Mr. Jocelyn's trouble to be congestion of the brain. He agreed to go with Roger to the old mansion and do what he could for the patient, although holding out slight hope of recovery.

"She is learning to associate me with misfortune, and will dread my presence as if I were a bird of ill-omen," Roger groaned mentally, as he recalled the several miserable occasions which, in the mind of Mildred, were inseparably connected with himself; "but some day—*some day*, if I have to strive for a lifetime—she shall also learn that it is not I who bring the trouble."

Christmas comes at the darkest and dreariest season of the year, making short, cold days, and longer, colder nights the holiday season, just as He, whose birth the day commemorates, comes to human hearts in the darkest and coldest hours of desolation. Even in the great city there were few homes so shadowed by poverty and sorrow that they were not brightened by some indications of the hallowed time. The old mansion, that once may have been embowered in evergreens, was again filled with the aromatic breath of the forest, for Roger had commissioned a friend in the country to send so large a supply to Belle that she was embarrassed with riches of hemlock, laurel, and pine, which, although given away prodigally, left enough to transform their rooms into the aspect of bowers. Since they had not money for toys, they could make the Christmas-tide a time of wonder and delight to Fred and Minnie in this inexpensive way, and Mildred, who would naturally shrink from the wild mountain home of the evergreen boughs, found in weaving and arranging them into tasteful decorations a pleasure alloyed by only one thought—she was indebted for it to Roger Atwood, the silent yet determined rival of the man she loved. Though he buried his feeling in such profound silence, and hid all manifestation so carefully that even her intuition could not lay hold of any one thing, and say, "This proves it," she nevertheless felt the presence of his love, and sometimes thought she felt it all the more because of its strong repression. It almost vexed her that he made no advances, and gave her nothing to resent, while all the time he was seeking her with the whole force of his will, or at least waiting for some possibility of the future. When Belle proposed that he should help decorate their living-room, since they, at this season, had only the remnants of evenings to give, and were wearied, too, almost beyond the power for extra effort, she felt that for Belle's sake she ought not to object, and that for her own sake she could not, so scrupulous had been the quiet, distant respect with which he had treated her. When he came he seemed to anticipate her thoughts and to obey her wishes in the arrangement of the greenery, even before she spoke, so keen was his observation and quick his sympathy with her mind.

These very facts increased her prejudice and dislike. He was too clever, too keen-sighted and appreciative. Had he been indifferent toward her, and not so observant, she would have soon learned to like him and enjoy his society, for he had a bright, piquant way of talking, and was seldom at a loss for words. In fact, he had plenty of ideas, and was fast gaining more. One reason why Mildred shrank from him in strengthening repulsion was because, in his absorbing interest and his quick comprehension of her thought and feeling, he came too near. Without intending it, and in spite of himself, he intruded on her woman's privacy;

for no matter how careful he might be, or how guarded she was in words or manner, she felt that he understood what was in her mind. Her natural impulse, therefore, was to shun his presence and suppress her own individuality when she could not escape him, for only an answering affection on her part could make such understanding appreciation acceptable.

Roger was not long in guessing quite accurately how he stood in her thoughts, and he was often much depressed. As he had said to Clara Bute, he had a downright dislike to contend against, and this might not change with his success. And now it was his misfortune to become associated in her mind with another painful event—perhaps a fatal one. She might thank him sincerely for his kindness and the trouble he had taken in their behalf, but, all the same, deep in her heart, the old aversion would be strengthened.

"That invertebrate, Arnold," he muttered, "represents to her the old, happy life; I, her present life, and it's my luck always to appear when things are at their worst. After to-night she will shudder with apprehension whenever she sees me. What *will* become of them if Mr. Jocelyn dies!"

Full of forebodings and distress at the shock and sorrow impending over those in whom he was so deeply interested, he and the physician placed Mr. Jocelyn in a covered express wagon that was improvised into an ambulance, and drove up town as rapidly as they dared.

In response to a low knock Mrs. Jocelyn opened the door, and the white, troubled face of Roger announced evil tidings before a word was spoken.

"My husband!" she gasped, sinking into a chair.

The young man knelt beside her and said, "Mrs. Jocelyn, his life may depend on your courage and fortitude."

He had touched the right chord, and, after a momentary and half-convulsive sob, she rose quietly, and said, "Tell me what to do—tell me the worst."

"I have brought him with me, and I have a physician

also. I found him on a steamer, by accident. They were about to send him to a hospital, but I was sure you would want him brought home."

"Oh, yes—God bless you—bring him, bring him quick."

"Courage. Good nursing will prevent the worst."

Roger hastened back to the patient, stopping on the way only long enough to ask Mrs. Wheaton to go to Mrs. Jocelyn's room instantly, and then, with the physician's aid, he carried the unconscious man to his room, and laid him on his bed.

"Oh, Martin! Martin!" moaned the wife, "how changed, how changed! Oh, God! he's dying."

"I hope not, madam," said the physician; "at any rate we must all keep our self-possession and do our best. While there is life there is hope."

With dilated eyes, and almost fierce repression of all aid from other hands, she took the clothing from the limp and wasted form.

"He *is* dying," she moaned; "see how unnatural his eyes are; the pupils are almost gone. Oh, God! why did I let him go from me when he was so ill!"

"Would you not like Belle and Miss Mildred summoned at once?" Roger asked.

"Yes, yes, they ought to be here now; every moment may be precious, and he may become conscious."

"At the same time I would like you to call on Dr. Benton in Twenty-third Street," added the physician. "He is a friend of mine, and has had much experience. In so serious a case I would like to consult him."

Roger, while on his way to Dr. Benton's office, passed a livery-stable with a coach standing just within the door, and he at once resolved that the weary girls should not be exhausted by flying home in terror-stricken haste. He took the carriage, obtained the physician, and explained to him what had happened while on the way to the shop in which Belle was employed. It was Christmas-eve, and the store was still crowded with eleventh-hour purchasers, on whom the weary child was waiting in a jaded, mechanical way. Her vacant look and the dark lines under her eyes proved how exhausted she was; but at the sight of Roger a flash of light and pleasure came into her face, and then his expression caused it to fade into extreme pallor.

"What is it?" she asked, turning from a garrulous customer.

"Don't be alarmed; get your things and come with me. I will make it all right with your employer."

"Belle," he said, when they were by the carriage door, "you must be a brave woman to-night. Your father is home, and he is very ill. Perhaps his life depends on quiet and freedom from all excitement. Dr Benton, an experienced physician, is in the carriage, and will go with us. You must tell your sister—I cannot."

If Belle had been herself she would not have failed him; but, after the long strain of the day, she became completely unnerved at his tidings, and sobbed almost hysterically. She could not control herself sufficiently to enter the shop where Mildred stood, unconscious of the approaching shadow, and so the heavy task of breaking the news fell upon Roger. "If Belle, naturally so strong, was white and faint from the long, toilsome day, how wan and ghost-like poor Mildred will appear!" was his thought as he sprang to the sidewalk.

They were closing up, and the discipline of the shop was over. Instead of pallor, there was an angry crimson in Mildred's cheeks, and an indignant fire in her eyes. She evidently was deeply incensed, and her companions apparently were as greatly amused. When she saw Roger the crimson deepened in her face, her brow knitted in strong vexation, and she went on with her task of putting the goods under her charge in order, as if she had not seen him; but the thought flashed through her mind: "Oh that he were to me what he is to Belle! Then he might punish my insolent persecutor, but he's the last one in the world to whom I can appeal. Oh, where is papa?"

"Miss Jocelyn—"

"Don't you see you have another beau?" whispered one of her companions as she passed out. "You won't treat this one with words and manner that are the same as a slap in the face, for he's too good-looking."

She paid no heed to the gibe, for the young man's tone was significant, and she had lifted her eyes to his with eager questioning. His grave, sad face banished the flush from hers instantly.

"Miss Jocelyn," Roger began again, in a low tone, "you have already learned to associate me with painful experiences. I cannot help it. But this, my misfortune, is nothing; you must nerve yourself for anxiety that will test even your strength. Your father is home, and ill. I will not explain further before strangers. Belle and a physician are awaiting you in the carriage."

How quiet and measured were his words; but even in her distress she was painfully conscious that the slight tremor in his voice was the low vibration of a feeling whose repressed intensity would sooner or later break forth. Beyond a momentary shrinking from what seemed to her but well-mastered vehemence, she gave him no thought in her overwhelming solicitude.

Scarcely a moment elapsed before she joined him at the door. As he placed her in the carriage he said, "Dr. Benton will explain to you what has happened."

"Roger—" sobbed Belle, but he sprang on the box with the driver, and in a few moments they were at the door of the old mansion.

"Dr. Benton," said the young man, "will you please accompany Miss Jocelyn? After the fatigue of the day and the shock of this evening she will need your support," and he saw that she leaned heavily on the physician's arm.

Having dismissed the carriage, he found Belle leaning against the side of the house, faint and trembling. The young athlete lifted her in his arms and bore her steadily and easily to the doorway, and then again up the winding stairway. "Belle," he whispered, "if you lose your father you shall at least have a brother."

She entwined her arm about his neck in mute acceptance of the relationship. Her every breath was a low sob, and she could not then tell him how his words reassured her, taking away, in part, the almost overwhelming terror of being left unprotected in the world.

During Mr. Jocelyn's absence his family had tried to banish from their minds the memory of his weakness, and thus they had come to think of him again as the strong, cheerful, genial man they had known all their lives. The months preceding his departure were like a hateful dream. It had been a dearly cherished hope that, after breathing his native air for a few weeks, he would return the same frank, clear-eyed, clear-brained man that had won his way, even among strangers, after the wreck and ruin of the war. To him their thoughts had turned daily, in the hope of release from toil that was often torture, and from anxieties that filled every waking hour with foreboding.

How bitter the disappointment then, and how terrible the shock, as they now looked upon his prostrate form, meagre, shrunken, and almost lifeless! Instead of the full, dark eyes that had beamed mirthfully and lovingly for so many years, there was an unnatural contraction of the pupils which rendered them almost invisible. His once healthful complexion was now livid, or rather of a leaden, bluish hue; his respirations stertorous and singularly deliberate.

"He is dying," Mildred moaned; "he is far, far away from us, even now. Oh, if we could have but one look, one sign of farewell!"

Belle and Mrs. Jocelyn became almost helpless with grief, for it did not seem possible to them that he could rally. "Oh, why did I let him go—why did I let him go!" was the wife's remorseful and often-repeated question.

The elderly and experienced physician whom Roger had brought ignored with professional indifference the grief-stricken household, and was giving his whole mind to the study of the case. After examining the pupils of Mr. Jocelyn's eyes, taking his temperature, and counting his pulse, he looked at his associate and shook his head significantly. Roger, who stood in the background, saw that Dr. Benton did not aaccept the young physician's diagnosis. A moment later Dr. Benton bared the patient's arm and pointed to many small scars, some old and scarcely visible, and others recent and slightly inflamed. The young practitioner then apparently understood him, for he said, "This is both worse and better than I feared."

"Worse, worse," growled Dr. Benton.

"What do you mean?" asked Mrs. Jocelyn, more dead than alive.

"Madam," began Dr. Benton very gravely, "have you never seen your husband using a little instrument like this?" and he produced from his pocket a hypodermic syringe.

"Never," was the perplexed and troubled reply.

The physician smiled a little satirically, and remarked, in a low aside, "I hope the drug has not affected the whole family. It's next to impossible to get at the truth in these cases."

"Do you think he will die?" was her agonized query.

"No, madam, we can soon bring him around, I think, and indeed he would probably have come out of this excess unaided; but he had better die than continue his excessive use of morphia. I can scarcely conceive how you could have remained ignorant of the habit."

Mildred bowed her head in her hands with a low, despairing cry, for a flash of lurid light now revealed and explained all that had been so strange and unaccountable. The terrible secret was now revealed, as far as she was able to comprehend it—her father was an opium inebriate, and this was but the stupor of a debauch! The thought of his death had been terrible, but was not this worse? She lifted her face in a swift glance at Roger, and saw him looking at her with an expression that was full of the strongest sympathy, and something more. She coldly averted her eyes, and a slow, deep flush of shame rose to her face. "Never shall I endure a humiliation but he will witness it, and be a part of it," was her bitter thought.

The physicians meanwhile changed their treatment, and were busy with professional nonchalance. Mrs. Jocelyn was at first too bewildered by their words and manner to do more than look at them, with hands clasping and unclasping in nervous apprehension, and with eyes full of deep and troubled perplexity. Then, as the truth grew clearer, that a reflection had been made upon her own and her husband's truth, she rose unsteadily to her feet, and said, with a pathetic attempt at dignity, "I scarcely understand you, and fear that you as little understand my husband's condition. He never concealed anything from me. He has been unfortunate and in failing health for months, and that is all. I fear, from your cruel and unjust surmises, that you do not know what you are doing, and that you are destroying his slender chances for life."

"Do you wish to discharge us, then?" was Dr. Benton's brusque response. He was a man of unusual skill, but blunt and unsympathetic, especially in cases wherein he suspected deception—an element almost inseparable from the morphia habit. The victim is almost invariably untruthful, and the family not unfrequently hide the whole truth in the desire to shield the disgracefaul weakness. Dr. Benton was too familiar with these facts to be easily moved, but when the sad-hearted wife clasped her hands and cried, in tones that would touch the coldest heart, "I wish him to live, for his death would be far worse than death to us all," the physician said kindly, "There, there, Mrs. Jocelyn, I have seen many cases like this. Your husband will live, and will soon be able to speak to you. If you then can induce him to leave morphia alone, he may become as sound a man as ever."

Mildred put her arm around her mother and drew her into her room, closing the door.

A few moments later Roger heard the wife's passionate protest, "I do not believe it—I will never believe it." Then Dr. Benton said to him, "Here, young man, run to my house for an electric battery."

When he returned Mr. Jocelyn was coming slowly out of his deep coma, and his appearance was changing rapidly for the better. There was a deep, indignant flush on Mrs. Jocelyn's face, and she took Roger aside and said earnestly, "Never believe the lies you have heard here to-night. I know that you will never repeat them."

"Never, Mrs. Jocelyn."

But Mildred was pale and almost stony in her cold, calm aspect; her heart, in her desperation, was hard toward every one. Belle had not comprehended the truth at all, having been too much overwhelmed by her emotions to heed the earlier remarks of the physicians, and Mildred had said to them significantly and almost sternly, "There is no need of giving your diagnosis any further publicity."

Dr. Benton had then looked at her more attentively, and muttered, "An unusual girl; more's the pity."

"Mr. Atwood," Mildred began, a few moments after his entrance, "we thank you for your aid in this painful emergency, but we need trouble you no further. Papa is rallying fast. I will thank you to inform me of all the expense which you have incurred in our behalf at your earliest convenience."

"Mildred," interposed Mrs. Jocelyn, suddenly appearing from beside her husband's couch, the unwonted fire still burning in her usually gentle eyes, "I cannot permit Mr. Atwood to be dismissed so coldly. He has been a true friend in the most terrible emergency of our lives. I must have a strong, kind hand to sustain me now that my husband, my life, has been foully slandered in his own home."

Belle, in even greater terror of being left alone, clung to his arm, and said, "He cannot leave us—he has made me a promise this night which will keep him here."

With a troubled and deprecating look at Mildred, Roger

replied, "I will not fail you, Mrs. Jocelyn, nor you, Belle; but there is no further need of my intruding on your privacy. I shall be within call all night."

"He can stay hin my room," said Mrs. Wheaton, who, although aiding the physicians, could not help overhearing the conversation.

"No, he shall stay here," cried Belle passionately; "I'm so unnerved that I'm almost beside myself, and he quiets me and makes me feel safer. Millie has no right to show her prejudice at such a time."

Mildred, white and faint, sank into a chair by the table and buried her face in her arms, leaving the young fellow in sore perplexity as to what course he ought to take. He believed the physicians were right, and yet Mrs. Jocelyn had taken it for granted that he shared her faith in her husband's truth, and he knew she would banish him from her presence instantly should he betray a doubt as to the correctness of her view. At the same time the expression of his face had shown Mildred that he understood her father's condition even better than she did. It seemed impossible to perform the difficult and delicate part required of him, but with love's loyalty he determined to do what he imagined the young girl would wish, and he said firmly, "Belle, I again assure you that you can depend upon my promise to the utmost. Mrs. Jocelyn, my respect for you is unbounded, and the privilege of serving you is the best reward I crave. At the same time I feel that it is neither right nor delicate for me to witness sorrows that are so sacred. My part is to help, and not look on, and I can help just as well if within call all the time. Belle," he whispered, "dear Belle, I know you are unnerved by weeks of overwork as well as by this great trouble, but be a brave little woman once more, and all may soon be well," and he was about to withdraw when Dr. Benton appeared and said:

"Mrs. Jocelyn, your husband is now out of all immediate danger, but everything depends upon his future treatment. I wish this young man to remain a little longer, for you must now decide upon what course you will take. We have been called in an emergency. There is no need that I should remain any longer, for the physician who accompanied him here is now amply competent to attend to the case. You have, however, expressed lack of confidence in us, and may wish to send for your own physician. If so, this young man can go for him at once. I can prove to you in two minutes that I am right, and I intend to do so; then my responsibility ceases. Everything depends on your intelligent and firm co-operation with whatever physician has charge of the case, and it is no kindness to leave you under a delusion that does your heart more credit than your head or eyes."

He stepped back through the curtained doorway, and returned with her husband's vest, from an inner pocket of which he took a hypodermic syringe, a bottle of Magendie's solution, and also another vial of the sulphate of morphia.

"I am an old physician," he resumed, "and know your husband's symptoms as well as you know his face. His possession of these articles should confirm my words. The slight scars upon his arms and elsewhere were made by this little instrument, as I can show you if you will come and observe—"

His medical logic was interrupted by a low cry from the stricken wife, and then she fainted dead away.

Mildred, on the contrary, stepped forward, with a pale, stern face, and said, "I will take charge of these," and she carried the agents of their ruin to her own room. Instantly she returned, and assisted Mrs. Wheaton in the restoration of her mother.

To Belle, who had looked on dazed, trembling, and bewildered, Roger whispered, "I shall be within call all night."

CHAPTER XXXI

AN OPIUM MANIAC'S CHRISTMAS

BENEATH his brusque manner Dr. Benton masked a kind heart when once its sympathies were touched. He soon became satisfied that Mr. Jocelyn's family were not trying to shield his patient, but were, on the contrary, overwhelmed with dismay and shame at the truth which he had made clear to them. He therefore set about helping them, in his own prosaic but effective way, and he did not leave them until they were all as well and quiet as the dread circumstances of the situation permitted. Opium slaves are subject to accidents like that which had overtaken Mr. Jocelyn, who, through heedlessness or while half unconscious, had taken a heavy overdose, or else had punctured a vein with his syringe. Not infrequently habitués carelessly, recklessly, and sometimes deliberately end their wretched lives in this manner. Dr. Benton knew well that his patient was in no condition to enter upon any radical curative treatment, and it was his plan to permit the use of the drug for a few days, seeking meanwhile to restore as far as possible his patient's shattered system, and then gain the man's honest and hearty co-operation in the terrible ordeal essential to health and freedom. If Mr. Jocelyn had not the nerve and will-power to carry out his treatment—which he much doubted—he would advise that he be induced to go to an institution where the will of others could enforce the abstinence required. He believed that Mr. Jocelyn would consent to this, when convinced of his inability to endure the ordeal in his own strength. Having explained his intentions and hopes to Mrs. Jocelyn and Mildred, he left them cast down indeed, but not utterly devoid of hope.

It seemed to them that the husband and father must renounce the fatal habit at once, in response to their appeals. They could not understand that it was already beyond his power to break his chains—that they must be broken by other hands, if broken at all.

It may well be doubted if the light of Christmas day dawned on a sadder household than that which was sheltered in the old mansion. Worn and exhausted to the last degree, and yet sleepless from anxiety, grief, and shame, the two women watched beside the fitful, half-conscious man. At last he appeared to throw off his stupor sufficiently to recognize his wife; but it was with a strange look, in which were blended fear, suspicion, and shame. A cold perspiration broke out over his whole form, for something in her expression, and especially in the aspect of Mildred's face, seemed to indicate that they knew all, and his own guilty fears and conscience made the surmise true for the moment; but the tender manner in which his wife wiped his brow and kissed him were reassuring, and with his rallying powers grew the hope that his weakness might yet be unknown and successfully concealed until, by his physician's aid, he had thrown off the curse. Fearing above and beyond all things else that his wife would learn his degradation, he slowly and fitfully tried to mature plans of deception; but his enfeebled mind rallied so slowly that he felt for a time that silence and observation were his best allies. He would cautiously and suspiciously feel his way, and having learned all that had transpired since he remembered being on the steamer, he could then decide more clearly how to shape his course. He therefore affected to regard his condition as the result of a severe illness, and murmured that "quiet and home life would soon bring him round."

Mildred kissed him also, and answered, "We cannot think otherwise, papa, for our love, our lives, and all are bound up in you."

The morning dragged heavily away, for all except the little ones were under the impression that dark and woful days were before them. Mr. Benton had not disguised the truth—that the problem with which they had to deal was one of great difficulty and much doubt. This prospect was depressing, but that which weighed like lead upon their hearts was the thought that one who had ever been their ideal of honor and truth had deceived them for months, and had steadily yielded to a habit which he knew must destroy his family's honor and leave them friendless, penniless, and disgraced. The weeks of pain that Mildred had endured were not the result of a hard necessity, but of a vicious indulgence of a depraved appetite. Not disease but sin had so darkened their lives and brought them to a pass where even daily bread and shelter for the future were doubtful questions.

A thousand times Mildred asked herself, "How can I go out and face the world with my name blackened by this great cloud of shame?" She felt as if she never wished to step into the open light of day again, and the thought of Vinton Arnold made her shudder. "There is now a great gulf between us," she moaned. "The truth that my father is an opium slave can never be hidden, and even were Vinton inclined to be faithful, his family would regard me as a leper, and he will yield to their abhorrence."

The wound in both her own and her mother's heart was deep indeed. Their confidence was shattered, their faith in human goodness and honor destroyed. While they still hoped much, they nevertheless harbored a desperate fear, and, at best, the old serene trust could never return. Even if Mr. Jocelyn could rally and reform, there would ever remain the knowledge that he had once been weak and false, and might be again. He would be one who must be watched, shielded, and sustained, and not one upon whom they could lean in quiet faith. The quaking earth which shatters into ruin the material home brings but a slight disaster compared with the vice that destroys a lifelong trust in a husband and father.

Mr. Jocelyn's nerves were much too weak and irritable to endure his children's voices, and their innocence and unconsciousness of danger smote him with unendurable remorse; they were, therefore, sent to Mrs. Wheaton's room. There, too, Belle met Roger, and was much reassured by his hopeful words. She only half comprehended the truth concerning her father, and now, feeling the worst was past, her mercurial nature was fast regaining its cheerfulness. She was one who might despair one day and be joyous the next. Like her father, she had unlimited courage, and but little fortitude. Although she did not know it, the outlook for her was more threatening than for any of the others, for she could not patiently submit to a slow, increasing pressure of poverty and privation. As her father feared, she might be driven to interpose the protest of a reckless life.

Mr. Jocelyn was greatly reassured when Dr. Benton called, and treated him with much respect; and when a liberal allowance of morphia was injected into his arm, he became quite cheerful, believing that not only his family but even the physician was unaware, as yet, of his weakness. By neither sign nor word did Dr. Benton indicate his knowledge, for it was his design to rally his patient into the best possible condition, and then induce him to yield himself up wholly to medical skill, naturally believing that in his present enfeebled state he would shrink from entering on the decisive and heroic treatment required. Promising to call in the evening, he left Mr. Jocelyn apparently very much improved.

In the afternoon Mildred went to her room to seek a little rest. The physician thought he had given enough of the drug to satisfy his patient until he returned, but he had not properly gauged the morbid craving with which he was trying to deal, and as the day declined Mr. Jocelyn became very restless. Finally, he said he felt so much better that he would rise and dress himself, and, in spite of his wife's remonstrances, he persisted in doing so. Although tottering from weakness, he said, irritably, and almost imperiously, that he needed no help, and wished to be alone. With sad foreboding his wife yielded, and waited tremblingly for his next step, for he had become to her an awful mystery.

Her fears were fulfilled, for he soon lifted the curtain door and looked at her in a strange, suspicious manner. "I miss some medicine from my vest pocket," he said hesitatingly.

Her face crimsoned, and she found no words with which to reply.

"Did you take it out?" he demanded sharply.

"No," she faltered.

His manner began to grow excited, and he looked like a distorted image of his former self. Anger, suspicion, fear, and cunning were all blended in his face, but he so far mastered himself as to assume a wheedling tone and manner as he came toward her and said, "Nan, it was only a little tonic that I found beneficial while in the South. You must know where it is. Please give it to me."

The poor woman was so overcome by her husband's appearance and falsehood that she felt sick and faint, and knew not what to say.

"Where is it?" he demanded angrily, for he felt that unless he had the support of the drug speedily, he would wholly lose his self-control.

"Oh, Martin," pleaded his wife, "wait till Dr. Benton comes; he will be here this evening."

"Why this ado about nothing? I merely wish to take a little tonic, and you look as if I proposed suicide."

"Martin, Martin, it is suicide of body and soul. It is worse than murder of me and your innocent children. Oh, Martin, my heart's true love, make me a Christmas gift that I will prize next to Him from whom the day is named. Give me the promise that you will never touch the vile poison again," and she knelt before him and sought to take his hand.

For a moment he was overwhelmed. She evidently knew all! He sank into a chair, and trembled almost convulsively. Then came the impulse—an almost inevitable effect of the drug upon the moral nature—to lie about the habit, and to strive to conceal it, even after an unclouded mind would see that deception was impossible.

"Nan," he began, as he grew a little quieter, "you take cruel advantage of my weak nerves. You must see that I am greatly reduced by illness, and I merely wish to take a little tonic as any sane man would do, and you treat me to a scene of high tragedy. Give me my medicine, and I know that I shall soon be much better."

"Oh, my husband, has it really come to this?" and the wretched wife buried her face in her arms, and leaned heavily on the table.

He was growing desperate. Through excess he had already reached a point where ordinary life became an unendurable burden without the stimulant; but facing a harrowing scene like this was impossible. He felt that his appetite was like a savage beast on which he held a weakening and relaxing grasp. With the strange, double consciousness of the opium maniac, he saw his wife in all her deep distress, and he had the remorse of a lost soul in view of her agony; he was almost certain that she knew how he had wronged her and his children, and he had all the shame and self-loathing of a proud, sensitive man; he knew that he was false to the sacred trusts of husband and father, and that awful thing we call a sense of guilt added its deep depression. It is not inability to comprehend his degradation, his danger, his utter loss of manhood, which opium imposes on its wretched slave, but an impossibility to do aught except gratify the resistless craving at any and every cost. All will-power has gone, all moral resistance has departed, and in its place is a gnawing, clamorous, ravening desire. The vitiated body, full of indescribable and mysterious pain, the still more tortured mind, sinking under a burden of remorse, guilt, fear, and awful imagery, both unite in one desperate, incessant demand for opium.

While his wife sat leaning upon the table, her face hidden, she was the picture of despair; and, in truth, she felt almost as if she were turning into stone. If her husband had been brought home a mangled, mutilated man, as she often feared he might be during the long years of the war, she would have bent over him with a tenderness equalled only by the pride and faith that had ever found in him their centre; but this strange apparition of a man with odd, sinister-looking eyes, who alternately threatened and cowered before her—this man, mutilated more horribly in the loss of truth and love, who was thus openly and shamelessly lying—oh, was he the chivalric, noble friend, who had been lover and husband for so many years! The contrast was intolerable, and the sense of his falseness stung her almost to madness. She did not yet know that opium, like the corruption of the grave, blackens that which is the fairest and whitest.

For a few minutes Mr. Jocelyn debated with himself. Was he strong enough to go out to the nearest drug store? After one or two turns up and down the room he found that he was not. He might fall in utter collapse while on the way, and yet his system, depleted by his recent excess, demanded the drug with an intensity which he could not restrain much longer without becoming wild and reckless. He therefore said to his wife, in a dogged manner, "Nan, I must have that medicine."

The gentle creature was at last goaded into such a burst of indignation that for a few moments he was appalled, and trembled before her. The fire in her blue eyes seemed to scorch away her tears, and standing before him she said passionately, "As you are a man and a Southern gentleman, tell me the truth. I never concealed a thought from you; what have you been concealing from us for weeks and months? I wronged you in that I did not think and plan day and night how to save instead of how to spend, and I can never forgive myself, but my fault was not deliberate, not intentional. There was never a moment when I tried to deceive you—never a moment when I would not have suffered hunger and cold that you and the children might be warmed and fed. What is this tonic for which you are bartering your health, your honor and ours, your children's bread and blood? Mildred sold her girlhood's gifts, the few dear mementoes of the old happy days, that you might have the chance you craved. That money was as sacred as the mercy of God. For weeks the poor child has earned her bread, not by the sweat of her face, but in agony of body and unhappiness of heart. If it were disease that had so cast us down and shadowed our lives with fear, pain, and poverty, we would have submitted to God's will and watched over you with a patient tenderness that would never have faltered or murmured; but it's not disease, it's not something that God sent. It is that which crimsons our faces with shame."

He sat cowering and trembling before her, with his face buried in his hands.

In a sudden revulsion of tenderness she sank again on her knees before him, and pleaded in tones of tenderest pathos: "Martin, I know all; but I am ready to forgive all if you will be true from this time forward. I know now the cause of all your strange moods which we attributed to ill-health; I know the worst; but if, in humble reliance upon God, you will win back your manhood, the past evil days shall be blotted out, even as God blots out our sins and remembers them no more against us. We will sustain your every effort with sympathy and loving faith. We will smile at cold and hunger that you may have time—Great God!" and she sprang to her feet, white, faint, and panting.

Her husband had taken his hands from his face, and glared at her like a famished wolf. In his desperate, unnatural visage there was not a trace of manhood left.

"Give me the bottle of morphia you took from my

pocket," he demanded, rising threateningly. "No words; you might as well read the Ten Commandments to an unchained tiger. Give it to me, or there is no telling what may happen. You talk as if I could stop by simply saying, coolly and quietly, I will stop. Ten thousand devils! haven't I suffered the torments of the damned in trying to stop! Was I not in hell for a week when I could not get it? Do you think I ask for it now as a child wants candy? No, it's the drop of water that will cool my tongue for a brief moment, and as you hope for mercy or have a grain of mercy in your nature, give it to me *now*, *now*, NOW!"

The poor wife tottered a step or two toward her daughter's room, and fell swooning at the threshold. Mildred opened the door, and her deep pallor showed that instead of sleeping she had heard words that would leave scars on memory until her dying day.

"The poison you demand is there," she said brokenly, pointing to her bureau. "After mamma's appeal I need not, cannot speak," and she knelt beside her mother.

Her father rushed forward and seized the drug with the aspect of one who is famishing. Mildred shuddered, and would not see more than she could help, but gave her whole thought and effort to her mother, who seemed wounded unto death. After a few moments, to her unbounded surprise, her father knelt beside her and lifted her mother to a lounge, and, with a steady hand and a gentle, considerate manner, sought to aid in her restoration. His face was full of solicitude and anxiety—indeed he looked almost the same as he might have looked and acted a year ago, before he had ever imagined that such a demon would possess him.

When at last Mrs. Jocelyn revived and recalled what had occurred, she passed into a condition of almost hysterical grief, for her nervous system was all unstrung. Mr. Jocelyn, meanwhile, attended upon her in a silent, gentle, self-possessed manner that puzzled Mildred greatly, although she ascribed it to the stimulant he had taken.

After a few minutes a strange smile flitted across his face, and he disappeared within his own apartment. A little later, Mildred, returning from a momentary absence, saw him withdraw his syringe from the arm of her half-conscious mother.

"What have you done?" she asked sternly, and hastening to his side.

Secreting the instrument as a miser would his gold, he answered, with the same strange smile, "She shall have a merry Christmas yet; I have just remembered the day. See how quiet she is becoming; see that beautiful flush stealing into her pale face; see the light dawning in her eye. Oh, I gauged the dose with the skill of the best of them; and see, my hand is as steady as yours. I'm not a wreck yet, and all may still be well. Come, this is Christmas night, and we will keep it in good old Southern style. Where are Belle and the children? Ah! here they are. Where have you been, Belle?"

"In Mrs. Wheaton's room," she replied, looking at her father in much surprise. "I was trying to keep the children quiet, so that you, mamma, and Millie might have a little rest."

"That was very kind and good of you, and you now see that I am much better; so is mamma, and with your help and Mildred's we shall have a merry Christmas night together after all."

"Papa is right," Mrs. Jocelyn added with vivacity. "I *do* feel much better, and so strangely hopeful. Come here, Belle. I've scarcely seen you and the children all day. Kiss me, darlings. I believe the worst is now past, that papa will soon be well, and that all our troubles will end in renewed prosperity and happiness. I have been looking on the dark side, and it was wrong in me to do so. I should have had more faith, more hope, more thankfulness. I should bless God for that sight—Fred and Minnie on their father's knees as in old times. Oh, what a strange, bright turn everything has taken."

"Mamma dear," said Belle, who was kneeling and caressing her, "can I not ask Roger in to see you? He has looked like a ghost all day, from anxiety about you."

"Oh, no, no," gasped Mildred.

"Now, Millie," began Mrs. Jocelyn in gentle effusion, "you carry your prejudice against Roger much too far. He has been the world and all to Belle since he came to town. Belle was like a prisoned bird, and he gave her air and room to fly a little, and always brought her back safe to the nest. Think of his kindness last night (suddenly she put her hand to her brow as if troubled by something half forgotten, but her serene smile returned). Papa, thanks to Roger's kindness, is here, and he might have been taken to a hospital. I now feel assured that he will overcome all his troubles. What we need is cheerfulness—the absence of all that is depressing. Roger is lonely away from his home and people, and he shall share our Christmas cheer; so call him, Belle, and then you and Millie prepare as nice a supper as you can;" and the girl flew to make good a prospect so in accordance with her nature.

Mildred almost as precipitately sought her room. A moment later Roger was ushered in, and he could scarcely believe his eyes. The unconscious man, whom he at this time on the previous day believed dying, had his children on his lap, and was caressing them with every mark of affection. Although he still appeared to be very much of an invalid, and his complexion had a sallow and unnatural hue, even in the lamplight, it was difficult to believe that twenty-four hours before he had appeared to be *in extremis.* When he arose and greeted Roger with a courtesy that was almost faultless, the young fellow was tempted to rub his eyes as if all were a dream. Mrs. Jocelyn, too, was full of cheerfulness and hope, and made him sit beside her while she thanked him with a cordiality and friendliness that seemed even tinged with affection. If memory could be silenced there would be nothing to dispel the illusion that he looked upon a humble but happy home, unshadowed by any thought of danger or trouble. As it was, the illusion was so strong that he entered into the apparent spirit of the occasion, and he chatted and laughed with a freedom and ease he had never yet known in their presence.

"Where is Millie?" Mrs. Jocelyn suddenly asked. "We must be all together on this happy occasion. Minnie, call her, for I do not wish a moment of this long-deferred hour marred or clouded."

"Millie," cried the child, opening the door, "mamma wants you to come right away. We are having a lovely time."

"Don't mind Millie's ways," said Mrs. Jocelyn, touching Roger's arm and giving him a little confidential nod. "You understand each other."

These words, with her manner, struck Roger as peculiar in one who had ever seemed to him the embodiment of delicacy, but he was too inexperienced to gauge them properly. When he turned, however, to bow to Mildred, who entered and took a seat in a distant corner, he was startled by her extreme pallor, but acting on Mrs. Jocelyn's advice he tried to act as before, resolving, nevertheless, that if his presence continued to be a restraint on one for whom he was ever ready to sacrifice himself, he would speedily depart. Belle was radiant in her reaction from the long, miserable day, and, with a child's unconsciousness, gave herself up to her happiness.

"Millie shall rest as well as yourself, mamma, for she was up all night, and I'll get supper and prove what a housewife I am. Roger, if you do not swallow everything I prepare without a wry face, and, indeed, with every appearance of relish, I shall predict for you the most miserable old bachelorhood all your days."

"I am afraid you will put Roger's gallantry to a very severe test," cried Mrs. Jocelyn gayly. "Indeed, I fear we have not very much for supper except the warmest good-will. Our poverty now, however, will not last long, for I feel that I can so manage hereafter as to make amends for all the past. I can see that I am the one who has been to blame; but all that's past, and with my clearer, fuller knowledge and larger opportunities I can do wonders."

Roger was much struck by the peculiar smile with which Mr. Jocelyn regarded his wife as she uttered these words.

"Lemme show you what Aunty Wheaton gave me dis mornin'," lisped Fred, pulling Roger up.

As he rose he caught a glimpse of Mildred's face, and saw that she was regarding her mother and father in undisguised horror. Something was evidently wrong—fearfully wrong. There was a skeleton in that cheerful lighted room, and the girl saw it plainly. Never would he forget her terrible expression. He trembled with apprehension as he stood over the child's toy and tried to imagine what it was that had suddenly filled the place with a nameless dread and foreboding. So quick and strong was his sympathy for Mildred, so unmistakable had been the expression of the girl's face, that he was sure something must soon occur which would explain her fears.

He was right, for at this moment Dr. Benton knocked, entered, and took the chair he had vacated. The physician looked with some surprise at his patient and Mrs. Jocelyn's flushed, smiling face. As he felt her pulse her sleeve fell back, and he saw the ominous little red scar, and then he understood it all, and fixed a penetrating glance on the face of her husband, who would not meet his eye.

"I have done you wrong, Dr. Benton," Mrs. Jocelyn began volubly, "for we all are indebted to your skill that my husband is so much better. This day, which promised to pass so sadly, has a bright ending, thanks to your timely remedies. We are once more a united household, and I can never thank our dear young friend here, Mr. Atwood, enough that he discovered my husband and brought him to us and to your able treatment. Surely, Millie, your prejudice against him must vanish now, for—"

"Mother," cried Mildred, "if you have a grain of reason

or self-control left, close your lips. Oh, what a mockery it all is!"

When Belle took her astonished eyes from Mildred's face, Roger, who stood near the door, was gone.

"You had better follow your daughter's advice, Mrs. Jocelyn," said the physician quietly and soothingly; "you are a little feverish, and I prescribe quiet. May I see you alone a moment or two, Mr. Jocelyn?"

"Yes, here in my room," added Mildred eagerly.

It was with the aspect of mingled fear and haughtiness that Mr. Jocelyn followed Dr. Benton into the apartment, and the door was closed.

"Mother, you are ill," said Mildred, kneeling beside her. "For my sake, for yours, pray keep quiet for a while."

"Ill! I never felt better in my life. It's all your unreasonable prejudice, Millie."

"I think so too," cried Belle indignantly. "We were just beginning to have a little sunshine, and you have spoiled everything."

"I am the only one who knows the truth, and I shall take the responsibility of directing our affairs for the next few hours," replied Mildred, rising, with a pale, impassive face. "Belle, my course has nothing to do with Roger Atwood. I exceedingly regret, however, that he has been present. Wait till you hear what Dr. Benton says;" and there was something so resolute and almost stern in her manner that even Mrs. Jocelyn, in her unnatural exaltation, yielded. Indeed, she was already becoming drowsy from the effects of the narcotic.

"You are not yourself, mamma. I'll explain all to-morrow," the young girl added soothingly.

"Mr. Jocelyn," said the physician, with quiet emphasis, "you have injected morphia into your wife's arm."

"I have not."

"My dear sir, I understand your case thoroughly, and so do your wife and daughter, as far as they can understand my explanations. Now if you will cease your mad folly I can save you, I think; that is, if you will submit yourself absolutely to my treatment."

"You are talking riddles, sir. Our poverty does not warrant any assumption on your part."

"I know the insane and useless instinct of those in your condition to hide their weakness; but can you not control it, and permit me as your friend and physician to help you? I am seeking your interests, not my own."

"Curse you!" cried Mr. Jocelyn, in a burst of uncontrollable anger; "if you had been my friend you would have let me die, but instead you have said things to my wife that have blasted me forever in her eyes. If she had not known, I could have made the effort you require; but now I'm a lost man, damned beyond remedy, and I'd rather see the devil himself than your face again. These are my rooms, and I demand that you depart and never appear here again."

The physician bowed coldly, and left the ill-fated family to itself.

Mildred, who overheard her father's concluding words, felt that it would be useless then to interpose. Indeed she was so dispirited and exhausted that she could do no more than stagger under the heavy burden that seemed crushing her very soul.

She assisted her mother to retire, and the latter was soon sleeping with a smile upon her lips. Mr. Jocelyn sat sullenly apart, staring out into the bleak, stormy darkness, and Mildred left him for the first time in her life without giving him his good-night kiss. As she realized this truth, she sank on her couch and sobbed so bitterly that Belle, who had been meditating reproaches, looked at her with tearful wonder. Suddenly Mildred arose in strong compunction, and rushed back to her father; but he started up with such a desperate look that she recoiled.

"Don't touch me," he cried. "Put your lips to the gutter of the streets, if you will, but not to such pitch and foulness as I have become."

"Oh, papa, have mercy!" she pleaded.

"Mercy!" he repeated, with a laugh that froze her blood, "there is no mercy on earth nor in heaven," and he waved her away, and again turned his face to the outer darkness.

"Millie, oh, Millie, what *is* the matter?" cried Belle, shocked at her sister's horror-stricken face.

"Oh, Belle, is there any good God?"

"Millie, I'm bewildered. What does it all mean? The evening that began so brightly seems ending in tragedy."

"Yes, tragedy in bitter truth. Hope is murdered, life poisoned, hearts made to bleed from wounds that can never heal. Belle, papa loves opium better than he does you or me, better than his wife and little helpless children, better than heaven and his own soul. Would to God I had never lived to see this day!"

CHAPTER XXXII

A BLACK CONSPIRACY

ON the following morning Mrs. Jocelyn was ill and much depressed from the reaction of the drug that had been given without her knowledge, and after learning all that had transpired she sank into an almost hopeless apathy. Mildred also was unable to rise, and Belle went to their respective employers and obtained a leave of absence for a day or two, on the ground of illness in the family. Mrs. Wheaton now proved herself a discreet and very helpful friend, showing her interest by kindly deeds and not by embarrassing questions. Indeed she was so well aware of the nature of the affliction that overwhelmed the family that she was possessed by the most dismal forebodings as well as the deepest sympathy.

Mr. Jocelyn had departed at an early hour, leaving a note wherein he stated that he might be absent some days seeking employment in a neighboring city. He had felt that it would be impossible to meet his family immediately after the experiences of the previous day. Indeed he had gone away with the desperate resolve that he would break his habit or never return; but alas for the resolves of an opium slave!

Time dragged heavily on, the family living under a nightmare of anxiety, fear, and horrible conjectures. What might he not do? What new phase of the tragedy would hereafter be developed?

Now that the busy season was over, the girls found that they could retain their position as saleswomen only by accepting whatever their employers chose to pay, and the thrifty shopkeepers satisfied their consciences with the thought that they could obtain scores of others at even lower prices. Mr. Schriven, in the multiplicity of other interests, had almost forgotten Belle, and she had become in his mind merely a part of the establishment. Her dejected face and subdued manner excited some remark among her companions when she again appeared, but her explanation, "Mother is ill," quieted all curiosity.

For a few days Mildred looked as white and crushed as a broken lily, and then the reserve strength and courage of the girl began to reassert themselves. With a fortitude that was as heroic as it was simple and unostentatious, she resolutely faced the truth and resolved to do each day's duty, leaving the result in God's hands. With a miser's care she husbanded her strength, ate the most nourishing food they could afford, and rested every moment her duties permitted. The economy they were now compelled to practice amounted almost to daily privation. Belle and the children were often a little petulant over this change, Mrs. Jocelyn apathetic, but Mildred was inflexible. "We must not run in debt one penny," she would often remark with compressed lips.

Although frequently unoccupied at the shop, she was nevertheless compelled to stand, and in spite of this cruel requirement she rallied slowly. Thanks, however, to her wise carefulness, she did gain steadily in her power to endure and to fight the hard battle of life.

One of the saddest features of their trouble was the necessity of reticence and of suffering in silence. Their proud, sensitive spirits did not permit them to speak of their shame even to Mrs. Wheaton, and she respected their reserve. Indeed, among themselves they shrank from mentioning the sorrow that oppressed every waking moment and filled their dreams with woful imagery.

During an absence of nearly two weeks Mr. Jocelyn occasionally wrote a line, saying that he was as well as they could expect, and that was all. Then he reappeared among them and began leading a desultory kind of life, coming and going in an aimless way, and giving but little account of himself. They saw with a deeper depression that he had not improved much, although apparently he had avoided any great excesses. Occasionally he gave Mildred a little money, but how it was obtained she did not know. It was well he was reticent, for had she known that it was often part of a small loan from some half-pitying friend of former days, and that it would never be repaid, she would not have used a penny of it. They were simply compelled to recognize the awful truth, that the husband and father was apparently a confirmed opium inebriate. At first they pleaded with him again and again, unable to understand how it was possible for him to continue in so fatal a course, but at last they despairingly desisted. He would at times weep almost hysterically, overwhelmed with remorse, and again storm in reckless anger and unreasoning fury. As in thousands of other homes wherein manhood and honor have been destroyed, they found no better resource than silent endurance. Under such inflictions resignation is impossible. For Mrs. Jocelyn and Mildred it was simply a daily martyrdom, but in her companionship with Roger, Belle had much to sustain, cheer, and even brighten her life.

He was in truth a loyal friend, and daily racked his brain for opportunities to show her and Mrs. Jocelyn some reassuring attention; and his kindness and that of Mrs. Wheaton were about the only glints of light upon their darkening way. Mildred was polite and even kind in her manner toward the young man, since for Belle's sake and her mother's she felt that she must be so. His course, moreover, had compelled her respect; but nevertheless her shrinking aversion did not diminish. The fact that an evil destiny had seemingly destroyed her hope of ever looking into the face of Vinton Arnold again made the revolt of her heart all the more bitter against an unwelcome love of which she was ever conscious when Roger was present. But he had won her entire respect; he knew so much, and he worked on and waited. The grasp of his mind upon his studies daily grew more masterful, and his industry and persistence were so steady that the old commission merchant began to nod to himself approvingly.

The current of time flowed sluggishly on, bringing only changes for the worse to the Jocelyns. Early spring had come, but no spring-tide hope, and in its stead a bitter humiliation. The pressure of poverty at last became so great that the Jocelyns were in arrears for rent and were compelled to move. In this painful ordeal Mrs. Wheaton was a tower of strength, and managed almost everything for them, since no dependence could be placed on Mr. Jocelyn. The reader's attention need not be detained by a description of their new shelter—for it could not be called a home. They had a living-room and two very small bedrooms in a brick tenement wedged in among others of like unredeemed angularity, and belonging to the semi-respectable, commonplace order. It was occupied by stolid working-people of various nationalities, and all engaged in an honest scramble for bread, with time and thought for little else. The house was simply a modern, cheap shelter, built barely within the requirements of the law, and, from its newness, unsoiled as yet with the grime of innumerable crowded families. Everything was slight, thin, and money-saving in the architecture; and if a child cried, a shrill-tongued woman vociferated, or a laborer, angry or drunk, indulged in the general habit of profanity, all the other inmates of the abode were at once aware of the fact. By the majority, such sounds were no more heeded than the rumble in the streets, but to poor Mrs. Jocelyn and Mildred, with natures like Æolian harps, the discords of such coarse, crowded life were often horrible. There was naught to do but exist from day to day, to win what bread they could wherewith to sustain a life that seemed to promise less and less. Mr. Jocelyn was steadily sinking, and Belle, at last, growing bitter and restless under the privations of her lot, in spite of Roger's unfaltering friendship.

Mr. Jocelyn was not one who could sin in a conservative, prudent way. He seemed utterly unable to rally and be a man in his own strength, and his remorse over his conduct was so great that he sought a refuge in almost continuous excess. The greater the height, the more tremendous the fall, and he had now reached the recklessness of despair. He had many stolid, slouching neighbors in the tenements, who permitted life to be at least endurable for their families because of the intervals between their excesses; but an interval to Mr. Jocelyn was a foretaste of perdition. Nevertheless, if the wretched man, by a kindly violence, could have been shut up and away for weeks, perhaps months, from all possibility of obtaining the poisons that were destroying him, and treated with scientific skill, he might have been saved even at this late hour. When the world recognizes that certain vices sooner or later pass from the character of voluntary evil into the phase of involuntary disease, and should be treated rigorously and radically under the latter aspect, many lives and homes will be saved from final wreck.

No principles are better known than the influences of soil, climate, darkness, and light upon a growing plant. If the truth could be appreciated that circumstances color life and character just as surely, marring, distorting, dwarfing, or beautifying and developing, according as they are friendly or adverse, the workers in the moral vineyard, instead of trying to obtain fruit from sickly vines, whose roots grope in sterility, and whose foliage is poisoned, would bring the richness of opportunity to the soil and purify the social atmosphere. Immature Belle, in spite of all the influences for good from her mother, her sister, and Roger, could scarcely reside where she did and grow pure and womanly. She was daily compelled to see and hear too much that was coarse, evil, and debasing.

She knew that Roger was a friend, and nothing more—that his whole heart was absorbed in Mildred—and her feminine nature, stimulated by the peculiarities of her lot, craved warmer attentions. In her impoverished condition, and with her father's character becoming generally known, such attentions would not naturally come from young men whom those who loved her best could welcome. She was growing restless under restrictions, and her crowded, half-sheltered life was robbing her of womanly reserve. These undermining influences worked slowly, imperceptibly, but none the less certainly, and she recognized the bold, evil admiration which followed her more and more unshrinkingly.

Mr. Jocelyn's condition was no longer a secret, and he often, in common with other confirmed habitués, increased the effects of opium by a free use of liquor. He therefore had practically ceased to be a protector to his daughters. Fred and Minnie, in spite of all the broken-hearted and failing mother could do, were becoming little street Arabs, learning all too soon the evil of the world.

Since the revelation of her father's condition Mildred had finally relinquished her class at the mission chapel. Her sensitive spirit was so shadowed by his evil that she felt she would be speechless before children who might soon learn to associate her name with a vice that would seem to them as horrible as it was mysterious. Bread and shelter she must obtain, but she was too fear-haunted, too conscious of the shame to which she was linked, to face the public on any occasion not connected with her daily toil.

The pride characteristic of American people who have lapsed from a better condition was intensified by her Southern birth and prejudices. More than hunger, cold, and even death, she feared being recognized, pointed out, stared at, and gossiped about, while the thought of receiving charity brought an almost desperate look into her usually clear blue eyes. Therefore she shrank from even Mr. Wentworth, and was reticent on all topics relating to their domestic affairs. She knew that there were many families whom he was almost sustaining through crises of illness and privation; she also knew that there were far more who sought to trade upon his sympathies. While she could take aid from him as readily as from any one, she also believed that before she could receive it she must be frank concerning her father. Rather than talk of his shame, even to her pastor, it might well be believed that the girl would starve. What she might do for the sake of the others was another question.

Mr. Wentworth in sadness recognized the barrier which Mildred's pride was rearing between them, but he was too wise and experienced to be obtrusively personal. He sought earnestly, however, to guard the young girl against the moral danger which so often results from discouragement and unhappiness, and he entreated her not to part with her faith, her clinging trust in God.

"A clinging trust is, indeed, all that I have left," she had replied so sadly that his eye suddenly moistened; "but the waves of trouble seem strong and pitiless, and I sometimes fear that my hands are growing numb and powerless. In plain prose, I'm just plodding on—God knows whither. In my weary, faltering way I am trying to trust Him," she added, after a brief silence, "and I always hope to; but I am so tired, Mr. Wentworth, so depressed, that I'm like the soldiers that have been described to me as marching on with heavy eyes and heavy feet because they must. There is no use in my coming to the chapel, for I haven't the heart to say a word of cheer to any one, and hollow words would hurt me, while doing no good. I am trying your charity sorely, but I can't help it. I fear you cannot understand me, for even your Christian sympathy is a burden. I'm too tired, too sorely wounded to make any response; while all the time I feel that I ought to respond gratefully and earnestly. It seems a harsh and unnatural thing to say, but my chief wish is to shrink away from everybody and everything not essential to my daily work. I think I shall have strength enough to keep up a mechanical routine of life for a long time, but you must not ask me to think or give way to feeling, much less to talk about myself and—and—the others. If I should lose this stolid self-control which I am gaining, and which enables me to plod along day by day with my eyes shut to what may be on the morrow, I believe I should become helpless from despair and grief."

"My dear child," the clergyman had replied, in deep solicitude, "I fear you are dangerously morbid; and yet I don't know. This approach to apathy of which you speak may be God's shield from thoughts that would be sharp arrows. I can't help my honest sympathy, and I hope and trust that I may soon be able to show it in some helpful way—I mean in the way of finding you more remunerative and less cruel work," he added quickly, as he saw a faint flush rising in the young girl's face. Then he concluded, gravely and gently, "Miss Mildred, I respect you—I respect even your pride; but, in the name of our common faith and the bonds it implies, do not carry it too far. Good-by. Come to me whenever you need, or your conscience suggests my name," and the good man went away wholly bent on obtaining some better employment for Mildred; and he made not a little effort to do so, only to find every avenue of labor suited to the girl's capacity already thronged. Meanwhile the needs and sorrows of others absorbed his time and thoughts.

Belle, because of her thorough liking and respect for Mr. Wentworth, and even more for the reason that he had obtained her promise to come, was rarely absent from her class, and the hour spent at the chapel undoubtedly had a good and restraining influence; but over and against this one or two hours in seven days were pitted the moral atmosphere of the shop, the bold admiration and advances in the streets, which were no longer unheeded and were scarcely resented, and the demoralizing sights and sounds of a tenement-house. The odds were too great for poor Belle. Like thousands of other girls, she stood in peculiar need of sheltered home life, and charity broad as heaven should be exercised toward those exposed as she was.

As Mr. Jocelyn sank deeper in degradation, Mildred's

morbid impulse to shrink, cower, and hide, in such poor shelter as she had, grew stronger, and at last she did little more than try to sleep through the long, dreary Sabbaths, that she might have strength for the almost hopeless struggle of the week. She was unconsciously drifting into a hard, apathetic materialism, in which it was her chief effort not to think or remember—from the future she recoiled in terror—but simply to try to maintain her physical power to meet the daily strain.

It is a sad and terrible characteristic of our Christian city, that girls, young, beautiful, and unprotected like Mildred and Belle, are the natural prey of remorseless huntsmen. Only a resolute integrity, great prudence and care, can shield them; and these not from temptation and evil pursuit, but only from the fall which such snares too often compass.

Of these truths Mildred had a terrible proof. A purer-hearted girl than she never entered the maelstrom of city life; but those who looked upon her lovely face looked again, and lingeringly, and there was one who had devoured her beauty daily with wolfish eyes. In charge of the department of the shop wherein she toiled, there was a man who had long since parted with the faintest trace of principle or conscience. He was plausible, fine-looking, after a certain half-feminine type, and apparently vigilant and faithful in his duties as a floor-walker; but his spotless linen concealed a heart that plotted all the evil his hands dared to commit. For him Mildred had possessed great attractions from the first; and, with the confidence bestowed by his power, and many questionable successes, he made his first advances so openly that he received more than one public and stinging rebuff. A desire for revenge, therefore, had taken entire possession of him, and with a serpent's cold, deadly patience he was waiting for a chance to uncoil and strike. Notwithstanding his outward civility, Mildred never met the expression of his eyes without a shudder.

From frank-tongued Belle, Roger had obtained some

hints of this man's earlier attentions, and of his present ill-concealed dislike—a latent hostility which gave Mildred no little uneasiness, since, by some pretext, he might cause her dismissal. She knew too well that they were in such straits now that they could not afford one hour's idleness. Roger therefore nursed a bitter antipathy against the fellow.

One evening, late in March, the former was taking his usual brief walk before sitting down to long hours of study. He was at liberty to go whither he pleased, and not unnaturally his steps, for the hundredth time, perhaps, passed the door through which he could catch a glimpse of the young girl, who, with apparent hopelessness, and yet with such pathetic patience, was fighting a long battle with disheartening adversity. He was later than usual, and the employés were beginning to leave. Suddenly the obnoxious floor-walker appeared at the entrance with a hurried and intent manner. Then he paused a second or two and concealed himself behind a show-case. Roger now saw that his eyes were fixed on a girl who had just preceded him, and who, after a furtive glance backward, hastened up the avenue. Her pursuer—for such he evidently was—followed instantly, and yet sought to lose himself in the crowd so that she could not detect him. Partly in the hope of learning something to the disadvantage of one who might have it in his power to injure Mildred, and partly from the motive of adding zest to an aimless walk, Roger followed the man.

The girl, with another quick glance over her shoulder, at last turned down a side street, and was soon walking alone where passengers were few and the street much in shadow; here her pursuer joined her, and she soon evinced violent agitation, stopping suddenly with a gesture of indignant protest. He said something, however, that subdued her speedily, and they went on together for some little distance, the man talking rapidly, and then they turned into a long, dark passage that led to some tenements in the rear of those fronting on the street. About midway in this narrow alley a single gas jet burned, and under its light Roger saw them stop, and the girl produce from beneath her waterproof cloak something white, that appeared like pieces of wound lace. The man examined them, made a memorandum, and then handed them back to the girl, who hesitated to take them; but his manner was so threatening and imperious that she again concealed them on her person. As they came out together, Roger, with hat drawn over his eyes, gave them a glance which fixed the malign features of the man and the frightened, guilty visage of the girl on his memory. They regarded him suspiciously, but, as he went on without looking back, they evidently thought him a casual passer-by.

"It's a piece of villany," Roger muttered, "but of what nature I have no means of discovering, even were it any affair of mine. I am satisfied of one thing, however—that man's a scoundrel; seemingly he has the girl in his power, and it looks as if she had been stealing goods and he is compounding the felony with her."

If he had realized the depth of the fellow's villany he would not have gone back to his studies so quietly, for the one nearest to his heart was its object. The scene he had witnessed can soon be explained. Goods at the lace counter had been missed on more than one occasion, and it had been the hope of Mildred's enemy that he might fasten the suspicion upon her. On this evening, however, he had seen the girl in question secrete two or three pieces as she was folding them up, and he believed she had carried them away with her. Immediately on joining her he had charged her with the theft, and in answer to her denials threatened to have her searched before they parted. Then in terror she admitted the fact, and was in a condition to become his unwilling accomplice in the diabolical scheme suggested by his discovery.

He had said to her, in effect, that he suspected another girl—namely, Mildred Jocelyn—and that if she would place the goods in the pocket of this girl's cloak on the following afternoon he would by this act be enabled to extort a confession from her also, such as he had received in the present case. He then promised the girl in return for this service that he would make no complaint against her, but would give her the chance to find another situation, which she must do speedily, since he could no longer permit her to remain in the employ of the house for whom he acted. She was extremely reluctant to enter into this scheme, but, in her confusion, guilt, and fear, made the evil promise, finding from bitter experience that one sin, like an enemy within the walls, opens the gate to many others. She tried to satisfy such conscience as she had with the thought that Mildred was no better than herself, and that the worst which could happen to the object of this sudden conspiracy was a quiet warning to seek employment elsewhere. The man himself promised as much, although he had no such mild measures in view. It was his design to shame Mildred publicly, to break down her character, and render her desperate. He had learned that she had no protector worthy of the name, and believed that he could so adroitly play his part that he would appear only as the vigilant and faithful servant of his employers.

Mildred, all unconscious of the pit dug beneath her feet, was passing out the following evening into the dreary March storm, when the foreman touched her shoulder and said that one of the proprietors wished to see her. In much surprise, and with only the fear of one whose position meant daily bread for herself and those she loved better than self, she followed the man to the private office, where she found two of the firm, and they looked grave and severe indeed.

"Miss Jocelyn," began the elder, without any circumlocution, "laces have been missed from your department, and suspicion rests on you. I hope you can prove yourself innocent."

The charge was so awful and unexpected that she sank, pale and faint, into a chair, and the appearance of the terror-stricken girl was taken as evidence of guilt. But she soon rallied sufficiently to say, with great earnestness, "Indeed, sir, I am innocent."

"Assertion is not proof. Of course you are willing, then, to be searched?"

She, Mildred Jocelyn, searched for stolen goods! Searched, alone, in the presence of these dark-browed, frowning men! The act, the indignity, seemed overwhelming. A hot crimson flush mantled her face, and her womanhood rose in arms against the insult.

"I do not fear being searched," she said indignantly; "but a woman must perform the act."

"Certainly," said her employer; "we do not propose anything indecorous; but first call an officer."

They were convinced that they had found the culprit, and were determined to make such an example of her as would deter all others in the shop from similar dishonesty.

Mildred was left to herself a few moments, faint and bewildered, a whirl of horrible thoughts passing through her mind; and then, conscious of innocence, she began to grow calm, believing that the ordeal would soon be over. Nevertheless she had received a shock which left her weak and trembling, as she followed two of the most trusty women employed in the shop to a private apartment, at whose door she saw a bulky guardian of the law. The majority, unaware of what had taken place, had departed; but such as remained had lingered, looking in wonder at the hasty appearance of the policeman, and the intense curiosity had been heightened when they saw him stationed near an entrance through which Mildred was speedily led. They at once surmised the truth, and waited for the result of the search in almost breathless expectation. The girl who had done Mildred so deep a wrong had hastened away among the first, and so was unaware of what was taking place; the chief conspirator, from an obscure part in the now half-lighted shop, watched with cruel eyes the working of his plot.

CHAPTER XXXIII

MILDRED IN A PRISON CELL

NOT from any sense of guilt, but rather from the trembling apprehensiveness of one whose spirit is already half broken by undeserved misfortune, Mildred tottered to a chair within the small apartment to which she had been taken. With an appealing glance to the two women who stood beside her she said, "Oh, hasten to prove that I am innocent! My burden was already too heavy, and this is horrible."

"Miss Jocelyn," replied the elder of the women, in a matter-of-fact tone, "it's our duty to search you thoroughly, and, if innocent, you will not fear it. There will be nothing 'horrible' about the affair at all, unless you have been stealing, and it seems to me that an honest girl would show more nerve."

"Search me, then—search as thoroughly as you please," cried Mildred, with an indignant flush crimsoning her pale, wan face. "I'd sooner starve a thousand times than take a penny that did not belong to me."

Grimly and silently, and with a half-incredulous shrug, the woman, whose mind had been poisoned against Mildred, began her search, first taking off the young girl's waterproof cloak. "Why is the bottom of this side-pocket slit open?" she asked severely. "What is this, away down between the lining and the cloth?" and she drew out two pieces of valuable lace.

Mildred looked at the ominous wares with dilated eyes, and for a moment was speechless with astonishment and terror.

"Your words and deeds are a trifle discordant," began the woman, in cold satire, "but your manner is more in keeping."

"I know nothing about that lace," Mildred exclaimed passionately. "This is a plot against—"

"Oh, nonsense!" interrupted the woman harshly. "Here, officer," she continued, opening the door, "take your prisoner. These goods were found upon her person, concealed within the lining of her cloak," and she showed him where the lace had been discovered.

"A mighty clear case," was his grinning reply; "still you must be ready to testify to-morrow, unless the girl pleads guilty, which will be her best course."

"What are you going to do with me?" asked Mildred, in a hoarse whisper.

"Oh, nothing uncommon, miss—only what is always done under such circumstances. We'll give you free lodgings to-night, and time to think a bit over your evil ways."

One of the seniors of the firm, who had drawn near to the door and had heard the result of the search, now said, with much indignation, and in a tone that all present could hear, "Officer, remove your prisoner, and show no leniency. Let the law take its full course, for we intend to stamp out all dishonesty from our establishment, most thoroughly."

"Come," said the policeman, roughly laying his hand on the shoulder of the almost paralyzed girl.

"Where?" she gasped.

"Why, to the station-house, of course," he answered impatiently.

"Oh, you can't mean *that.*"

"Come, come, no nonsense, no airs. You knew well enough that the station-house and jail were at the end of the road you were travelling. People always get found out, sooner or later. If you make me trouble in arresting you, it will go all the harder with you."

"Can't I—can't I send word to my friends?"

"No, indeed, not now. Your pals must appear in court to-morrow."

She looked appealingly around, and on every face within the circle of light saw only aversion and anger, while the cruel, mocking eyes of the man whose coarse advances she had so stingingly resented were almost fiendish in their exultation.

"It's of no use," she muttered bitterly. "It seems as if all the world, and God Himself, were against me," and giving way to a despairing apathy she followed the officer out of the store—out into the glaring lamplight of the street, out into the wild March storm that swept her along toward prison. To her morbid mind the sleet-laden gale seemed in league with all the other malign influences that were hurrying her on to shame and ruin.

"Hi, there! Look where you are going," thundered the policeman to a passenger who was breasting the storm, with his umbrella pointed at an angle that threatened the officer's eye.

The umbrella was thrown back, and then flew away on the gale from the nerveless hands of Roger Atwood. Dumb and paralyzed with wonder, he impeded their progress a moment as he looked into Mildred's white face.

At last a time had come when she welcomed his presence, and she cried, "Oh, Mr. Atwood, tell them at home—tell them I'm innocent."

"What does this outrage mean?" he demanded, in a tone that cause the officer to grasp his club tightly.

"It means that if you interfere by another word I'll arrest you also. Move on, and mind your business."

"Miss Jocelyn, explain," he said earnestly to her, without budging an inch, and the comparatively few passers-by began to gather around them.

"You can have no communication with the prisoner on the street," said the arm of the law roughly; "and if you don't get out of my way you'll be sorry."

"Please don't draw attention to me," entreated Mildred

hurriedly. "You can do nothing. I'm falsely accused—tell them at home."

He passed swiftly on her side, and, as he did so, whispered, "You shall not be left alone a moment. I'll follow, and to-morrow prove you innocent," for, like a flash, the scene he had witnessed the evening before came into his mind.

"Quit that," warned the officer, "or I'll—" but the young man was gone. He soon turned, however, and followed until he saw Mildred led within the station-house door. The storm was so severe as to master the curiosity of the incipient crowd, and only a few street gamins followed his example. He was wary now, and, having regained his self-control, he recognized a task that would tax his best skill and tact.

Having watched until he saw the officer who had made the arrest depart, he entered the station-house. To the sergeant on duty behind the long desk he said, with much courtesy, "I am a friend of Miss Jocelyn, a young woman recently brought to this station. I wish to do nothing contrary to your rules, but I would like to communicate with her and do what I can for her comfort. Will you please explain to me what privileges may be granted to the prisoner and to her friends?"

"Well, this is a serious case, and the proof against her is almost positive. The stolen goods were found upon her person, and her employers have charged that there be no leniency."

"Her employers could not have wished her treated cruelly, and if they did, you are not the man to carry out their wishes," Roger insinuated. "All that her friends ask is kindness and fair play within the limits of your rules. Moreover, her friends have information which will show her to be innocent, and let me assure you that she is a lady by birth and breeding, although the family has been reduced to poverty. She has influential friends."

His words evidently had weight with the sergeant, and

Roger's bearing was so gentlemanly that the official imagined that the young man himself might represent no mean degree of social and political influence.

"Yes," he said, "I noticed that she wasn't one of the common sort."

"And you must have observed also that she was delicate and frail looking."

"Yes, that, too, was apparent, and we have every disposition to be humane toward prisoners. You can send her some supper and bedding, and if you wish to write to her you can do so, but must submit what you write to the captain of the precinct. I'm expecting him every minute."

Roger wrote rapidly:

"MISS JOCELYN—Your friends fully believe in your innocence, and I think I can say without doubt that they have the means of proving it. Much depends on your maintaining strength and courage. Bedding will be sent to make you comfortable, and, for the sake of your mother and those you love at home, I hope you will not refuse the supper that shall soon be sent also. I have ever believed that you were the bravest girl in the world, and now that so much depends on your fortitude and nerve, I am sure you will second the efforts of those who are trying to aid you. With the strongest respect and sympathy,

"ROGER ATWOOD."

The captain, who soon appeared, saw no objection to this note, and promised that it should be sent to Mildred.

Roger then went to the nearest restaurant, and procured a delicate and inviting supper, which, with a generous pot of coffee, he carried so swiftly through the storm that it was sent smoking hot to the cell in which Mildred was confined.

He then hastened to a livery-stable, and, having obtained a carriage, was driven rapidly to the tenement in which the Jocelyns had their rooms. Mr. Jocelyn, fortunately, was absent; for Mildred's natural protector would only have made matters far worse. If the guardians of the law had looked upon the wrecked and fallen man they would have felt that the daughter's alleged crime was already half explained. But a visit from Mrs. Jocelyn would make a far different impression, and he determined that she alone should accompany him to the station-house.

It would be useless to pain the reader with Mrs. Jocelyn's distress, and for a time Roger thought the tidings would crush the already stricken woman; but in answer to his appeal she soon rallied in defence of her child. At his request she assumed, as far as possible, the garb of a lady—the appearance and bearing of one was inseparable from her. It was with much difficulty that he persuaded the weeping and indignant Belle to remain with the children, for he well knew that she was far too excitable to deal with the police. Having made every provision possible for Mildred's comfort, they soon reached the station-house, and the sergeant in charge greeted them politely; but on learning their errand he frowned, and said to Mrs. Jocelyn, "No, you can't see her till she is brought into court to-morrow."

In answer to the mother's appeals and Roger's expostulations he remarked impatiently, "Do you think I'm going to disobey orders? Either take my answer or wait till the captain comes in again."

They had no other resource, and sat down to weary waiting, the mother weeping silently, and Roger, with sternly knit brows, deep in thought.

At last the captain returned, and the sergeant rose and said, "Here's the mother of the girl who was taken with stolen goods on her person. She wishes to speak with you."

"Well, what is it?" demanded the police-captain a little harshly, turning toward Mrs. Jocelyn; but his manner softened as he looked upon the thin, delicate features which had not yet lost their old, sweet charm, and which now were eloquent with a mother's unspeakable grief and solicitude. "Don't be frightened, madam," he added, somewhat kindly, as he saw the poor woman's ineffectual efforts to rise and speak. "I'm human, and not more hard-hearted than my duties require."

At last Mrs. Jocelyn burst forth: "If you have a heart at all, sir, save mine from breaking. My child is innocent —it will be proved to-morrow. A year ago we had a happy, beautiful home, and my girl a father whom all men respected. We've had misfortunes, that, thank God, fall to the lot of few, but my child has kept herself spotless through them all. I can prove this. She is in prison to-night through no fault of hers. Oh, sir, in the name of mother-love, can you keep me from my child? Can I not see her even for a moment, and say to her one reassuring word? She may go mad from fear and shame. She may die. Oh, sir, if you have the heart of a man, let me see her, let me speak to her. You, or any one, may be present and see that I mean no harm."

"There certainly has been some dreadful mistake," Roger put in hastily, as he saw the man was irresolute, and was regarding the suppliant sympathetically. "People who must command your respect will be glad to testify that Miss Jocelyn's character is such as to render impossible anything dishonorable on her part."

"Let me warn you," said the officer keenly, "that any such negative testimony will have but little weight against the positive facts in the case."

"Oh, let me see my child," cried Mrs. Jocelyn, in tones of such passionate pathos that his scruples gave way, and he said to the sergeant, "Let her see the girl! I'd be a brute to deny her, even if it is against our rules. The door-man need not stand near enough to embarrass them."

As Mrs. Jocelyn eagerly descended to the cells in the basement, the captain remarked to Roger, "The girl's friends will have to bestir themselves if they clear her. The evidence is so strong that she'll be committed for further trial, without doubt."

"I think she'll be discharged to-morrow," replied Roger quietly. "I thank you for your kindness to Mrs. Jocelyn."

"Mere statements as to the girl's previous character will not clear her," resumed the captain emphatically. "You are a relative, lover, or something, I suppose. This poor woman has knocked my routine methods a little out of gear. One rarely sees a face like hers in a station-house. She evidently comes of no common stock, and I'd like to hear that the charge is all a mistake, as you claim; but, young man, you can't meet criminal charges with generalities. You've got to show that she didn't steal that lace. I wish you success, for the mother's sake at least," and he passed into his private room.

As Mildred was about to enter the station-house she had looked back, hoping, for the first time in her life, that Roger Atwood was near. The eager and reassuring wave of his hand satisfied her that he would know the place of her imprisonment, and that he would do for her all within his power. Again he had appeared in the hour of misfortune and bitter humiliation. But, inspite of her heart, she now did justice to his sturdy loyalty, and she was comforted and sustained by the thought that not quite all the world was against her. She also knew that he would relieve her mother and Belle from unendurable anxiety on account of her absence, and that he would summon Mr. Wentworth to her aid. His promise to prove her innocent had meant nothing to her more than that he would inform and rally all of her friends. That he could know anything that would throw light on the evil mystery did not seem possible. She was then too miserable and depressed to do much more than wait, in a sort of stunned torpor, for what might next occur. Mechanically she answered such questions as were put to her in order that a record of the case might be made, and then was led to the cells below. She shuddered as she saw the dimly lighted stairway, and it seemed to her morbid fancy that she was to be thrust into a subterranean dungeon. Such, in a certain sense, it was; for in some of the older station-houses the cells are located in the basement. At the end of the corridor, nearest the street, she saw several women, and, unkempt and disgusting as these station-house tramps appeared, the fact that some of her own sex were near was reassuring. A prison was to her a place full of nameless horrors, for the romances she had read in brighter days gave to it the associations of medieval dungeons. Of the prosaic character of a modern jail she knew nothing, and when she was placed within a bare cell, and the grated iron door was locked upon her, the horrible desolation of her position seemed as complete and tragic a fate as had ever overtaken the unfortunate in the cruel past. She sat down upon the grimy wooden bench, which was the only provision made for rest or comfort, and the thought of spending a lonely night in such a place was overpowering. Not that she could hope for sleep, even if there were downy pillows instead of this unredeemed couch of plank on which some beastly inebriate may have slept off his stupor the night before, but she felt weak and faint, and her overtaxed physical nature craved some support and rest.

Distress of mind, however, soon made her forget all this, as her faculties slowly rallied from the shock they had received, and she began to realize that she was charged with a crime of which it might be difficult—perhaps impossible—to prove her innocence. At best, she feared she would always be so clouded with suspicion that all would refuse to employ her, and that her blighted life and undeserved shame, added to her father's character, would drag the family down to the lowest depths. The consequences to them all, and especially to Belle, seemed so threatening and terrible that she wrung her hands and moaned aloud.

At every sound she started up, nervous and morbidly apprehensive. The grating of the key in the iron door had given her a sense of relief and refuge. The massive bars that shut her in also shut out the brutal and criminal, who were associated with a prison in her mind; the thoughts of whom had filled her very soul with terror, when she was first arrested. As it was early in the evening she happened to be the first prisoner, and she prayed that there might be no others, for the possibility that some foul, drunken man might be thrust into an adjoining cell made her flesh creep. How many long, sleepless hours must pass before morning could bring any hope of release! And yet she dreaded the coming day unspeakably, for her path to freedom lay through a police court, with all its horrible publicity. Her name might get into the papers, and proud Mrs. Arnold treasure up every scrap of such intelligence about her. The tidings of her shame might be sent to her who as Miss Wetheridge had been her friend, and even she would shrink from one around whom clung such disgraceful associations. Again and again she asked herself, How could the charge against her be met? How could the family live without her? What would become of them? Belle, alas, would be rendered utterly reckless, because hopeless. The unhappy prisoner was far beyond tears. Even her faith in God failed her, for, seemingly, He had left her the victim of cruel wrong and unredeemed misfortune. With her hot, dry eyes buried in her hands she sat motionless and despairing, and the moments passed like hours.

At this crisis in her despair Roger's note was handed to her, and it was like the north star suddenly shining out on one who is benighted and lost. It again kindled hope, without which mind and body give way in fatal dejection. She kissed the missive passionately, murmuring, with eyes heavenward, "If he can clear my name from dishonor, if he will rescue my loved ones from the poverty and shame which are now threatening such terrible evils, I will make any sacrifice that he can ask. I will crush out my old vain love, if I die in the effort. My heart shall not prove a traitor to those who are true and loyal at such a time. He can save mamma, Belle, and the children from hopeless poverty, and perhaps destruction. If he will, and it is his wish, I'll give all there is left of my unhappy self. I will be his loyal wife—would to God I could be his loving wife!

Oh, would to God he had loved Belle instead of me! I could be devotion itself as his sister. But surely I can banish my old fond dream—which was never more than a dream—when one so deserving, so faithful, is willing to give me his strong, helpful hand. We are both very young; it will be years before—before—and, surely, in so long a time, I can conquer my infatuation for one who has left me all these dreary months without a word. A woman's heart cannot be proof against reason, gratitude, and the sacred duty owed to those she loves best. At any rate, mine shall not be, and if he still craves the loyalty and—and—yes, the love of one so shamed and impoverished as I am, he shall have all—*all*," and her face grew stern with her purpose of self-mastery. She forced down some of the food he sent, and drank the coffee. "I will be brave," she murmured. "I will try to second his efforts to clear my name, for death were better than shame. I shall, at least, try to deserve his respect."

Then musingly she added, "How can my friends have gained any information that would prove me innocent? Mother and Belle cannot know anything definite, nor can Mr. Wentworth. He promised in that brief whisper when he passed me in the street that he would prove it. Can he have learned anything in his strange vigilance? It seems impossible. Alas, I fear that their best hope is to show that I have hitherto borne a good character, and yet if my present home and our poverty are described, if—worse than all—papa appears in the court-room, I fear they will think the worst," and something of her old despair began to return when she heard approaching footsteps.

"Millie!" cried a loved and familiar voice. The key grated in the lock, and in another moment she was sobbing on her mother's breast, and her bruised heart was healed by the unutterable tenderness of a mother's love. It filled the dark cell with the abounding, undoubting, unquestioning spirit of unselfish devotion, which was akin to the fragrance diffused from the broken box of alabaster.

When sufficiently calm, Mildred told her mother what had happened, and she in turn whispered that Roger had strong hopes that he could prove her innocence on the following day, though how she did not know. "And yet, Millie," she concluded, "for some reason he inspires me with confidence, for while he feels so deeply, he is quiet and thoughtful about the least thing. Nothing seems to escape his mind, and he says he has some information of which he does not think it best to speak at present. He entreats you to take courage, and says that if you will 'keep up and be your brave, true self, gentle and strong,' you can do much to aid him. We will all stand by you, and Mr. Wentworth will be with us."

"Where—where is papa?" faltered Mildred, with a slight flush. "I don't know," responded the wife, with a deep sob.

"Alas, mother, it's cruel to say it, but it will be best that he should not appear at all. Keep him away if possible. I hope he may never know anything about it, unless you think this terrible result of his course may awaken him to a final struggle to do right. I would gladly suffer anything to save him."

"No, Millie, he would not be his old self if he came into court," said her mother dejectedly, "and his appearance and manner might turn the scale against you. Our best hope is to let Roger manage everything. And now, good-by, my darling. God sustain you. Do not fear anything to-night. Roger says you are safe, and that his only dread is that you may become nervously prostrated, and he relies on your help to-morrow. I can't stay any longer. Oh, God, how glad I would be if I could hold you in my arms all night! Belle is strongly excited, and says she will never believe a word against you, nor will any of your true friends—alas! I wish we had more."

"Time is up," warned the doorman.

"Tell Mr. Atwood that I am deeply grateful for his aid, and more grateful for his trust," said Mildred.

"Courage, Millie; you can sustain me by keeping up yourself. You will find us in the court-room waiting for you."

With an embrace in which heart throbbed against heart they separated, and the poor girl was comforted and more hopeful in spite of herself, for while she would shrink from Roger, her confidence in his shrewdness and intelligence had made such growth that she half believed he would find some way of proving her innocent, although how he had obtained any evidence in her favor she could not imagine. The bedding brought by her mother transformed the cell-bunk into a comfortable couch, and she lay down and tried to rest, so as to be ready to do her part, and her overtaxed nature soon brought something like sleep. She was startled out of her half-consciousness by a shrill cry, and sprang to her feet. There was a confused sound of steps on the stairs, and then again the same wild cry that almost made her heart stand still. A moment later two policemen appeared, dragging a woman who was resisting and shrieking with demoniacal fury.

The sight was a horrible one. The faces of the great, stalwart men were reddened by exertion, for the woman seemed to possess supernatural strength, and their familiarity with crime was not so great as to prevent strong expressions of disgust. Little wonder, for if a fiend could embody itself in a woman, this demented creature would leave nothing for the imagination. Her dress was wet, torn, and bedraggled; her long black hair hung dishevelled around a white, bloated face, from which her eyes gleamed with a fierceness like that of insanity.

With no little difficulty they thrust her into a cell opposite the one in which Mildred was incarcerated, and as one of the men turned the key upon her he said roughly, "Stay there now, you drunken she-devil, till you are sober," and breathing heavily from their efforts they left the poor wretch to the care of the jailer.

Mildred shrank away. Not for the world would she

encounter the woman's frenzied eyes. Then she stopped her ears, that she might not hear the horrid din and shameful language, which made the place tenfold more revolting. The man in charge of the cells sat dozing stolidly by the stove, some distance away. His repose was not to be disturbed by such familiar sounds.

At last the woman became quiet, and Mildred breathed more freely, until some mysterious sounds, suggesting that her terrible neighbor was trying to open her door, awakened her fears, for even the thought of her coming any nearer made her tremble. She therefore sprang up and looked between the iron bars. At first she was perplexed by what she saw, and then her heart stood still, for she soon made out that the woman was hanging by the neck, from the highest bar of her cell door. "Help," Mildred shrieked; "quick, if you would save life."

The man by the stove sprang up and rushed forward.

"There, see—oh, be quick!"

The jailer comprehended the situation at once, unlocked the door, and cut the parts of her clothing which the woman had improvised into a halter. She soon revived, and cursed him for his interference. He now watched her carefully, paying no heed to her horrible tongue, until the crazed stage of her intoxication passed into stupor.[1] To Mildred he said, reassuringly, "Don't be afraid; you're as safe as if you were at home."

"Home, home, home!" moaned the poor girl. "Oh, what a mockery that word has become! My best hope may soon be to find one in heaven."

---

[1] The writer saw the cell in which, on the evening before, the woman described tried twice to destroy herself. He also saw the woman herself, when brought before the police justice. She had seen twenty-five years, but in evil she seemed old indeed. According to her story, she was a daughter of the Puritans.

CHAPTER XXXIV

"A WISE JUDGE"

WHEN the interminable night would end Mildred could not guess, for no dawning was visible from her basement cell. The woman opposite gradually became stupid and silent. Other prisoners were brought in from time to time, but they were comparatively quiet. A young girl was placed in a cell not far away, and her passionate weeping was pitiful to hear. The other prisoners were generally intoxicated or stolidly indifferent, and were soon making the night hideous with their discordant respiration.

The place had become so terrible to Mildred that she even welcomed the presence of the policeman who had arrested her, and who at last came to take her to the police court. Must she walk with him through the streets in the open light of day? She feared she would faint on what, in her weakness, would be a long journey, and her heart gave a great throb of gratitude as she saw Roger awaiting her in the large general room, or entrance, to the station-house. Nor was her appreciation of his kindness diminished when she saw a man in attendance—evidently a waiter from a restaurant—with a plate of sandwiches and a pot of coffee. Roger came forward, eagerly grasping her hand, and there was so much solicitude and sympathy in his dark eyes that her tears began to gather, and a faint color to suffuse the pallor that at first had startled him.

"Mr. Atwood," she murmured, "you are kindness itself, and I have not deserved it. Forgive me. I will try not to fail you to-day, for your respect sustains me, and I would not lose it."

"I knew your brave spirit would second all our efforts," he said in like low tones, and with a bright, grateful look. "Here, waiter—come, Miss Jocelyn, it's by just such prosaic means that soldiers sustain the fight. You'll dine at home."

"Yes, hurry up," added the officer; "we have no time now for words or ceremony."

She ate a few mouthfuls, and drank some coffee. "I cannot take any more now," she said to Roger.

Oh, how plainly her womanly instinct divined his unbounded loyalty; and, with bitter protest at her weakness, she knew with equal certainty that she shrank from his love with her old, unconquerable repugnance. With a dissimulation which even he did not penetrate, she looked her thanks as the officer led the way to the street, and said, "Since your friends provide the carriage, you can ride, miss; only we can't part company."

She stepped into the coach, the policeman taking the opposite seat.

"Oh, God, how pale and wan she is! This will kill her," Roger groaned, as she sprang up on the box with the driver.

It was so early that few were abroad, and yet Mildred would not look up. How could she ever look up again! The leaden clouds seemed to rest upon the steeples of the churches. Churches! and such scenes as she had witnessed, and such a wrong as hers, were taking place under the shadow of their spires!

Roger had passed as sleepless a night as had fallen to Mildred's lot, and bitterly he regretted that he had been able to accomplish so little. Mr. Wentworth was out of town, and would not be back for a day or two. Then he sought the judge before whom Mildred would appear the following morning, and learned, with dismay, that he, too, had gone to a neighboring city, and would return barely in time to open court at the usual hour! He had hoped that, by telling his story beforehand, the judge would adopt his plan of discovering the real culprit. This was still his hope, for, after long thought, he determined not to employ counsel, fearing it would lead to a prolongation of the case. His strong characteristic of self-reliance led him to believe that he could manage the affair best alone, and he was confident from his own inexperience. The rain had ceased, and for hours he paced the wet pavement near the station-house, finding a kind of satisfaction in being as near as possible to the one he loved, though utterly unable to say a reassuring word.

Having learned that the prisoners might ride to court if the means were provided, he had a carriage ready long before the appointed time, and his presence did much to nerve Mildred for the ordeal she so much dreaded.

On reaching the entrance at which the prisoners were admitted, he sprang down to assist Mildred to alight; but the officer said gruffly, "Stand back, young man; you must have your say in the court-room. You are a little too officious."

"No, sir; I'm only most friendly."

"Well, well, we have our rules," and he led the trembling girl within the stony portals, and she was locked up in what is termed "the box," with the other female prisoners, who were now arriving on foot.

This was, perhaps, the worst experience she had yet endured, and she longed for the privacy of her cell again. Never before had she come in contact with such debased wrecks of humanity, and she blushed for womanhood as she cowered in the furthest corner and looked upon her companions—brutal women, with every vice stamped on their bloated features. The majority were habitual drunkards, filthy in person and foul of tongue. True to their depraved instincts, they soon began to ridicule and revile one who, by contrast, proved how fallen and degraded they were. And yet, not even from these did the girl recoil with such horror as from some brazen harpies who said words in her ear that made her hide her face with shame. The officer in charge saw that she was persecuted, and sternly interfered in her behalf, but from their hideous presence and contact she could not escape.

By some affinity not yet wholly obliterated, the girl she had heard weeping in the night shrank to her side, and her swollen eyes and forlorn appearance could not hide the fact that she was very young, and might be very pretty. Mildred knew not what to say to her, but she took her hand and held it. This silent expression of sympathy provoked another outburst of grief, and the poor young creature sobbed on Mildred's shoulder as if her heart were breaking. Mildred placed a sustaining arm around her, but her own sustaining truth and purity she could not impart.

A partition only separated her from the "box"—which was simply a large wooden pen with round iron bars facing the corridor—to which the male prisoners were brought, one after another, by the policemen who had arrested them. The arrival of the judge was somewhat delayed, and may the reader never listen to such language as profaned her ears during the long hour and a half before the opening of the court.

Fortunately her turn came rather early, and she at last was ushered to the doorway which looked upon the crowded court-room, and her heart throbbed with hope as she singled out her mother, Belle, Mrs. Wheaton, and Roger, from among long lines of curious and repulsive faces. The former kissed their hands to her, and tried to give wan, reassuring smiles, which their tears belied. Roger merely bowed gravely, and then, with an expression that was singularly alert and resolute, gave his whole attention to all that was passing. After recognizing her friends, Mildred turned to the judge, feeling that she would discover her fate in his expression and manner. Was he a kindly, sympathetic man, unhardened by the duties of his office? She could learn but little from his grave, impassive face. She soon feared that she had slight cause for hope, for after what seemed to her an absurdly brief, superficial trial, she saw two of her companions of the "box" sentenced to three months' imprisonment. The decision, which to her had such an awful import, was pronounced in an offhand manner, and in the matter-of-fact tone with which one would dispose of bales of merchandise, and the floods of tears and passionate appeals seemingly had no more effect on the arbiter of their fates than if he had been a stony image. She could not know that they were old offenders, whose character was well known to the judge and the officers that had arrested them. Such apparent haphazard justice or injustice had a most depressing effect upon her and the weeping girl who stood a little in advance.

The next prisoner who appeared before the bar received very different treatment. He was a middle-aged man, and had the appearance and was clothed in the garb of a gentleman. With nervously trembling hands and bowed head, he stood before the judge, who eyed him keenly, after reading the charge of intoxication in the streets.

"Have you ever been arrested before?" he asked.

"No indeed, sir," was the low, emphatic reply.

"Come up here; I wish to speak with you."

The officer in attendance took the half-comprehending man by the elbow and led him up within the bar before the long desk which ran the whole width of the courtroom, and behind which the judge sat with his clerks and assistants.

"Now tell me all about it," said the judge, and the man in a few words told his story without any palliation. With a gleam of hope Mildred saw the expression of the judge's face change as he listened, and when at last he replied, in tones so low that none could hear them save he to whom they were addressed, she saw that look which wins all hearts—the benignant aspect of one who might condemn for evil, but who would rather win and save from evil. The man slowly lifted his eyes to the speaker's face, and hope and courage began to show themselves in his bearing. The judge brought his extortation to a practical conclusion, for he said, "Promise me that with God's help you will never touch the vile stuff again."

The promise was evidenly sincere and hearty. "Give me your hand on it," said his Honor.

The man started as if he could scarcely believe his ears, then wrung the judge's hand, while his eyes moistened with gratitude. "You are at liberty. Good-morning, sir;" and the man turned and walked through the crowded court-room, with the aspect of one to whom manhood had been restored.

Hope sprang up in Mildred's heart, for she now saw that her fate was not in the hands of a stony-hearted slave of routine. She looked toward her relatives, and greeted their tearful smiles with a wan glimmer of light on her own face, and then she turned to watch the fortunes of the weeping girl who followed next in order. She did not know the charge, but guessed it only too well from the judge's face, as the officer who had arrested her made his low explanation. She, too, was summoned within the rail, and the judge began to question her. At first she was too greatly overcome by her emotions to answer. As she cowered, trembled, and sobbed, she might well have been regarded as the embodiment of that shame and remorse whch overwhelm fallen womanhood before the heart is hardened and the face made brazen by years of vice. Patiently and kindly the judge drew from her faltering lips some pitiful story, and then he talked to her in low, impressive tones, that seemed to go straight to her despairing soul. A kind, firm, protecting hand might then have led her back to a life of virtue, for such had been her bitter foretastes of the fruits of sin that surely she would have gladly turned from them, could the chance have been given to her. The judge mercifully remitted her punishment, and gave her freedom. Who received her, as she turned her face toward the staring throng that intervened between her and the street? Some large-hearted woman, bent on rescuing an erring sister? Some agent of one of the many costly charities of the city?

No, in bitter shame, no. Only the vile madam who traded on the price of her body and soul, and who, with vulture-like eyes, had watched the scene. She only had stood ready to pay the fine, if one had been imposed according to the letter of the law. She only received the weak and friendless creature, from whom she held as pledges all her small personal effects, and to whom she promised immediate shelter from the intolerable stare that follows such victims of society. The girl's weak, pretty face, and soft, white hands were but too true an index to her infirm will and character, and, although fluttering and reluctant, she again fell helpless into the talons of the harpy. Hapless girl! you will probably stand at this bar again, and full sentence will then be given against you. The judge frowned heavily as he saw the result of his clemency, and then, as if it were an old story, he turned to the next culprit. Mildred had been much encouraged as she watched the issue of the two cases just described; but as her eyes followed the girl wistfully toward the door of freedom she encountered the cold, malignant gaze of the man who had charge of her department at the shop, and who she instinctively felt was the cause of her shameful and dangerous position. By his side sat the two women who had searched her and the leading foreman of the store. Sick and faint from apprehension, she turned imploringly toward Roger, who was regarding the floor-walker with such vindictive sternness that she felt the wretch's hour of reckoning would soon come, whatever might be her fate. This added to her trouble, for she feared that she was involving Roger in danger.

No time was given for thoughts on such side issues, for the prisoner preceding her in the line was sentenced, after a trial of three minutes—a summary proceeding that was not hope-inspiring.

The name of Mildred Jocelyn was now called, and there was a murmur of expectant interest in the court-room, for she was not by any means an ordinary prisoner in appearance, and there were not a few present who knew something of the case. The young girl was pushed before the bar, and would gladly have clung to it, in order to support her trembling form. But while she could not infuse vigor into her overtaxed muscles, her brave spirit rallied to meet the emergency, and she fixed her eyes unwaveringly upon the judge, who now for the first time noticed her attentively, and it did not escape her intensely quickened perceptions that his eyes at once grew kindly and sympathetic. Sitting day after day, and year after year, in his position, he had gained a wonderful insight into character, and in Mildred's pure, sweet face he saw no evidence of guilt or of criminal tendencies. It was, indeed, white with fear, and thin from wearing toil and grief; but this very pallor made it seem only more spiritual and free from earthliness, while every feature, and the unconscious grace of her attitude, bespoke high breeding and good blood.

First, the officer who arrested her told his story, and then the elder of the two women who searched her was summoned as the first witness. The judge looked grave, and he glanced uneasily at the prisoner from time to time; but the same clear, steadfast eyes met his gaze, unsullied by a trace of guilt. Then the second woman corroborated the story of her associate, and the judge asked, "How came you to suspect the prisoner so strongly as to search her?" and at this point the floor-walker was summoned.

The vigilant magistrate did not fail to note the momentary glance of aversion and horror which Mildred bestowed upon this man, and then her eyes returned with so deep and pathetic an appeal to his face that his heart responded, and his judgment led him also to believe that there was error and perhaps wrong in the prosecution. Still he was compelled to admit to himself that the case looked very dark for the girl, who was gaining so strong a hold on his sympathy.

"I must inform your Honor," began the witness plausibly, after having been sworn, "that laces had been missed from the department in which this girl was employed, and

I was keenly on the alert, as it was my duty to be. Some suspicious circumstances led me to think that the prisoner was the guilty party, and the search proved my suspicions to be correct."

"What were the suspicious circumstances?"

The man seemed at a loss for a moment. "Well, your Honor, she went to the cloak-room yesterday afternoon," he said.

"Do not all the girls go to the cloak-room occasionally?"

"Yes, but there was something in her face and manner that fastened my suspicions upon her."

"What evidences of guilt did you detect?"

"I can scarcely explain—nothing very tangible. The evidences of guilt were found on her person, your Honor."

"Yes, so much has been clearly shown."

"And she was very reluctant to be searched, which would not have been the case had she been conscious of innocence."

The woman who searched her was now asked, "Did she shrink from search, in such a manner as to betoken guilt?"

"I can't say that she did show any fear of being searched by us," was the reply. "She refused to be searched in the private office of the firm."

"That is, in the presence of men? Quite naturally she did." Then to the floor-walker, "Have your relations with this girl been entirely friendly?"

"I am glad to say I have no relations with her whatever. My relations are the same that I hold to the other girls—merely to see that they do their duty."

"You are perfectly sure that you have never cherished any ill-will toward her?"

"So far from it, I was at first inclined to be friendly."

"What do you mean by the term friendly?"

"Well, your Honor" (a little confusedly), "the term seems plain enough."

"And she did not reciprocate your friendship?" was the keen query.

"After I came to know her better, I gave her no occasion to reciprocate anything; and, pardon me, your Honor, I scarcely see what bearing these questions have on the plain facts in the case."

A slight frown was the only evidence that the judge had noted the impertinent suggestion that he did not know his business.

"Are you perfectly sure that you cherish no ill-will toward the prisoner?"

"I simply wish to do my duty by my employers. I eventually learned that her father was an opium-eater and a sot, and I don't fancy that kind of people. That is my explanation," he concluded, with a large attempt at dignity, and in a tone that he evidently meant all should hear.

"Her father is not on trial, and that information was uncalled for. Have you any further testimony?" the judge asked coldly.

"No, sir," and he stepped down amid a suppressed hiss in the court-room, for the spectators evidently shared in the antipathy with which he had inspired the keen-eyed but impassive and reticent magistrate, who now beckoned Mildred to step up close to him, and she came to him as if he were her friend instead of her judge. He was touched by her trust; and her steadfast look of absolute confidence made him all the more desirous of protecting her, if he could find any warrant for doing so. She said to him unmistakably by her manner, "I put myself in your hands."

"My child," the judge began seriously, yet kindly, "this is a very grave charge that is brought against you, and if it is your wish you can waive further trial before me at this stage of proceedings, for unless you can prove yourself innocent at this preliminary examination, your case must be heard before a higher court. Perhaps you had better obtain counsel, and have the whole matter referred at once to the grand jury."

"I would rather be tried by you, sir," Mildred replied, in a vibrating voice full of deep, repressed feeling; "I am innocent. It would be like death to me to remain longer under this shameful charge. I have confidence in you. I know I am guiltless. Please let me be tried now, *now*, for I cannot endure it any longer."

"Very well, then;" and he handed her a small, grimy Bible, that, no doubt, had been kissed by scores of perjured lips. But Mildred pressed hers reverently upon it, as she swore to "tell the truth, the whole truth, and nothing but the truth."

After a few preliminary questions as to age, etc., the justice said, reassuringly, "Now tell your story briefly and clearly."

It was indeed a brief story, and it had the impress of truth; but his Honor looked very grave as he recognized how little there was in it to refute the positive testimony already given. "Have you witnesses?" he asked.

"My mother and sister are present, and—and—a young man who thinks he knows something in my favor."

"I will hear your mother first," said the judge, believing that in her he would find the chief source of character; and when the sad, refined gentlewoman stood beside her daughter, he was all the more convinced that the girl ought to be innocent, and that all his insight into character and its origin would be at fault if she were not. In low, eager tones, Mrs. Jocelyn spoke briefly of their misfortunes, and testified as to Mildred's conduct. "She has been an angel of patience and goodness in our home," she said, in conclusion; "and if this false charge succeeds, we shall be lost and ruined indeed. My daughter's pastor is out of town, and in our poverty we have few friends who could be of any service. An old neighbor, Mrs. Wheaton, is present, and will confirm my words, if you wish; but we would thank your Honor if you will call Mr. Roger Atwood, who says he has information that will aid my child."

"Very well, madam," responded the judge kindly, "we will hear Mr. Atwood."

Roger was now sworn, while Mrs. Jocelyn returned to

her seat. In the young fellow's frank, honest face the judge found an agreeable contrast with the ill-omened visage of the floor-walker, whose good looks could not hide an evil nature.

"I must beg your Honor to listen to me with patience," Roger began in a low tone, "for my testimony is peculiar, and does not go far enough unless furthered by your Honor's skill in cross-questioning;" and in eager tones, heard only by the judge, he told what he had seen, and suggested his theory that if the girl, whom he had followed two evenings before, could be examined previous to any communication with her accomplice, she would probably admit the whole guilty plot.

The judge listened attentively, nodding approvingly as Roger finished, and said, "Leave me to manage this affair. I wish you to go at once with an officer, point out this girl to him, and bring her here. She must not have communication with any one. Nor must anything be said to her relating to the case by either you or the officer. Leave her wholly to me."

A subpœna was made out immediately and given to a policeman, with a few whispered and emphatic injunctions, and Roger was told to accompany him.

"This case is adjourned for the present. You may sit with your mother within the railing," he added kindly to Mildred.

The floor-walker had been watching the turn that the proceedings were taking with great uneasiness, and now was eager to depart, in order to caution the girl that Roger was in pursuit of against admitting the least knowledge of the affair; but the judge was too quick for him, and remarked that he was not through with him yet, and requested that he and the representative of the firm should remain. The two women who had testified against Mildred were permitted to depart. Then, as if dismissing the case from his mind, he proceeded to dispose of the other prisoners.

Belle joined her sister, and greeted her with great effusiveness, looking ready to champion her against the world; but they at last quieted her, and waited with trembling impatience and wonder for the outcome of Roger's mission.

The girl who had been led to wrong Mildred so greatly returned to the shop that morning with many misgivings, which were much increased when she learned what had occurred. She also felt that her accomplice had dealt treacherously in allowing such serious proceedings against Mildred, for he had promised that she should be merely taxed with theft and warned to seek employment elsewhere. "If he deceives in one respect he will in another, and I'm not safe from arrest either," she said to herself, and she made so many blunders in her guilty preoccupation that she excited the surprise of her companions. As she was waiting on a customer she heard a voice remark, "That's the girl," and looking up she grew faint and white as she saw, standing before her, a policeman, who served his subpœna at once, saying, "You must go with me immediately."

Frightened and irresolute, she stammered that she knew nothing about the affair.

"Well, then, you must come and tell his Honor so."

"Must I go?" she appealed to one of the firm, who happened to be near.

"Certainly," he replied, examining the subpœna; "go and tell all you know, or if you don't know anything, say so."

"I don't see why I should be dragged into the case—" she began brazenly.

"There's the reason," said the officer impatiently; "that subpœna has the power of bringing any man or woman in the city."

Seeing that resistance was useless, she sullenly accompanied them to a street-car, and was soon in readiness to be called upon for her testimony. The judge having disposed of the case then on trial, Mildred was again summoned to the bar, and the unwilling witness was sent for. She only had time to cast a reproachful glance at the man who, she feared, had betrayed her, and who tried, by his manner, to caution her, when the judge demanded her attention, he having in the meantime noted the fellow's effort.

"Stand there," he said, placing her so that her back was toward the man who sought to signal silence. "Officer, swear her. Now," he resumed severely, "any deviation from the truth, and the whole truth, will be perjury, which, you know, is a State-prison offence. I can assure you most honestly that it will be better for you, in all respects, to hide nothing, for you will soon discover that I know something about this affair."

After the preliminary questions, which were asked with impressive solemnity, he demanded, "Did you not leave the shop on Tuesday evening, and pass up the Avenue to —— Street?"

"Yes, sir."

"Did you not look back twice, to see if you were followed?"

"I may have looked back."

"You don't deny it, then?"

"No, sir."

"Did not Mr. Bissel, the floor-walker, join you in —— Street, before you had gone very far?"

"Ye—yes, sir," with a start.

"Did he not say something that agitated you very much?"

"He may have frightened me," she faltered.

"Yes, he probably did; but why? Did you not make a strong gesture of protest against what he said?"

'Yes, sir," with a troubled stare at the judge.

"Did you not go on with him very quietly and submissively, after a moment or two?"

"Yes, sir," and her face now was downcast, and she began to tremble.

"Did you not enter a covered alley-way, that led to tenements in the rear?"

"Yes, sir," with increasing agitation.

"Well, what did you do there?"

"Has he told on me, your Honor?" she gasped, with a sudden flood of tears.

"What he has done is no concern of yours. You are under oath to tell the whole truth. There was a single gas-jet burning in the covered passage-way, was there not?"

"Yes, sir," sobbing violently.

"Has Miss Mildred Jocelyn ever wronged you?"

"N—no, sir, not that I know of."

"Now tell me just what occurred under that gas-jet."

"I'll tell your Honor the whole truth," the girl burst out, "if your Honor'll let me off this time. It's my first offence, and we're poor, and I was driven to it by need, and he promised me that Miss Jocelyn wouldn't suffer anything worse than a warning to find another place."

Believing that her accomplice had betrayed her, she told the whole story without any concealment, fully exonerating Mildred. Although the judge maintained his stern, impassive aspect throughout the scene, he hugely enjoyed the floor-walker's dismay and confusion, and his tortured inability to warn the girl to deny everything.

"Please, your Honor, forgive me this time," sobbed the trembling witness in conclusion, "and I'll never do wrong again."

"I have no right or power to punish you," replied the judge; "it rests wholly with your employers whether they will prosecute you or not. Send that floor-walker here" (to an officer). "Well, sir, what have you to say to this testimony?" he asked, as the fellow shuffled forward, pale and irresolute. "Remember, you are still under oath."

The wily villain, caught in his own trap, hesitated. He was tempted to deny that the plot against Mildred was at his instigation; but, like the girl, he saw that the judge had mysterious information on the subject, and he could not tell how far this knowledge went. If he entered on a series of denials he might be confronted by another witness. The young man who had been sent to identify the girl, and whose unexpected presence had brought such disaster, might have been concealed in the passage-way, and so have seen and heard all. With the fear of an indictment for perjury before his eyes the fellow began to whine.

"I was only trying to protect the interests of my employers. I had suspected the Jocelyn girl—" At this there arose from the court-room a loud and general hiss, which the judge repressed, as he sternly interposed,

"We have nothing to do with your suspicions. Do you deny the testimony?"

"No, sir; but—"

"That's enough. No words; step down." Then turning to Mildred, he said kindly and courteously, "Miss Jocelyn, it gives me pleasure to inform you that your innocence has been clearly shown. I should also inform you that this man Bissel has made himself liable to suit for damages, and I hope that you will prosecute him. I am sorry that you have been subjected to so painful an ordeal. You are now at liberty."

"I thank—oh, I thank and bless your Honor," said Mildred, with such a depth of gratitude and gladness in her face that the judge smiled to himself several times that day. It was like a burst of June sunshine after a storm. While the witness was admitting the facts which would prove her guiltless, Mildred was scarcely less agitated than the wretched girl herself; but her strong excitement showed itself not by tears, but rather in her dilated eyes, nervously trembling form, and quickly throbbing bosom. Now that the tension was over she sank on a bench near, and covering her eyes, from which gushed a torrent of tears, with her hands, murmured audibly, "Thank God! oh, thank God! He has not deserted me after all."

Looks of strong sympathy were bent upon her from all parts of the room, and even the judge himself was so much affected that he took prompt refuge in the duties of his office, and summoning the foreman of the shop, said, "You may inform your employers how matters stand." This functionary had been regarding the later stage of the proceedings in undisguised astonishment, and now hastened to depart with his tidings, the floor-walker following him with the aspect of a whipped cur, and amid the suppressed groans and hisses of the spectators. The girl, too, slunk away after them in the hope of making peace with her employers.

The judge now observed that Roger had buttonholed a reporter, who had been dashing off hieroglyphics that meant a spicy paragraph the following day. Summoning the young man, he said, as if the affair were of slight importance, "Since the girl has been proved innocent, and will have no further relation to the case, I would suggest that, out of deference to her friends and her own feelings, there be no mention of her name," and the news-gatherer good-naturedly acceded to the request.

A new case was called, and new interests, hopes, and fears agitated the hearts of other groups, that had been drawn to the judgment-seat by the misfortunes or crimes of those bound to them by various ties.

Mrs. Jocelyn would not leave the place, which she had so dreaded, until Roger could accompany them, and they chafed at every moment of delay that prevented their pouring out their thanks. But Mildred's heart was too full for words. She fully understood how great a service he had rendered her. She bitterly reproached herself for all her prejudice in the past, and was in a mood for any self-sacrifice that he would ask. Tears of deep and mingled feeling fell fast, and she longed to escape from the staring crowd. Not before such witnesses could she speak and look the gratitude she felt.

With downcast eyes and quivering lips she followed her mother—to whom Roger had given his arm—from the courtroom. A carriage stood at the door, into which Mrs. Jocelyn was hurried before she could speak; then turning so promptly that there was no chance even for exuberant Belle or the effervescing Mrs. Wheaton to utter a syllable, Roger seized Mildred's hand, and said earnestly, "Thanks for your aid, Miss Jocelyn. I thought you were the bravest girl in the world, and you have proved it. I am as glad as you are, and this is the happiest moment in my life. I've just one favor to ask—please rest, and don't worry about anything—not *anything.* That's all. Good-by, for I must be off to business;" and before she or any of them could speak he caught a swiftly passing street-car and disappeared.

CHAPTER XXXV

"I AM SO PERPLEXED"

THE little group that Roger left on the sidewalk looked after him in a dazed manner for a moment, and then Belle exclaimed, a trifle indignantly, "Well, I declare, if he hasn't thanked you, instead of you thanking him."

Mildred sprang into the carriage, feeling that she must have some refuge at once, and, burying her face on her mother's shoulder, burst into another passion of tears.

"There, there," said Mrs. Wheaton, as they were driven toward their home; "the poor child's 'eart is too full for hany neat speeches now. Ven they meets hagain she'll thank him with heyes an' 'and, better than hany vords 'ere hon the street. He vas too bright a chap to take his thanks in this 'ere public place."

To their surprise, Mildred raised her head, and replied, in strong protest, "You do him wrong, Mrs. Wheaton. He was so modest and manly that he wished to escape all thanks. He has taken a noble revenge on me for all my stupid prejudice."

"That's right," cried ecstatic Belle. "Honest confession is good for the soul. I'll admit that most men and women are made of dust—street dust at that—but Roger Atwood is pure gold. He has the quickest brain and steadiest hand of any fellow in the world, and he'll stand up at the head before he's gray."

Fortunately, Mr. Jocelyn was not at home when they returned, and they had a chance to take a quiet breath after their strong excitement. Mrs. Wheaton, with many hearty congratulations and words of cheer, took her departure. Mrs. Jocelyn was justly solicitous about Mildred, fearing that the reaction from an ordeal that would tax the strongest might bring utter prostration to her delicate and sensitive organism. Mildred's manner soon threatened to realize her worst fears. She had passed a sleepless night, and was faint from fatigue, and yet, as the hours lapsed, she grew more nervously restless. Her eyes were hot and dry, sometimes so full of resolution that they were stern in their steadfastness, and again her face expressed a pathetic irresoluteness and sadness that made the mother's heart ache.

"Millie," she whispered, as she came to the bed on which the girl was tossing restlessly, "there's something on your mind. Mother's eyes are quick in reading the face of her child. You are thinking--you are debating something that won't let you rest, when you need rest so much. Oh, Millie darling, my heart was growing apathetic—it seemed almost dead in my breast. I've suffered on account of your father, till it seemed as if I couldn't suffer any more; but your peril and your troubled face teach me that it is not dead, and that my best solace now is devotion to my children. What is it, Millie, that you are turning over in your mind, which makes you look so desperately sad and fearful, and again—and then your expression frightens me—so determined as if you were meditating some step, which, I fear, you ought not to take? Oh, Millie, my child, the worst that I know about is bad enough, God knows, but your face makes me dread that you may be led by your troubles to do something which you would not think of were you less morbid and overwrought. I may have seemed to you a poor, weak woman in all of our troubles, but mother's love is strong, if her mind and body are not."

"Mamma, mamma, do not judge me or yourself so harshly. You have always been my ideal, mamma, and

I was thinking of nothing worse than how to rescue you and the others from your desperate straits. How can we go on living in this way, your heart breaking, your poor, frail body overtaxed with coarse labor, and Belle, Minnie, and Fred becoming contaminated by our dreadful surroundings. The shock I've received has awakened me from my old apathy. I see that while I just toiled for daily bread, and a little of it too, we were drifting down, down. Papa grows worse and worse. Belle is in danger; and what will become of Fred and Minnie if they remain long amid such scenes? Only yesterday morning I heard Fred quarrelling with another little boy on the landing, and lisping out oaths in his anger. Oh, mamma, we must be able to look forward to some escape from all this, or else you will soon give way to despair, and the worst will come. Oh that I were a man! Oh that I knew how to do something, through which I could earn enough to put papa into an institution, such as I have read of, and give you a home worthy of the name. But I cannot. I can only do what thousands of others can do, and take my chances with them in getting work. And now I seem so broken down in body and soul that I feel as if I could never work again. There seems to be one way, mamma, in which I can help you." And then she hesitated, and a deep, burning flush crimsoned the face that was so pale before. "Well," she said, at last, in a kind of desperation, "I might as well speak plainly, if I speak at all. It's no secret to you how Roger Atwood feels toward me, and also, mamma, you know my heart. While I could kiss his hand in gratitude, while I would not shrink from any suffering for his sake, to show how deeply I appreciate the priceless service he has rendered me, still, mamma, mamma, I'm only a woman, and am cursed with all the perversity of a woman's heart. Oh, what a loyal friend, what a devoted sister I could be to him! Mamma, can't you understand me?"

"Yes, Millie," sadly answered her mother.

"Well, mamma, I'm so perplexed. It seems for his

sake, since we have become so poor and disgraced, that I ought to refuse his suit. To the world, and especially to his friends, it will appear dreadfully selfish that we should link our wretched fortunes to his, and so cloud his prospects and impede his progress. I can't tell you how I dread such criticism. And yet, mamma, you know—no, mamma, even you cannot understand how great would be my self-sacrifice, when to others it will appear that I am only too glad to cling to one who gives some promise of better days. But the turning point has now come. Hitherto my manner toward Mr. Atwood has been unmistakable, and he has understood me; and were he obtuseness itself he could not fail to understand me. But after what has happened I cannot treat him so any longer. It would be shameful ingratitude. Indeed, in my cell last night I almost vowed that if he would prove me innocent—if he would save you and Belle and the children, I would make any sacrifice that he would ask. If I feel this way he will know it, for he almost reads my thoughts, he is so quick, and his feeling for me is so deep. And yet, mamma, now that I have thought more I fear that in sacrificing my own heart I am also sacrificing him. His friends will think so, at least. He is so young, chivalric, and unworldly that he may think it a noble thing to help us fight out our battle; but will he think so in coming years? Will he think so if the struggle is long and hard? Will he think so if we impede and retard him? Alas, will he think so if he finds that I can give him only gratitude and respect? Oh, mamma, I am *so* perplexed. I don't want to wrong him; I can't see you suffer on hopelessly and helplessly, and therefore it seems I ought to give him the right to help us should he seek for it, as I feel sure he will if I show any relenting. We could not be married for a long time; but if we were engaged he could do much to shield and protect us all; and now, alas, we have no protector. Belle needs one—oh, how sorely she needs one—and what would have been my fate had he not come to my aid? It would seem heartless in me to say simply, Thank you, sir; and yet, what heart have I to give in exchange for his devotion? He deserves so much, and I can give so little. Oh, mamma, will an old love die and a new one grow because they—because you wish it, and pray for it? I am so perplexed, so tossed and torn by my conflicting thoughts and feelings that my poor brain reels, and it seems as if I should lose my reason. And yet I must decide upon some course, for if, after his loyalty to me, I give him hope, I'll not disappoint him if I died a thousand times—no, not if Vinton Arnold came and laid all his wealth at my feet; I can see his love in every glance of his eye, still more can I feel it when he is near me; and if I offer him friendship or a sister's affection, it will seem to him like giving a stone for bread. But I must offer him only these or else give him hope—a hope that it would now be dishonor to disappoint. Mamma, mamma, what shall I do—what ought I to do?"

During this outpouring of her child's soul Mrs. Jocelyn was much agitated, and wiped tear after tear from her eyes. The impulse of her loyal, unworldly heart was first to take sides with Mildred's faithfulness to her earliest love, but her reason condemned such a course so positively that she said all she could against it. "Millie," she began, falteringly at first, "I feel with you and for you deeply. I know your rare quality of fidelity—of constancy. You are an old-fashioned Southern girl in this respect. While I would not have you wrong your heart, you must not blindly follow its impulses. It is often said that women have no reason, though some are calculating enough, Heaven knows. Surely, Millie, this is a case in which you should take some counsel of your reason, your judgment; and believe me, darling, I speak more for your sake than ours. While I admit that Roger has become very dear to me, I would not sacrifice you, my love, even in our sore straits. It is of you I think chiefly. I cannot endure the thought that the future of my darling child may be utterly blighted. I cannot bear to think of your settling down into a weary working-woman, with nothing to look forward to but daily drudgery for daily bread."

"I do not dread that so much, mamma—oh, nothing like so much—as a long and perhaps a vain effort to love one who has a sacred right to love as well as loyalty."

"Millie, you don't know how lonely and desolate your life might become. Millie—forgive me for saying it—your old love is utterly vain."

"I know it, mamma," said Mildred, with a low sob.

"Therefore, my darling, the sweetness and goodness of your young life ought not to be wasted on that which is vain and empty. If Mr. Arnold were worthy of your affections he would not have left you all this time without even a word. And, Millie, we may as well face the truth: we never belonged to the Arnolds' world, and it was wicked folly, for which I suffer hourly remorse, that we ever tried to approach it. If, instead of attempting to live like our rich neighbors, I had saved a goodly portion of your father's income, all might have been so different; but I was never taught to save, and I was just blind—blind. I never see your father but the thought comes, like a stab in the heart, I might have prevented it. Oh, if I had only stayed with him! It was during that fatal separation that he formed the habit which will cause his death and mine." (Poor Mrs. Jocelyn always remained under this illusion.)

"Oh, mamma, mamma, don't talk that way: I can't bear it."

"I must prepare you, Millie, darling, for what I clearly foresee. Martin is destroying himself, and I shall not long survive him. Oh, Millie, it's a terrible thing to love a weak man as I love your father. I love him so that his course is killing me. It could not be otherwise, for I am much to blame. Don't interrupt me; I am speaking these bitter words for your ultimate good. Your life is before you—"

"Mamma, how can my life be before me if you die broken-hearted?"

"Because you are young. You know that it would add tenfold bitterness to my already overflowing cup if I saw no chance for you, Belle, and the little ones. You may soon have to be mother and sister both. I forewarn you, because, as Roger says, you are strong as well as gentle, and you must not just drift helplessly toward we know not what. Oh, Millie, my poor crushed heart must have one consolation before it is at rest. Roger is not, and never will be, a weak man. It is not in his nature to give way to fatal habits. I, too, with a woman's eye, have seen his deep, strong affection for you, and with a mother's jealous love I have studied his character. He is a young giant, Millie, whom you unconsciously awoke to manhood. He comes of a sturdy, practical race, and unites to their shrewdness a chivalric Southern heart and large brain. He doesn't begin to know, himself, how much of a man he is, but the experience of life will fast develop him. He is one who will master circumstances, and not be molded by them. Obstacles will only stimulate his will. Your prejudice and dislike have not made him falter a moment. In the heart of a girl like you, Millie, I truly believe that a new love for such a man will surely spring up, and grow and strengthen with each succeeding year, and you would be worthy of him. You could make him happy, and eventually add greatly to his success. He is sure to become eminent, and be burdened with many large affairs, and the home you could make for him would be a refuge and a resting-place from which he would go out daily, strong and refreshed. Let his friends say what they please at first. He has his own career to make, and in his choice of you he has shown how unerring and sound his instincts are, and you can prove them so, and will, I think, when time has given your morbid and unhappy heart its healthful tone. Mrs. Wheaton has done much work at his uncle's house, and Mrs. Atwood talks to her quite freely. Mrs. Wheaton says they are wealthy, although they live so plainly, and that Mr. Atwood, Roger's uncle, is wonderfully taken with the young man, and means to give him a chance to climb among the highest, if he continues to be so steady and persevering. Of course you know that Roger will never be anything else than steady. And Mrs. Wheaton also says that Mr. Atwood will, no doubt, leave everything to him, for he has no children."

"I am sorry you have told me this," sighed Mildred; "it would have been hard enough at best, but I should feel almost mercenary now."

"Oh, Millie, you are too morbid and proud for anything," expostulated Mrs. Jocelyn, in whom no misfortune or sorrow could wholly blot out her old, mild passion for making good matches for her daughters—good matches in the right sense of the word—for she would look for worth, or what seemed worth to her, as well as the wealth that is too often considered solely. She had sought to involve Vinton Arnold by innocent wiles, and now, in pathetic revival of her old trait, she was even more bent on providing for Mildred by securing a man after her own heart. Love for her daughter, far more than ambition, was the mainspring of her motive, and surely her gentle schemes were not deserving of a very harsh judgment. She could not be blamed greatly for looking with wistful eyes on the one ray of light falling on her darkening path.

After a brief, troubled silence Mrs. Jocelyn resumed, with pathos and pleading in her voice, "Millie, darling, if this could all be, it would brighten my last days."

"There, there, mamma; as far as I *can* carry out your wishes, it shall be. I had already virtually promised it, and I should be perverse indeed could I not do all—all in my power to brighten your sad life. But, darling mamma, you must promise to live in return. A palace would be desolate if you were not seated in the snuggest corner of the hearth. I'll try to love him; I know I ought to give my whole heart to one who is so worthy, and who can do so much to brighten your life."

"Blessings on you, Millie. You will soon learn to return all his affection. You are both young, and it will probably be years before you can be married. In the meantime you will have a protector and friend who will have the right to aid you. You were slowly dying for want of air and change and hope. You worked all day, and shut yourself up in this miserable place at night, and it could not last; as your affianced he can take your part against the world, and protect Belle; and during the years while he is making his way upward, you will learn to love him. You will become interested in his studies, hopes, and prospects. You will encourage, and at the same time prevent undue application, for no man knows how to take care of himself. He can be our deliverer, and you his good angel. Your relations and long engagement may not be exactly conventional; but he is not conventional, neither is your need nor our sad fortunes. Since God has put within our reach this great alleviation of our sorrow, ought we to refuse it?"

"Set your mind at rest, mamma; you have made duty plain. I will do my best, and it now all rests with Roger."

"Millie, you are a dear, good child," said the mother brokenly, and with smiles shining like light through her tears; and after a close embrace she went out, closing the door that the weary girl might rest at last.

When alone, Mildred turned her face to the wall and breathed, like the lowest and saddest note of a wind-touched harp, "Vinton, Vinton Arnold, farewell forever. I must look for you no more—I must think of you no more. Oh, perverse heart, be still!"

But a decision had been reached, and her perplexed mind had at last found the rest of a fixed resolve. Then nature asserted her right, and she slept long and heavily. When she awoke, the lamp was lighted in the one living-room, from which came the sounds of an unsteady step and a thick, rough voice. She trembled, for she knew that her father had come home again intoxicated—an event that was becoming terribly frequent of late. She felt too weak and nerveless to go out and look upon their living disgrace, and lay still with long, sighing breaths. "Even Mr. Atwood will turn from us in disgust, when he realizes papa's degradation," she thought. "Alas! can it be right to cloud his bright young life with such a shameful stain! Oh, if it were not selfish, I could wish to die and escape from it all."

At last the heavy, shuffling step passed into the adjoining bedroom, and soon the wretched man was in stupor. As Mildred came out she saw Belle, who had returned from her work, looking toward the room in which her father slept, with a lowering, reckless expression that made her sister shudder.

Mildred tried to banish evil thoughts by putting her arm around the young girl's neck and kissing her between the eyes. "Don't look so, Belle," she whispered.

"Where is that to end?" Belle asked, in a strange, harsh voice, pointing toward the room. "Millie, I can't stand this life much longer."

"Oh, Belle, don't forget there is a heaven beyond this life."

"It's too far beyond. Look here, Millie; since God don't answer mamma's prayers, I haven't much faith in anything. See what undeserved trouble came upon you too. If it hadn't been for Roger you would have been in prison to-night, and we'd have been alone here with a drunken father. How can one have faith and try to be good when such things happen?"

"Belle," said Mildred, with a solemnity that made the reckless, discouraged girl turn pale, "you had better take a knife from that table and stab mamma than do anything wrong."

"Oh, hush!" whispered Belle, for Mrs. Jocelyn now entered with the children, whom she was glad to have away when the unnatural father returned, even though she knew they were with the wild young Arabs of the tenement.

CHAPTER XXXVI

A WOMAN'S HEART

MRS. JOCELYN and her daughters were silent and depressed during their meagre supper, for they never could become accustomed to the terrible skeleton in their household. When Mr. Jocelyn confined himself solely to opium he was not so revolting, but common, beastly intoxication was unendurable. They felt that it was brutalizing his very soul, and becoming a millstone around their necks which must drag them down to some unknown abyss of infamy. Mechanically they went through the motions of eating, the mother and daughters forcing down the little food they could afford, and the children ravenously devouring all that was given to them. As Mildred saw the mother trying to slip unnoticed her almost untasted supper from her plate to Fred's, she laid a hand upon her arm and said:

"No, mamma; remember you are to live," she added in a low whisper, and the poor creature tried to smile and was submissive.

With a pathetic maintenance of their old-time habits, they had scarcely cleared away the supper-table, put the children to rest, and made the poor little place as neat and inviting as possible, when Mr. Wentworth appeared, followed by Roger. Mildred had been expecting the latter with trepidation, Belle with impatience; and the hard, lowering look on the face of the young girl gave way to one of welcome and pleasure, for if Belle's good moods were apt to be transient, so were her evil ones, and the hearty, healthy spirits of the young fellow were contagious.

Mildred was greatly relieved to see Mr. Wentworth, for while she had fully resolved to yield to Roger's suit, her heart, despite her will, welcomed delay. She was also glad that her pastor was present, for she could now show her strong gratitude without fear of immediate and embarrassing results. She was therefore more prompt even than Belle, and, taking the young man's hand in both of her own, she said, with tears in her eyes:

"Why didn't you let me thank you this morning? My gratitude has been growing every moment, and you must take it all or I shall sink under it. Mr. Wentworth, I should have been in some horrible prison to-night, with my heart breaking from sorrow and shame, if it were not for this kind, generous friend, Mr. Atwood. I long cherished an unreasoning prejudice against you, and showed it openly. You have taken a strange revenge. No Southern gentleman could have acted more nobly, and a Southern girl could not use stronger praise than that."

Roger's hand, usually so strong and steady, trembled. These words, warm from the heart of the girl who had hitherto been so distant and unapproachable, almost took away his breath. "Please don't," he faltered. "Such gratitude—such words—from you oppress me. I don't deserve such thanks. Any decent man would have been glad to save one who was so good and so wronged, and I shall always regard it as the luckiest event of my life that I happened to be the one to aid you. Oh, you don't know, you never can know what immense good-fortune it was." Then, as if fearing he might lose his self-control, he broke hastily away to greet Mrs. Jocelyn, but Belle caught him with the impulse of the warm-hearted sister she had become, and throwing her arm around his neck exclaimed, "I'm going to pay you with the best coin I have." And she kissed him again and again.

"Oh, Jupiter!" gasped the blushing youth. "Bless that floor-walker and all his deviltry! I shall let him off just a little for this."

"No, don't. I'll give you another kiss if you'll get even with him," Belle whispered.

"It's a bargain," he said in her ear, and Belle ratified the compact immediately.

"Oh," thought Mildred, in the depths of her heart, "if it were only Belle instead of me!"

Mrs. Jocelyn's greeting was scarcely less demonstrative than Belle's, but there was a motherly tenderness in it that brought tears into the young fellow's eyes. "Blessings on you, my dear good boy," she murmured, "and a mother's blessing will do you no harm."

"Look here," said Roger brusquely, "if you don't let up on a fellow I shall make a confounded fool of myself." And his lip quivered as if he were a boy in truth.

Mr. Wentworth, who in their strong feeling had been quite ignored, at first looked on with smiling sympathy. Mildred had given him the hand that Roger released, and holding it in a warm clasp he did not speak at first, but watched a scene that had for him the attractions of a real drama. He now did not help Roger much by saying, in his hearty way, "That's right; lay it on strong; he deserves all, and more. Miss Mildred, I have been yellow with envy for the last two hours because I was absent. I would have eulogized you so in court that the judge would have addressed you as Saint Mildred, and yet it's but honest to say that you would have gone to jail like many a saint before you had not Roger got hold of the facts which enabled the judge to prove you innocent. The law is awfully matter-of-fact, and that lace on your person had to be accounted for."

"Yes, yes," cried Belle, "tell us everything. We've been dying with curiosity all day, and you've been so mysterious and important, and have put on such airs, that you quite awed me. Seems to me that for a country boy you are blossoming fast."

"It isn't necessary for a country boy to be a fool, especially when he has eyes," replied Roger in an off-hand way.

"It's all simple enough. I happened to be passing the store where Miss Mildred—"

"Happened to be passing! How often did you happen to pass?" Belle interrupted, with a face full of mischief.

"You are not a judge, ma'am, and so can't cross-question," he answered, with a quick blush but a defiant little nod, "and if you were, no one is obliged to incriminate himself. I was merely passing, and the movements of that scamp, Bissel, slightly awakened my curiosity, and I followed him and the girl. I was exceedingly fortunate, and saw enough to enable the judge to draw from the girl the whole story. Now you see what a simple, prosaic part I played. Miss Jocelyn, in keeping up so bravely through scenes and experiences that were perfectly horrible to her, is the heroine of the piece. By Jove!—beg your pardon, Mr. Wentworth—it was as good as a play to see how she looked her innocence into the heart and mind of the judge. I saw the judicial frost in his eyes melting like two icicles on the south side of a barn. Oh, the judge could see as far into a millstone as the next man," he continued, laughing, as if he relished the memory hugely. "After those horrid old hags were sent along so fast to where they belonged, he looked when Miss Jocelyn appeared as if a whole picture gallery were before him. He could keep up his official regulation manner, but his eyes paid a certain prisoner many compliments."

"Roger, you've got the eyes of a lynx," said Belle, and Mildred was human enough to show the pleasure she felt at his words.

"Nonsense," replied the young fellow in sudden confusion. "Any one who has learned to hunt well gets a quick eye."

"The judge's eyes at least were not at all to blame," added Mr. Wentworth, laughing, and looking at Mildred so kindly and admiringly that the color which was stealing into her face deepened rapidly. "Well, to come down to business. Roger and I have been to see your employers, and we talked to them rather strongly. While they insist that they were misled and not to blame, they felt remorseful, and we struck while they were in their regretful mood. They give you a week's vacation, and send you twenty-five dollars as a small compensation for what you have suffered."

"I don't want it," cried Mildred indignantly.

"Oh yes, you do; besides it's only spoiling the Philistines. They had already discharged that scoundrel Bissel, and they intend prosecuting the girl. They apologize to you, and promise to raise your wages, but I think I can obtain enough sewing and fancy work to render it unnecessary for you to go back unless you prefer it. I don't want to think of your being subjected to that barbarous rule of standing any longer. I know of a lady on Fifth Avenue who is a host if she once becomes interested in any one, and through her I think I can enlist enough people to keep you busy. I feel sure she will be our ally when she knows all."

"Oh, if I could only stay with mamma and work at home, I should be so glad," was the young girl's response.

"Well, I must have one promise first, and your conscience should lead you to make it honestly. You must give me your word that you will not shut yourself up from light, air, and recreation. You must take a walk every day; you must go out with your sister and Roger, and have a good time as often as possible. If I find you sewing and moping here all the time, I shall feel hurt and despondent. Miss Millie, the laws of health are just as much God's laws as the Ten Commandments."

"I feel you are right," she faltered. Then she covered her face with her hands and sobbed, "But papa, papa. Mr. Wentworth, since all know it now, you must know the truth that is worse than death to us. I feel as if I wanted to hide where no one could ever see me again; I fear we do Mr. Atwood a wrong in permitting him to be so friendly."

Roger towered up until he "looked six feet six," as Belle

remarked afterward, and, coming straight to the speaker, he took her hand and said, "Miss Jocelyn, when I'm ashamed to be seen with you and Belle, I'll strike hands with Bissel in the sneak-thieving line. I ask for no prouder distinction than to be trusted by your mother and by you."

"Roger has settled that question, and shown himself a sensible fellow," resumed Mr. Wentworth, with an emphatic and approving nod. "Since you have spoken of a subject so deeply painful, I will speak plainly too. There are plenty of people, I admit, who treat the family of wrong-doers as if their unspeakable misfortune were their fault; and in a certain sense this tendency is wholesome, for it has a great restraining influence on those tempted to give way to evil. But this tendency should not be carried to cruel lengths by any one, and there are those who are sufficiently just to discriminate and feel the deepest sympathy—as I do. While it would be in bad taste for you and Miss Belle to ignore this trouble, and flaunt gayly in public places, it would be positively wicked to let your trouble crush out health, life, and hope. You are both young, and you are sacredly bound to make the best and the most of the existence that God has bestowed upon you. You have as good a right to pure air and sunshine as I have, and as good a right to respect while you maintain your present character. It would do your father no good, it would break your mother's heart, if you followed your morbid impulses. It would only add to your father's remorse. I fear his craving for the poisons that are destroying him has become a disease, and that it is morally impossible for him to refrain."

"Do you think—would it be possible to put him into an institution," Mildred faltered.

"Well, it would be expensive, and yet if he will go to one and make an honest effort to be cured, perhaps the money might be raised."

"Oh," cried Mildred, "we'd starve almost, we'd work night and day to give him a chance."

"The money shall be raised," said Roger quietly. "I've saved nearly all my wages, and—"

"Oh, Mr. Atwood," burst out Mildred impetuously, "this would be far better than saving me from prison. I would pay you back every penny if I toiled all my life, and if papa could be his old self once more we would soon regain all that we have lost." Then a sudden passion of sobs shook her slight form. "Oh," she gasped brokenly, "I could die—I could suffer anything to save papa."

"Mr. Wentworth," said the wife, with a look in her large tearless blue eyes which they never forgot, "we will live in one room, we'll spend only enough for bare existence, if you'll help us in this matter." Then putting her arms around Roger's neck she buried her face on his breast and murmured, "You are like a son to me, and all there is left of my poor crushed heart clings to you. If I could see Martin the man he was, I could die in peace."

"He shall have the chance of the best and richest," said Roger brokenly. "I ask nothing better than to have a hand in saving such a man as Mr. Jocelyn must have been."

Then was Roger's hour and opportunity, and he might at that time have bound Mildred to him by vows that the girl would sooner perish than break. Indeed in her abounding gratitude, and with every generous, unselfish chord in her soul vibrating, even his eyes could have been deceived, and he might easily have believed that he had won her heart. But there was neither policy nor calculation in his young enthusiasm. His love truly prompted his heart, but it was a heart abounding in good, unselfish impulses, if sufficient occasion called them forth. He loved Mrs. Jocelyn and Belle scarcely less than his own mother and sister, and yet with a different affection, a more ideal regard. They appealed to his imagination; their misfortunes made them sacred in his eyes, and aroused all the knightly instincts which slumber in every young, unperverted man. Chief of all, they belonged to Mildred, the girl who had awakened his manhood, and to whom he had felt, even when she was so cold and prejudiced, that he owed his larger life and his power to win a place among men. Now that she was so kind, now that she was willing to be aided by him in her dearest hopes, he exulted, and life grew rich in tasks for which the reward seemed boundless. The hope would come to him, as Mildred rose to say good-by with a look that he had never seen on any human face before, that she might soon give him something warmer and better than gratitude; but if she could not soon, he would wait, and if she never could return his love, he proposed to be none the less loyal as a friend.

Indeed the young girl's expression puzzled him. The old pride was all gone, and she gave him the impression of one who is conquered and defenceless, and who is ready to yield anything, everything to the victor. And this ill-defined impression was singularly true, for she was in a passion of self-sacrifice. She felt that one who had been so generous and self-forgetful had a right to all that a true man could ask, and that it would be base in her to refuse. The greater the sacrifice the more gladly she would make it, in order that she too might prove that a Southern girl could not be surpassed in *noblesse oblige* by a Northern man. She was in one of those supreme moods in which men and women are swayed by one dominant impulse, and all other considerations become insignificant. The fact that those she loved were looking on was no restraint upon her feeling, and the sympathizing presence of the clergyman added to it. Indeed her emotion was almost religious. The man who had saved her from prison and from shame—far more: the man who was ready to give all he had to rescue her fallen father—was before her, and without a second's hesitation she would have gone into a torture-chamber for the sake of this generous friend. She wanted him to see his absolute power. She wanted him to know that he had carried her prejudice, her dislike by storm, and had won the right to dictate his terms. Because she did not love him she was so frank in her *abandon*. If he had held her heart's love she would have been shy, were she under tenfold greater obligations. She did not mean to be unmaidenly—she was not so, for her unconscious delicacy saved her—but she was at his feet as truly as the "devotee" is prostrate and helpless before the car of Juggernaut. But Roger was no grim idol, and he was too inexperienced, too modest to understand her. As he held her throbbing palm he looked a little wonderingly into her flushed face and tear-gemmed eyes that acknowledged him lord and master without reserve; then he smiled and said in a low, half-humorous tone, "I shan't be an ogre to you—you won't be afraid of me any longer, Miss Mildred?"

"No," she replied impetuously; "you are the truest and best friend a woman ever had. Oh, I know it—I know it now. After what you said about papa, I should despise myself if I did not know it."

She saw all his deep, long-repressed passion leap into his face and eyes, and in spite of herself she recoiled from it as from a blow. Ah, Mildred, your will is strong, your gratitude is boundless, your generous enthusiasm had swept you away like a tide, but your woman's heart is stronger and greater than all, and he has seen this truth unmistakably. The passion died out of his face like a flame that sinks down to the hidden, smouldering fire that produced it. He gave her hand a strong pressure as he said quietly, "I am indeed your friend—never doubt it;" then he turned away decidedly, and although his leave-taking from Mrs. Jocelyn and Belle was affectionate, they felt rather than saw there was an inward struggle for self-mastery, which made him, while quiet in manner, anxious to get away.

Mr. Wentworth, who had been talking with Mrs. Jocelyn, observed nothing of all this, and took his leave with assurances that they would see him soon again.

Mildred stood irresolute, full of bitter self-reproach. She took an impulsive step toward the door to call Roger back, but, checking herself, said despairingly, "I can deceive neither him nor myself. Oh, mamma, it is of no use." And indeed she felt that it would be impossible to carry out the scheme that promised so much for those she loved. As the lightning flash eclipses the sun at noonday, so all of her gratitude and self-sacrificial enthusiasm now seemed but pale sickly sentiment before that vivid flame of honest love—that divine fire which consumes at touch every motive save the one for the sacred union of two lives.

"I wish I could see such a man as Roger Atwood look at me as he looked at you," said Belle indignantly. "I would not send him away with a heartache."

"Would to Heaven it had been you, Belle!" replied Mildred dejectedly. "I can't help it—I'm made so, and none will know it better than he."

"Don't feel that way," remonstrated Mrs. Jocelyn; "time and the thought of what Roger can do for us will work great changes. You have years before you. If he will help us save your father—"

"Oh, mamma, I could shed for him all the blood left in my body."

"Nonsense!" cried the matter-of-fact Belle. "He doesn't want your blood; he only wants a sensible girl who will love him as he deserves, and who will help him to help us all"

Mildred made a despairing gesture and went to her room. She soon reappeared with a quilt and a pillow, and placing them on the floor beside the low bed in which the children slept, said, "I'll stay here, and you take my place with Belle, mamma. No," she added resolutely, as her mother began to remonstrate; "what I resolve upon I intend to do hereafter, even to the least thing. You shall not go near the room where papa is to-night."

Throughout the evening, while love, duty, and generous sympathy planned for his redemption; throughout the long night, while the sad-hearted wife prayed for success in their efforts, the husband and father lay shrouded in the heavy, rayless darkness of a drunken stupor.

CHAPTER XXXVII

STRONG TEMPTATION

"WELL, I must admit that I have rarely been so touched and interested before," said Mr. Wentworth, as he and Roger walked homeward together; "and that is saying much, for my calling brings human life before me in almost every aspect. Mildred Jocelyn is an unusual girl. Until to-day I thought her a trifle cold, and even incapable of very deep feeling. I thought pride—not a common pride, you know, but the traditional and proverbial pride of a Southern woman—her chief characteristic, but the girl was fairly volcanic with feeling to-night. I believe she would starve in very truth to save her father, though of course we won't permit any such folly as they are meditating, and I do not believe there is any sacrifice, not involving evil, at which she would hesitate. She's a jewel, Atwood, and in winning her, as you will, you will obtain a girl for whom a prince might well sue. She's one of a thousand, and beneath all her wonted self-control and reserve she has as true and passionate a heart as ever beat in a woman's breast."

"Good-night," said Roger, a little abruptly. "I agree with all you can say in regard to Miss Jocelyn's nobility, and I shall not fail her, nor shall I make bargains or conditions in my loyalty. The privilege of serving such a woman is enough. I will see you again soon," and he walked rapidly down the street on which his uncle resided.

Roger and Mr. Wentworth had become very good friends, and the latter had been of much service to the young fellow by guiding him in his reading and study. The clergyman had shown his usual tact in dealing with Roger. Never once had he lectured or talked religion at him, but he preached interestingly, and out of the pulpit was the genial, natural, hearty man that wins the respect and goodwill of all. His interviews with Roger were free from the faintest trace of religious affectation, and he showed that friendly appreciation and spirit of comradeship which young men like. Roger felt that he was not dealing with an ecclesiastic, but with a man who was as honest, earnest, and successful in his way as he ever hoped to be in his. He was therefore being drawn by motives that best accorded with his disposition toward the Christian faith—by a thorough respect for it, by seeing its practical value as worked out in the useful busy life of one who made his chapel a fruitful oasis in what would otherwise have been a moral desert. In his genuine humanity and downright honesty, in his care of people's bodies as well as souls, and temporal as well as spiritual interests, the minister was a tower of strength, and his influence for good over the ambitious youth, now fast developing the character which would make or mar him for life, was most excellent. While Roger spoke freely to him of his general hopes and plans, and gave to him more confidence than to any one else, there was one thing that, so far as words were concerned, he hid from all the world—his love for Mildred. The sagacious clergyman, however, at last guessed the truth, but until to-night never made any reference to it. He now smiled to think that the sad-hearted Jocelyns might eventually find in Roger a cure for most of their troubles, since he hoped that Mr. Jocelyn, if treated scientifically, might be restored to manhood.

Mr. Ezra Atwood, Roger's uncle, sat in his small parlor far beyond his usual hour for retiring, and occasionally he paced the floor so impatiently as to show that his mind was deeply perturbed. While his nephew had studied books he had studied his nephew, and in the process the fossilization of his heart had been arrested, and the strong, steady youth had suggested hopes of something like a filial relation to the childless man. At first he had growled to himself, "If the boy were only mine I'd make a man of him," and then gradually the idea of adopting and making a man of him, had presented itself and slowly gained full possession of his mind. Roger was capable, persevering, and tremendously ambitious—qualities that were after the old man's heart, and, after maintaining his shrewd furtive observation for months, he at last muttered to himself, "I'll do it, for he's got the Atwood grit and grip, and more brains than any of us. His father is shrewd and obstinate enough, but he's narrow, and hasn't breadth of mind to do more than pinch and save what he can scratch out of that stony farm of his. I'm narrow, too. I can turn an honest penny in my line with the sharpest in the market, and I'm content; but this young fellow is a new departure in the family, and if given a chance and kept from all nonsense he can climb to the top notch. There's no telling how high a lawyer can get in this country if he has plenty of brains and a ready tongue."

Thus the old man's dominant trait, ambition, which he had satisfied in becoming known as one of the most solid and wealthy men of his calling, found in his nephew a new sphere of development. In return for the great favors which he proposed to confer, however, he felt that Roger should gratefully accept his wishes as absolute law. With the egotism and confidence of many successful yet narrow men, he believed himself perfectly capable of guiding the young fellow's career in all respects, and had little expectation of any fortunate issue unless he did direct in all essential and practical matters. Mr. Atwood worshipped common-sense and the shrewd individuality of character which separates a man from his fellows, and enables him to wrap himself in his own interests and pursuits without babbling to others or being impeded by them. Influenced by his wife, he was kind to the poor, and charitable in a certain methodical way, but boasted to her that in his limited circle he had no "hangers-on," as he termed them. He had an instinctive antipathy to a class that he called "ne'er-do-weels," "havebeens," and "unlucky devils," and if their misfortunes and lack of thrift resulted from causes like those destroying Mr. Jocelyn he was sternly and contemptuously implacable toward them. He was vexed that Roger should have bothered himself with the sick man he had discovered on shipboard the day before Christmas. "It was no affair of his," he had grumbled; but as the young fellow had been steady as a clock in his business and studies after Mr. Jocelyn had recovered, he had given no further thought to these friends, nor had it occurred to him that they were more than passing acquaintances. But a letter from Roger's father, who had heard of Mr. Jocelyn's condition and of his son's intimacy with the family, awakened the conservative uncle's suspicions, and that very afternoon the well-meaning but garrulous Mrs. Wheaton had told his wife all about what she regarded as brilliant performances on the part of Roger at the police court. Mrs. Atwood was a kind-hearted woman, but she had much of her husband's horror of people who were not respectable after her strict ideal, and she felt that she ought to warn him that Roger's friends were not altogether desirable. Of course she was glad that Roger had been able to show that the young girl was innocent, but shop-girls living in low tenements with a drunken father were not fit companions for their nephew and possible heir. Her husband indorsed her views with the whole force of his strong, unsympathetic, and ambitious nature, and was now awaiting Roger with the purpose of "putting an end to such nonsense at once." The young man therefore was surprised to find, as he entered the hallway, that his uncle was up at an hour late for him.

"I wish to see you," was the prompt, brief greeting from Mr. Atwood, who was uneasily tramping up and down the small stiff parlor, which was so rarely used that it might almost have been dispensed with as a part of the residence.

Roger came forward with some anxiety, for his uncle lowered at him like a thunder-cloud.

"Sit there, where I can see your face," was the next curt direction. There was neither guilt nor fear in the frank countenance that was turned full upon him. "I'm a man of few words," he resumed more kindly, for Roger's expression disarmed him somewhat. "Surely," he thought, "when the boy gets a hint of what I can do for him, he'll not be the fool to tangle himself up with people like the Jocelyns."

"Where have you been to-night?" he asked bluntly. Roger told him. "Where were you last night and this morning?" Roger briefly narrated the whole story, concluding, "It's the first time I've been late to business, sir."

The old man listened grimly, without interruption, and then said, "Of course I'm glad you got the girl off, but it's bad management to get mixed up in such scrapes. Perhaps a little insight into court-room scenes will do you no harm since you are to be a lawyer. Now that the affair is over, however, I wish you to drop these Jocelyns. They are of no advantage to you, and they belong to a class that is exceedingly disagreeable to me. I suppose you know what kind of a man Mr. Jocelyn is?"

"Yes, sir; but you do not know what kind of a woman Mrs. Jocelyn is. She is—"

"She is Jocelyn's wife, isn't she?"

"Certainly; but—"

"And the girl is his daughter. They live in a dowdy tenement, and are as poor as crows."

"Misfortune and the wrong of others might make all this true of us," began the youth impetuously; "and yet if old friends should turn their backs—"

"You are not an old friend," his uncle again interrupted, in his hard, business-like tones. "They are merely accidental acquaintances, who happened to board at your father's house last summer. They haven't the ghost of a claim upon you. It looks far more as if you were in love with the girl, and were making a romantic fool of yourself."

Roger's face grew very white, but he controlled himself, and asked, "Uncle, have I ever treated you with disrespect?"

"Certainly not; why should you?"

"With some right I may also ask why you treat me with such disrespect?"

The old man opened his eyes, and was somewhat taken aback by this unexpected question, and yet a moment's reflection showed him that he had given cause for it. He also misunderstood his nephew, and resumed, with a short conciliatory laugh, "I guess I'm the fool, to be imagining all this nonsense. Of course you are too much of an Atwood to entangle yourself with such people and spoil your prospects for life. Look here, Roger. I'll be frank with you, and then we'll understand each other. You know I've neither chick nor child, and I've turned a good big penny in business. When you first came I thought you were a rattle-pated country boy that wanted a lark in the city, and I took you more to keep you out of mischief than for any other cause. Well, I've watched you closely, and I was mistaken. You've got the stuff in you to make a man, and I see no reason why you should not be at the top of the heap before you reach my years, and I mean to give you a chance. You've got a little soft place in your head and heart, or you wouldn't be getting yourself mixed up in other people's troubles. I tell you what it is, my boy, a man who gets ahead in these times must strike right out for himself, and steer clear of all fouling with 'ne'er-do-weels,' as if they had a pestilence. Hook on to the lucky ones, the strong ones, and they'll help you along. Now if you'll take this course and follow my advice right along, I'll give you a chance with the first. You shall go to the best college in the land, next to the law-school, and then have money enough to enable you to strike high. By the time you are thirty you can marry an heiress. But no more Jocelyns and shop-girls who have been at station-houses, if you please. The girl may have been innocent of that offence; but, plain man as I am, I don't like this style of people at all, and I know human nature well enough to be sure that they'll try to tie themselves on to you if they can. I've thought it all out in my slow way, and, since you've got it in you, I'm going to give you a chance to put the Atwood name where I can't, with all my money."

Roger was deeply moved, for he had no idea that his uncle was cherishing such far-reaching plans in his behalf. While he had little sympathy with the cold, selfish side of the programme, his strong ambition responded powerfully to the prospect held out to him. He knew that the hopes inspired were not vain, for his uncle was a man whose deeds always outstripped his words, and that his fortunes were practically assured if he would follow the worldly-wise policy to which he had listened. His ambition whispered, "Mildred Jocelyn does not love you, and never will. Even now, after you have done so much for her, and her gratitude is boundless, her heart shrinks from you. She may not be able to help it, but it is true nevertheless. Why should you throw away such prospects for the sake of one who loves another man, and who, until in a time of desperate need, treated you with undisguised coldness and dislike? Besides, by yielding to your uncle's will you can eventually do more for the family than if thrown on your own resources." It was indeed the great temptation of his life, and he wavered.

"Uncle," he said irresolutely, "you have indeed opened a very alluring prospect, and I am grateful that you think so well of me, and that you are willing to do so much. Since you have been so frank with me, I will be equally so with you," and he told him all about his relations with the Jocelyns, and tried to make the shrewd old merchant understand that they were not common people.

"They are the most dangerous people of all," he interrupted impatiently. "Having once been up in the world, they think they are still as good as anybody, and are wild to regain their old position. If they had always been poor and commonplace, they would not be so likely to presume. What you say about the girl's not caring for you is sheer nonsense. She'd marry you to-morrow if she could. The one idea of such people is to get out of the slough into which they have fallen, and they'll marry out of it the first chance they get, and like enough they'll do worse if they can't marry. I tell you they are the most dangerous kind of people, and Southern at that. I've learned all about them; the father has gone to the devil for good and all, and, with your feeling and weakness toward them, you'll never be safe a moment unless you drop them completely and finally. Come, young man, let this affair be the test between us. I've worked hard for nearly a lifetime, and have a right to impose some conditions with what has been earned by forty years of toil, early and late. I never speculated once. Every dollar I had to spare I put in paying real estate and governments, and, Roger, I'm worth to-day a good half a million. Ha, ha, ha! people who look at the plain old man in the plain little house don't know that he could afford a mansion on the Avenue better than most of them. This is between ourselves, but I want you to act with your eyes open. If you are such a soft-headed fool as to let that girl, who you admit does not like you or care a rap for you personally, stand between you and such prospects, then I'm mistaken in you, and the sooner I find it out the better. Come, now, I'll be good-natured and liberal in the matter, for young men will be a little addle-pated and romantic before they cut their wisdom teeth. Through that English woman who works for your aunt occasionally you can see to it that these people don't suffer, but beyond that you must drop them once for all. What is more, your father and mother take the same view that I do, and your filial duty to them requires what I ask. While we naturally refuse to be mixed up with such people, we are seeking chiefly to promote your welfare; for the worst thing that can happen to a young man starting in life is to have a helpless lot of people hanging on him. So, come, give me your promise—the promise of an Atwood—and it will be all right."

Roger was not a self-sacrificing saint by any means. Moreover, he had inherited the Atwood characteristics sufficiently to feel all the worldly force of his uncle's reasoning, and to be tempted tremendously by his offers. They promised to realize his wildest dreams, and to make the path to fame and wealth a broad, easy track instead of a long, steep, thorny path, as he had expected. He was virtually on the mountain-top, and had been shown "all the kingdoms of the world and the glory of them."

But against this brilliant background he saw the thin, pale face of Mrs. Jocelyn, as she looked up to him with loving trust and gratitude, and the motherly kiss that she had imprinted on his cheek was a seal to her absolute faith. He felt the pressure of Belle's arm about his neck, and remembered his promise to give her a brother's regard and protection, and justly he feared that if deserted now the impulsive, tempted girl would soon meet shipwreck. She would lose faith in God and man. But that which touched him most nearly were his words to Mildred—words spoken even when she showed him most plainly that her heart was not his, and probably never could be—"I am your friend; never doubt it." How false he would seem to them; how false and selfish to his friend, the great-hearted clergyman, who was like Christ himself in his devoted labors; how false and base he would ever feel himself to be in his own soul!

For a time there was a terrible conflict in his breast as he paced the floor in long strides, with hands clenched and brow heavily contracted. His uncle watched him curiously and with displeased surprise, for that he could hesitate at all seemed to the worldly man an evidence of fatal weakness.

Roger fought it out like a genuine Atwood, and was nearer akin to his uncle than the old merchant would ever suspect. His heart craved the kingdoms of the world unspeakably, but he now realized that he must barter for them his honor, his manhood, and love. Thus far he had a right to love Mildred, and it was not her fault she could not return it. But, poor and shamed as she was, he knew that she would despise him if he yielded now, even though he rose to be the foremost man of the nation. Not with any chivalric, uncalculating impulse did he reach his conclusion, but by the slow, deliberate reasoning of a cool-headed, sturdy race that would hold to a course with life-long tenacity, having once chosen it.

Turning to his uncle, he asked quietly. "What did you mean by 'the promise of an Atwood'?"

"You ought to know. Our family, for generations, have lived up among the granite hills of Forestville, and, although poor, our promises, whether spoken or written, are like them."

"I'm glad to hear you say that—I'm glad to be reminded of it," his nephew replied. "Well, my promise has already been given. I have promised that poor broken-hearted woman, Mrs. Jocelyn, that I'd try to help her through her terrible misfortunes. I've promised her daughter Belle that I'd give her a brother's care and affection. I've promised the girl I love that I would at least be her friend, since I cannot be more. I'll prove myself a true Atwood, worthy to sustain the family name and honor by keeping my promises, and if I break them, you yourself, deep in your heart, would despise me."

For a moment the old merchant was nonplussed, so adroitly and unexpectedly had Roger turned his words against him. Then, like most men suddenly put in a false position, he grew angry, and blurted out, "Nonsense! It doesn't apply at all. These artful women have come it over you—have entrapped you." The young man here made a strong gesture of protest. "Oh, don't try to deceive me," his uncle proceeded, more loudly and passionately; "I know the world. If I'd blindly made promises to adventurers who would compass my ruin, ought I to keep them? If I find I've indorsed a forged check, ought I not to stop its payment? In the name of your parents and as your uncle, I protest against this folly, for I see well enough where it will end. Moreover, I tell you plainly that you must choose between me and my offers, and that old sot of a Jocelyn and his scheming wife and daughters. If you can be carried away by such absurdity, you are weaker than water, and the sooner you learn by bitter experience the better, for you certainly belong to that class which only hard experience can teach. But I'd like to see those brazen-faced creatures and give them a piece of—"

"Stop!" thundered Roger; "beware how you say another word against those whom sorrow should render sacred. You know less about them than about heaven. Do you forget that I am of age? You made me an offer, and I thanked you for it honestly and gratefully. What's more, I was base enough to be tempted by it. Oh, yes"—with a bitter laugh—"I was an Atwood enough for that. If you had not coupled it with the condition that I should, like a coward, desert helpless and unfortunate women to whom my word is given, I would have fulfilled your best hopes and ambitions, and have made your age glad with my grateful love and service. In your cold-hearted worldliness you have overreached yourself, and you wrong yourself more than me, even though I perish in the streets. But I won't starve. Mark my words: I'll place the Atwood name where you can't, with all your money, and I shall not make broken faith with those who trust me, the foundation of my fortunes."

"Very well, then," said his uncle, who had quieted down into an anger of white heat; "since you prefer those disreputable strangers to your family, go to them. I wash my hands of you, and shall write to your father to this effect to-night. I'm a prompt man and don't dilly-dally."

"Mrs. Jocelyn and her daughters are no more disreputable than you are, sir, and calling me 'soft-headed fool' doesn't make me one. I know the duty I owe my parents, and shall perform it. I shall write to them also. They shall hear both sides, and were your fortune multiplied a thousand times, I won't sell my manhood for it. Am I to have shelter another night, or do you wash your hands of me here and now?"

"Oh, stay by all means, or you may find yourself in the same cell in which your paragon spent last night," replied his uncle, whose rage now passed all bounds.

"Those words are brutal," said Roger sternly, "and if you are not ashamed of them after thinking them over, you are not the man I took you to be," and he stalked out of the room and out of the house, slamming the door after him.

The old merchant sank into a chair, trembling with both anger and chagrin, for he felt that he had been worsted in the encounter. He did regret the words as soon as spoken, and a certain rude sense of justice made him feel, even in his excitement, that his nephew, although an egregious fool of course, had been true to his sense of right and honor. He was assuredly the victim of a designing lot of women, but believing them to be true, his course had been manly, and the thought would come, "Since he was so faithful to them, he would have been equally so to me, and he might have found the hussies out in time to prevent trouble." And now he had said words which in effect turned his brother's son out of doors at midnight. With something like a groan and an oath he resolved not to write that night, and to see how he felt in the morning. His nephew on provocation had proved as great a Tartar as he knew himself to be, and he now remembered that the former had some excuse in his hot young blood, and that he had a right to choose against his offer, if fool enough to do it, without being reviled and insulted.

After a wretched night he found on the breakfast-table a brief, cold note from Roger, saying that he would inform him in a day or two where to send his effects and such part of his salary as remained unpaid. The old man frowned, and the Atwood pride and obstinacy took possession of him like evil spirits. In grim reticence he resumed his old routine and life, and again gave himself up to the mechanical accumulation and saving of money.

CHAPTER XXXVIII

NO "DARK CORNERS"

FROM his uncle's house Roger went to a small hotel and obtained a room in which to spend a sleepless night. After the excitement of anger passed, he recognized the difficulties of his position. He was worse than friendless in the great city, for when he sought employment and gave an account of his antecedents, people would ask suspiciously why he left his uncle. The reasons were of too delicate a nature to be babbled about in business offices.

At first he was much depressed, and complained that "luck was dead against him." Moreover he felt that he had responded too harshly to his uncle, who, after all, was only trying to aid him in his cold-blooded way. Nevertheless he, too, had his share of the Atwood pride and obstinacy, and he resolved that the man who had called him a "soft-headed fool" for sacrificing himself to his sense of honor and duty must apologize before there could be any reconciliation. His good sense led him to make one wise resolution, and early in the morning he carried it out by making a clean breast of it to Mr. Wentworth. The good man listened with deep interest, and heartened the young fellow wonderfully by clapping him on the shoulder and saying, "You are made of the right stuff, Atwood, and although the material is yet a little raw and crude, experience and Christian principle will temper it in time into the finest metal."

"Don't ascribe Christian principle to me," growled Roger, "for I'm tempted to swear like a pirate."

"Very likely, and not without some reason. I occasionally feel a little that way myself, but I don't do it; neither have you."

Roger stared. "You're not a bit like a minister," he burst out.

"Sorry to hear it."

"That isn't what I mean. You are a *man*. Our dominie up at Forestville was only a minister."

"I have my share of human nature, Roger, and am glad of it, for I know from experience just how you young fellows feel. But it involves many a big fight. Christian principle doesn't mean a cotton-and-wool nature, or a milk-and-water experience, to put it in a homely way. It's Christian principle that makes Mildred Jocelyn, as you say, one of the bravest and best girls in the world. She's worth more than all your uncle's money, and you needn't be discouraged, for you'll win her yet. A young fellow with your pluck can make his way unaided, and thousands have done so without your motives or your ability. I'll stand by you, for you are the kind of man that I believe in. To make your course completely blameless, you must write a long filial letter to your mother, explaining everything; and if you'll take my advice you will send something like this to your uncle;" and sitting down he scratched off the following words:

"On calmer reflection I perceive that your intentions toward me were kindly and friendly. I should have remembered this, and the respect due to your years, and not have spoken so harshly. For all that it was not right for me to say, I apologize. At the same time it is my undoubted right and unwavering purpose to be guided by my own conscience. Our views of life and duty vary so widely that it will be best for me to struggle on alone, as I can. This, however, is no reason why we should quarrel, or forget the ties of blood which unite us, or our characters as gentlemen."

"Such a note will put you right with your own conscience and your people at home," resumed Mr. Wentworth, "and there's nothing like starting right."

Roger complied at once, for the clergyman's "human nature" had gained his unlimited confidence.

"Now I'm going out," said his friend. "You stay and make my study your own. There is paper, etc. I think I know of a room that you can obtain for a small sum from a nice, quiet family, and perhaps it will just suit you. I'll see; but don't take it if you don't like it. You'll stay and lunch with us, and we'll drink to your success in generous cups of coffee that only my wife knows how to make," and he left Roger cheered, hopeful, and resolute. What was better still, the young man was starting right, as was well proved by the long, affectionate, yet firm and manly letter written to his mother.

After a genial lunch, at which he was treated with a respect and kindness which did him a world of good, he went with Mr. Wentworth to see the room, and was well pleased with it, and he added his future address to the note to his uncle. He then said:

"I keep my promise about Mr. Jocelyn, and the sooner that man is put under treatment the better."

"Why, Roger!" exclaimed his friend, "you can't do anything now."

"I can do just what I promised. I have a hundred dollars in the bank, and there is about twenty-five still due me. With the latter sum I can get along until I can find employment."

"Hold on, Roger; it seems to me that your generosity is getting the better of you now. Circumstances have greatly changed since you made your promise."

"I've not changed, and my promises don't change with circumstances. It may be some time before you can raise the money, even if you can get it at all in these hard times, and it's something that ought to be done at once."

"Give me your hand again, old fellow. The world would say we were a pair of fools, but we'll wait and see who's right. Come to me at nine to-morrow morning."

Mr. Wentworth had several things on hand that he

meant to do, but he dropped everything and started for the offices of some lawyers whom he knew, determined to find a foothold at once for his plucky protégé. Roger went to call on Mrs. Jocelyn, feeling that he would like to get the matter relating to her husband settled, so that he might give all his thought and energy to the problem of making his way unaided. In response to his knock a light step crossed the floor, and the door was opened a little, revealing Mildred's face, then it was thrown open hospitably. "Oh, Mr. Atwood," she exclaimed, "I am very glad to see you. Forgive me that I opened the door so suspiciously, but you have never lived in a tenement, and do not know what awful neighbors are often prowling around. Besides, I was alone, and that made me more timid. I am so troubled about something, and perhaps you can help me, for you seem to be able to help every one," Mildred continued hastily, for she dreaded an embarrassing silence between them unspeakably. "I've been to see my employers in the hope they would forgive that poor girl who put the lace in my cloak, and they won't. They were polite and kind to me, and offered me better wages if I would come back, but were relentless toward the girl, saying they 'meant to break up that kind of thing once for all.' Don't you think something might be done?"

"If you failed there would be no use of my trying," said Roger, smiling. "I think it was wonderfully good of you to go on such an errand."

"I've had some lessons in goodness lately," she replied, with a little friendly nod. "As I talked with those stern men, I realized more than ever what an escape I've had, and I've thanked you in my heart a thousand times."

The young fellow looked as if he had been repaid a thousand times, and wondered that he could have been so tempted by his uncle's terms, for it now seemed impossible that he could ever do aught else than serve the sweet, sad girl who looked into his eyes with the trust and friendliness which he had sought for so long in vain. His face became so expressive of his feelings that she hurried on to speak of another matter weighing on her mind.

"Mr. Atwood," she said hesitatingly, "I have another trouble. You looked so vindictively at that Mr. Bissel in the court-room that I have feared you might do something that you would afterward regret. I know how one with your honorable spirit would feel toward such a wretch, but, believe me, he is beneath your notice. I should feel so badly if you got into any trouble on my account. Indeed it seems that I couldn't stand it at all," and she said it with so much feeling that he was honestly delighted. His spirits were rising fast, for this frank, strong interest in his welfare, in contrast with her old constraint and coldness, was sweet to him beyond all words.

With a mischievous and rather wicked look in his dark eyes, he said, "You must leave that fellow to me. I'm not a saint as you are."

Mildred proved that she was not altogether a saint by inwardly relishing his spirit, for she never could overcome some of the traits of her Southern blood; but she said, honestly and anxiously, "I should feel very badly if you got into any trouble."

"That thought will make me prudent," he replied gratefully. "You would never feel badly again about anything, if I had my way."

"I believe you, Mr. Atwood, and I can't see why I did not understand you better before," said Mildred, the words slipping out almost before she knew it.

"I don't think you understand me yet," he answered, very gently.

She did not reply, but he saw her fingers trembling with nervous apprehension as she tried to go on with her sewing; he also saw that she was growing very pale. Indeed she had almost the sick, faint look of one who is about to submit to some painful operation.

"Don't be frightened, Miss Mildred," he remarked, after watching her keenly for a moment or two. She looked up and saw him smiling broadly at her. In answer to her perplexed look he continued quietly, "I can tell you what has been the matter between us, and what is the matter now—you are afraid of me."

"Mr. Atwood—" faltered Mildred, and then words failed her, and her pale face crimsoned.

"Don't you think it would be best for us to understand each other, now that we are to be friends?" he asked.

"Yes," gasped the young girl faintly, fearing every moment that he would lose his self-control and pour out a vehement declaration of his love. She was prepared to say, "Roger Atwood, I am ready to make any sacrifice within my power that you can ask," but at the same time felt that she could endure slow torture by fire better than passionate words of love, which would simply bruise the heart that could make no response. If he would only ask quietly, "Mildred, will you be my wife when the right time comes? I'll be content with such love as you can give," she would have replied with the calmness of an unalterable purpose, "Yes, Roger, and I'll do my best," believing that years of effort might be crowned with success. But now, to have him plead passionately for what she could no more bestow than if she were dead, gave her an indescribable sense of fear, pain, and repugnance; and she cowered and shrank over the sewing which she could scarcely hold, so great was her nervous apprehension.

Instead of the vehement declaration there came a low, mellow laugh, and she lifted her eyes and stared at him, her work dropping from her hands.

Roger understood the situation so well, and was so thoroughly the master of it in his generous self-control and kindly intentions, that he should scarcely be blamed if he got out of it such bitter-sweet enjoyment as he could, and he said, with a twinkle in his eyes, "Miss Millie, I wasn't going to strike you."

"I don't understand you at all," cried Mildred, with a

pathetically perplexed expression and starting tears, for the nervous strain was becoming a little too prolonged.

Roger became grave at once, and with a quiet, gentle manner he came to her side and took her hand. "Will you be as honest with me as I shall be with you?" he asked.

"I'll try to be."

"Well, then, I'll soon solve for you my poor little riddle. Miss Mildred, you know that I have loved you ever since you waked up an awkwad, lazy, country fellow into the wish to be a man."

His words were plain enough now, surely, but she was no longer frightened, for he spoke in such a kindly natural voice that she looked him straight in the eyes, with a delicate bloom in her face, and replied:

"I didn't wish to mislead you, Mr. Atwood, and I wouldn't trifle with you."

"You have been truth and honesty itself."

"No, I've not," she answered impetuously; "I cherished an unreasoning prejudice against you, and—and—I disliked you, though why, I can't see now, and nobly you have triumphed over both prejudice and dislike."

"It will ever be the proudest triumph of my life; but, Miss Mildred, you do not love me in the least, and I fear you never will."

"I am so sorry, so very sorry," she faltered, with a crimson face and downcast eyes.

"I am, too; but that which I want to say to you is, that you are not to blame, and I don't blame you. I could not love a girl simply because she wanted me to, were such a thing possible, and why should I demand of you what I couldn't do myself? All I asked in the first place—don't you remember it in the old front walk at home?—was friendship. Let us go back to that. Let me become your simple, honest friend, and help you in every way within my power. Don't let me frighten you any more with the dread of high tragedy. Now you've had all the declaration you ever need fear. I won't break loose or explode under any provocation. I can't help my love, and you must not punish me for it, nor make yourself miserable about it, as if it were a powder magazine which a kind word or look might touch off. I want to put your heart to rest, for you have enough to bear now, Heaven knows; I want you to feel safe with me—as free from fear and annoyance as Belle is. I won't presume or be sentimental."

"Oh, my perverse, perverse heart!" wailed Mildred. "I could tear it out of my breast and throw it away in disgust. I want to love—it would be a poor return for all that you are and have done for me—but it is of no use. I will not deceive one so true as you are, by even a trace of falseness. You deserve the love of the best woman in the world, and some day you'll find her—"

"I have found her," he put in quietly.

"No, no, no!" she cried passionately; "but I am as nature made me, and I can't seem to help myself. How strange it seems that I can say from the depths of my soul I could die for you, and yet that I can't do just the one thing you deserve a thousand times! But, Roger, I will be the most devoted sister that ever a man had."

"No," he said, smiling, "that won't answer at all. That wouldn't be honest, as far as I am concerned. Belle is my sister, but you can never be. I know you don't love me now, and, as I've said, perhaps you never can, but I'm too persistent in my nature to give up the hope. Time may bring changes, and I've got years of up-hill work before I can think of marrying. You are in a self-sacrificing mood now. I saw it in your eyes and manner last night—I see it now. Mildred, I could take a very great advantage of you if I chose."

"Indeed you could. You don't know how generous you are. You have conquered me, overwhelmed me by your kindness, and I couldn't say No to anything in your nature to ask."

For a moment he looked sorely tempted, and then he said brusquely, "I'll put a spoke in that wheel. I'd give all the world for this little hand, but I won't take it until your heart goes with it. So there!"

The young girl sighed deeply. "You are right," she murmured, "when you give so much I can give so little."

"That is not what I was thinking of. As a woman you have sacred rights, and I should despise myself if I tried to buy you with kindness, or take advantage of your gratitude. I'll admit, too, since we are to have no dark corners in this talk, that I would rather be loved as I know you can love. I'd rather have an honest friendship than a forced affection, even though the force was only in the girl's will and wishes. I was reading Maud Muller the other night, and no woman shall ever say of her life's happiness, that but for me 'it might have been.' "

"I don't think any woman could ever say that of you."

"Mildred, you showed me your heart last night, and it has a will stronger than your will, and it shall have its way."

The girl again sighed. "Roger," she said, "one reason why I so shrank from you in the past was that you read my thoughts. You have more than a woman's intuition."

"No," he said, laughing a little grimly, "I'm not a bit feminine in my nature. My explanation may seem absurd to you, but it's true, I think. I am exceedingly fond of hunting, and I so trained my eyes that if a leaf stirred or a bird moved a wing I saw it. When you waked me up, and I determined to seek my fortunes out in the world, I carried with me the same quickness of eye. I do not let much that is to be seen escape me, and on a face like yours thoughts usually leave some trace."

"You didn't learn to be a gentleman, in the best sense of the word, in the woods," she said, with a smile.

"No, you and your mother taught me that, and I may add, your father, for when I first saw him he had the perfection of manners." He might also have referred to Vinton Arnold, whom he had studied so carefully, but he could not bring himself to speak of one whom in his heart he knew to be the chief barrier between them, for he was well aware that it was Mildred's involuntary fidelity to her first love that made his suit so dubious. At his reference to her father Mildred's eyes had filled at once, and he continued gently, "We understand each other now, do we not? You won't be afraid of me any more, and will let me help you all to brighter days?"

She put both of her hands in his, and said earnestly, "No, I will never be afraid of you again, but I only half understand you yet, for I did not know that there was a man in the world so noble, so generous, so honest. You have banished every trace of constraint, and I'll do everything you say."

There was a look of almost boyish pleasure on his face as she spoke, and in imitation of the heroes of the interminable old-time romances that once had formed the larger part of his reading, he was about to raise her hand to his lips when she snatched it away, and as if mastered by an impulse not to be controlled, put her arms around his neck and kissed him, then burst into tears with her head upon his shoulder.

He trembled a moment, and said, in low tones, "God bless you, Millie." Then he gently placed her in her chair. "You mustn't do that again," he said gravely. "With you it was but a grateful sisterly impulse, but if I were Samson I'd not be strong enough—well, you understand me. I don't want to give the lie to all I've said."

"Oh, Roger, Roger," sobbed the girl, "I can do nothing for you and yet you have saved me from shame and are giving us all hope and life."

"You are responsible for all there is good in me," he tried to say lightly, "and I'll show you in coming years if you have done nothing for me. Good-by now. It's all right and settled between us. Tell Mrs. Jocelyn that one hundred dollars are ready as soon as she can induce her husband to take the step we spoke of." And he hastened away, feeling that it was time he retreated if he would make good the generous words he had spoken.

CHAPTER XXXIX

"HOME, SWEET HOME!"

"OH, MILLIE," cried Mrs. Jocelyn, entering with the children and throwing herself into a chair, fatigued and panting from her walk and climb of the stairs, "I've so much to tell you. Oh, I'm so distressed and sorry. It seems that evil has become our lot, and that we bring nothing but evil to others. You, too, look as if you had been crying as if your heart would break."

"No, mamma, I feel much better—more at rest than I have been for a long time. My tears have done me good."

"Well, I'm sorry I must tell you something that will grieve you dreadfully, but there's no help for it. It does seem when things are going wrong in one's life, there's no telling where they'll stop. You know Mrs. Wheaton works for Roger's aunt, Mrs. Atwood. Well, she was there this morning, and Mrs. Atwood talked dreadfully about us, and how we had inveigled her nephew into the worst of folly. She told Mrs. Wheaton that Mr. Atwood had intended to give Roger a splendid education, and might have made him his heir, but that he demanded, as his condition, that he should have nothing more to do with such people as we were, and how Roger refused, and how after a bitter quarrel the latter left the house at midnight. She also said that his uncle would have nothing more to do with him, and that his family at home would be almost equally angry. Oh, I feel as if I could sink into the earth with shame and worry. What shall we do?"

"Surely, mamma, there is some mistake. Roger was here much of the afternoon, and he never said one word about it," Mildred answered, with a troubled face.

"It's just like him. He didn't want to pain you with the news. What did he say?" she asked, with kindling interest, and Mildred told her substantially all that had occurred.

"Well, Millie," said her mother emphatically, "you will be the queerest girl on the face of the earth if you can't love him now, for he has given up everything for you. He might have been richer than Vinton Arnold."

"He must not give up anything," said Mildred resolutely. "There is reason in all things. He is little more than a boy in years, and he has a boy's simplicity and unworldliness. I won't let him sacrifice himself for me. He doesn't know what he is doing. His aunt's estimate of such people as we have become is correct, and I'll perish a thousand times before I'll be the means of dragging down such a man as Roger Atwood. If I knew where to find him I'd go and tell him so this moment."

That was a dreary hour in the poor little home, but worse things were in store for them, for, as Mrs. Jocelyn said, when things are going wrong there is a terrible logic about them, and malign events follow each other with almost inevitable sequence. All was wrong with the head of the family, and terrible were the consequences to his helpless wife and children. Mr. Jocelyn heard a rumor of Mildred's experience in the police court, and he went to the place that day and obtained some account of the affair. More clearly and awfully than ever before he comprehended the depths into which he had fallen. He had not been appealed to—he had not even been told. He did not stop to consider how good the reasons were for the course his family had taken, but, blind with anger and despair, he sought his only refuge from the hell within his breast, and began drinking recklessly. By the time he reached the tenement where he dwelt he was in a state of wild intoxication. A man at the door called him a drunken beast, at which Mr. Jocelyn grasped him by the throat and a fierce scuffle ensued. Soon the whole populous dwelling was in an uproar, while the man retreated, fighting, up the stairways, and his infuriated assailant followed with oaths and curses. Women and children were screaming, and men and boys pouring out of their rooms, some jeering and laughing, and others making timid and futile efforts to appease and restrain the liquor-crazed man.

Suddenly a door opened, and a pale face looked out; then a slight girlish figure darted through the crowd and clasped Mr. Jocelyn. He looked down and recognized his daughter Mildred. For a moment he seemed a little sobered, and then the demon within him reasserted itself. "Get out of my way!" he shouted. "I'll teach that infernal Yankee to insult a Southern officer and gentleman. Let me go," he said furiously, "or I'll throw you down the stairway," but Mildred clung to him with her whole weight, and the men now from very shame rushed in and overpowered him.

He was speedily thrust within his own doorway, and Mildred turned the key after him and concealed it. Little recked the neighbors, as they gradually subsided into quiet, that there came a crash of crockery and a despairing cry from the Jocelyns' room. They had witnessed such scenes before, and were all too busy to run any risk of being summoned as witnesses at a police court on the morrow. The man whom Mr. Jocelyn had attacked said that he would see the agent of the house in the morning and have the Jocelyn family sent away at once, because a nuisance, and all were content with this arrangement.

Within that locked door a terrible scene would have been enacted had it not been for Mildred's almost supernatural courage, for her father was little better than a wild beast. In his mad rush forward he overturned the supper-table, and the evening meal lay in a heap upon the floor. The poor wife, with a cry in which hope and her soul itself seemed to depart, fell swooning on the children's bed, and the little ones fled to the darkest corner of Mildred's room and cowered in speechless fear. There was none to face him save the slight girl, at whom he glared as if he would annihilate her.

"Let me out!" he said savagely.

"No," said the girl, meeting his frenzied gaze unwaveringly, "not until you are sober."

He rushed to the door, but could not open it. Then turning upon Mildred he said, "Give me the key—no words —or I'll teach you who is master."

There were no words, but only such a look as is rarely seen on a woman's face. He raised his hand to strike her, but she did not shrink a hair-breadth. "Papa," she said, in a low, concentrated tone, "you called yourself a Southern gentleman. I did not dream you could strike a woman, even when drunk."

The effect of her words was magical. His hand sank to his side. Then he raised it and passed it over his brow as if it all were a horrid dream. Without a word he went with unsteady step to his own room, and again Mildred locked the door upon him.

Mrs. Jocelyn's swoon was long and death-like, and before Mildred could restore her, Belle, returning from her work, tried to enter, and finding the door locked called for admittance. When she crossed the threshold and saw the supper dishes broken and scattered on the floor: when she saw her mother looking as if dead, the little ones crying at her side, and Mildred scarcely less pale than the broken-hearted woman, with a desperate look in her blue eyes, the young girl gave a long, low cry of despair, and covering her face with her hands she sank into a chair murmuring, "I can't endure this any longer—I'd rather die. We are just going to rack and ruin. Oh, I wish I could die, for I'm getting reckless—and—and wicked. Oh, oh, oh!—"

"Belle, come and help me," said Mildred, in the hard, constrained tones of one who is maintaining self-control by the utmost effort. Belle complied, but there was an expression on her face that filled her sister's soul with dread.

It were well perhaps to veil the agony endured in the stricken household that night. The sufferings of such women as Mrs. Jocelyn and Mildred cannot be portrayed in words, and the dark chaos that had come into poor Belle's tempted, despairing, immature soul might well make her good angel weep. With a nature craving sunshine and pleasure like the breath of life, she felt herself being dragged hopelessly into darkness, shame, and abject poverty. The poor child was not deliberately contemplating evil—she was scarcely capable of doing good or evil deliberately—but a youth who had sought her once before, and of whom she had long been shy, was again hovering around her.

She was more wary now, yet bolder, and received his advances with a manner tinged with mocking coquetry. He was profuse with promises, and she tried to believe them, but in her heart she could not, and yet she did not repulse him with that stern, brief decision which forms the viewless, impassable wall that hedges virtue.

The sisters tried to remove the outward traces of their wrecked home, and mechanically restored such order as was within their power, but in their secret souls they saw their household gods overturned and trampled upon, and, with the honor and manhood of their father, they felt that night as if they had lost everything.

After they had quieted their mother and brought the poor creature a brief oblivion, Mildred made a passionate appeal to Belle to stand by her. The warm-hearted girl cried and wrung her hands passionately, but all her trembling sister could obtain from her were the words,

"Millie, we are being dragged down I don't know where."

Events followed rapidly. Before Mr. Jocelyn, sullen, nerveless, racked with headache and tortured with heartache, could leave his room on the morrow, the agent of the tenement served a notice on him to the effect that he must vacate his rooms at once; that the other tenants complained of him as a nuisance; and that he (the agent) would be content to lose the rent for the few days that had elapsed since the last regular payment if they would all go out at once. The angry reply was that they would move that day, and, without a word, he left his family in suspense. In the course of the forenoon he returned with a furniture van, and had so braced himself with opium that he was able to assist effectively, yet morosely, in the packing and removing of their fast-dwindling effects, for everything not essential had been sold. His wife and daughter did not remonstrate—they were too dispirited for that—but in dreary apathy did his bidding as far as their strength permitted, feeling meanwhile that any change could scarcely be for the worse.

Mildred almost felt that it was for the better, for their new shelter was in a small rear tenement not far from the old mansion, and was reached from the street by a long covered passageway. To her morbid fancy it suggested the hiding-place that her heart craved. She now scarcely heeded the facts that the place was anything but cleanly and that their neighbors were more unpromising in appearance than those they had just left. Mrs. Jocelyn was so ill and weak that she ought not to raise her hands, and Mildred felt that her strength was unequal to the task of even arranging their household articles so as to make the poor little nook inhabitable. She therefore went for their old stanch ally Mrs. Wheaton, who returned with her and wrought such miracles as the wretched place permitted of. In just foreboding she shook her head over the prospects of her friends in such a neighborhood, for her experienced eyes enabled her to gauge very correctly the character of the people who lived across the hall and in the upper and lower stories. They were chiefly ignorant and debased Irish families, and the good woman's fears were not wholly due to race antipathy. In the tenement from which they came, the people, although poor, were in the main stolid, quiet, and hard-working, but here on every side were traces and hints, even at midday, of degraded and vicious lives. The classes in the tenements appear to have a moral gravity or affinity which brings to the same level and locality those who are alike, and woe be to aliens who try to dwell among them. The Jocelyns did not belong to the tenement classes at all, and Mrs. Wheaton correctly feared that the purgatory which was the corner-stone in their neighbors' creeds would be realized in the temporal experience of the Southern family. Now that the step had been taken, however, she concealed her anxieties, and did her best to avoid collisions with the burly, red-faced women and insolent children whose officious offers of help were but thin veils to a coarse curiosity and a desire for petty pilfering. Mildred shuddered at the people about her, and was cold and brief in her words. As it was, Fred nearly brought on general hostilities by resisting a shock-headed little urchin who had not the remotest regard for the principles of *meum* and *tuum*. As the sun declined the general verdict of the neighbors was, "They thinks themselves too foine for the loikes o' us, but we'll tache 'em."

After Mrs. Wheaton had departed with many misgivings, Mildred took her father aside and told him plainly what had occurred the evening before. He sat with his face buried in his hands, and listened without a word. Indeed, he was so overwhelmed with shame and remorse that he was speechless. "Papa, look at me," she said at last.

Slowly he raised his bloodshot, fearful eyes to hers, and the expression of his child's face made him tremble.

"Papa," she said slowly, and her tones were both sad and stern, "you must never come home drunk again. Another such scene might cost mamma her life. If you *will* take opium, we cannot help it, but you must drink no more vile liquor. I have now learned from bitter experience what the latter means, and what it must lead to. I shall not fail in love and duty to you, but I cannot permit mamma, Belle, and the children to be utterly destroyed.

You may do some wild, reckless deed that would blast us all beyond remedy; therefore, if you have a particle of self-control left, let rum alone, or else we must protect ourselves. We have endured it thus far, not with patience and resignation, but in a sort of apathetic despair. This apathy has been broken. Belle is becoming reckless, mamma is dying of a broken heart, and the little ones are exposed to influences that threaten to blight their lives. There must be some change for the better. We must at least be relieved from the fear of bodily harm and the intolerable shame of such scenes as occurred last night. In our hard struggle we must find some kind of a refuge and some degree of quiet and peace in what we call home. It is no kindness to you to endure in silence any longer, and I now see that it will be fatal to those we both love. You may not be able to refrain from opium, but you can and must give up liquor. If you cannot, and there is a remedy in the land, we must avail ourselves of it. I do not know what kind of a place you have brought us to, but I feel sure that we shall need protection. If you should come home again as you did last night, I am satisfied, from the looks of the people in this house, that we should have a scene of violence that I shudder to think of. You had better—it would be more merciful to stab mamma to her heart than to cause her death by drunkenness."

Her words were not threatening, but were spoken with the calmness of inexorable resolve, and he sat before her with an ashen face, trembling like an aspen, for it was like the Day of Judgment to him. Then in gentler and pleading accents she told him of their plan to place him under skilful treatment, and besought him to yield himself up to the care of one who had won much reputation in dealing with cases like his own; but all the encouragement she could obtain were the words, "I'll think of it."

The memory of those fearful days on shipboard, when he was without morphia, made him recoil with unspeakable dread from a like ordeal again, but he promised earnestly that he would indulge no more in liquor. With the cunning of an opium maniac he understood his danger, knowing that further scenes of violence would lead to his arrest and imprisonment. Of his gentle wife he had no fears, but this frail, resolute girl subdued him. He saw that he was driving a strong nature to desperation—saw it with all the agony and remorse of a naturally good father whose better nature was bound hand and foot by depraved appetites. He was conscious of the terrible wrong that he was inflicting on those for whom he once would have died to shield them from a breath of dishonor. But, come what might, he must have opium *now*, and to counteract the words of his daughter he took enough morphia to kill all the wretched inmates of the tenement. Under its slight exhilaration he felt some hope of availing himself of the proposition that he should go to a curative institution, and he half promised that he would before long. At this point the painful interview ended, and Mildred went for Belle, who as yet had no knowledge of their change of abode.

As the two girls returned, in the dusk of evening, to the long dark passageway that led to the tenement in which they now had rooms, Mildred trembled with fear as she saw that its entrance was surrounded and blocked by a group of rough-looking young men and boys. Belle pushed boldly through them, although they leered, laughed, and made coarse jests. Mildred followed shrinkingly, with downcast eyes. "We'll tache 'em to be neighborly," were the last words she heard, showing that the young ruffians had already obtained their cue from their depraved and low-lived parents.

They looked forward to a dismal evening, but a loyal friend came to their rescue. Roger, having arranged the room selected for him by Mr. Wentworth, could not resist the temptation to see those who were ever uppermost in his thoughts. In dismay and anxiety he learned of their hasty removal and something of the causes which led to it. From the janitor he obtained their present address, and the appearance of his broad shoulders and fearless face had a restraining influence on the mischief-making propensities of the rowdies who kennelled in the vicinity. The alien new-comers evidently were not friendless, and there was hesitation in the half-formed measures for their annoyance.

Roger remained an hour or two, aiding the girls in trying to make the rooms more homelike, which, however, was rather a hopeless task. Mr. Jocelyn, half stupefied by opium, retreated to one of the small dark closet bedrooms, and left the scene unembarrassed by his presence. Roger remarked emphatically that the tenement was no place for them, but Mildred told him that the rent had been paid for a month in advance, and that they must try to endure it, adding, "The twenty-five dollars that you and Mr. Wentworth obtained for me has been, after all, a perfect Godsend."

He was touched, and bound to her with bands of steel by the perfect trust she now reposed in him, and he determined to watch over her like an amiable dragon, making it his first and constant thought how to rescue them all from their wretched condition. He was much surprised, however, when Mildred said to him, as he was preparing to leave, "Mr. Atwood, there is something I wish to say to you. Will you let me walk a block or two with you, and then bring me back again?"

Roger tried to disguise his feelings by saying laughingly that he would "walk to Spuyten Duyvil" with her, but added, "You are too tired to go out at all to-night. I will come to-morrow evening," and he remonstrated so earnestly and kindly that she yielded, promising to rest much of the following day.

"Oh, Millie," said her mother, with a faint smile, "it does my heart good to see that there is some one who knows how and has the will to take care of you."

"Yes," cried Belle, "this place is a perfect hole. It's not fit for nice girls to be seen in, and if Roger gives us a chance to get out of it you had better take it as soon as possible. I give you fair warning."

"What do you mean, Belle?" asked her mother.

Belle made no answer, but went to her closet bedroom with a morose, sullen look on her face. The poor woman looked inquiringly at Mildred, who said soothingly, "Don't worry, mamma. Belle is a little tired and discouraged to-night. She'll be in a better mood in the morning."

When all were sleeping from the fatigues of the day, she sat alone with clasped hands and eyes so wide and troubled that it seemed as if she could never close them again. "Alas!" she sighed, "what must I do? He is our good genius, and yet I must drive him away. He must not sacrifice all his prospects for us. It would be most cruel and unjust to let him do so. I must reason with him and show him plainly that it would not be right, and absolve him from every shadow of blame for leaving us to such fate as God permits. Because he is so generous and brave he shall not suffer a loss which he cannot now comprehend."

At last, from utter weariness, she fell into a broken sleep.

CHAPTER XL

NEIGHBORS

PROMPTLY the following evening Roger appeared, and with glowing cheeks told his friends that Mr. Wentworth had found him employment in a lawyer's office, which would enable him to pay his way and at the same time give him much practical insight into his chosen profession. Mildred looked at him wistfully, but her resolution was not shaken, and they went out together, Roger saying, with a smiling nod at Belle, "It will be your turn to-morrow evening."

"Roger," said Mildred, "I've much to say to you, and it is of great importance that you should listen calmly and sensibly."

"All right," he answered laughingly. "You will find me as quiet and impressible as the oysters over which we'll have our talk, but only on this condition. You shall not fatigue yourself by a word here in the street." Nevertheless she felt the phlegmatic creature's arm trembling under her hand. After a moment he went on, in the same light way, "I want you to understand I am not going to be a friend in name merely; I intend to assert my rights, and you had better learn from the start that I am the most tremendously obstinate fellow in the city."

"But you must listen to reason."

"Certainly; so must you."

"To begin with," she resumed, "I've had my supper, and so don't need any more."

"I haven't had mine, and am ravenous. The idea of

talking reason to a hungry man! I know of a nice quiet restaurant which, at this hour, we'll have almost to ourselves. You surely won't be so unsocial as to let me eat alone."

"Well, if I yield in trifles you must yield in matters that are vital. Why did you not get your supper before?"

"Too busy; and then, to be honest, I knew I'd enjoy it a hundredfold more with you. I'm a social animal."

Mildred sighed, for this good-comradeship was making her duty very hard.

They soon reached the place in question, and Roger ordered enough for four.

"You don't realize what you are doing in any respect," said Mildred in smiling reproof.

"Wait half an hour before you settle that question," he replied with a confident nod. "I'll soon prove to you what an unsentimental being I am."

"Oh," thought Mildred, "how can I give up his friendship when he acts in this way? And yet I must. He must be shown just how he is wronging himself." When the waiter had departed she looked straight into his eyes with one of her steadfast glances, and said earnestly, "Roger, I appreciate your generous kindness far more than any words can tell you, but the time has come for me to act resolutely and finally. Sad experience has taught me more within a year than most women learn in a lifetime. Mrs. Wheaton, who often works for your aunt, has told us of the sacrifice you have made in our behalf, and we cannot permit it. If not in years, I'm much older than you in other respects, and you don't realize—"

Roger interrupted her by leaning back in his chair and breaking out into an irrepressible laugh. "So you are going to interfere in behalf of the small boy's interests? My venerable friend, permit me to remind you that I am six feet high in my stockings, and have lately reached the mature age of twenty-one."

"Roger," replied Mildred, with a pained look on her

face, "I'm in earnest, and I've lain awake nearly all of two nights thinking about it."

"Millie, your oysters are getting cold. You don't know anything about boys, much less about men. Don't you know I'll be much more amiable after supper? It's the nature of the male animal, and what's the use of going against nature?"

"Oh, Roger, listen to me. I'm desperately in earnest. To let you sacrifice such prospects as Mrs. Wheaton said your uncle held out to you for our sakes oppresses me with guilt. I can't eat anything—you don't realize—"

"Millie Jocelyn," said Roger, his face becoming grave and gentle, "I know what you are driving at. You might as well try to stop Spring from coming on. I'm going to be your honest, faithful friend, so help me God! Even if you left me now and refused to speak to me again, I'd watch over you and yours in every way I could. It's my good destiny, and I thank God for it, for I feel it's making a man of me. I won't deceive you in one iota, and I admit to my shame that my worldly old uncle tempted me that night, especially after I saw from your face just how you felt. Even then my hope was that I could do more for you by yielding to his views than if I stood out against them, but a little thought convinced me that you would starve rather than take aid from one who would not give open friendship and companionship, and you would be right. Oh, I exult in your pride, and respect you for it. You are my ideal woman, Millie, and if my uncle had owned this island, and had offered it all to me, I'd have made a wretched bargain in giving up for it the privilege of being here this evening, with the right to look you straight in the eyes without shame. If I had yielded to him then, as the devil tempted me to, I'd never have known another day of self-respect or happiness. I'm building now on the rock of honor and manhood, and you can't say anything that will change my purpose. I know what I am about if I am only a 'boy'; and Mr.

Wentworth, who has been told all, approves of my course. So eat your oysters, Millie, and submit to the inevitable."

"Oh, Roger, Roger, what shall I say to you?"

"Look here, Millie; if you were in my place, would you desert a brave, true girl in misfortune? No; unlike me, you would never have hesitated a moment."

"But, Roger, as you say you—you—saw in my face a truth that absolved you—"

"What I saw in your face," he said gravely, "is my misfortune. It is not anything for which you are to blame in the least. And, Millie, I'd rather have your friendship than any other woman's love. I'm choosing my own course with my eyes open, and, thank God, I've chosen rightly. I'd have been the most miserable fellow in the whole city if I had chosen otherwise. Now I'm happy. It's all right. I've vowed to be a brother to Belle, and to do all in my power for your sweet, gentle mother. I've vowed to be your true friend in all respects, and if you protested till Doomsday it wouldn't make any difference. I've written to my mother, and I know her well enough to be sure that she will approve of my course. So will my father by and by. He isn't bad at heart, but, like uncle, a dollar is so large in his eyes that it hides the sun. Be that as it may, I'm just as much of an Atwood as he is, and can be just as obstinate in doing what I know to be right as he can be in requiring a course that would spoil my life. Millie, there never was a soldier, in all the past, braver than you have shown yourself to be, and you are a delicate girl that I could carry like a child. Do you advise a young, strong-handed fellow to play the coward, and desert the women I love and honor in their sore need and danger? You have looked on only one side of this question, and you must not think so meanly of me as to even suggest anything of the kind again."

"Roger, Roger, can you realize what you are saying?" Mildred faltered, a slow, painful flush crimsoning her face. "How can you honor those who are so disgraced? You don't know what papa has become. The world will share your uncle's views concerning us."

"I do know all about your father, Millie, and I pity him from the depths of my soul. He is the dark background which brings out your absolute truth and purity. I do honor you and Mrs. Jocelyn as I honor my own mother, and I intend to prove myself worthy of your respect at least, for its loss would be fatal to me. I even honor your rare fidelity, though it stands so awfully in my way. Now, surely, we understand each other. But, come, this is far too serious talk for a restaurant and the supper-table. I am now going to give my whole soul to oysters, and I adjure you by our bonds to do the same. Here's to our friendship, Millie, and may I be choked the moment I'm false to it!" and he drained a generous cup of coffee.

"You won't listen to me, then," she said, with a face wherein perplexity, relief, and gratitude were blended.

"I won't listen to a word that will make me the most miserable wretch in the world, and you won't get rid of me as long as I live. So, there, you might as well submit to fate and eat your oysters."

Her expression became very grave and resolute. "Roger," she said slowly, "I did not know there was so kind and true a man in the world. I will do anything that you can ask."

His eyes suddenly became infinitely wistful and tender, and then he gave himself a little characteristic shake as he said, rather brusquely, "I accept that promise, and shall at once tax it to the utmost with the request that you eat a jolly good supper and call on me every time I can aid you."

Her glance in response warmed his soul, and then she gave herself up to socal friendliness in a way which proved that a great burden had been taken from her heart. On their way home, however, she hinted her fears in regard to Belle, and Roger understood her thoroughly. For the next few days he watched the young girl, and soon satisfied himself as to the character of the man who was pursuing her. His object now was to obtain some ground for brotherly interference, and one Saturday evening, while following Belle home, he saw a young man join her and receive an undoubted welcome. He soon became aware that matters were progressing fast and far, for the young people wandered off into unfrequented streets, and once, where the shadows were deepest, he saw Belle's attendant steal his arm about her waist and kiss her. Belle's protest was not very vigorous, and when at last they parted in the passageway that led to Belle's home the kiss was repeated and not resented at all.

Roger followed the young man, and said, "You have just parted from Miss Belle Jocelyn."

"Well, that's my affair."

"You will find yourself so greatly mistaken that you had better answer my questions honestly. What are your intentions toward her? I have the right to ask."

"None of your business."

"Look here, young man, she has acknowledged me as her brother, and as a brother I feel toward her. I've only a few plain words to say. If your intentions are honorable I'll not interfere, although I know all about you, and you are not my style of man by any means. If your intentions are not honorable, and you do not cease your attentions, I'll break every bone in your body—I swear it by the God who made me."

"Go to the devil!" muttered the fellow.

"No, sir, nor shall I permit you to take one dear to me to the devil, but I pledge my word to send you straight to him if you harm Belle Jocelyn. Here, stop and look me in the eyes under this lamp. You kissed her twice to-night. Do you intend to make her your wife?"

There was no answer, but the sullen, half-frightened face was an unmistakable response. "I understand you now," said Roger savagely, taking the fellow by the throat, "and I'll send you swiftly to perdition if you don't promise to let that girl alone," and his gleaming eyes and iron grasp awed the incipient roué so completely that he quavered out:

"Oh, let go. If you feel the girl is your property, I'll let her alone."

Roger gave him a wrathful push which precipitated his limp form into the gutter, and growled as he walked of, "If you value your life, keep your promise."

An evening or two later Roger said to Belle, whom he had taken out for a stroll, "I kept my word—I cowhided that fellow Bissel, who played such a dastardly part toward your sister. Of course I did not want to get myself into trouble, or give him any power over me, so I found out his haunts and followed him. One night, as he was returning rather late from a drinking saloon, I spoiled his good looks with a dozen savage cuts. He was too confused to see who it was in the dark, and to mislead him more thoroughly I said, with the last blow, 'Take that for lying and causing a poor girl to be sent to prison.' He thinks, no doubt, that some friend of the thief was the one who punished him. What's more, he won't forget the lashing I gave him till his dying day, and if I mistake not his smooth face will long bear my marks."

Belle gave but a languid approval, for she had missed her lover for the last two evenings. "Belle," he continued, gravely but gently, "I was tempted to choke the life out of a fellow the other night, and it was the life of one who kissed you twice."

She dropped her hand from his arm, but he replaced it and held it tightly as he resumed, "I'm no make-believe brother, you know. I'm just such a brother as I would be if I had been born with you on a Southern plantation. Though the young man was not to my mind, I told him that if his intentions were honorable I would not interfere, but I soon learned that he was an out-and-out scoundrel, and I said words to him that will make him shun you as he would death. Belle, I would kill him as I used to club rattlesnakes in the country, if he harmed a hair of your head, and he knows it."

"You misjudge him utterly," cried Belle in a passion,

"and you have just driven away the one friend that I had in all the world. I won't stand it. I'm not a baby, and I won't be treated like one."

Roger let her storm on without a word, but at last, when she concluded, "I've no father worthy of the name, and so I'll take care of myself," he asked quietly:

"How about your mother, Belle?"

In strong revulsion the impulsive girl gave way to an equally passionate outburst of grief. "Oh," she cried, "I wish I were dead!"

"Belle," said Roger, very gently now, "if you listened to that fellow you would soon make that wish in earnest. Now in your heart you don't mean it at all. You don't love such a man, and you know it. Why should you throw your young, beautiful life into the gutter? It is a mere reckless protest against your unhappy life. Belle, you are not seventeen, and you may live till you are seventy if you take care of yourself. Think of the changes for the better that may come in that time. They shall come, too. I shall share with you all my fortunes, and you have told me many a time that I was sure to succeed. I pledge you my word that before many years you shall have good honest men at your feet," and he reasoned with her so sensibly, and petted and soothed her so kindly, that at last she clung to his arm as if it were a defence indeed, and said, with tearful eyes, "You *are* a brother in the best sense of the word, and I wonder you have patience with such a reckless, passionate fool as I am. I'm not fit for you to speak to."

"No, Belle, you are not bad at heart—far from it. You are half desperate from your present misfortunes, and in your blind impulse to escape you would make matters infinitely worse. Be patient, dear. It's a long lane that has no turning. To one so young as you are life promises very much, if it is not spoiled at the beginning, and Mr. Wentworth would tell us that there is a heaven beyond it all."

The influence of this interview did not speedily pass from

her mind, and by her gentler and more patient bearing Mildred was taught again how much she owed to one whom she had so long repelled.

Mr. Wentworth succeeded in interesting the lady to whom he had referred in Mildred, and a visit from the young girl confirmed her good impressions. As a result, sufficient work was found or made to give Mildred steady employment. Mr. Jocelyn was comparatively quiet and much at home. Often he was excessively irritable and exasperating in words and manner, but no longer violent from bestial excess. He put off the project of going to a curative institution, with the true opium inertia and procrastination, and all efforts to lead him to definite action proved fruitless. His presence, however, and his quiet, haughty ways, with Roger's frequent visits, did much for a time to restrain the ill-disposed people around them, but the inevitable contact with so much depravity and coarseness was almost unendurable.

Now that Mildred no longer went out to her work, she taxed her ingenuity to the utmost to amuse Fred and Minnie, that she might keep them from the horrible associations beyond their door, but her father's irritability often rendered it impossible for them to remain in the room, and, childlike, they would assimilate somewhat with the little heathen among whom their lot was now cast.

Poor Mrs. Jocelyn was sinking under her sorrows. She did not complain: she blamed herself with a growing morbidness for the ruin of her husband and the hard lot of her children, and hope deferred was making her heart sick indeed. Her refined, gentle nature recoiled with an indescribable repugnance from her surroundings, and one day she received a shock from which she never fully recovered.

Her husband was out, and Mildred had gone to deliver some work. The children, whom she tried to keep with her, broke away at last and left the door open. Before she could close it a drunken woman stumbled in, and, sinking into a chair, she let a bundle slip from her hands. It fell on the floor, unrolled, and a dead infant lay before Mrs. Jocelyn's horrified gaze. Her cries for help brought a stout, red-faced woman from across the hallway, and she seemed to understand what was such a fearful mystery to Mrs. Jocelyn, for she took the unwelcome intruder by the shoulder and tried to get her to go out hastily, but the inebriated wretch was beyond shame, fear, or prudence. Pulling out of her pocket a roll of bills, she exclaimed, in hideous exultation:

"Faix, I'oive had a big day's work. Trhree swell families on the Avenue guv me all this to burry the brat. Burry it? Divil a bit. It's makin' me fortin'. Cud we ony git dead babbies enough we'd all be rich, Bridget, but here's enough to kape the pot bilin' for wakes to come, and guv us a good sup o' whiskey into the bargain. Here, take a drap," she said, pulling out a black bottle and holding it up to Mrs. Jocelyn. "What yer glowrin' so ghostlike for? Ah, let me alone, ye ould hag," she said angrily to the red-faced woman, who seemed in great trepidation, and tried to put her hand over the drunken creature's mouth. "Who's afeard? Money'll buy judge and jury, an' if this woman peaches on us I'll bate her brains out wid the dead babby."

Finding that words were of no avail, and that she could not move the great inert mass under which Mrs. Jocelyn's chair was creaking, the neighbor from across the way snatched the money and retreated to her room. This stratagem had the desired effect, for the woman was not so intoxicated as to lose her greed, and she followed as hastily as her unsteady steps permitted. A moment later the red-faced woman dashed in, seized the dead child and its wrappings, and then shaking her huge fist in Mrs. Jocelyn's face, said, "If yees ever spakes of what yer've sane, I'll be the death of ye—by the Vargin I will; so mum's the word, or it'll be worse for ye."

When Mildred returned she found her mother nervously prostrated. "I've had a bad turn," was her only explanation. Her broken spirit was terrified by her awful neighbors, and not for the world would she add another feather's weight to the burdens under which her family faltered by involving them in a prosecution of the vile impostor who had sickened her with the exposure of a horrible trade.[1]

"Mamma," cried Mildred, in sharp distress, "we must leave this place. It's killing you."

"I wish we could leave it, dear," sighed the poor woman. "I think I'd be better anywhere else."

"We shall leave it," said the girl resolutely. "Let the rent go. I had already about decided upon it, and now I'll go with Mrs. Wheaton to-morrow and find rooms among more respectable people."

The events of the evening confirmed her purpose, for the young roughs that rendezvoused nightly at the entrance of the long passageway determined that they would no longer submit to the "uppish airs" of the sisters, but "tache 'em" that since they lived in the same house they were no better than their neighbors. Therefore, as Belle boldly brushed by them as usual on her return from the shop, one young fellow, with a wink to his comrades, followed her, and where the passage was darkest put his arm around her waist and pressed upon her cheek a resounding kiss. In response there came from the entrance a roar of jeering laughter. But the young ruffian found instantly to his sorrow that he had aroused a tigress. Belle was strong and furious from the insult, and her plump hand came down on the fellow's nose with a force that caused the blood to flow copiously. After the quick impulse of anger and self-defence passed she ran sobbing like a child to Mildred, and declared she would not stay another day in the vile den. Mildred was white with anger, and paced the room excitedly for a few moments.

"Oh, God, that we had a father!" she gasped. "There,

[1] This character is not an imaginary one, and, on ample authority, I was told of an instance where the large sum of fifty dollars was obtained from some kindly family by this detestable method of imposition.

Belle, let us be patient," she continued after a few moments; "we can't contend with such wretches. I promise you that this shall be your last day in this place. We ought to have left before."

Then, as the girls grew calmer, they resolved not to tell either their father or Roger, fearing that they might become embroiled in a dangerous and disgraceful quarrel involving their presence in a police court. Mildred had given her mother a sedative to quiet her trembling nerves, and she was sleeping in one of the bedrooms, and so happily was not aware of Belle's encounter.

Mr. Jocelyn soon came in, and, for the first time since Mildred's warning, was a little the worse for liquor, but he had the self-control to keep quiet, and after a few mouthfuls of supper went to his room overcome by the stupor he had sought. After the children were sleeping the girls gladly welcomed Roger, for he had become the chief source of light and hope in their saddened lives. And he did brighten and cheer them wonderfully, for, content with a long and prosperous day's work, and full of the hopefulness and courage of youth, he imparted hope and fortitude to them in spite of all that was so depressing.

"Come, girls," he said at last, "you need some oxygen. The air is close and stifling in this den of a house, and outside the evening is clear and bracing. Let's have a stroll."

"We can't go far," said Mildred, "for mamma is sleeping, and I would not have her wake and be frightened for anything."

"Well, we'll only go around a block or two. You'll feel the stronger for it, and be in a better condition to move to-morrow," for Mildred had told him of her purpose, and he had promised to help them get settled on the following evening. When they reached the end of the dark passageway they feared that trouble was brewing, for a score of dark, coarse faces lowered at them, and the fellow that Belle had punished glared at her above his bandaged face. Paying no heed to them, however, they took a brief, quick walk, and returned to find the entrance blocked by an increasing number of dangerous-looking young ruffians.

"Stand aside," said Roger sternly.

A big fellow knocked off his hat in response, and received instantly a blow in the eye which would have felled him had he not been sustained by the crowd, who now closed on the young man.

"Run up the street and call for police," he said to the girls, but they were snatched back and held by some of the gang, and hands placed over their mouths, yet not before they had uttered two piercing cries.

Roger, after a brief, desperate struggle, got his back to the wall and struck blows that were like those of a sledgehammer. He was dealing, however, with some fairly trained pugilists, and was suffering severely, when a policeman rushed in, clubbing right and left. The gang dispersed instantly, but two were captured. The girls, half fainting from excitement and terror, were conducted to their room by Roger, and then they applied palliatives to the wounds of their knight, with a solicitude and affection which made the bruises welcome indeed to the young fellow. They were in terror at the idea of his departure, for the building was like a seething caldron. He reassured them by promising to remain until all was quiet, and the police also informed them that the house would be under surveillance until morning.

On the following day, with Mrs. Wheaton's aid, they found rooms elsewhere, and Roger, after appearing as witness against the rowdies that had been captured, and informing his employers of what had occurred, gave the remaining hours to the efficient aid of his friends.

CHAPTER XLI

GLINTS OF SUNSHINE

THEIR new rooms at first promised remarkably well. They were on the ground-floor of a large tenement that fronted on a rather narrow street, and their neighbors seemed quiet, well-disposed people. Mr. Wentworth soon called and congratulated them on the change. Mrs. Wheaton frequently came to give Mrs. Jocelyn a "'elping 'and," as she phrased it, but her eliminations did not extend to her work, which was rounded out with the completeness of hearty goodwill. Roger rarely missed an evening without giving an hour or two to the girls, often taking them out to walk, with now and then a cheap excursion on the river or a ramble in Central Park. In the latter resort they usually spent part of Sunday afternoon, going thither directly from the chapel. Mildred's morbidness was passing away. She had again taken her old class, and her face was gaining a serenity which had long been absent.

One of the great wishes of her heart now had good prospect of being fulfilled, for her father had at last consented to go to an institution wherein he could receive scientific treatment suited to his case. The outlook was growing so hopeful that even Mrs. Jocelyn was rallying into something like hopefulness and courage, and her health was slowly improving. She was one whose life was chiefly sustained by her heart and the well-being of those she loved.

Belle also was improving greatly. The memorable interview with Roger, already described, had a lasting influence, and did much to banish the giddiness of unthinking, ignorant girlhood, and the recklessness arising from an unhappy life. Now that the world was brightening again, she brightened with it. Among his new associates Roger found two or three fine, manly fellows, who were grateful indeed for an introduction to the handsome, lively girl, and scarcely a week passed during May and June that some inexpensive evening excursion was not enjoyed, and thoroughly enjoyed too, even by Mildred. Roger was ever at his best when in her society. His talk was bright and often witty, and his spirit of fun as genuine and contagious as that of Belle herself. He was now sincerely happy in the consciousness of Mildred's perfect trust and strong affection, believing that gradually, and even before the girl was aware of it, she would learn to give more than friendship. It was his plan to make himself essential to her life, indeed a part of it, and he was apparently succeeding. Mildred had put her fate into his hands. She felt that she owed so much to him that she was ready to keep her promise literally. At any time for months he might have bound her to him by promises that would never have been broken; he knew it, and she was aware of his knowledge, but when, instead of taking advantage of her gratitude, he avoided all sentiment, and treated her with a cordial frankness as if she were in truth simply the friend he had asked her to become, all of her old constraint in his presence was unthought of, and she welcomed the glances of his dark, intent eyes, which interpreted her thoughts even before they were spoken. The varying expressions of his face made it plain enough to her that he liked and appreciated her thoughts, and that his admiration and affection were only strengthened by their continued companionship. Moreover, she was well content with what she regarded as her own progress toward a warmer regard for him.

One moonlight night in June they made up a little party for an excursion on a steamer plying down the Bay. Belle had had two attendants, and would have been just as well pleased had there been two or three more. As she once asserted, she could have kept them "all jolly." During the earlier hours Roger had been as merry and full of nonsense as Belle, but on their return he and Mildred had taken seats a little apart from the others and drifted into some talk relating to one of his studies, he in a simple, lucid manner explaining to her the latest theories on a disputed question. She surprised and pleased him by saying, with a little pathetic accent in her voice,

"Oh, Roger, you are leaving me far, far behind."

"What do you mean, Millie?"

"Why, you are climbing the peaks of knowledge at a great pace, and what's to become of poor little me, that have no chance to climb at all worth naming? You won't want a friend who doesn't know anything, and can't understand what you are thinking about."

"I'll wait for you, Millie; rest assured you shall never be left alone."

"No, that won't do at all," she replied, and she was in earnest now. "There is one thing wherein you will find me as obstinate as an Atwood, and that is never to let our friendship retard your progress or render your success doubtful, now that you have struck out for yourself. Your relatives think that I—that we shall be a drag upon you; I have resolved that we shall not be, and you know that I have a little will of my own as well as yourself. You must not wait for me in any sense of the word, for you know how very proud I am, and all my pride is staked on your success. It ought to have been dead long ago, but it seems just as strong as ever."

"And I'm proud of your pride. You are a soldier, Millie, and it isn't possible for you to say, 'I surrender.'"

"You are mistaken. When you saved me from prison; when you gave nearly all you had that papa might have the chance which I trust will restore his manhood, I surrendered, and no one knew it better than you did."

"Pardon me, Millie; the gates of the citadel were closed, and ever have been. Even your will cannot open them—

no, not even your extravagant sense of gratitude for what it would be my happiness to do in any case. That something which was once prejudice, dislike, repulsion, has retreated into the depths of your heart, and it won't yield—at least it hasn't yet. But, Millie, I shall be very patient. Just as truly as if you were the daughter of a millionaire, your heart shall guide your action."

"You are a royal fellow, Roger," she faltered. "If you were not so genuinely honest, I should think you wonderfully shrewd in your policy."

"Well, perhaps the honest course is always the shrewdest in the long run," he replied laughingly, and with a deep gladness in his tone, for her words gave a little encouragement. "But your charge that I am leaving you behind as I pursue my studies has a grain of truth in it as far as mere book learning goes. In your goodness, Millie, and all that is most admirable, I shall always follow afar off. Since I can't wait for you, as you say, and you have so little time to read and study yourself, I am going to recite my lessons to you—that is, some of them, those that would interest you—and by telling you about what I have learned I shall fix it all in my mind more thoroughly."

Mildred was exceedingly pleased with the idea. "I don't see why this isn't possible to some extent," she said gladly, "and I can't tell you how much hope and comfort it gives me. That I've had so little time to read and cultivate my mind has been one of the great privations of our poverty, but if you will patiently try to make me understand a little of what you are studying, I won't relapse into barbarism. Oh, Roger, how good you are to me!"

"That is like saying, How good I am to myself! Let me tell you, Millie, in all sincerity, that this plan promises as much for me as for you. Your mind is so quick, and you look at things so differently, that I often get new and better ideas of the subject after talking it over with you. The country boy that you woke up last summer was right in believing that you could be an invaluable friend, for I can't tell you how much richer life has become to me."

"Roger, how I misunderstood you! How blind and stupid I was! God was raising up for me the best friend a girl ever had, and I acted so shamefully that anybody but you would have been driven away."

"You do yourself injustice, and I wouldn't let any one else judge you so harshly."

After reaching her room that night, Mildred thought, "I do believe mamma was right, and that an old-fashioned Southern girl, such as she says that I am, can learn to love a second time. Roger is so genuinely good and strong! It rests me to be with him, and he gives some of his own strength and courage. To-night, for the first time since he told me everything so gently and honestly, has anything been said of that which I can see is in his mind all the time, and I brought on all that was said myself. I can now read his thoughts better than he can read mine, and it would be mean not to give him a little of the hope and encouragement that he so richly deserves. It troubles me, however, that my mind and heart are so tranquil when I'm with him. That's not the way I once felt," she sighed. "He seems like the dearest brother a girl ever had—no, not that exactly; he is to me the friend he calls himself, and I'd be content to have things go on this way as long as we lived."

"Millie," cried Belle roguishly, "what did Roger say to you to call out such sweet smiles and tender sighs?"

The young girl started, and flushed slightly. "We were talking about astronomy," she said brusquely.

"Well, I should think so, for the effects in your appearance are heavenly. If he could have seen you as you have appeared for the last ten minutes, he would be more desperately in love than ever. Oh, Millie, you are so pretty that I am half in love with you myself."

"Nonsense! you are a giddy child. Tell me about your own favorites, and which of them you like best."

"I like them all best. Do you think I'm going to be

such a little goose as to tie myself down to one? These are but the advance guard of scores. Still I shall always like these ones best because they are kind to me now while I'm only a 'shop-lady,'"

"You mustn't flirt, Belle."

"I'm not flirting—only having a good time, and they know it. I'm not a bit sentimental—only jolly, you know. When the right time comes, and I've had my fun, I'm going to take my pick of the best."

"Well, that's sensible. Belle, darling, are not Roger's friends better than those underhanded fellows who could not look mamma in the eyes?"

"Oh, Millie," said the impulsive girl with a rush of tears, "don't speak of those horrid days. I was an ignorant, reckless fool—I was almost beside myself with despair and unhappiness; I could kiss Roger's hands from gratitude. Look here, Millie, if you don't marry him I will, for there's no one that can compare with him."

"Come, now, don't make me jealous."

"I wish I could. I've a great mind to flirt with him a little, just to wake up your old stupid heart. Still I think you are coming on very well. Oh, Millie, how I could dance at your wedding! Solid as I am, my feet would scarcely touch the floor."

Mildred laughed, and said softly, "It would be a pity to deny you so much pleasure, Belle." Then she added resolutely, "No more talk about weddings, if you please. For long, long years Roger must give his whole mind to his studies. His relatives say that we shall hang helplessly upon him and spoil his life, but we'll prove them mistaken, Belle. I'd work my fingers off to give him the chance that he'll make so much of, for I'm as proud of him as you are."

"That's the way to talk," exulted Belle. "I see how it's all coming out. He'll stand up head, as I told you, and I told you, too, that he'd win you in spite of yourself. Roger Atwood does all he undertakes—it's his way."

"Well, we'll see," was the half-smiling, half-sighing

answer; but sanguine Belle had no doubt concerning the future, and soon her long eyelashes drooped over her glowing cheeks in untroubled sleep.

"Oh, how good for us all is the sunlight of a little happiness and hope!" Mildred thought. "Darling mamma is reviving, Belle is blossoming like a blush rose, and I—well, thank God for Roger Atwood's friendship. May I soon be able to thank Him for his love."

Ah, Mildred Jocelyn, you have still much to learn. A second love can grow up in the heart, but not readily in one like yours.

Within a month from the time that Mr. Jocelyn entered a curative institution, he returned to his family greatly changed for the better. His manner toward his family was full of remorseful tenderness, and he was eager to retrieve his fortunes. They welcomed him with such a wealth of affection, they cheered and sustained him in so many delicate and sympathetic ways, that he wondered at the evil spell which had bound him so long and made him an alien among those so lovable and so dearly beloved. He now felt sure that he would devote body and soul to their welfare for the rest of his days, and he could not understand why or how it was that he had been so besotted. The intense sufferings during the earlier stage of his treatment at the institution made him shrink with horror from the bare thought of his old enslavement, and during the first weeks after his return he did not dream it was possible that he could relapse, although he had been warned of his danger. His former morbid craving was often fearfully strong, but he fought it with a vindictive hatred, and his family, in their deep gladness and inexperience, felt assured that husband and father had been restored to them.

It seemed as if he could not thank Roger enough, and his eyes grew eloquent with gratitude when the young fellow's name was mentioned, and when they rested on his bright, honest face. Mr. Wentworth went out among his business friends, and so interested one of them that a position was in a certain sense made for the poor man, and although the salary was small at first, the prospect for its increase was good if he would maintain his abstinence and prove that he had not lost his old fine business powers. This he bade so fair to do that hope and confidence grew stronger every day, and they felt that before very long they would be able to move into more commodious quarters, situated in a better part of the city, for by reason of the neglect of the streets and sewerage on the part of the authorities, the locality in which they now were was found to be both very disagreeable and unwholesome. They would have removed at once, but they were eager to repay Roger the money he had loaned them, although he protested against their course. Not realizing their danger, and in the impulse of their pride and integrity, they remained, practicing the closest economy.

Early in July, Roger obtained a vacation, and went home on a visit, proposing to harden his muscles by aiding his father through the harvest season. He was so helpful and so kind and considerate that even grim, disappointed Mr. Atwood was compelled to admit that his boy had become a man. Mrs. Atwood tenderly and openly exulted over him, and, obeying her impulse, she wrote a friendly letter to Mildred, which made the young girl very happy.

Susan became more than reconciled to Roger's course, for he promised that some day she should often come to the city and have splendid times. Clara Bute had become the happy wife of a well-to-do farmer, and she sent an urgent request to Belle and Mildred to visit her. The latter would not leave her parents, but Belle accepted gladly, and the gay, frolicsome girl left more than one mild heartache among the rural beaux that vied with each other in their attentions.

CHAPTER XLII

HOPES GIVEN AND SLAIN

THE skies seemed serene and bright, with promise to all for many happy days, but clouds were gathering below the horizon, and, most unexpectedly to him, the first bolt fell upon Roger. A day or two before his return to the city he found at the village office a letter with a foreign post-mark, addressed, in his care, to Miss Mildred Jocelyn. He knew the handwriting instantly, and he looked at the missive as if it contained his death-warrant. It was from Vinton Arnold. As he rode away he was desperately tempted to destroy the letter, and never breathe a word of its existence. He hoped and half believed that Mildred was learning to love him, and he was sure that if Arnold did not appear he would win all that he craved. The letter, which he had touched as if it contained nitro-glycerine, might slay every hope. Indeed he believed that it would, for he understood Mildred better than she understood herself. She believed that Arnold had given her up. Her heart had become benumbed with its own pain, and was sleeping after its long, weary waiting. He was sure, however, that if not interfered with he could awaken it at last to content and happiness. This letter, however, might be the torch which would kindle the old love with tenfold intensity. Long hours he fought his temptation like a gladiator, for fine as had been Mildred's influence over him, he was still intensely human. At last he gained the victory, and went home quiet, but more exhausted than he had ever been from a long hot day's toil in the harvest-field. He had resolved to keep absolute faith with Mildred, and having once reached a decision he was not one to waver.

As his mother kissed him good-by she held him off a moment, then whispered, "Roger, Miss Jocelyn has given you something better than all your uncle's money. I am content that it should be as it is."

On the afternoon of the day of his arrival in the city he went to meet his fate. Mrs. Jocelyn greeted him like the mother he had just left, and Mildred's glad welcome made him groan inwardly. Never before had she appeared so beautiful to him—never had her greeting been so tinged with her deepening regard. And yet she looked inquiringly at him from time to time, for he could not wholly disguise the fear that chilled his heart.

"Belle had a perfectly lovely time in the country," said Mrs. Jocelyn. "She has told us all about your people, and what a farmer you became. She said everybody was proud of you up at Forestville, and well they might be, although they don't know what we do. Oh, Roger, my dear boy, it does my heart good to see you again. We have all missed you so much. Oh, you'll never know—you never can know. Good-by now, for a little while. I promised Mrs. Wheaton that I'd bring the children over and spend the afternoon with her. She is going to show me about cutting some little clothes for Fred. What a dear kind soul she is, with all her queer talk. God bless you, my boy. You bring hope and happiness back with you."

But the poor fellow was so conscious of his own coming trouble that tears came into his eyes, and after Mrs. Jocelyn had gone he looked at Mildred in a way that made her ask, gently and anxiously:

"What is it, Roger?"

After a moment's hesitation he said grimly, "Millie, it's rough on a fellow when he must be his own executioner. There, take it. It's the heaviest load I ever carried in my life," and he threw the letter into her lap.

After a moment's glance she trembled violently, and

became pale and red by turns, then buried her face in her hands.

"I knew it would be so," he said doggedly. "I knew what was the matter all along."

She sprang up, letting the letter drop on the floor, and clung to him. "Roger," she cried, "I won't read the letter. I won't touch it. No one shall come between us—no one has the right. Oh, it would be shameful after all—"

"Millie," he said almost sternly, replacing her in her chair, "the writer of that letter has the right to come between us—he is between us, and there is no use in disguising the truth. Come, Millie, I came here to play the man, and you must not make it too hard for me. Read your letter."

"I can't," she said, again burying her burning face in her hands, and giving way to a sudden passion of tears.

"No, not while I'm here, of course. And yet I'd like to know my fate, for the suspense is a little too much. I hope he's written to tell you that he has married the daughter of the Great Mogul, or some other rich nonentity," he added, trying to meet his disappointment with a faint attempt at humor; "but I'm a fool to hope anything. Good-by, and read your letter in peace. I ought to have left it and gone away at once, but, confound it! I couldn't. A drowning man will blindly catch at a straw."

She looked at him, and saw that his face was white with pain and fear.

"Roger," she said resolutely, "I'll burn that letter without opening it if you say so. I'll do anything you ask."

He paced the room excitedly with clenched hands for a few moments, but at last turned toward her and said quietly, "Will you do what I ask?"

"Yes, yes indeed."

"Then read your letter."

She looked at him irresolutely a moment, then made a little gesture of protest and snatched up the missive almost vindictively.

After reading a few lines her face softened, and she said, in accents of regret which she was too much off her guard to disguise, "Oh, he never received my answer last summer."

"Of course not," growled Roger. "You deserved that, for you gave your note to that old blunderbuss Jotham, when I would have carried it safely."

"Oh, Roger, I can't go on with this; I am wronging you too shamefully."

"You would wrong me far more if you were not honest with me at this time," he said almost harshly.

His words quieted and chilled her a little, and she replied sadly, "You are right, Roger. You don't want, nor should I mock you with the mere semblance of what you give."

"Read the letter," was his impatient reply, "or I shall go at once."

She now turned to it resolutely, proposing to read it with an impassive face, but, in spite of herself, he saw that every word was like an electric touch upon her heart. As she finished, the letter dropped from her hands, and she began crying so bitterly that he was disarmed, and forgot himself in her behalf. "Don't cry so, Millie," he pleaded. "I can't stand it. Come, now; I fought this battle out once before, and didn't think I could be so accursedly weak again."

"Roger, read that letter."

"No," he answered savagely; "I hate him—I could annihilate him; but he shall never charge me with anything underhanded. That letter was meant for your eyes only. Since it must be, God grant he proves worthy; but his words would sting me like adders."

She sprang to him, and, burying her face upon his shoulder, sobbed, "Oh, Roger, I can't endure this. It's worse than anything I've suffered yet."

"Oh, what a brute I am!" he groaned. "His letter ought to have brought you happiness, but your kind heart is breaking over my trouble, for I've acted like a passionate boy. Millie, dear Millie, I will be a brave, true man, and, as I promised you, your heart shall decide all. From this time forth I am your brother, your protector, and I shall protect you against yourself as truly as against others. You are not to blame in the least. How could I blame you for a love that took possession of your heart before you knew of my existence, and why has not Millie Jocelyn as good a right to follow her heart as any other girl in the land? And you shall follow it. It would be dastardly meanness in me to take advantage of your gratitude. Come now, wipe your eyes, and give a sister's kiss before I go. It's all right."

She yielded passively, for she was weak, nerveless, and exhausted. He picked up the open letter, replaced it within the envelope, and put it in her hand. "It's yours," he said, "by the divine right of your love. When I come this evening, don't let me see a trace of grief. I won't mope and be lackadaisical, I promise," and smilingly he kissed her good-by.

She sat for an hour almost without moving, and then mechanically put the letter away and went on with her work. She felt herself unequal to any more emotion at that time, and after thinking the affair all over, determined to keep it to herself, for the present at least. She knew well how bitterly her father, mother, and Belle would resent the letter, and how greatly it would disquiet them if they knew that her old love was not dead, and seemingly could not and would not die. With the whole force of her resolute will she sought to gain an outward quietude, and succeeded so well that the family did not suspect anything. She both longed for and dreaded Roger's appearance, and when he came she looked at him so kindly, so remorsefully, that she tasked his strength to the utmost; but he held his own manfully, and she was compelled to admit that he had never appeared so gay or so brilliant before. For an hour he and Belle kept them all laughing over their bright nonsense, and then suddenly he said, "Vacation's over; I must begin work to-morrow," and in a moment he was gone.

"Millie," cried Belle, "you ought to thank your stars, for you have the finest fellow in the city," and they all smiled at her so brightly that she fled to her room. There Belle found her a little later with red eyes, and she remarked bluntly, "Well, you *are* a queer girl. I suppose you are crying for joy, but that isn't my way."

After her sister was asleep Mildred read and re-read Arnold's letter. At first she sighed and cried over it, and then lapsed into a long, deep reverie. "Hard as it is for Roger," she thought, "he is right—I am not to blame. I learned to love Vinton Arnold, and permitted him to love me, before I had ever seen Roger. I should have a heart of stone could I resist his appeal in this letter. Here he says: 'You did not answer my note last summer—I fear you have cast me off. I cannot blame you. After insults from my mother and my own pitiful exhibitions of weakness, my reason tells me that you have banished all thoughts of me in anger and disgust. But, Millie, my heart will not listen to reason, and cries out for you night and day. My life has become an intolerable burden to me, and never in all the past has there been a more unhappy exile than I. The days pass like years, and the nights are worse. I am dragged here and there for the benefit of my health—what a miserable farce it is! For half the money I am spending here I could live happily with you, and, sustained by your love and sympathy, I might do something befitting my man's estate. One day, when I said as much to my mother, her face grew cold and stern, and she replied that my views of life were as absurd as those of a child! I often wish I were dead, and were it not for the thought of you I half fear that I might be tempted to end my wretched existence. Of course my health suffers from this constant unhappiness, repression, and humiliation. The rumor has reached me that your father has become very poor, and that he is in ill health. The little blood I have left crimsons my face with shame that I am not at your side to help and cheer you. But I fear I should be a burden to you, as I am to every one else. My fainting turns—one of which you saw—are becoming more frequent. I've no hope nor courage to try to get well—I am just sinking under the burden of my unhappy, unmanly life, and my best hope may soon be to become unconscious and remain so forever. And yet I fully believe that one kind word from you would inspire me with the wish, the power to live. My mother is blind to everything except her worldly maxims of life. She means to do her duty by me, and is conscientious in her way, but she is killing me by slow torture. If you would give me a little hope, if you would wait—oh, pardon the selfishness of my request, the pitiable weakness displayed in this appeal! Yet, how can I help it? Who can sink into absolute despair without some faint struggle—some effort to escape? I have had the happiness of heaven in your presence, and now I am as miserable as a lost soul. You have only to say that there is no hope, and I will soon cease to trouble you or any one much longer.'

"How can I tell him there is no hope?" she murmured. "It would be murder—it would be killing soul and body. What's more, I love him—God knows I love him. My heart just yearns for him in boundless pity and sympathy, and I feel almost as if he were my crippled, helpless child as well as lover. It would be cruel, selfish, and unwomanly to desert him because of his misfortune. I haven't the heart to do it. His weakness and suffering bind me to him. His appeal to me is like the cry of the helpless to God, and how can I destroy his one hope, his one chance? He needs me more than does Roger, who is strong, masterful, and has a grand career before him. In his varied activities, in the realization of his ambitious hopes, he will overcome his present feelings, and become my brother in very truth. He will marry some rich, splendid girl like Miss Wetheridge by and by, and I shall be content in lowly, quiet ministry to one whose life and all God has put into my hands. His parents treat Vinton as if he were a child; but he has reached the age when he has the right to choose for himself, and, if the worst comes to the worst, I could support him myself. Feeling as I do now, and as I ever shall, now that my heart has been revealed to me, I could not marry Roger. It would be wronging him and perjuring myself. He is too grand, too strong a man not to see the facts in their true light, and he will still remain the best friend a woman ever had."

Then, with a furtive look at Belle to see that she was sleeping soundly, she wrote: "DEAR VINTON: My heart would indeed be callous and unwomanly did it not respond to your letter, over which I have shed many tears. Take all the hope you can from the truth that I love you, and can never cease to love you. You do yourself injustice. Your weakness and ill health are misfortunes for which you are not responsible. So far from inspiring disgust, they awaken my sympathy and deepen my affection. You do not know a woman's heart—at least you do not know mine. In your constant love, your contempt for heartless, fashionable life, and your wish to do a man's part in the world, you are manly. You are right also in believing that if you lived in an atmosphere of respect and affection you would so change for the better that you would not recognize yourself. For my sake as well as your own, try to rally, and make the most of your sojourn abroad. Fix your mind steadily on some pursuits or studies that will be of use to you in the future. Do not fear; I shall wait. It is not in my nature to forget or change." And with some reference to their misfortunes, a repetition of her note which Jotham had lost, and further reassuring words, she closed her letter.

"I am right," she said; "even Roger will say I am doing right. I could not do otherwise."

Having made a copy of the letter that she might show it to Roger, she at last slept, in the small hours of the night. As early as possible on the following day she mailed the letter, with a prayer that it might not be too late.

A day or two later she sought a private interview with

her friend, and whispered, "Roger, dear Roger, if you do not fail me now you will prove yourself the best and bravest man in the world. I am going to repose a trust in you that I cannot share at present with any one else—not even my mother. It would only make her unhappy now that she is reviving in our brighter days. It might have a bad influence on papa, and it is our duty to shield him in every way."

She told him everything, made him read the copy of her letter to Arnold. "You are strong, Roger," she said in conclusion, "and it would kill him, and—and I love him. You know now how it has all come about, and it does not seem in my nature to change. I have given you all I can—my absolute trust and confidence. I've shown you my whole heart. Roger, you won't fail me. I love you so dearly, I feel so deeply for you, I am so very grateful, that I believe it would kill me if this should harm you."

He did not fail her, but even she never guessed the effort he made.

"It's all right, Millie," he said with a deep breath, "and I'll be a jolly bachelor for you all my life."

"You must not say that," she protested. "One of these days I'll pick you out a far better wife than I could ever be."

"No," he replied decisively, "that's the one thing I won't do for you, if you picked out twenty score."

He tried to be brave—he was brave; but for weeks thereafter traces of suffering on his face cut her to the heart, and she suffered with him as only a nature like hers was capable of doing. Events were near which would tax his friendship to the utmost.

August was passing with its intense heat. The streets of the locality wherein the Jocelyns lived were shamefully neglected, and the sewerage was bad. Mr. Jocelyn was one of the first to suffer, and one day he was so ill from malarial neuralgia that he faltered in the duties of his business.

"I can't afford to be ill," he said to himself. "A slight dose of morphia will carry me through the day; surely I've strength of mind sufficient to take it once or twice as a medicine, and then plenty of quinine will ward off a fever, and I can go on with my work without any break or loss; meanwhile I'll look for rooms in a healthier locality."

His conscience smote him, warned him, and yet it did not seem possible that he could not take a little as a remedy, as did other people. With the fatuity of a self-indulgent nature he remembered its immediate relief from pain, and forgot the anguish it had caused. He no more proposed to renew the habit than to destroy his life—he only proposed to tide himself over an emergency.

The drug was taken, and to his horror he found that it was the same as if he had kindled a conflagration among combustibles ready for the match. His old craving asserted itself with all its former force. His will was like a straw in the grasp of a giant. He writhed, and anathematized himself, but soon, with the inevitableness of gravitation, went to another drug store and was again enchained.[1]

For a few days Mr. Jocelyn tried to conceal his condition from his family, but their eyes were open now, and they watched him at first with alarm, then with terror. They pleaded with him; his wife went down on her knees before him; but, with curses on himself, he broke away and rushed forth, driven out into the wilderness of a homeless life like a man possessed with a demon. In his intolerable shame and remorse he wrote that he would not return until he had regained his manhood. Alas! that day would never come.

---

[1] It is a sad fact that more than half of those addicted to the opium habit relapse. The causes are varied, but the one given is the most common: it is taken to bridge over some emergency or to give relief from physical pain or mental distress. The infatuated victim says, "I will take it just this once," and then he goes on taking it until it destroys him. I have talked with several who have given way for the second and third time, and with one physician who has relapsed five times. They each had a somewhat different story to tell, but the dire results were in all cases the same. After one indulgence, the old fierce craving, the old fatal habit, was again fixed, with more than its former intensity and binding power.

CHAPTER XLIII

WAS BELLE MURDERED?

MRS. WHEATON, Mr. Wentworth, and Roger did what they could for the afflicted family, and Roger spent the greater part of several nights in a vain search for the absent man, but he had hidden himself too securely, and was drowning reason, conscience, his entire manhood, in one long debauch. The young man grew more haggard than ever in his deep sympathy for his friends, for they clung to him with the feeling that he only could help them effectually. He begged them to move elsewhere, since the odors of the place were often sickening, but they all said No, for the husband and father might return, and this now was their one hope concerning him.

In the second fall of her husband Mrs. Jocelyn seemed to have received her death-wound, for she failed visibly every day.

One night Belle was taken with a severe chill, and then fever and delirium followed. When Roger came the ensuing evening, Mildred sobbed on his shoulder.

"Oh, Roger, my heart is paralyzed with dread. The skies you were making so bright for us have become black with ruin. You are the only one who brings me any hope or comfort. Come with me. Look at Belle there. She doesn't know any of us. For the last hour her mind has wandered. Half the time she is thanking you for all that you have done for us; then she calls for papa, or is away in the country. The doctor has been here, and he looked very grave. He says it's all due to the bad sanitary condition of this part of the city, and that there are other cases just like it, and that they are hard to manage. Why didn't we move before? Oh, oh, oh!" and she cried as if her heart would break.

"Don't grieve so, Millie," Roger faltered. "I never could stand it to see tears in your eyes. Belle is young and vigorous; she'll pull through."

"I hope so. Oh, what should we do if she should— But the doctor says the fever takes a stronger hold on persons of full habit like Belle, and now that I've made inquiries I find that it has been fatal in several instances. We have been so troubled about papa that we thought of nothing else, and did not realize our danger. There are two cases like Belle's across the way, and one in this house, and none of them are expected to live."

"Millie," said Roger resolutely, "I won't even entertain the thought of Belle's dying. I'm going to stay with you every night until she is out of danger. I can doze here in this chair, and I should be sleepless with anxiety anywhere else. You must let me become a brother now in very truth."

"No, Roger, we can't permit it. You might catch the fever."

"Millie, I will stay. Do you think I could leave you to meet this trouble alone? I can relieve you in many ways, and give you and your mother a chance for a little rest. Besides, what is the fever to me?" he added, with a touch of recklessness which she understood too well.

"Roger," she said gravely, "think what your life and health are to me. If you should fail me I should despair."

"I won't fail you," he replied, with a little confident nod. "You will always find me on hand like a good-natured dragon whenever you are in trouble. The first thing to do is to send these children to the country, and out of this poisoned air," and he sat down at once and wrote to his mother and Clara Wilson, formerly Clara Bute.

Then, true to his word, he watched with Mildred and Mrs. Jocelyn every night. Frequently his hand upon the brow of the delirious girl would quiet her when nothing else could, and Mildred often saw his tears falling fast on the unconscious face.

Mrs. Wilson answered his letter in person. "I couldn't wait a minute," she said. "I went right over to Mrs. Atwood's and told her that no one could have the children but me, and my husband says they can stay until you want them back. He is so good to me! Dear little Belle!" she sobbed, bending over the sufferer, "to think that I once so misjudged you! A better-hearted girl never breathed. As soon as she's able to be moved you must bring her right to me, and I'll take care of her till she's her old rosy, beautiful self. No, I'll come for her. I wish I could take her in my arms and carry her home now."

"She often speaks of you," faltered Mildred. "Indeed she seems to be living all her old life over again."

The doctor looked graver every day, and at last held out no hope. Late one night they saw that the crisis was near. Belle was almost inanimate from weakness, and Mrs. Jocelyn, Mildred, and Roger sat beside her in the large living-room, into which they had moved her bed, so that if possible she might get a little air—air that was laden with vile, stifling odors. At last the feeble tossings of the poor sufferer ceased, and she looked around intelligently. Her mother kissed her, and said soothingly, "Sleep, dear, and you'll soon be better."

She shook her head, and continued to look as if in search of some one, and then whispered,

"Where is papa?"

"You are not strong enough to see him now," her mother replied with pallid lips, while Mildred put her hand to her side from the intolerable pain in her heart.

Belle lay still a few moments, and they breathed low in their suspense. Her mother kept her soothing touch upon her brow, while Mildred held her hand. At last two great tears rolled down the poor girl's face, and she said faintly, "I remember now."

"Oh, Belle, darling, sleep," murmured her mother, "and you will soon get well." Again she slowly shook her head. "Dear little mother," she whispered, "forgive naughty Belle for all her wild ways. You were always patient with me. Pray God to forgive me, for I'm going fast. If He's like you—I won't fear Him."

Mrs. Jocelyn would have fallen on her child if Roger had not caught her and placed her gently on the lounge, where she lay with dry, tearless eyes and all the yearnings of the mother-heart in her wan face. Belle's eyes followed her wistfully, then turned to Mildred.

"Good-by, Millie darling, best of sisters. You will have a long—happy life—in spite of all."

Mildred clung to her passionately, but at Belle's faint call for Roger she knelt at the bedside and looked with streaming eyes on the near approach of death.

"Roger," Belle whispered, "lift me up. I want to die on your breast—you saved me—you *know*. Take care Millie—mamma—little ones. Don't wake them. Now—tell me—some—thing—comforting out of—the Bible."

"'God is not willing that one of His little ones should perish,'" said the young fellow brokenly, thankful that he could recall the words.

"That's sweet—I'm—one of His—littlest ones. It's—getting—very dark—Roger. I know—what it—means. Good—by. We'll—have—good—times—together—yet."

Then came that absolute stillness which he understood too well. He bowed his head upon the cold brow of the dead girl, and wept as only strong men weep in their first great sorrow. Mildred almost forgot her own grief in trying to lead him away and to comfort him, but he clung convulsively to Belle's lifeless form. At last he broke almost frantically away.

"Roger, Roger," cried Mildred, "where are you going? What are you going to do?"

"I don't know—I must have air or my heart will break; I'll go mad. She's just been murdered, *murdered*," and he rushed out.

After a little while he returned, and said, "There, Millie, I'm better. I won't give way again," and he took her in his arms and let her cry away some of the pain in her heart.

Mrs. Jocelyn still lay upon the sofa, white as marble, and with dry, dilated eyes. She was far beyond tears.

. . . .

On the day following Belle's death the Hon. —— —— sat down to a sumptuous dinner in one of the most fashionable of the Saratoga hotels. A costly bottle of wine added its ruddy hue to his florid complexion. The waiters were obsequious, the smiling nods of recognition from other distinguished guests of the house were flattering, and as the different courses were brought on, the man became the picture of corpulent complacence. His aspect might have changed could he have looked upon the still form of the once frolicsome, beautiful girl, who had been slain because he had failed so criminally in fidelity to his oath of office. It would not have been a pleasant task for him to estimate how much of the money that should have brought cleanliness and health among the tenements of the poor was being worse than wasted on his own gross personality.

CHAPTER XLIV

THE FINAL CONSOLATIONS OF OPIUM

THE glowing September sun had rarely revealed a sadder group than that which still watched beside poor Belle. At last Roger looked at his watch and said:

"I will now go and see Mr. Wentworth, and bring Mrs. Wheaton."

"Very well, Roger," Mildred replied, "we leave everything in your hands."

"Millie, I can't bear to have Belle placed in one of the crowded city cemeteries. Would you not be willing to have her sleep in our tree-shadowed graveyard at Forestville? We could keep flowers on her grave there as long as we lived."

"Oh, Roger, how kind of you to think of that! It would be such a comfort to us!"

"I will take her there myself on the evening boat," he said decisively, and he hastened away feeling that he must act promptly, for his aching head and limbs led him to fear that Belle's fever was already in his veins. Mr. Wentworth overflowed with sympathy, and hastened to the afflicted family with nourishing delicacies. Mrs. Wheaton soon followed, tearful and regretful.

"I didn't know," she said; "I've 'ad a sick child or I'd a been hover before. Not 'earing from you I thought hall vas vell, and there's the poor dear dead, an' I might 'ave done so much for 'er."

"No, Mrs. Wheaton, all was done that could be done in this poisoned air. We feared you might catch the fever if you came, and we knew you would come."

"Hindeed I vould, if you hall 'ad the small-pox. Now I'm going to do heverything," and she fretted at every effort of the exhausted watchers to help her.

Roger telegraphed his father to meet him at the boat with the village hearse. The news spread fast, and the little community was soon deeply stirred with sympathetic interest. Mrs. Jocelyn was too weak to endure the journey, and Mildred would not leave her. Therefore Mr. Wentworth held a simple, heartfelt service over the one they all so loved, and Roger departed on his sad errand. He was eager to get away, and, if the thought of Belle had not been uppermost in all minds, it would have been seen that he was far from well in spite of his almost desperate efforts to hide his illness. His father found him on the boat delirious with fever. The old man's face was haggard and drawn as he returned to Forestville with his two helpless burdens, grieving far more for the one that was ill than for the one that was dead. "It's turning out just as brother Ezra said," he growled. "A man's a fool to mix himself up with other people's troubles." The interest in the village deepened into strong excitement when it became known that Roger was ill with the fever that had caused Belle's death, some timid ones fearing that a pestilence would soon be raging in their midst. But the great majority yielded to their good impulses, and Mrs. Atwood was overwhelmed with offers of assistance. Several young farmers to whom Belle had given a heartache a few weeks before volunteered to watch beside her until the funeral, and there was a deeper ache in their hearts as they sat reverently around the fair young sleeper. The funeral was a memorable one in Forestville, for the most callous heart was touched by the pathos of the untimely death.

Meanwhile poor Roger was tossing in fever and muttering constantly of his past life. The name, however, oftenest on his lips was that of Millie Jocelyn.

Never before in all the troubled past did the poor girl so need his sustaining love as on the night he left her.

Mr. Wentworth spent an hour with the sad mother and daughter after the others had gone, and then sorrowfully departed, saying that he had an engagement out of town, and that he would come again immediately on his return. Mrs. Wheaton had gone home, promising that she would come back in the evening and spend the night with them, for she had a neighbor who would take care of the children, and so at last the two stricken women were left alone.

Mildred was bathing her mother's head and trying to comfort her when the door opened, and a haggard, unkempt man stood before them. For a second they looked at him in vague terror, for he stood in a deep shadow, and then Mrs. Jocelyn cried, "Martin! Martin!" and tears came to her relief at last.

He approached slowly and tremblingly. Mildred was about to throw herself into his arms, but he pushed her away. His manner began to fill them with a vague, horrible dread, for he acted like a spectre of a man.

"Where are the children?" he asked hoarsely.

"We have sent them to the country. Oh, papa, do be kind and natural—you will kill mamma."

"There is crape on the door-knob," he faltered. "Where's Belle?"

"Oh, oh, oh!" sobbed Mildred. "Papa, papa, have mercy on us. Can't you sustain and help us at such a time as this?"

"She is dead, then," he whispered, and he sank into a chair as if struck down.

"Yes, she's dead. You were the first one she asked for when she came out of her fever."

"Great God! my punishment is greater than I can bear," he groaned.

"Oh, Martin," pleaded his wife, "come to me," and too weak to rise from her couch she held out her arms to him.

He looked at her with a remorse and agony in his expression that were indescribable. "No, Nan," he said, "I'm not fit for you to touch now. I'm murdering you all," and he went hastily to his room and locked the door.

They waited, scarcely breathing in their deep apprehension.

In a few moments he came out, and his face was rigid and desperate in its aspect. In spite of his repelling gesture Mildred clasped him in her arms. The embrace seemed to torture him. "Let me go!" he cried, breaking away. "I poison the very air I breathe. You both are like angels of heaven and I—O God! But the end has come," and he rushed out into the gathering darkness. Mrs. Jocelyn tried to follow him, and fell prostrate with a despairing cry on the floor.

Mildred's first impulse was to restore her mother, without seeking help, in the faint hope that her father would return, for she had learned what strange alternations of mood opium produces; but as the sense of his words grew clearer she was overpowered, and trembled so violently that she was compelled to call to her help a neighbor—a plain, good-hearted woman who lived on the same floor. When at last Mrs. Jocelyn revived she murmured piteously:

"Oh, Millie, why didn't you let me die?"

"Mamma," pleaded the girl, "how can you even think of leaving me?"

"Millie, Millie darling, I fear I must. My heart feels as if it were bleeding internally. Millie"—and she grasped her child's shoulder convulsively, "Millie, look in his room for—for—his pistol."

"Oh, mamma, mamma!"

"Look, look!" said her mother excitedly. "I can't bear the suspense."

Thinking that her mother was a little hysterical, and that compliance would quiet her, Mildred went to the place where her father always kept his cavalry revolver—the one memento left of his old heroic army life. *It was gone!*

She almost sank to the floor in terror, nor did she dare return to her mother.

"Millie, Millie, quick!" came in a faint cry from the outer room.

The poor girl rushed forward and buried her face in her mother's bosom, sobbing, "Mamma, oh mamma, live for my sake."

"I knew it, I knew it," said the stricken wife, with a long low cry. "I saw it in his desperate face. Oh, Martin, Martin, we will die together!"

She clasped Mildred tightly, trembled convulsively a moment, and then her arms fell back, and she was as still as poor Belle had been.

"Oh, mamma!" Mildred almost shrieked, but she was far beyond recall, and the suffering heart was at rest.

When the woman returned with the cup of tea she had gone to prepare for Mrs. Jocelyn, she found the young girl leaning forward unconscious on the bosom of the dead mother.

When she revived it was only to moan and wring her hands in despair. Mrs. Wheaton soon appeared, and having learned what had happened she threw her apron over her head and rocked back and forth in her strong sympathetic grief. But her good heart was not long content with tears, and she took Mildred into her arms and said:

"I vill be a mother to you, and you shall never vant a 'ome vile I 'ave von," and the motherless girl clung to her in a way that did the kind soul a world of good.

Before the evening was very far advanced a boy brought a note to the door. Mildred seized it and asked:

"Who gave it to you?"

"I don't know—a man. He pointed to this door, and then he went away very fast."

She tore it open, and read in horror: "My darling wife, dear beyond all words in these my final despairing moments. My love for you and those left is the only trace of good remaining in my heart. I die for your sakes. My continued existence would be a curse, for I have lost my manhood. I am possessed by a devil that I can't control. I cannot ask you to forgive me. I can never forgive myself. Farewell. After I am gone, brighter days will come to you all. Pity me if you can, forgive me if you can, and remember me as I was before—" And there the terrible missive ended.

For an hour the girl lay moaning as if in mortal pain, and then the physician who was summoned gave her a sedative which made her sleep long and heavily. It was quite late in the morning when she awoke, and the events that had passed first came to her like a horrid dream, and then grew into terrible reality. But she was not left to meet the emergency alone, for Mrs. Wheaton and Clara Wilson watched beside her. The latter in her strong sympathy had come to the city to take Mildred and her mother to the country, and she said to Mrs. Wheaton that she would now never leave her friend until she was in the breezy farmhouse.

After a natural outburst of grief Mildred again proved that Arnold's estimate of her was correct. She was equal to even this emergency, for she eventually grew quiet and resolute. "I must find papa," she said.

"Shall I?" Mrs. Wilson asked Mrs. Wheaton significantly.

"Yes, Millie is more hof a soldier than hany hof us."

"Well," continued Mrs. Wilson, "Mrs. Wheaton found this in the morning paper: 'An unknown man committed suicide on the steps of No. 73 —— Street. His remains have been taken to the Morgue for identification.' "

For a few moments Mildred so trembled and looked so crushed that they feared for her exceedingly. "Poor papa!" she moaned, "he was just insane from remorse and opium. Seventy-three —— Street! Why, that was the house in which we used to live. It was there that papa spent his first happy years in this city, and it was there he went to die. Oh, how dreadful, how inexpressibly sad it all is! What shall we do?"

"Leave hall to me," said Mrs. Wheaton. "Mrs. Wilson, you stay 'ere with the poor dear, an' I'll hattend to heverything."

Mildred was at last too overpowered to do more than lie on the lounge, breathing in long tremulous sighs.

Mrs. Wheaton went at once to the Morgue and found that the "unknown man" was indeed Mr. Jocelyn, and yet he had so changed, and a bullet-hole in his temple had given him such a ghastly appearance, that it was difficult to realize that he was the handsome, courtly gentleman who had first brought his beautiful daughter to the old mansion.

Mrs. Wheaton represented to the authorities that he was very poor, that his daughter was an orphan and overcome with grief, and that she now was the nearest friend of the afflicted girl. Her statement was accepted, and then with her practical good sense she attended to everything.

During her absence Mildred had sighed, "Oh, I do so wish that Roger Atwood were here. He gives me hope and courage when no one else can."

"Millie," said Mrs. Wilson tearfully, "for his sake you must rally and be braver than you have ever been before. I think his life now depends upon you. He has the fever, and in his delirium he calls for you constantly."

At first Mrs. Wilson thought the shock of her tidings would be more disastrous to the poor girl, already so unnerved and exhausted, than all the terrible events which had thus far occurred. "I have brought him nothing but suffering and misfortune," she cried. "He gave up everything for us, and now we may cost him his life."

"Millie, he is not dead, and you, if any one, can bring him life."

She had touched the right chord, for the young girl soon became quiet and resolute. "He never failed me," she said in a low voice, "and I won't fail him."

"That is the right way to feel," said Mrs. Wilson eagerly. "I now think that everything depends on your courage and fortitude. Mrs. Wheaton and I have planned it all out. We'll go to Forestville on the evening boat, and take your father's and mother's remains with us."

Mrs. Wheaton learned from the undertaker connected with Mr. Wentworth's chapel that the clergyman would not be back until evening, and she told the former to tell their pastor all that had occurred, and to ask him to keep the circumstances of Mr. Jocelyn's death as quiet as possible.

The man was discreet and energetic, and they were all so expeditious that the evening saw them with their sad freight on the way to Forestville, the keys of Mildred's rooms having been left with the kind woman who had befriended her in the sudden and awful emergency. Mrs. Wheaton parted from Mildred as if she were her own child, and went mournfully back to her busy, useful life. Mr. and Mrs. Jocelyn were buried with a quiet, simple service beside poor Belle, and sensible Mrs. Wilson soon inspired the good-hearted village people with the purpose to spare the feelings of the stricken girl in every possible way. Mildred caressed her little brother and sister with the tenderness of a mother added to her sisterly affection, and she was comforted to see how much they had already improved in the pure country air. "Oh, Clara," she said, "what a friend you have been to me! God alone can repay you."

"Millie," Mrs. Wilson earnestly replied, "I owe you a debt I can never pay. I owe you and darling Belle happiness and prosperity for this life, and my hope of the life to come. My husband is strong and prosperous, and he says I shall do all that's in my heart for you. Oh, Millie, he is so good to me, and he cried over Belle like a child. I thought I loved him before, but when I saw those tears I just worshipped him. He has a man's heart, like Roger. Now, Millie, I'm going to keep these children as long as you'll let me, and treat them as my own. I feel that the promise has been given to me that they'll grow up to be a great comfort to us both."

On the evening after the funeral Mildred went to aid in the care of Roger, and Mrs. Atwood greeted her with all the warmth and tenderness that a daughter would have received. Even Mr. Atwood drew his sleeve across his eyes as he said, "If you'll help us save our boy, you'll find that I'm not as crabbed and crooked a stick as I seem."

Mildred was shocked and her heart chilled with fear at the change in Roger, but her hand upon his brow and her voice did more to quiet him than all the physician's remedies. She became his almost tireless watcher, and she said hopefully that the bracing autumn winds rustled around the farmhouse like the wings of ministering angels, and that they would bring life and health to the fever-stricken man. They all wondered at her endurance, for while she looked so frail she proved herself so strong. At last the crisis came, as it had in Belle's case, but instead of waking to die he passed from delirium into a quiet sleep, Mildred holding his hand, and when he opened his eyes with the clear glance of intelligence, they first looked upon her dear face. "Millie," he whispered.

She put her fingers upon her lips, smiled, and said, "I won't leave you if you will be good and do all I say. You never failed me yet, Roger, and you must not now."

"I'll surely get well if you stay with me, Millie," he answered contentedly, and soon he slept again as quietly as a child.

CHAPTER XLV

MOTHER AND SON

OUR story passes rapidly over the events of the ensuing months. In his native mountain air, and under the impulse of his strong, unbroken constitution, Roger recovered rapidly and steadily. As soon as he was strong enough he went to the village cemetery, and, leaning his head on Belle's grave, sobbed until Mildred led him away. For a long time tears would come into his eyes whenever the names of Mrs. Jocelyn and the young girl he loved so fondly were mentioned. He and Mildred planted the sacred place thick with roses and spring-flowering bulbs.

Mildred resisted all entreaties to remain in the country, saying that she was a city girl at heart, and that, with Mr. Wentworth's aid, she could easily earn her livelihood in town, and do much for Fred and Minnie. Moreover, she felt that she could not be parted from Roger, for seemingly he had become an inseparable part of her life. The experiences he had shared with her were developing within him a strong and noble manhood, and he vowed that the young girl who had known so much sorrow should have all the happiness that he could bring to pass.

When Mrs. Wheaton learned of Mildred's purpose to return to town, she took more commodious apartments in the old mansion, and set apart a room for the young girl. She also sold most of her own things and took Mildred's furniture out of storage, so that the place might seem familiar and homelike to her friend.

When Roger had almost recovered his wonted health,

Mrs. Atwood told her husband that he must go with her to visit his brother in town, for the worthy woman had a project on her mind which she carried out with characteristic directness and simplicity.

They surprised Mr. and Mrs. Ezra Atwood at breakfast, and partook of the cheer offered them rather grimly and silently. After the meal was over Roger's mother said, without any circumlocution:

"Brother-in-law, I've come to have a plain, honest talk with you, and if you're a true Atwood you'll listen to me. I want your wife and my husband to be present. We are nigh of kin, but we are forgetting ties which the Lord hath ordained. Ezra, I believe you are a good man at heart, but, like my husband, you set too much store by things that perish in the using. My boy has taught me that there are better things in this world, and we'll all soon be where we may look on money as a curse. You have not spoken to my son since last spring, and you've been cold toward us. I want you to know the truth, and realize what you're doing; then if you go on in this way, you must settle it with your own conscience;" and with a homely pathos all her own she told the whole story.

The uncle at first tried to be grim and obstinate, but he soon broke down completely. "I'm glad you've come," he said huskily. "My conscience hasn't given me any peace for months, and I wanted to give in, but you know that it's like drawing an eye-tooth for an Atwood to give in. I'm proud of the boy, and he'll be a blessing to us all. He *is* a new departure in the family; he's got more brains than any of us, and with it all a big, brave heart. He shall marry the girl if he wants to; and now that her old wretch of a father is dead, no harm need come of it. But they're young; they must wait until Roger is educated up to the best of 'em. Well, now that I've given in, there shall be no half-way work," and he insisted on sending for his lawyer and making his will in Roger's favor at once.

"I didn't come for any such purpose as this," said

Roger's mother, wiping her eyes, while his father could scarcely conceal his exultation; "but I felt that it was time for us to stop living like heathen," and after a visit of a very different nature from the one they had feared, the worthy couple returned to Forestville well content with the results of their expedition.

Roger was jubilant over the news, and he hastened to impart it to Mildred, who was spending the remaining weeks of her sojourn in the country with her friend Mrs. Wilson.

"Millie," he said, "you shall never want again. My good fortune would be nothing to me unless I shared it with you."

But she disappointed him by saying, "No, Roger, you must let me live the independent life that my nature requires," and the only concession that he could obtain from her was a promise to receive his aid should any emergency require it.

Before Mildred's return a letter from Vinton Arnold was forwarded to her at Forestville, and it must be admitted that it gave her sad heart something like a thrill of happiness. It was an eloquent and grateful outpouring of affection, and was full of assurances that she had now given him a chance for life and happiness.

When she told Roger, he looked very grim for a moment, and then by a visible effort brightened up and said, "It's all right, Millie." After pacing the room for a few moments with a contracted brow, he continued, "Millie, you must grant me one request—you must not say anything to Arnold about me."

"How can I say anything then about myself?" she answered. "I want him to know that I owe everything to you, and I hope to see the day when you will be the closest of friends."

"Well, that will be a good way on. I must see him first, and learn more about him, and—well, friends related as Arnold will be to me are not common. I've too much of the old untamed man in me to go readily into that kind of thing. I will do anything in the world for you, but you must not expect much more till I have a few gray hairs in my head. Come now, you must humor me a little in this affair; you can say generally that some friends were kind, and all that, without much personal reference to me. If you should write as you propose, he might be jealous, or —worse yet—write me a letter of thanks. It may prevent complications, and will certainly save me some confoundedly disagreeable experiences. After I've seen him and get more used to it all, I may feel differently."

"You certainly will, Roger. Your life will gradually become so rich, full, and happy, that some day you will look back in wonder at your present feelings."

"Life will be full enough if work can make it so; but you must not expect me to outgrow this. It will strengthen with my years. It's my nature as well as yours. But I foresee how it will be," he continued despondently; "I shall inevitably be pushed further and further into the background. In your happy home life—"

Before he could utter another word Mildred was sobbing passionately. "Roger," she cried, "don't talk that way. I can't bear it. If Vinton is jealous of you, if he fails in manly appreciation of you, I will never marry him. Strong as my love is for him, such a course would destroy it. There are certain kinds of weakness that I can't and won't tolerate."

He was surprised and deeply touched, for her manner was usually so quiet and well controlled that even he was at times tempted to forget how strong and passionate was her nature on occasions sufficient to awaken it. "There, Millie, I've hurt your feelings," he said remorsefully. "Even I do not half understand your good, kind heart. Well, you must have patience with me. When the right time comes my deeds will satisfy you, I think, though my words are now so unpromising. But please don't deny me—don't say anything about me until I give you permission. What has occurred between us is sacred to me—it's our affair."

"Very well, if you so wish it; but never even think again that you will ever be less to me than you are now."

Nevertheless he went sadly away, saying to himself, "She's sincere, Heaven knows, but what I said will be true in spite of her best intentions."

The next day, after many farewells and an hour spent beside Belle's grave, Roger returned to the city, far better prepared for life's battle than when he first left his native village. Two or three days later Mildred followed him, accompanied by Mrs. Wilson, who was determined to see her safely settled in Mrs. Wheaton's care. Pain and pleasure were almost equally blended in Mildred's experience as she looked upon the furniture and the one or two pictures that had escaped their poverty—all of which were so inseparable, in their associations, from those who were gone, yet never absent long from memory. But the pleasure soon got the better of the pain, for she did not wish to forget. Mrs. Wheaton's welcome was so hearty as to be almost overpowering, and when Roger appeared in the evening with a beautiful picture for her walls she smiled as she once thought she never could smile again. Mr. Wentworth also called, and was so kind and sympathetic that the young girl felt that she was far from friendless. "I so managed it," he whispered in parting, "that there was little public reference to your father's sad end. Now, Millie, turn your thoughts toward the future. Let Roger make you happy. Believe me, he's pure gold."

"Just what poor Belle said," she thought sighingly after he had gone. "I must disappoint them all. But Roger will help me out. He deserves a far better wife than poor shamed, half-crushed Millie Jocelyn can ever make him, and he shall have her, too, for he is much too young and strong not to get over all this before many years elapse."

Life soon passed into a peaceful, busy routine. Roger was preparing himself for the junior class in college under the best of tutors, and his evenings, spent with Mildred, were usually prefaced by a brisk walk in the frosty air. Then he either read aloud to her or talked of what was Greek to good-natured Mrs. Wheaton, who sat knitting in a corner discreetly blind and deaf. Unknown to Mildred, he was able to aid her very efficiently, for he taxed Mrs. Wentworth's ingenuity in the invention of all kinds of delicate fancy work, and that good lady, in the most business-like manner, gave the orders to Mildred, who thought that, considering the hard times, she was wonderfully prosperous.

Twice during the winter she went with Roger to Forestville, and she had her little brother and sister spend the Christmas week with her. It was the brightest experience the little people ever remembered, although, unnoted by them, Mildred, with sad memories that do not belong to childhood, often wiped bitter tears from her eyes as she recalled the terrible events of the preceding holiday season. She became an efficient ally of Mr. Wentworth, and was almost as glad to aid him, in return for his stanch friendship, as the cause he represented.

She and Vinton Arnold maintained quite a regular correspondence, and the fact occasioned the young man more than one stormy scene. His mother saw Mildred's letter before he received it, and the effect of the missive upon him, in spite of his efforts at concealment, were so marked that she at once surmised the source from which it came. The fact that a few words from Mildred had done more for the invalid than all the expensive physicians and the many health resorts they had visited would have led most mothers to query whether the secret of good health had not been found. Mrs. Arnold, on the contrary, was only angered and rendered more implacable than ever against the girl. She wrote to her husband, however, to find out what he could about her family, believing that the knowledge might be useful. Mr. Arnold merely learned the bare facts that the Jocelyns had become greatly impoverished, that they were living in low tenements, that the father had become a wretched sot, and, worse than all, that the girl herself had been in a station-house, although he believed she was proved innocent of the charge against her. He therefore wrote to his wife that the correspondence must cease at once, since it might involve the family in disgrace—certainly in disgraceful associations. He also wrote to his son to desist, under the penalty of his heaviest displeasure. With an expression of horror on her face, Mrs. Arnold showed this letter to her son. In vain he tried to protest that not one evil thing against Mildred could be proved; that she was innocence and purity itself; that her misfortunes and the wrong of others were no reason for desertion on his part. His mother for once lost her frigid politeness. "What!" she almost screamed, "do you think we would ever let that horrid creature bear our name? A woman who has been in a prison cell, and mixed up with the vilest and lowest people in the city, should not even be named in my presence."

Her son gave her a strange, vindictive look. "You unnatural mother," he muttered between his teeth, "thus to speak of the girl to whom your son has given his best love, and who is worthy of it!" and he turned on his heel and left her.

Mrs. Arnold became somewhat hysterical, and wrote home that she believed that Vinton was losing his mind. She soon learned, however, that she would have no ground for such a charge, although her son was becoming greatly changed. His politeness to her was scrupulous to a nicety, but was unrelenting in its icy coldness. At the same time she knew that he was continuing the correspondence, and she saw, too, that he was making the most studied and careful effort to gain in physical strength. One day she began to upbraid him bitterly for his disobedience, but he interrupted her by saying sternly:

"Madam, there is no child present. I treat you with respect. I also demand respect."

The proud, resolute woman admitted to herself that his

management was becoming a difficult and dubious problem, and at last, discouraged and exasperated by the unwavering steadfastness of his course and manner, she wrote that they might as well return home, for "he was beyond her influence."

Therefore, thrilling with glad expectation, Arnold found himself in his native city much sooner than he had expected. He had no very definite plans. If he could only become sufficiently well to earn his own livelihood the future would be comparatively clear. If this were impossible, his best hope was to wait, secure in Mildred's faith, for the chances of the future, believing that his father might relent if his mother would not. For this event, however, the outlook was unpromising. Mr. Arnold was incensed by his wife's fuller account of his son's behavior, and the proof she had obtained, in spite of his precautions, that he was in frequent correspondence with Mildred. He had since learned the circumstances of Mr. Jocelyn's wretched death, and that Mildred was but a sewing-girl, living with an ignorant English woman in a dilapidated old tenement, and his bitter revolt at the whole affair was quite natural in view of his superficial inquiries and knowledge. Both he and his wife judged from their proud and worldly standpoint solely, and therefore on the day following Vinton's arrival they summoned him to a private interview. At first Mr. Arnold proposed to reason with his son, but the cold, unyielding face soon so irritated him that he became almost violent in his anger. After he and his mother had nearly exhausted themselves, Vinton said quietly:

"Now that you have both lectured and threatened me as if I were a boy, I would like to ask one question. Have I ever disgraced you yet?"

The husband and wife looked at each other, and were not a little perplexed how to meet this passive resistance. In the same low, incisive tones, Vinton continued, "If you propose to turn me into the streets for loving Miss Jocelyn, do so at once, for I do love her, and I shall ever love her."

"She shall not touch a penny of our money," said Mrs. Arnold, with an implacable look.

"With me," replied her son, with the same old vindictive glance, "it is not a question of pennies, but of life and death. I feel toward Miss Jocelyn as I suppose my father once felt toward you, although what heart you had to win I cannot understand from your manner toward me. I have seen considerable of society, but have never met a woman who could compare with Mildred Jocelyn in all that constitutes a true lady. I shall not waste any words concerning the virtues of her heart upon such unsympathetic listeners, but I am at least a man in years, and have the right to love her."

"Oh, certainly," said Mrs. Arnold angrily, "there is no law which can prevent your disgracing yourself and us."

"Nor is there any law or gospel, madam, for your unnatural, unsympathetic course toward your own flesh and blood. Good-evening."

"Now you see how strange and infatuated he has become," she said to her husband after her son's departure; but the old merchant shook his head in trouble and perplexity.

"We have been too hard upon him, I fear," he said.

"If you weaken in this matter, I shall not," she answered decisively. "If he gives way to this folly, both I and my children will disown all kith and kin."

"Well, well," he replied impatiently, "it will have to be so, I suppose; but nevertheless I believe we have been too hard with him."

CHAPTER XLVI

A FATAL ERROR

THE next morning Arnold started out to visit the one rarely absent from his thoughts. It was a lovely day in the latter part of June, and his heart grew glad and hopeful in spite of the discouraging conditions of his lot. All the world could not prevent his loving Mildred, or destroy her faith, and at some time and in some way they would attain their happiness. These hopes were like the bright summer sun, and he walked with a firmer and more elastic tread than he had ever known before.

When he reached the haggard old mansion his heart misgave him. "Can it be reality," he asked himself, "that she has been living in places like this?" and the half-defined fear entered his mind that she might have changed somewhat with her fortunes, and might no longer be in appearance the delicate, refined, beautiful girl that he had left so long since. But his impatient heart gave him no time for such imaginings, and he hastened to gratify his intense desire to look upon her face.

In response to a low knock Mildred opened the door, and found herself in the arms of her lover. Then he held her off and looked at her earnestly. "Oh, Millie!" he exclaimed, "you have only grown more beautiful, more womanly in these long, weary years. Your face is the reflex of the letters on which I have lived, and which gave me the power to live."

Then in the excess of his joy he sank into a chair, and, putting his hand upon his heart, looked very pale. She sprang to his side in alarm. "Don't worry, Millie," he said, taking her hand. "It's passing. I don't have them very often now. I'm much better, thanks to you. Happiness rarely kills."

It was well that Mrs. Wheaton and the children were out. This scene would have been a great shock to the good woman, for she was Roger's ally, heart and soul, and did not even know of Arnold's existence. Since Arnold and Mildred were so fortunate as to be alone, they talked frankly over their old happy days, and as far as she could without breaking her promise to Roger, Mildred spoke of the deep sorrows which had almost overwhelmed her during his absence.

"How my heart aches for you!" Arnold said. "I never realized before what sad experiences you have passed through. The part which I can't endure is that I have been of no help to you. On the contrary, you reached out this little hand and saved me. Everything has been just the opposite of what it ought to have been, and even now in these surroundings you are like a diamond in a dust-heap. Oh, how different it would all be if I had my way!" and he in turn told her quite frankly how he was situated.

"Vinton," she said earnestly, "you must do all in your power to grow strong and make a place for yourself in the world. As you say, I cannot punish you for the pride and hostility of your parents; I don't think of them, and I could never take any favors at their hands. As a man you have the right to choose for yourself, and can do so while maintaining the utmost courtesy and respect toward your family. I don't fear poverty—I'm used to it. The thing for you to do is to find some honest work that won't tax you too greatly, and gain strength in its performance."

"Oh, Millie, how strong and true you are! I will take your advice in this as in all respects. But we shall have to wait a long time, I fear. I have so little knowledge of business, and I think my father, influenced by my mother, will thwart rather than help me."

"Very well, I can wait," she answered smilingly. "Indeed I'd rather wait."

Now that her happiness seemed assured, however, she sighed over Roger so often and remorsefully that at last Arnold said,

"You have some trouble on your mind, Millie?"

"You must not expect to find me a light-hearted girl any more," she replied evasively.

"Well," he said, as he clasped her closely in farewell, "my every waking thought shall now be how best to banish sighs and bring smiles."

That evening, while they were out for a walk, Mildred said to Roger, with a little tremor in her voice, "He's come."

He gave her a swift look, and then he turned as quickly away, but his arm grew rigid under her hand.

"Don't fail me, Roger," she pleaded.

"It's unexpected—I wasn't prepared," he said, in a low tone, and then he was silent. He felt her hand trembling so greatly that he soon mastered himself for her sake. "It's all right, Millie," he said heartily. "Be just as happy as you can."

"How can I be truly happy when you are not?" she sighed.

"Bless your kind heart! do you think I am going to stand off and lower at your happiness like a black cloud? Do you think I'm going to droop, look forlorn and deserted, and heave great sighs in dark corners? By all the powers! if I were capable of such meanness toward you, I'd whip myself worse than I did that fellow Bissel."

"Do you think I'll feel for you any the less because you are so good and brave about it?"

"Oh, confound it!" he said impatiently, "you must not feel too much. Spoiling your happiness won't do me any good; it would just make me savage."

She leaned her head for a second against his shoulder and said, "I'm not a bit afraid of you, Roger."

"There, Millie," he said quietly, "you always get the better of the old Satan in me, but I sometimes feel as if I could more easily tame a whole menagerie than my own nature. Come to think of it, it's all turning out for the best. To-morrow I go home on quite a long vacation. Father isn't very well this summer, and I'm to take charge of the harvest for him."

"Isn't this plan a little sudden?" she asked.

"Not more so than your news," he replied grimly.

"Are you not willing to meet him yet?"

"Not quite. After a few weeks in the fields I shall come back with the stoicism and appearance of a wild Indian. Come, Millie, I said I wouldn't fail you, nor shall I. Leave it all to me. I will explain to Mrs. Wheaton to-night, and to our other friends when the right time comes, and I will make it appear all right to them. If I justify you, they should have nothing to say. And now you have nothing to do but accept your happiness and make the most of it. I still request that you do not speak of me to Arnold except in a casual way. When we meet you can introduce me simply as a friend who was kind during your troubles. I'll soon know after we meet whether we can get on together, and if we can't it will save complications for you as well as myself. You must let me serve you in my own way, and I think my judgemnt will be better than yours in this matter."

She was silent for a few moments, and by the light of a lamp he saw that her eyes were full of tears. "Roger," she said softly after a while, "I sometimes think that my affection for you is greater than my love for Vinton, but it is so different. It seems almost like my religion. You are a refuge for me, no matter what happens."

"Thank you, Millie, but I don't deserve such honor."

Mrs. Wheaton could not be brought to look at the situation as Roger did, and she accepted the fact of Vinton Arnold with but a grim acquiescence, which was not mollified by the young man's manner toward her. While meaning to be very kind and polite, he was unconsciously patronizing. She belonged to a class with which he had never had much to do, and in his secret soul he chafed at her presence and her relations to Mildred. While in the abstract he might say that Mildred's associations made no difference to him, he could not in fact overcome his lifelong prejudices, and Mildred's surroundings were not at all to his taste. Luxury and the absence of all that was rude and coarse had become essential to him, and Mrs. Wheaton's cockney English and homely life often gave him cold chills.

Mildred in one respect disappointed him also, for she would take no aid from him, and would in no way deviate from her retired, independent life. "Even if my feelings and principles were not involved," she said, "good taste requires that I conform to my circumstances."

She would take such quiet walks with him as his strength permitted, but would visit no places of public resort. In view of his family's hostility to his course, Arnold did not so much regret this, and so it came about that they spent many of their evenings on the platform over the roof, with the old German astronomer, star-gazing and oblivious, not far away.

While Mildred maintained her loyalty to her old friends, and her resolute plainness and simplicity of life, she considerately recognized that it was all so foreign to her lover's previous experience that she could not expect him to feel as she did. Moreover, his presence renewed her old love for the refined and beautiful, and her heart, that had been so sad and preoccupied, awoke at last to the truth that she was out of her sphere—an exile far from the world her nature craved. Arnold seemed an inseparable part of that old world of beauty and elegance. His every act and word brought it back, and it caused a deepening regret that he was compelled to seek her in her present situation; therefore she also began to share his ill-concealed wish that she might soon escape. Honestly as she loved Mrs. Wheaton, and would love her for all her kindness, the good woman's talk and ways often jarred discordantly on her nerves. Arnold soon discovered this fact, and it made him very impatient over the prospect of life long continued under its present aspects. He was conscious of Mrs. Wheaton's latent hostility, and he had not the tact to conciliate her, nor indeed did he make very great effort to do so. Mildred was very sorry for this, but did not blame him greatly, for she knew her plain old friend could never be to him what she was to those who had learned her goodness and worth in emergencies that had levelled all external differences.

But in spite of the ingredients brought by these facts and the memories of the past, Mildred found the cup of happiness which Arnold pressed to her lips sweet indeed. She had been exceedingly sorrowful for a long time, and it is contrary to nature that the young should cling to sorrow, however true and constant they may be. Her love was a part of her happy girlhood, and now it seemed to have the power to bring back some of her former girlish lightness of heart. The prospects offered by Arnold certainly had little to do with the returning tide of gladness which seemed bearing her from the dark, rugged shores on which she had been nearly wrecked. It was a buoyancy inherent within the love she cherished, and her joy was so sweet, so profound, that she shut her eyes to the future and thought, "For a few days, for a few weeks, we'll just drink deeply at this life-giving fountain. After our long separation it will do us both more good than anything else."

She had said to Arnold that she was willing to wait, that she would rather wait, but she soon began to feel differently. Arnold infused into her nature some of his own dreamy, enervated spirit, and sometimes he would describe to her an imaginary home so exactly to her taste that she would sigh deeply; and one day she remonstrated, "Don't tantalize me with any more such exquisite mirages. Let us rather think of the best and quickest way to secure a real home, and let us be content in it, however humble it must be." But Arnold was far better able to construct an imaginary palace than an ordinary cottage. Although he seemed gaining steadily under the impulse of his happiness, she often trembled to see how frail he was in body and how untrained and impracticable in mind. He was essentially the product of wealth, luxury, and seclusion, and while his intentions might be the best, she was sometimes compelled to doubt his ability to make much headway in the practical, indifferent world. Instead of being discouraged, she only thought, "No one can ever doubt the genuineness of my love. Roger is rich already, and he is certain to become eminent, and yet my love is more than all the world to me, and I so long for a little nook of a home that I could call all my own, that I would be willing to marry Vinton at once and support him myself if his health required it. I don't think I can be like other girls. I shall never get over my pride, but I haven't a particle of ambition. The world at large is nothing to me, and instead of wishing to shine in it, I am best pleased to escape its notice altogether."

Arnold's family were as deeply perplexed as they were incensed at his course. He would not leave the city for any fashionable resort, and they well knew the reason. His father and mother hesitated in their departure, not knowing what "folly," as they termed it, he might be guilty of in their absence. They felt that they must bring the matter to some issue, and yet how to do so puzzled them greatly, for, as he had said, he had done nothing as yet to disgrace them, and his bearing toward them was as irreproachable as it was cold and dignified.

At last, unknown to them, an elder brother undertook to solve the problem. He was a thorough man of the world, and his scrupulous compliance with the requirements of fashionable society led his mother to regard him as a model of propriety. In his private, hidden life he was as unscrupulous as the ultra fashionable often are.

"Vinton," he said one day, "what a fool you are making of yourself in this affair! You have been brought up like a girl, and you are more simple and innocent than they average. I've seen your charmer, and I admit that she is a fine creature. As far as looks go, you show as much judgment as any man in town, but there your wits desert you. Girls in her position are not nice as to terms when they can greatly better themselves. You have money enough to lodge her like a princess compared with her present condition. *Verbum sat sapienti.*"

Vinton replied indignantly that he knew nothing about Mildred.

"Oh, I know all about women," was the confident reply; "have forgotten more than you ever knew."

Nevertheless this thought, like an evil seed, sprang up into a speedy but not rank growth. Arnold saw that his family would regard his marriage as an outrage which they would resent in every possible way, and that their hostility now was but an ill-concealed, smouldering fire. The relation to him would not be what his brother suggested, but as sacred and binding as marriage. His unhealthful reading, his long years abroad, and the radical weakness of his nature prepared him to accept this solution as the easiest and best that circumstances permitted of. He justly doubted whether he would soon, if ever, gain the power of being independent. He knew nothing of business, and hated its turmoil and distractions, and while for Mildred's sake he would attempt anything and suffer anything, he had all the unconquerable shrinking from a manful push out into the world which a timid man feels at the prospect of a battle. He had been systematically trained into weakness, and he felt that men, when he came to compete with them, would discover and take advantage of his defects. His cold, haughty reticence was but disguised timidity. In Mildred's presence he ever showed the best side of his nature, and his lonely, repressed life had always touched the tenderest chords of her heart. If their love had been smiled upon from the first, how different would have been his fate! She would have tenderly developed his dwarfed, crushed manhood, and the result would have been happiness for them both.

"Millie," said Arnold, one starlight night, "do you care very much for the world's opinions?" They were sitting on the platform above the old mansion. The German astronomer, after grumbling awhile at an obscuring haze, had gone downstairs in disgust, and left the lovers to themselves.

"No, Vinton, I never cared much for the world at any time, and now I have an almost morbid impulse to shrink from it altogether. I'm like my dear mamma. Home was her world. Poor, dear mamma!" and she buried her face on his shoulder and shed tears that his presence robbed of much of their bitterness.

"I not only do not care for the world," he said impetuously, "but I hate it. I've been dragged through it, and have ever found it a desert, stony place. My heart just aches for the sweet quiet and seclusion of such a home as you could make, Millie. As it is, I have no home. A hollow iceberg could not be more cold and joyless than my present abode. Neither have you a home. It is only in stolen moments like these, liable to interruption, that we can speak of what is in our hearts;" and then, prompted by his feelings, longings, and the apparently friendless condition of the girl whose head rested so trustingly on his breast, he broached the scheme of life that had taken possession of his imagination.

At first, in her faith and innocence she scarcely understood him, but suddenly she raised her head, and looked at him with startled eyes. "What!" she said, in trembling alarm, "no marriage? Mr. Wentworth and Roger Atwood not present?"

"No minister could make our union more sacred than it would be to me," he faltered, "and as soon as my obdurate parents—"

She sprang to her feet, and exclaimed passionately, "I'd rather die ten thousand deaths than bring a blush of shame to Roger Atwood's face." Then she sank into her chair in an uncontrollable outburst of grief. He pleaded with her, but she was deaf; he tried to caress her, but although half unconscious from her agony, she repulsed him. "Oh, oh," she moaned, "is this the sole reward of my fidelity?"

"Millie, Millie," he entreated, "you will kill me if you cannot control yourself. I will do anything you say—submit to any terms. Oh, pity me, or I shall die."

"Leave me," she said faintly.

"Never," he cried; "I'd sooner cast myself down from this height."

By visible and painful effort she at last grew calm enough to say firmly:

"Mr. Arnold, I do pity you. Even at this moment I will try to do you justice. My heart seems broken, and yet I fear you will suffer more than I. My own womanhood would make your words the sufficient cause for our final separation, and had I not a friend in the world we could never meet again. But I have a friend, a brother to whom I owe more than life, and whom I love better than life. He would have made me rich if I would have let him, but I loved you too well. Not for my hope of heaven would I make him blush for me. I would have married you and lived in a single room in a tenement. I would have supported you with my own hands. The weaknesses for which you were not to blame drew my heart toward you, but you have shown a defect in your character to-night which creates an impassable gulf between us. In view of the wrong done you by others I forgive you—I shall pray God to forgive you—but we have fatally misunderstood each other. If you have any manhood at all, if you have the ordinary instincts of a gentleman, you will respect the commands of an orphan girl, and leave me, never to approach me again."

Speechless, almost paralyzed in his despair, he tottered to the steps and disappeared.

CHAPTER XLVII

LIGHT AT EVENTIDE

AS Mrs. Wheaton crossed the hallway from a brief call on a neighbor, Vinton Arnold passed her. She noted by the light of the lamp in her hand that his pallor was ghostlike, and she asked quickly:

"Vere is Miss Jocelyn?"

He paid no more heed to her than if he were a shadow of a man, and went by her with wavering, uncertain steps, without a word. In sudden alarm she hastened to the roof, and found Mildred kneeling by her chair, weeping and almost speechless from grief. She took the girl in her arms, and said excitedly, "Vat did he say to you?"

"Oh," sobbed Mildred, "my heart is broken at last. I feel as mamma did when she said her heart was bleeding away. Mrs. Wheaton, I shall stay with you now as long as I live, and it seems as if it wouldn't be very long. Never speak of him again—never speak of it to a living soul. He asked that which would banish you and Roger—dear, brave, patient Roger—from my side forever, and I will never see his face again. Oh, oh, I wish I could die!"

"I'm a plain voman," Mrs. Wheaton said grimly, "but I took the measure of 'im soon as I clapped my heyes on 'im; but, Millie, me darlin', you couldn't be so cruel as to break hour 'earts by dying for sich a man. You vould make the vorld black for us hall, yer know. Come, dear, come vith me. I'll take care hof yer. I'm not fine like 'im that's gone, thank the Lord, but I'll never ax ye to do haught that Mr. Ventvorth vouldn't bless," and she half supported the exhausted, trembling girl to her room, and there was tender and tireless in her ministrations. In the early dawn, when at last Mildred slept for an hour or two, she wrote, in a half-eligible scrawl, to Roger, "Come back. Millie wants you."

His presence in response was prompt indeed. On the second morning after the events described, Mildred sat in her chair leaning back with closed eyes. Mrs. Wheaton was away at work, and her eldest daughter was watching the little brood of children on the sidewalk. A decided knock at the door caused the young girl to start up with apprehension. She was so nervously prostrated that she trembled like a leaf. At last she summoned courage and opened the door slightly, and when she saw Roger's sunburned, honest face she welcomed him as if he were a brother indeed.

He placed her gently in her chair again, and said, with a keen look into her eyes, "How is this, Millie? I left you happy and even blooming, and now you appear more pale and broken than ever before. You look as if you had been seriously ill. Oh, Millie, that couldn't be, and you not let me know," and he clasped her hand tightly as he spoke.

She buried her burning face on his shoulder, and said, in a low, constrained tone, "Roger, I've told Mr. Arnold this much about you—I said I'd die ten thousand deaths rather than cause you to blush for me."

He started as if he had been shot. "Great God!" he exclaimed, "and did he ask you aught that would make you blush?"

Bitter tears were Mildred's only answer.

The young man's passion for a few moments was terrible, but Mildred's pallid face soon calmed him. "You could not harm him," she said sadly. "What is one blow more to a man who is in torture? I pity him from the depths of my soul, and you must promise me to let him alone. Never for a moment did I forget that you were my brother."

In strong revulsion of feeling he bent one knee at her

side and pleaded, "Oh, Millie, give me the right to protect you. I'll wait for you till I'm gray. I'll take what love you can give me. I'll be devotion itself."

"Don't, Roger," she said wearily. "I love you too well to listen. Such words only wound me. Oh, Roger, be patient with me. You don't understand, you never will understand. I do give you the right to protect me; but don't talk that way again. I just long for rest and peace. Roger, my friend, my brother," she said, lifting her eyes appealingly to his, and giving him both of her hands, "don't you see? I can give you everything in this way, but in the way you speak of—nothing. My heart is as dead as poor Belle's."

"Your wish shall be my law," he said gently.

"And you'll not harm Mr. Arnold?"

"Not if it will hurt you."

"I never wish to see or hear from him again, and you'll never have cause to fear any one else."

"Millie," he said sadly, "it is for you I fear most. You look so sad, pale, and broken-hearted. There isn't a sacrifice I wouldn't make for you. Millie, you won't let this thing crush you? It would destroy me if you did. We will resume our old quiet life, and you shall have rest of body and soul;" and he kept his word so well that, before many months passed, her mind regained sufficient tone and strength to enable her to engage in the simple duties of life with something like zest. He talked to her about many of his studies, he searched the stores for the books which he thought would be to her taste, and took her to see every beautiful work of art on exhibition. In spite of her poverty, he daily made her life richer and fuller of all that he knew to be congenial to her nature. While she gained in serenity and in capability for quiet enjoyment, he was positively happy, for he believed that before many years passed she would be ready to spend the rest of life at his side. He meantime was pursuing his studies with a vigor and success that inspired his friends with the most sanguine hopes.

Vinton Arnold, on that terrible night when his false dream of life was shattered, went through the streets as oppressed with shame and despair as if he were a lost spirit. As he was slowly and weakly climbing the stairs his father called him to the sitting-room, where he and his wife were in consultation, feeling that matters must be brought to some kind of a settlement, Mrs. Arnold urging extreme measures, and her husband bent on some kind of compromise. As his son entered, the old gentleman started up, exclaiming:

"Good God, my boy, what is the matter?"

"He's going to have one of his bad turns," said his mother, rising hastily.

"Hush, both of you," he commanded sternly, and he sat down near the door. Fixing a look of concentrated hatred on his mother, he said slowly, "Madam, you are not willing that I should marry Mildred Jocelyn."

"And with very good reason," she replied, a little confused by his manner.

"Well, let it rejoice such heart as you have—I shall never marry her."

"What do you mean?"

"I mean never to speak to you again after this brief interview. I am a lost man—lost beyond hope, and you are the cause. If you had had a mother's heart my father would not have been so obdurate. Since you would not let me marry her, I was tempted by my love and the horrible life I lead in this house to offer her a relation which would have been marriage to me, but from which her proud, pure spirit recoiled, as I recoil from you, and I shall never see her face again in this world or in any world. Your work is finished. You need not scheme or threaten any more. While she is as good as an angel of heaven, she is as proud as you are, and you have murdered my hope—my soul. Father, I have but one request to make to you. Give me money enough to live anywhere except under this roof. No, no more words to-night, unless you would have me die in your presence with curses on my lips. I have reached the utmost limit;" and he abruptly left the room.

Mrs. Arnold took refuge in hysterics, and her husband rang violently for her maid, and then locked himself up in his library, where he walked the floor for many an hour. The next morning he tried to make overtures to his son, but he found the young man deaf and stony in his despair. "It's too late," was all that he would say.

"Oh, let him alone," protested his wife irritably, as her husband came down looking sorely troubled; "Vinton will indulge in high tragedy for a few months, and then settle down to sensible life," and in the hope of this solution the old merchant went gloomily to his business.

That day Vinton Arnold left his home, and it was years before he returned.

Two years or more passed away in quiet, toilsome days for Mildred. She had gained serenity, and apparently had accepted her lot without repining. Indeed, thanks to Roger's unfaltering devotion, it was not a monotonous or a sad one. He let her heart rest, hoping, trusting that some day it would wake from its sleep. In compliance with her wish he was in semblance a brother, and his attentions were so quiet and frank, his manner toward her so restful, that even she half believed at times that his regard for her was passing into the quiet and equable glow of fraternal love. Such coveted illusions could not be long maintained, however, for occasionally when he was off his guard she would find him looking at her in a way that revealed how much he repressed. She shed many bitter tears over what she termed his "obstinate love," but an almost morbid conviction had gained possession of her mind that unless she could return his affection in kind and degree she ought not to marry him.

At last she began to grow a little restless under her rather aimless life, and one day she said to her pastor, Mr. Wentworth, "I want a career—isn't that what you call it? I'm tired of being a sewing-woman, and soon I shall be a wrinkled spinster. Isn't there something retired and quiet which a girl with no more brains and knowledge than I have can do?"

"Yes," he said gravely; "make a home for Roger."

She shook her head. "That is the only thing I can't do for him," she replied very sadly. "God only knows how truly I love him. I could give him my life, but not the heart of a wife. I have lost everything except truth to my womanly nature. I must keep that. Moreover, I'm too good a friend of Roger's to marry him. He deserves the strong first love of a noble woman, and it will come to him some day. Do you think I could stand before you and God's altar and promise what is impossible? No, Mr. Wentworth, Roger has a strength and force of character which will carry him past all this, and when once he sees I have found a calling to which I can devote all my energies, he will gradually become reconciled to the truth, and finally accept a richer happiness than I could ever bring him."

"You are an odd girl, Mildred, but perhaps you are right. I've learned to have great faith in you. Well, I know of a career which possibly may suit you. It would open an almost limitless field of usefulness," and he told her of the Training School for Nurses in connection with Bellevue Hospital.

The proposition took Mildred's fancy greatly, and it was arranged that they should visit the institution on the following afternoon. Roger sighed when he heard of the project, but only remarked patiently, "Anything you wish, Millie."

"Dear old fellow," she thought; "he doesn't know I'm thinking of him more than myself."

Mildred made her friend Clara Wilson and her brother and sister a long visit the following summer, and in the fall entered on her duties, her zest greatly increased by the prospect of being able before very long to earn enough to give Fred and Minnie a good education. The first year of her training passed uneventfully away, she bringing to her tasks genuine sympathy for suffering, and unusual aptness and ability. Her own sorrowful experience made her tender toward the unfortunate ones for whom she cared, and her words and manner brought balm and healing to many sad hearts that were far beyond the skill of the hospital surgeons.

During the first half of the second year, in accordance with the custom of the School, she responded to calls from wealthy families wherein there were cases of such serious illness as to require the services of a trained nurse, and in each instance she so won the confidence of the attending physician and the affection of the family as to make them personal friends. Her beautiful face often attracted to her not a little attention, but she was found to be as unapproachable as a Sister of Charity. Roger patiently waited, and filled the long months with unremitting toil.

One evening toward the latter part of the first six months of her outside work, Mildred returned from nursing a patient back to health. She found the lady in charge of the institution in much tribulation. "Here is Mrs. Sheppard, from one of the most influential families on Fifth Avenue, offering anything for a nurse. Her brother is dying with consumption, she says. He has a valet in attendance, but the physician in charge says he needs a trained nurse, for he wants constant watching. He is liable to die at any moment. We haven't a nurse unemployed. Do you feel too tired to go?"

"Oh, no," said Mildred. "My patient improved so much that for the last week I've almost been resting."

"And you think you can go?"

"Certainly."

"I'll tell Mrs. Sheppard then to send for you in a couple of hours. That will give you time to get ready."

Two hours later Mildred was driven rapidly by a coachman in livery to a mansion on Fifth Avenue, and she was speedily ushered into the room where the patient lay. He was sleeping at the time, with curtains drawn and his face turned away. Mildred only glanced at him sufficiently to see that he was very much emaciated. A middle-aged lady who introduced herself as Mrs. Sheppard received her, saying, "I'm so glad you are here, for I am overcome with fatigue. Last night he was very restless and ill, and would have no one near him except myself. His valet is in that room just across the hall, and will come at the slightest summons. Now while my brother is sleeping I will rest at once. My room is here, opening into this. Call me if there is need, and don't mind if he talks strangely. Your room is there, just beyond this one," and with a few directions, given with the air of extreme weariness, she passed to her own apartment, and was soon sleeping soundly.

Mildred sat down in the dim room where the light fell upon her pure, sweet profile, which was made a little more distinct by the flickering of the cannel-coal fire, and began one of the quiet watches to which she was becoming so accustomed. Her thoughts were very painful at first, for they seemed strangely inclined to dwell on Vinton Arnold. From the time they parted she had heard nothing of him, and since the brief explanation that she had been compelled to give to Roger, his name had not passed her lips. He had been worse than dead to her, and she wondered if he were dead. She had never cherished any vindictive feelings toward him, and even now her eyes filled with tears of commiseration for his wronged and wretched life. Then by a conscious effort she turned her thoughts to the friend who had never failed her. "Dear Roger," she murmured, "he didn't appear well the last time I saw him. He is beginning to look worn and thin. I know he is studying too hard. Oh, I wish my heart were not so perverse, for he needs some one to take care of him. He can't change; he doesn't get over it as I hoped he would," and her eyes, bent on the fire, grew dreamy and wistful.

Unknown to herself, she was watched by one who scarcely dared to breathe lest what seemed a vision should vanish. The dying man was Vinton Arnold. His married sister, overcome by weariness and the stupor of sleep, had inadvertently forgotten to mention his name, and Mildred was under the impression that the name of her patient was Sheppard. She had never been within the Arnold mansion, nor was she specially familiar with its exterior. Entering it hastily on a stormy night, she had not received the faintest suggestion that it was the home to which she and her mother had once dreamed she might be welcomed.

When at last Arnold had awakened, he saw dimly, sitting by the fire, an unfamiliar form, which nevertheless suggested the one never absent from his thoughts. Noiselessly he pushed the lace curtain aside, and to his unspeakable wonder his eyes seemed to rest on Mildred Jocelyn. "She is dead," he first thought, "and it is her spirit. Or can it be that my reason is leaving me utterly, and the visions of my tortured mind are becoming more real than material things? Oh, see," he murmured, "there are tears in her eyes. I could almost imagine that a good angel had taken her guise and was weeping over one so lost and wrecked as I am. Now her lips move—she is speaking softly to herself. Great God! can it be real? Or is it that my end is near, and long-delayed mercy gives me this sweet vision before I die?"

His sombre and half-superstitious conjectures were almost dispelled by a little characteristic act on Mildred's part—an act that contained a suggestion of hope for Roger. In awakening the stronger traits of manhood in the latter she had also evoked an appreciation of beauty and a growing love for it. Mildred was human enough not to regret that this developing sense should find its fullest gratification in herself. Though so determined to become a wrinkled spinster, she found a secret and increasing pleasure in the admiring glances that dwelt upon her face and dainty figure, and this fact might have contained for him, had he known it, a pleasing hint. It must be confessed that she no longer wished to go into his presence without adding a little grace to her usually plain attire; and now that she was thinking so deeply of him she involuntarily raised her hand to adjust her coquettish nurse's cap, which by some feminine magic all her own she ever contrived to make a becoming head-dress rather than a badge of office.

Even to Vinton Arnold's perturbed and disordered mind the act was so essentially feminine and natural, so remote from ghostly weirdness, that he raised himself on his elbow and exclaimed, "Millie, Millie Jocelyn!"

"Ah," cried Mildred starting from her chair and looking fearfully toward the half-closed door of Mrs. Sheppard's room. In her turn her heart beat quickly, with the sudden superstitious fear which the strongest of us cannot control when we seem close to the boundaries of the unseen world. "It was *his* voice," she murmured.

"Millie, oh, Millie, are you real, or is it a dream?"

She took two or three steps toward the bed, stopped, and covered her face with her hands.

"Oh, speak!" he cried in agony. "I do not know whether I am dreaming or awake, or whether I now see as if before me the one ever in my thoughts. You hide your face from me," he groaned, sinking back despairingly. "You have come for a brief moment to show me that I can never look upon your face again."

Mildred thought swiftly. Her first impulse was to depart at once, and then her womanly pity and sense of duty gained the mastery. Vinton Arnold was now a dying man, and she but a trained nurse. Perhaps God's hand was in their strange and unexpected meeting, and it was His will that the threads of two lives that had been bound so closely should not be severed in fatal evil. Should she thwart His mercy?

"Mr. Arnold," she said, in an agitated voice, "this is a strange and undreamed-of meeting. Let me quiet your mind, however, by telling you how simple and matter-of-fact are the causes which led to it. I am now a professional nurse from the Training School connected with Bellevue Hospital, and your sister, having sent to the School for assistance, obtained my services as she might those of any of my associates. In view—perhaps—it would be best for one of them to take my place."

He was strongly moved, and listened panting and trembling in his weakness. "Millie," at last he faltered, "is there any God at all? Is there any kind or merciful spirit in nature? If so, you have been sent to me, for I am dying of remorse. Since you bade me leave you I have suffered tortures, day and night, that I cannot describe. I have often been at the point of taking my own life, but something held me back. Can it be that it was for this hour? Mildred, I am dying. The end of a most unhappy life is very near. Is there no mercy in your faith—no mercy in your strong, pure womanly heart?"

"Vinton," she said gently, "I believe you are right. God has sent me to you. I will not leave you until it is best."

"Millie, Millie," he pleaded, "forgive me. I cannot believe in God's forgiveness until you forgive me."

"I forgave you from the first, Vinton, because I knew there was no cold-blooded evil in your mind, and I have long felt that you were more sinned against than sinning. If I stay I must impose one condition—there must be no words concerning the past. That is gone forever."

"I know it, Mildred. I killed your love with my own hand, but the blow was more fatal to me than to you."

"Can you not rally and live?" she asked tearfully.

"No," he said, with a deep breath. "Moreover, I have no wish to live. The dark shadow of my life will soon fall on you no more, but the hope that I may breathe my last with you near brings a deep content and peace. Does any one yet suspect who you are?"

"No. I fear Mrs. Arnold will not think it best."

"I have never spoken to Mrs. Arnold since that awful night, and if she interferes now I will curse her with my last breath. This is my one hope—my one gleam of light in the life she has cursed—"

"Hush, oh hush! Unless my presence brings quietness I cannot stay," for at the name of his mother he became dangerously agitated. "I will tell Mrs. Sheppard in the morning, and I think she will arrange it so that I can do all in my power for you."

"No," he replied, after a little thought, "I will tell her. She is unlike my mother and other sisters, and has a good heart. She has taken entire charge of me, but I was in such a hell of suffering at the thought of dying without one word from you that I was almost a maniac. I will be quiet now. Leave all to me; I can make her understand."

When Mrs. Sheppard entered, as the late dawn began to mingle with the gaslight, she found her brother sleeping quietly, his hand clasping Mildred's. To her slight expression of surprise the young girl returned a clear, steadfast look, and said calmly, "When your brother awakes he has some explanations to make. I am Mildred Jocelyn."

The lady sank into a chair and looked at her earnestly. "I have long wished to see you," she murmured. "Vinton has told me everything. I was so overcome with sleep and fatigue last night that I neither told you his name nor asked yours. Did you not suspect where you were?"

"Not until he awoke and recognized me."

"Was he greatly agitated?"

"Yes, at first. It was so unexpected that he thought me a mere illusion of his own mind."

"Miss Jocelyn, I believe God sent you to him."

"So he thinks."

"You won't leave him till—till— It can't be long."

"That depends upon you, Mrs. Sheppard. I am very, very sorry for him," and tears came into her eyes.

Low as was the murmur of their voices, Arnold awoke and glanced with troubled eyes from one to the other before it all came back to him; but his sister brought quiet and rest by saying gently, as she kissed him:

"Vinton, Miss Jocelyn shall not leave you."

CHAPTER XLVIII

"GOOD ANGEL OF GOD"

THE young nurse soon became known through the house simply as Miss Mildred. With the exception of Mrs. Sheppard, the valet, and the physician, no one entered the sick-room except Mr. Arnold, and the old man often lingered and hovered around like a remorseful ghost. He had grown somewhat feeble, and no longer went to his business. His son had tolerated his presence since he had come home to die, but had little to say to him, for the bitterness of his heart extended to the one who had yielded to his mother's hardness and inveterate worldliness. In the secrecy of his heart the old merchant admitted that he had been guilty of a fatal error, and the consequences had been so terrible to his son that he had daily grown more conscience-smitten; but his wife had gained such an ascendency over him in all social and domestic questions that beyond occasional protests he had let matters drift until Vinton returned from his long exile in Europe. The hope that his son would get over what his wife called "an absurd youthful folly" was now rudely dispelled, and in bitterness he reproached himself that he had not adopted a different course.

From the way in which he came in and looked at his son when he was sleeping, it was soon revealed to Mildred how he felt, and she pitied him also.

Mrs. Sheppard was a wealthy widow, and the eldest daughter. She was for the present making her home under the paternal roof. Unlike her mother, she had quick, strong sympathies, which sorrows of her own had deepened. She had assumed the care of her brother, and infused into her ministry a tenderness which at last led the imbittered heart to reveal itself to her. She was therefore already prepared to be Mildred's sincere ally in bringing a little light into the late evening-tide of her brother's clouded day.

Most of the time she sat in her own room with the door ajar, leaving Vinton to the ministrations of his nurse. He required far less care now, for he seemed content to rest as one might during a respite from torture. His eyes would follow Mildred with a pathetic longing when he was awake, and when she took his hand and told him to sleep he would obey like a child. He seemed better because so quiet, but he grew weaker daily. All knew, and none better than himself, that life was slowly ebbing. His father came in more frequently than ever, for his son showed no restlessness at his presence now. At Mildred's request Vinton even began to greet him with something like a welcome, and the young girl did all in her power to make the old gentleman feel at home; sometimes she would place a large easy-chair by the fire and ask him to sit with them. He was glad to comply, and often looked wonderingly and earnestly at the fair young nurse that was working such a transformation in the patient. He once or twice tried to become better acquainted with her, but ever found her gentle, deferential, and very reserved.

Twice Mildred asked Vinton to let her send for Mr. Wentworth, but he shook his head and said that she alone could do him any good. "Read the Bible to me when you feel like it. I'll listen to you, but my best hope is to sleep so quietly that I shall have no dreams. If that cannot be, I'll remember that you forgave me."

"Such words make me very sad," she replied, on the latter occasion, tears rushing into her eyes.

"I am not worthy that you should care so much," he said. "What am I but a flickering rush-light which your hand is shielding that it may burn out quietly?"

"Vinton, you are wrong. The life which God has given you cannot cease. I am not wise and learned, and I have an almost unconquerable diffidence in speaking on these subjects, except to children and the poor and ignorant. But since you won't see any one else, I must speak. You say God sent me to you, and I accept your belief, but He did not send me to you merely to relieve physical pain and mental disquiet. If a man is stumbling toward an abyss of darkness, is it any great kindness to hold a lamp so that his last steps may be easier? There is for each one of us a vital truth and a sacred duty, and in shutting your eyes to these and living in the present hour, you show—pardon an honest friend for saying it—you show a more fatal weakness than you have yet manifested."

"You are mistaken, Mildred," he said bitterly. "As far as I am concerned, what truth is there for me to contemplate except a wasted, unhappy life, wrecked and shamed beyond remedy, beyond hope. I long ago lost what trace of manhood I once had. Never dream that because you have forgiven me I shall forgive myself. No, no," he said, with a dark vindictiveness in his eyes, "there are three that I shall never forgive, and I am one of them. As for duty, the word is torment. What can I do—I who can scarcely raise my hand? My day is over, my chance has gone by forever. Don't interrupt me. I know you would speak of the consolations of religion, but I'd rather go to the devil himself—if there is one—than to such a God as my mother worships; and she has always been a very religious woman. The whole thing long since became a farce to me at our church. It was just as much a part of the fashionable world that blighted me as the rest of society's mummeries. You never went there after you had real trouble to contend with. It was the last place that you would think of going to for comfort or help. The thought of you alone has kept me from utter unbelief, and I would be glad to believe that there is some kindly power in existence that watches over such beings as you are, and that can reward your noble life; but as far as I am concerned it's all a mystery and a weariness. You are near—you are merciful and kind. This is all the heaven I expect. It is far more than I deserve. Let me rest, Mildred. It will be but for a few more days. Then when you close my eyes, may I sleep forever," and he leaned back faint and exhausted. He would not let her interrupt him, for he seemed bent on settling the question as far as he was concerned, and dismissing it finally.

She listened with fast-falling tears, and answered sighingly, "Oh, I do wish you would see Mr. Wentworth. You are so wrong—so fatally mistaken."

"No," he said firmly, "I will see no one but you."

"Oh, what shall I say to you?"

"Do not grieve so about me. You cannot change anything. You cannot give me your strong, grand nature any more than you can your beautiful life and perfect health. I could become a Catholic and worship St. Mildred," he added with a smile, trying to banish her tears. "The only duty that I am capable of is to try to make as little trouble as possible, and to cease making it altogether soon. Go and rest, and I will too, for I'm very tired."

"No," she said resolutely. "My mission to you must not end so weakly, so uselessly. Will you do me a favor?"

"I?"

"Yes; listen quietly and honestly;" and she read the first verses of the nineteenth chapter of St. John, ending with the words, "Behold the man."

"Vinton," she said eagerly, "the truth to which I referred was embodied truth, and your first sacred duty is to look to Him and live. To the last conscious moment of life this will remain your first and most sacred duty, and were you the strongest man in this city you could not do more. It's not a question of religions at all, or of what other people are or believe. The words I have read have brought you face to face with this Divine Man, who came to seek and save that which was lost. Never did a despairing human soul cry out to Him in vain. He is as real as I am. His tender pity is infinitely beyond mine. Far better and wiser would it be for you to turn from me than from Him. Oh, merciful Christ, how the world wrongs Thee'" and she buried her face in her hands and sobbed bitterly.

"Millie, please don't," he entreated. "I can't endure to see you so grieved."

"Forgive me—I am forgetting myself sadly; but how can I see you so hopeless, so despairing, when there is no more need of it than of your refusing what I try to do for your comfort? There, rest now, but think of what I've said. I may have done wrong to tire you so, but to minister to the body only, when the soul, the man within you, is in such infinite need seems but a mockery. If you continue to wrong Him who should be the one great hope of every human heart, you will sadden all my days. My mission will be but a poor one indeed."

He was very much exhausted, but he said gently, "I will think of it, and may the One you serve so faithfully bless you for your divine pity. What you have said seems to make everything different; you appear to have something real and definite in your mind. Give me your hand and I will rest; then, my good angel, teach me your faith."

This Mildred did almost wholly from God's own word. At first it was hard for him to believe that there were any possibilities for one like him, but at last he accepted the truth that God is not willing that the least should perish. "The mystery of life is something that the wisest cannot solve," she said to him, "but the best hopes of the world have ever centred about this Divine Friend. Burdened hearts have gone to Him in every age and found rest. Oh, how often He has comforted me when mine seemed breaking! In response to a simple trust He gives a hope, a life which I do not think can be found elsewhere, and in the limitless future that which was all wrong here may be made right and perfect."

"So this is your revenge, Millie. You come and bring me this great hope."

"No, God sent me."

Mildred's mission to the sad-hearted Mrs. Sheppard was almost as sacred and useful as to her brother, and they had many long talks which possessed all the deep interest which is imparted by experiences that leave a lasting impress on memory.

Every day increased the bitter regret that short-sighted worldliness had blighted one life and kept from others one who had such rare powers of creating all that constitutes a home.

To Roger Mildred had written almost daily, telling him everything. Her letters were so frank and sincere that they dispelled the uneasiness which first took possession of his mind, and they gradually disarmed him of his hostility to the dying man. There is a point in noble souls beyond which enmity falters and fails, and he felt that Mildred's course toward Arnold was like the mercy of God. He reverenced the girl who like an angel of mercy was bringing hope to a despairing soul.

"Laura," said old Mr. Arnold to Mrs. Sheppard one evening as she was sitting with him in his library, "this young nurse is a continual surprise to me."

"What do you mean, papa?"

"Well, she impresses me strangely. She has come to us as a professional nurse, and yet I have never seen a more perfect gentlewoman. There is a subtle grace and refinement about her which is indescribable. No wonder Vinton has been made better by her care. I wouldn't mind being sick myself if I could have her about me. That girl has a history. How comes she in such a position?"

"I think her position a very exalted one," said his daughter warmly. "Think what an infinite blessing and comfort she has been in our household."

"True, true enough; but I didn't expect any such person to be sent to us."

"I am perfectly ready to admit that this young girl is an unusual character, and have no doubt that she has had a history that would account for her influence. But you are in error if you think that these trained nurses are recruited from the ranks of commonplace women. Many of them come from as good families as ours, and have all the instincts of a true lady. They have a noble calling, and I envy them."

"Well, you know more about it than I do, but I think this Miss Mildred a rare type of woman. It's not her beautiful face, for she has a charm, a winsomeness that is hard to define or account for. She makes me think of some subtle perfume that is even sweeter than the flower from which it is distilled. Would to God Vinton had met such a girl at first! How different it all might have been!"

Mrs. Sheppard left the room so hastily as to excite her father's surprise.

One day Vinton said to Mildred, "How can I be truly forgiven unless I forgive? I now see that I have wronged God's love even more than my mother has wronged me, and in my deep gratitude from the consciousness of God's forgiveness I would like to forgive her and be reconciled before I die. To my brother I will send a brief message—I can't see him again, for the ordeal would be too painful. As for my father, I have long ceased to cherish enmity against him. He, like myself, is, in a certain sense, a victim of our family pride."

"Vinton," Mildred replied, "I cannot tell you how glad I am to hear you speak so. I have been waiting and hoping for this, for it is proof that your feeling is not mere emotion and sentiment. You now propose to do something that is more than manly—it is divine. God's greatest, dearest, most godlike prerogative is to forgive, and man's noblest act is to forgive a great wrong. Vinton, you have now won my respect."

She never forgot his answering glance. "Millie," he said softly, "I can die happy now. I never expected more than your pity."

"If you will do this, your memory will become sweet

and ennobled in my heart. Your action will show me how grandly and swiftly God can develop one who has been wronged by evil."

"God bless you, my good angel. Ask my sister to send for my father and mother at once. I feel a little stronger this evening, and yet I think the beginning of my new life is very near."

Mildred went into Mrs. Sheppard's room and told her of Vinton's purpose. She looked at the young girl for a moment with eyes blinded by tears, and then clasped her in a close, passionate embrace which was more eloquent than any words. "Oh, Mildred," she said, with a low sob, "if you only could have been my sister!" Then she hastened to carry out her brother's wishes.

The fire burned brightly in the grate, the softened lights diffused a mild radiance through the room, and the old impression of gloom was utterly absent when Vinton's parents entered. Neither Mrs. Arnold nor her husband was quite able to hide the surprise and embarrassment felt at the unexpected summons, but Mr. Arnold went promptly to the bedside, and, taking his son's hand, said huskily, "I'll come any time you wish, my dear boy, be it night or day."

Vinton gave as warm a pressure in answer as his feebleness permitted, and then he said gravely, "I wish you and mother to sit here close to me, for I must speak low, and my words must be brief. I have but a little fragment of life left to me, and must hasten to perform the few duties yet within my power."

"Had not this young woman better retire?" suggested Mrs. Arnold, glancing coldly at Mildred, who stood in the background, Mrs. Sheppard detaining her by a strong, warm clasp of her hand.

"No," said Vinton decisively, "she must remain. Were it not for the influence of this Christian—not religious, but Christian—girl, you would never have seen my face again, with my consent. In showing me how God forgives the sinful, she has taught me how to forgive. Mother, I never expected to forgive you, but I do from my heart. I am far beyond the world and all worldly considerations. In the clear light of the endless life to which we are all hastening, I see as never before how small, petty, and unworthy are those unnatural principles which blight human life at fashion's bidding. Mother, I wish to do you justice. You tried to care for me in my childhood and youth. You spared yourself no expense, no trouble, but you could not seem to understand that what I needed was sympathy and love —that my heart was always repressed and unhappy. The human soul, however weak, is not like an exotic plant. It should be tended by a hand that is as gentle as it is firm and careful. I found one who combined gentleness with strength; stern, lofty principle with the most beautiful and delicate womanhood; and you know how I lost her. Could I have followed the instincts of my heart, my fate would have been widely different. But that is now all past. You did not mean to wrong me so terribly. It was only because your own life was all wrong that you wronged me. Your pride and prejudice prevented you from knowing the truth concerning the girl I loved. Mother, I am dying, and my last earnest counsel to you and father is that you will obey the words of the loftiest and greatest, 'Learn of me, for I meek and lowly in heart, and ye shall find rest unto your souls.' If you cannot do this, your lives will be a more wretched failure than mine has been. Bury your worldly pride in my grave, and learn to be gentle and womanly, and may God forgive you as truly as I do."

As he spoke slowly and feebly, the cold, proud woman began to tremble and weep, and when his words ceased she sank on her knees at his bedside and sobbed, "Oh, what have I done? Must I bear the remorse of having murdered my own child?"

"No, mother, you were blinded as I was. You will be forgiven as I have been. In the better home of heaven we'll find the secret of our true relationship which we missed here. Good-by now. I must hasten, for I am very weak."

Mrs. Arnold rose, put her arms around her son and kissed him, and her daughter supported her from the room, Vinton's eyes following her sorrowfully until she disappeared. Then he said, "Dear old father, come and sit close beside me."

He came, and bowed his head upon his son's hand.

"Millie," he called feebly to the young girl who stood by the fire with her face buried in her hands. She came at once. "God bless you for those tears. They fall like dew into my soul. Millie, I feel as if—I don't know what it means—it seems as if I might go to my rest now. The room is growing dark, and I seem to see you more in my mind than with my eyes. Millie, will you—can you so far forgive me as to take my head upon your bosom and let me say my last words near your heart?"

"Great God!" cried his father, starting up, "is he dying?"

"Father, please be calm. Keep my hand. Let my end come as I wish. Millie, Millie, won't you?"

Her experienced eyes saw that his death was indeed at hand—that his life had but flickered up brightly once more before expiring. Therefore she gratified his final wish, and took his head upon her breast.

"Rest, rest at last," he sighed.

"Father," he said after a moment or two, "look at this dear girl who has saved my soul from death." The old man lifted his head and gazed upon the pure, sweet face at which he had looked so often and questioningly before.

"Oh, Vinton, Vinton, God forgive me! I see it all. Our insane pride and prejudice kept a good angel from our home."

"Yes, father, this is Mildred Jocelyn. Was I wrong to love her?"

"Oh, blind, blind fool that I've been!" the old man groaned.

"Don't grieve so, father. If you will listen to her words, her mission to us all will be complete. She is fatherless. Be kind to her after I am gone."

The old man rose slowly and leaned his brow on Mildred's head. "My child," he said brokenly, "all my love for Vinton shall now go to you, and his portion shall be yours."

"God bless you, father. Good-by now. Let me sleep," and his eyes closed wearily.

"That's right, my boy; you'll be better in the morning," and with feeble, faltering steps he left the room, murmuring, "Oh, that I had only known in time!"

Mrs. Sheppard now entered and took his place. For a little time Vinton seemed to sleep. Then he opened his eyes and looked slowly around. They kindled into loving recognition as they rested on his sister. "Laura, your patience and mercy toward me have been rewarded," he whispered. "Say to Mansfield and my other brother and sisters what I told you. Be as kind to Mildred as you have been to me. Good-by."

"Millie, Millie, good angel of God to me, farewell for a little while."

His eyes closed again, his breath came more and more slowly, and at last it ceased. His sister put her hand over his heart. His sad, thwarted life had ended on earth.

Mildred kissed him for the first time in her ministry, and murmured, as she gently laid his head back upon the pillow, "Thank God, it has not ended as I feared!"

CHAPTER XLIX

HOME

WE take up the thread of our story after the lapse of several months. Mildred left the Arnold family softened and full of regret. Even proud Mrs. Arnold asked her forgiveness with many bitter tears, but beyond a few little significant gifts they found it impossible to make the one toward whom their hearts were now so tender take more than the regular compensation that went toward the support of the institution to which she belonged. Mr. Arnold and Mrs. Sheppard would not give her up, and often came to see her, and the old gentleman always made her promise that when he became ill she would take care of him; and once he whispered to her, "You won' take anything from me now, but in my will I can remember my debt. All my wealth cannot pay what I owe to you."

"Money has nothing to do with my relations to you," she replied gently.

"Vinton's portion belongs to you," was his quiet reply. "The poor boy so understood it, and I shall not break faith with the dead."

"Then his portion shall go toward relieving suffering in this city," was her answer.

"You can do what you please with it, for it shall be yours."

While Mildred quietly performed her duties as head-nurse in one of the wards during the last six months of the two years of her sojourn at the Training School, some important changes had occurred in Roger's circumstances. He had, more than a year before, graduated second in his class at college, and had given the impression that he would have been first had he taken the full four years' course. His crotchety uncle, with whom since the reconciliation he had resided, had died, and after a few months his wife followed him, and Roger found himself a wealthy man, but not a happy one. Beyond giving his parents every comfort which they craved, and making his sister Susan quite an heiress, he scarcely knew what to do with the money. His uncle's home was not at all to his taste, and he soon left it, purchasing a moderate-sized but substantial and elegant house in a part of the city that best suited his convenience. Here he installed Mrs. Wheaton as housekeeper, and, with the exception of his own suite of rooms and the sleeping apartments, left all the rest unfurnished. After placing himself in a position to offer hospitalities to his country relatives, he determined that the parlors should remain empty, as a mute reproach to Mildred.

One evening, a week before she graduated, he induced her to go with him to see his house. "It's not a home," he whispered; "I merely stay here." Then, without giving time for reply, he ushered her into the hall, which was simply but very elegantly furnished. Mildred had time only to note two or three fine old engravings and a bronze figure, when Mrs. Wheaton, bustling up from the basement, overwhelmed her with hospitality. They first inspected her domains, and in neatness and comfort found them all that could be desired. "You see," said the good woman, as she and Mildred were hidden from view in a china closet, "I could get hup quite a grand dinner, but I hain't much use fur these 'ere things, for he heats less and less hevery day. I'm troubled habout Mr. Roger, fur he seems kinder low hin 'is spirits and discouraged like. Most young men vould feel like lords hin 'is shoes, but he's a-gettin' veary and listless-like. Vun day he vas so down that I vanted 'im to see a doctor, but he smiled kinder strange and said nothin'.

He's a-gettin' thin and pale. Vat vould I do hif he should get sick?"

Mildred turned in quick alarm and glanced at the young man, who stood looking at the glowing kitchen-range, as if his thoughts were little interested in the homely appliances for his material comfort. His appearance confirmed Mrs. Wheaton's words, for his features were thinner than they had been since he recovered from his illness, and there was a suggestion of lassitude and dejection in his manner. She went directly to him and said:

"Mrs. Wheaton tells me you are not well."

He started, then threw off all depression, remarking lightly, "Mrs. Wheaton is fidgety. She prepares enough food for four men. I'm well—have been working rather late at night, that's all."

"Why do you, Roger?" she asked, in a voice full of solicitude.

"If I don't feel sleepy there is no use in wasting time. But come, you have seen enough of the culinary department. Since Mrs. Wheaton has charge of it you can know beforehand that everything will be the best of its kind. I think I can show you something in my sitting-room that will interest you more."

Mrs. Wheaton preceded them, and Mildred took his arm in a way that showed that he had not been able to banish her anxiety on his behalf. "Let me see your parlors, Roger," she said when they again reached the hall. "I expect to find them models of elegance."

He threw open the door and revealed two bare rooms, the brilliantly burning gas showing frescoes of unusual beauty, but beyond these there was nothing to relieve their bleak emptiness. "I have no use for these rooms," he remarked briefly, closing the door. "Come with me," and he led her to the apartment facing the street on the second floor. The gas was burning dimly, but when he had placed her where he wished her to stand, he suddenly turned it up, and before her, smiling into her eyes from the wall, were three exquisitely finished oil portraits—her father and mother and Belle, looking as she remembered them in their best and happiest days.

The effect upon her at first was almost overpowering. She sank into a chair with heart far too full for words, and looked until tears so blinded her eyes that she could see them no longer.

"Roger," she murmured, "it's almost the same as if you had brought them back to life. Oh, Roger, God bless you—you have not banished papa; you have made him look as he asked us to remember him," and her tender grief became uncontrollable for a few moments.

"Don't cry so, Millie," he said gently. "Don't you see they are smiling at you? Are the likenesses good?"

"They are lifelike," she answered after a little. "How could you get them so perfect?"

"Belle and your mother gave me their pictures long ago, and you remember that I once asked you for your father's likeness when I was looking for him. There were some who could aid me if they knew how he looked. Then you know my eye is rather correct, and I spent a good deal of time with the artist. Between us we reached these results, and it's a great happiness to me that they please you."

Her eyes were eloquent indeed as she said, in a low tone: "What a loyal friend you are!"

He shook his head so significantly that a sudden crimson came into her face, and she was glad that Mrs. Wheaton was busy in an adjoining room. "Come," he said lightly, "you are neglecting other friends;" and turning she saw fine photographs of Mr. Wentworth, of Clara Wilson, Mrs. Wheaton, and her little brother and sister; also oil portraits of Roger's relatives.

She went and stood before each one, and at last returned to her own kindred, and her eyes began to fill again.

"How rich you are in these!" she at last said. "I have nothing but little pictures."

"These are yours, Millie. When you are ready for them I shall place them on your walls myself."

"Roger," she said a little brusquely, dashing the tears out of her eyes, "don't do or say any more kind things to-night, or my self-control will be all gone."

"On the contrary, I shall ask you to do me a kindness. Please sit down on this low chair by the fire. Then I can add the last and best picture to this family gallery."

She did so hesitatingly, and was provoked to find that her color would rise as he leaned his elbow on the mantel and looked at her intently. She could not meet his eyes, for there was a heart-hunger in them that seemed to touch her very soul. "Oh," she thought, "why doesn't he—why can't he get over it?" and her tears began to flow so fast that he said lightly:

"That will do, Millie. I won't have that chair moved. Perhaps you think an incipient lawyer has no imagination, but I shall see you there to-morrow night. Come away now from this room of shadows. Your first visit to me has cost you so many tears that you will not come again."

"They are not bitter tears. It almost seems as if I had found the treasures I had lost. So far from being saddened, I'm happier than I've been since I lost them—at least I should be if I saw you looking better. Roger, you are growing thin; you don't act like your old self."

"Well, I won't work late at night any longer if you don't wish me to," he replied evasively.

"Make me that promise," she pleaded eagerly.

"Any promise, Millie."

She wondered at the slight thrill with which her heart responded to his low, deep tones.

In the library she became a different girl. A strange buoyancy gave animation to her eyes and a delicate color to her face. She did not analyze her feelings. Her determination that Roger should have a pleasant evening seemed to her sufficient to account for the shining eyes she saw reflected in a mirror, and her sparkling words. She praised his selection of authors, though adding, with a comical look, "You are right in thinking I don't know much about them. The binding is just to my taste, whatever may be the contents of some of these ponderous tomes. There are a good many empty shelves, Roger."

"I don't intend to buy books by the cartload," he replied. "A library should grow like the man who gathers it."

"Roger," she said suddenly, "I think I see some fancy work that I recognize. Yes, here is more." Then she darted back into the sitting-room. In a moment she returned exclaiming, "I believe the house is full of my work."

"There is none of your work in the parlors, Millie."

She ignored the implied reproach in words, but could not wholly in manner. "So you and Mrs. Wentworth conspired against me, and you got the better of me after all. You were my magnificent patron. How could you look me in the face all those months? How could you watch my busy fingers, looking meanwhile so innocent and indifferent to my tasks? I used to steal some hours from sleep to make you little gifts for your bachelor room. They were not fine enough for your lordship, I suppose. Have you given them away?"

"They are in my room upstairs. They are too sacred for use."

"Who ever heard of such a sentimental brother!" she said, turning abruptly away.

Mrs. Wheaton was their companion now, and she soon gave the final touches to a delicate little supper, which, with some choice flowers, she had placed on the table. It was her purpose to wait upon them with the utmost respect and deference, but Mildred drew her into a chair, with a look that repaid the good soul a hundred times for all the past.

"Roger," she said gayly, "Mrs. Wheaton says you don't eat much. You must make up for all the past this evening. I'm going to help you, and don't you dare to leave anything."

"Very well, I've made my will," he said, with a smiling nod.

"Oh, don't talk that way. How much shall I give the delicate creature, Mrs. Wheaton? Look here, Roger, you should not take your meals in a library. You are living on books, and are beginning to look like their half-starved authors."

"You are right, Miss Millie. 'Alf the time ven I come to take havay the thinks I finds 'im readin', and the wittles 'ardly touched."

"Men are such foolish, helpless things!" the young girl protested, shaking her head reprovingly at the offender.

"I must have some company," he replied.

"Nonsense," she cried, veiling her solicitude under a charming petulance. "Roger, if you don't behave better, you'll be a fit subject for a hospital."

"If I can be sent to your ward I would ask nothing better," was his quick response.

Again she was provoked at her rising color, for his dark eyes glowed with an unmistakable meaning. She changed the subject by saying, "How many pretty, beautiful, and costly things you have gathered in this room already! How comes it that you have been so fortunate in your selections?"

"The reason is simple. I have tried to follow your taste. We've been around a great deal together, and I've always made a note of what you admired."

"Flatterer," she tried to say severely.

"I wasn't flattering—only explaining."

"Oh dear!" she thought, "this won't do at all. This homelike house and his loneliness in it will make me ready for any folly. Dear old fellow! I wish he wasn't so set, or rather I wish I were old and wrinkled enough to keep house for him now."

Conscious of a strange compassion and relenting, she hastened her departure, first giving a wistful glance at the serene faces of those so dear to her, who seemed to say,

"Millie, we have found the home of which you dreamed. Why are not you with us?"

Although she had grown morbid in the conviction that she could not, and indeed ought not to marry Roger, she walked home with him that night with an odd little unrest in her heart, and an unexpected discontent with the profession that heretofore had so fully satisfied her with its promise of independence and usefulness. Having spent an hour or two in her duties at the hospital, however, she laughed at herself as one does when the world regains its ordinary and prosaic hues after an absorbing day-dream. Then the hurry and bustle of the few days preceding her graduation almost wholly occupied her mind.

A large and brilliant company was present in the evening on which she received her diploma, for the Training School deservedly excited the interest of the best and most philanthropic people in the city. It was already recognized as the means of giving to women one of the noblest and most useful careers in which they can engage.

Mildred's fine appearance and excellent record drew to her much attention, and many sought an introduction. Mr. Wentworth beamed on her, and was eloquent on the credit she had brought to him. Old Mr. Arnold and Mrs. Sheppard spoke to her so kindly and gratefully that her eyes grew tearful. Mrs. Wheaton looked on exultantly as the proudest and richest sought the acquaintance of the girl who had so long been like her own child.

But the first to reach and greet her when the formalities of the evening were over was her old friend who had been Miss Wetheridge. "We have just arrived from a long absence abroad," she exclaimed, "and I'm glad and thankful to say that my husband's health is at last restored. For the first year or two he was in such a critical condition that I grew selfish in my absorption in his case, and I neglected you—I neglected everybody and everything. Forgive me, Mildred. I have not yet had time to ask your story from Mr. Wentworth, but can see from the way he looks at you that you've inflated him with exultation, and now I shall wait to hear all from your own lips,'' and she made the girl promise to give her the first hour she could spare.

In spite of all the claims upon her time and attention, Mildred's eyes often sought Roger's face, and as often were greeted with a bright, smiling glance, for he had determined that nothing should mar her pleasure on this evening. Once, however, when he thought himself unobserved, she saw a look of weariness and dejection that smote her heart.

When the evening was quite well advanced she came to him and said, "Won't you walk with me a little in this hallway, where we can be somewhat by ourselves? It so happens that I must go on duty in a few moments, and exchange this bright scene for a dim hospital ward; but I love my calling, Roger, and never has it seemed so noble as on this evening while listening to the physician who addressed us. There is such a deep satisfaction in relieving pain and rescuing life, or at least in trying to do so; and then one often has a chance to say words that may bring lasting comfort. Although I am without a home myself, you do not blame me that I am glad it is my mission to aid in driving away shadows and fear from other homes?"

"I am homeless, too, Millie."

"You! in that beautiful house, with so many that you love looking down upon you?"

"Walls and furniture cannot make a home; neither can painted shadows of those far away. I say, Millie, how sick must a fellow be in order to have a trained nurse?"

She turned a swift, anxious glance upon him. "Roger, tell me honestly," she said, "are you well?"

"I don't know," he replied, in a low tone; "I fear I'll make you ashamed of me. I didn't mean to be so weak, but I'm all unstrung to-night. I'm losing courage—losing zest in life. I seem to have everything, and my friends consider me one of the luckiest of men. But all I have oppresses me and makes me more lonely. When I was sharing your sorrows and poverty, I was tenfold happier than I am now. I live in a place haunted by ghosts, and everything in life appears illusive. I feel to-night as if I were losing you. Your professional duties will take you here and there, where I cannot see you very often."

"Roger, you trouble me greatly. You are not well at all, and your extreme morbidness proves it."

"I know it's very unmanly to cloud your bright evening, but my depression has been growing so long and steadily that I can't seem to control it any more. There, Millie, the lady superintendent is looking for you. Don't worry. You medical and scientific people know that it is nothing but a torpid liver. Perhaps I may be ill enough to have a trained nurse. You see I am playing a deep game," and with an attempt at a hearty laugh he said good-night, and she was compelled to hasten away, but it was with a burdened, anxious mind.

A few moments later she entered on her duties in one of the surgical wards, performing them accurately from habit, but mechanically, for her thoughts were far absent. It seemed to her that she was failing one who had never failed her, and her self-reproach and disquietude grew stronger every moment. "After all he has been to me, can I leave him to an unhappy life?" was the definite question that now presented itself. At last, in a respite from her tasks, she sat down and thought deeply.

Roger, having placed Mrs. Wheaton in a carriage, was about to follow on foot, when Mr. Wentworth claimed his attention for a time. At last, after the majority of the guests had departed, he sallied forth and walked listlessly in the frosty air that once had made his step so quick and elastic. He had not gone very far before he heard the sound of galloping horses, then the voices of women crying for help. Turning back he saw a carriage coming toward him at furious speed. A sudden recklessness was mingled with his impulse to save those in extreme peril, and he rushed from the sidewalk, sprang and caught with his whole weight the headgear of the horse nearest to him. His impetuous onset combined with his weight checked the animal somewhat, and before the other horse could drag him very far, a policeman came to his aid, dealing a staggering blow behind the beast's ear with his club, then catching the rein.

Roger's right arm was so badly strained that it seemed to fail him, and before he could get out of the way, the rearing horse he was trying to hold struck him down and trampled upon him. He was snatched out from under the iron-shod hoofs by the fast gathering crowd, but found himself unable to rise.

"Take me to Bellevue," he said decisively.

The hospital was not far away, and yet before an ambulance could reach him he felt very faint.

Mildred sat in her little room that was partitioned off from the ward. Her eyes were wide and earnest, but that which she saw was not present to their vision.

Suddenly there were four sharp strokes of the bell from the hospital gate, and she started slightly out of her revery, for the imperative summons indicated a surgical case which might come under her care. There was something so absorbing in the character of her thoughts, however, that she scarcely heeded the fact that an ambulance dashed in, and that the form of a man was lifted out and carried into the central office. She saw all this obscurely from her window, but such scenes had become too familiar to check a deep current of thought. When, a few moments later, the male orderly connected with the ward entered and said, "Miss Jocelyn, I've been down and seen the books, and accordin' to my reckonin' we'll have that case," she sprang up with alacrity, and began assuring herself that every appliance that might be needed was in readiness. "I'm glad I must be busy," she murmured, "for I'm so bewildered by my thoughts and impulses in Roger's behalf, that it's well I must banish them until I can grow calm and learn what is right."

The orderly was right, and the "case" just brought in was speedily carried up on the elevator and borne toward the ward under her charge. With the celerity of well-trained hands she had prepared everything and directed that her new charge should be placed on a cot near her room. She then advanced to learn the condition of the injured man. After a single glance she sprang forward, crying,

"Oh, merciful Heaven! it's Roger!"

"You are acquainted with him then?" asked the surgeon who had accompanied the ambulance, with much interest.

"He's my brother—he's the best friend I have in the world. Oh, be quick—here. Gently now. O God, grant his life! Oh, oh, he's unconscious; his coat is soaked with blood—but his heart is beating. He will, oh, he will live; will he not?"

"Oh, yes, I think so, but the case was so serious that I followed. You had better summon the surgeon in charge of this division, while I and the orderly restore him to consciousness and prepare him for treatment."

Before he ceased speaking Mildred was far on her way to seek the additional aid.

When she returned Roger's sleeve had been removed, revealing an ugly wound in the lower part of his left arm, cut by the cork of a horseshoe, made long and sharp because of the iciness of the streets. A tourniquet had been applied to the upper part of the arm to prevent further hemorrhage, and under the administration of stimulants he was giving signs of returning consciousness.

The surgeon in charge of the division soon arrived, and every effort of modern skill was made in the patient's behalf. Bottles of hot water were placed around his chilled and blood-drained form, and spirits were injected hypodermically into his system. The fair young nurse stood a little in the background, trembling in her intense anxiety, and yet so trained and disciplined that with the precision of a veteran she could obey the slightest sign from the attendant surgeons. "He never failed me," she thought; "and if loving care can save his life he shall have it night and day."

At last Roger knew her, and smiled contentedly; then closed his eyes in almost mortal weariness and weakness. As far as he was able to think at all, he scarcely cared whether he lived or died, since Mildred was near him.

The physicians, after as thorough examination as was possible, and doing everything in their power, left him with hopeful words. The most serious features in the case were his loss of blood and consequent great exhaustion. The division surgeon said that the chief danger lay in renewed hemorrhage, and should it occur he must be sent for at once, and then he left the patient to Mildred's care, with directions as to stimulants and nourishment.

Mildred would not let Roger speak, and he lay in a dreamy, half-waking condition of entire content. As she sat beside him holding his hand, she was no longer in doubt. "My 'stupid old heart,' as Belle called it, is awake at last," she thought. "Oh, how awful would be my desolation if he should die! Now I know what he is to me. I loved Vinton as a girl; I love Roger as a woman. Oh, how gladly I'd take his place! What could I not sacrifice for him! Now I know what he has suffered in his loneliness. I understand him at last. I was hoping he would get over it—as if I could ever get over this! He said he was losing his zest in life. Oh, what an intolerable burden would his loss make of life for me! O God, spare him; surely such love as this cannot be given to two human souls to be poured out like water on the rock of a pitiless fate."

"Millie," said Roger faintly, "your hand seems alive, and its pulsations send little thrills direct to my heart. Were it not for your hand I would think my body already dead."

"Oh, Roger," she murmured, pressing her lips on his hand, "would to God I could put my blood into your veins. Roger, dear beyond all words, don't fail me, now that I need you as never before. Don't speak, don't move. Just rest and gain. Hush, hush. Oh, be quiet! I won't leave you until you are stronger, and I'll always be within call."

"I'll mind, Millie. I was never more contented in my life."

Toward morning he seemed better and stronger, and she left him a few moments to attend to some other duties. When she returned she saw to her horror that hemorrhage had taken place, and that his arm was bleeding rapidly. She sprang to his side, and with trained skill pressed her fingers on the brachial artery, thus stopping further loss of blood instantly. Then calling to the orderly, she told him to lose not a second in summoning the surgeon.

Roger looked up into her terror-stricken face, and said quietly, "Millie, I'm not afraid to die. Indeed I half think it's best. I couldn't go on in the old way much longer—"

"Hush, hush," she whispered.

"No," he said decisively, "my mission to you is finished. You will be an angel of mercy all your days, but I find that after all my ambitious dreams I'm but an ordinary man. You are stronger, nobler than I am. You are a soldier that will never be defeated. You think to save my life by holding an artery, but the wound that was killing me is in my heart. I don't blame you, Millie—I'm weak—I'm talking at random—"

"Roger, Roger, I'm not a soldier. I am a weak, loving woman. I love you with my whole heart and soul, and if you should not recover you will blot the sun out of my sky. I now know what you are to me. I knew it the moment I saw your unconscious face. Roger, I love you now with a love like your own—only it must be greater, stronger, deeper; I love you as a woman only can love. In mercy to me, rally and live—*live!*"

He looked at her earnestly a moment, and then a glad smile lighted up his face.

"I'll live now," he said quietly. "I should be dead indeed did I not respond to that appeal."

The surgeon appeared speedily, and again took up and tied the artery, giving stimulants liberally. Roger was soon sleeping with a quietude and rest in his face that assured

Mildred that her words had brought balm and healing to a wound beyond the physician's skill, and that he would recover. And he did gain hourly from the time she gave him the hope for which he had so long and so patiently waited. It must be admitted that he played the invalid somewhat, for he was extremely reluctant to leave the hospital until the period of Mildred's duties expired.

A few months later, with Mrs. Heartwold—the Miss Wetheridge of former days—by her side, she was driven to Roger's house—her home now. The parlors were no longer empty, and she had furnished them with her own refined and delicate taste. But not in the midst of their beauty and spaciousness was she married. Mr. Wentworth stood beneath the portraits of her kindred, and with their dear faces smiling upon her she gave herself to Roger. Those she loved best stood around her, and there was a peace and rest in her heart that was beyond joy.

When all were gone, Roger wheeled the low chair to its old place beside the glowing fire, and said:

"Millie, at last we both have a home. See how Belle is smiling at us."

"Dear sister Belle," Mildred murmured, "her words have come true. She said, Roger, when I was fool enough to detest you, that you 'would win me yet,' and you have—all there is of me."

Roger went and stood before the young girl's smiling face, saying earnestly:

"Dear little Belle, 'we *shall* have good times together yet,' or else the human heart with its purest love and deepest yearning is a lie."

Then turning, he took his wife in his arms and said, "Millie darling, we shall never be without a home again. Please God it shall be here until we find the better home of Heaven."

APPENDIX

CHRISTIAN men and women of New York, you—not the shopkeepers—are chiefly to blame for the barbarous practice of compelling women, often but growing girls, to stand from morning until evening, and often till late in the night. The supreme motive of the majority of the men who enforce this inhuman regulation is to make money. Some are kind-hearted enough to be very willing that their saleswomen should sit down if their customers would tolerate the practice, and others are so humane that they grant the privilege without saying, By your leave, to their patrons.

There is no doubt where the main responsibility should be placed in this case.

Were even the intoxicated drayman in charge of a shop, when sober he would have sufficient sense not to take a course that would drive from him the patronage of the "best and wealthiest people in town." Upon no class could public opinion make itself felt more completely and quickly than upon retail merchants. If the people had the humanity to say, We will not buy a dime's worth at establishments that insist upon a course at once so unnatural and cruel, the evil would be remedied speedily. Employers declare that they maintain the regulation because so many of their patrons require that the saleswoman shall always be standing and ready to receive them. It is difficult to accept this statement, but the truth that the shops wherein the rule of standing is most rigorously enforced are as well patronized as others is scarcely a less serious indictment, and it is also a depressing proof of the strange apathy on the question.

No labored logic is needed to prove the inherent barbarity of the practice. Let any man or woman—even the strongest—try to stand as long as these frail, underfed girls are required to be upon their feet, and he or she will have a demonstration that can never be forgotten. In addition, consider the almost continual strain on the mind in explaining about the goods and in recommending them, in making out tickets of purchase correctly while knowing that any errors will be charged against their slender earnings, or more than made good by fines. What is worse, the organs of speech are in almost constant exercise, and all this in the midst of more or less confusion. The clergyman, the lecturer, is exhausted after an hour of speech. Why are not their thunders directed against the inhumanity of compelling women to spend ten or twelve hours of speech upon their feet? The brutal drayman was arrested because he was inflicting pain on a sentient being. Is not a woman a sentient being? and is any one so ignorant of physiology as not to have some comprehension of the evils which must result in most cases from compelling women—often too young to be mature—to stand, under the trying circumstances that have been described?

An eminent physician in New York told me that ten out of twelve must eventually lose their health; and a proprietor of one of the shops admitted to me that the girls did suffer this irreparable loss, and that it would be better for them if they went out to service.

The fact that cashiers who sit all day suffer more than those who stand proves nothing against the wrong of the latter practice. It only shows that the imperative law of nature, especially for the young, is change, variety. Why not accept the fact, and be as considerate of the rights of women as of horses, dogs, and cats? While making my investigations on this subject, I asked a gentleman who was in charge of one of the largest retail shops in the city, on what principle he dealt with this question. "On the principle of humanity," he replied. "I have studied hygienic science, and know that a woman can't stand continuously except at the cost of serious ill-health."

Later I asked the proprietor if he did not think that his humanity was also the best business policy, for the reason that his employés were in a better condition to attend to their duties.

"No," he said; "on strict business principles I would require constant standing; but this has no weight with me, in view of the inhumanity of such a rule. If I had the room for it in the store, I'd give all my employés a good slice of roast beef at noon; but I have not, and therefore I give them plenty of time for a good lunch."

The manager of another establishment, which was furnished with ample means of rest for the girls, said to me, "A man that compels a girl to stand all day ought to be flogged."

He also showed me a clean, comfortable place in the basement in which the girls ate their lunches. It was supplied with a large cooking-stove, with a woman in constant attendance. Each girl had her own tea or coffee-pot, and time was given for a substantial and wholesome meal. I would rather pay ten per cent more for goods at such shops than to buy them at others where women are treated as the cheapest kind of machines, that are easily replaced when broken down.

Granting, for the sake of argument, that customers may not be waited on quite so promptly, and that the impression of a brisk business may not be given if many of the girls are seated, these are not sufficient reasons for inflicting torment on those who earn their bread in shops. I do not and cannot believe, however, that the rule is to the advantage of either employer or customer in the long run. It is not common-sense that a girl, wearied almost beyond endurance, and distracted by pain, can give that pleasant, thoughtful attention to the purchaser which she could bestow were she in a normal condition. At very slight expense the proprietors of large shops could give all their employés a generous plate of soup and a cup of good tea or coffee. Many bring meagre and unwholesome lunches; more dine on cake, pastry, and confectionery. These ill-taught girls are just as prone to sin against their bodies as the better-taught children of the rich. If employers would give them something substantial at midday, and furnish small bracket seats which could be pulled out and pushed back within a second of time, they would find their business sustained by a corps of comfortable, cheerful, healthful employés; and such a humane, sensible policy certainly ought to be sustained by all who have any sympathy with Mr. Bergh.

The belief of many, that the majority of the girls are broken down by dissipation, is as superficial as it is unjust. Undoubtedly, many do carry their evening recreation to an injurious excess, and some place themselves in the way of temptations which they have not the strength to resist; but every physician knows that some recreation, some relief from the monotony of their hard life, is essential. Otherwise, they would grow morbid in mind as well as enfeebled in body. The crying shame is that there are so few places where these girls can go from their crowded tenement homes and find innocent entertainment. Their dissipations are scarcely more questionable, though not so elegantly veneered, as those of the fashionable, nor are the moral and physical effects much worse. But comparatively few would go to places of ill-repute could they find harmless amusements suited to their intelligence and taste. After much investigation, I am satisfied that in point of morals the working-women of New York compare favorably with any class in the world. To those who do not stand aloof and surmise evil, but who acquaint themselves with the facts, it is a source of constant wonder that in their hard and often desperate struggle for bread they still maintain so high a standard.

Tenement life with scanty income involves many shadows at best, but in the name of manhood I protest against taking advantage of the need of bread to inflict years of pain and premature death. We all are involved in this wrong to the degree that we sustain establishments from which a girl is discharged if she does not or cannot obey a rule which it would be torture for us to keep.

I shall be glad, indeed, if these words hasten by one hour the time when from the temple of human industry all traders shall be driven out who thrive on the agonies of girls as frail and impoverished as Mildred Jocelyn.

THE END